THE RINGS OF SATURN

PART TWO

BY APRIL ADAMS

First Print Edition: August 2018

ISBN: 978-0-692-15863-0

Cover design by Tracey Thompson

For my sister Sarah, and sister in-laws Allison and Laura.
For my brothers Will and Eric and Jacob, and El Cuñado - Robert.
For the bond we share.

TABLE OF CONTENTS

v

 ONE

During my time on Esodire, I picked up three new books for my collection. All with hard covers and paper pages. All three from Earth, verified, and not cheap. One especially intrigued me because much of the story took place in the country that my grandparents had come from – France.

What intrigued me more was the first line of the book which started, "It was the best of times, it was the worst of times..." No statement could be truer regarding the hundred and fifty years after GwenSeven's manufacture and sale of the human constructs called The Pantheon. Personally, I thought of those years as mostly best times – punctuated with watershed moments, intervals of pure joy, and what I came to think of as the knife in the dark.

The ship we traveled on was not over-extravagant but much more luxurious than any I would have booked on my own. It was built like a wheel, with all the living quarters on the outer rim. Those rooms encircled a ring of larger rooms that were used for a variety of purposes. Some were offices, three served as a small and temporary lab for Faith, and a number of them made up a medical center – one where Mira had what seemed like constant checks. The next inner ring had fewer, but larger, areas that included a sizeable movie room, a considerable exercise facility, a separate area with a swimming pool, and even a small park with grass and trees. These bordered a wide walkway that gave access to a hub of eateries: a coffeeshop with a café and four restaurants. They all circled a gargantuan kitchen, which was the very center of the wheel. Upstairs, the captain did his stuff directly on top of the hub and the machinery that ran it all was somewhere down below - along with all the cargo.

Thankfully, it was all on Faith's dime.

Faith de Rossi, the eldest granddaughter of Cronus, was the mastermind behind GwenSeven – the first company in the known universe to successfully manufacture artificial humans. With her two sisters and their biodentical twins, they had made seven of these constructs, so perfect that six of them had sold for billions. Most of those billions had gone to Cronus since he had funded the project. The rest was invested in what they publicly announced as Pantheon II. Behind the curtains we were simply calling them the second run.

The second run of creating artificial humans would take place on Dione, one of Saturn's moons. I was in charge of building the manufacturing plant to which we were currently en route.

One of the First Seven, Mira, turned out to be the love of my life. She was sold and worked as a personal assistant to one of the wealthiest men in the universe, and she was carrying my child. We were blessed by the fact that she was able to wok remotely for an entire year.

I saw Mira every day on the journey back to my home galaxy. After breakfast together, she would work in the office Faith had arranged for her while I was on the other side of the ship, drinking pots of weak coffee and going over plans and talking with my subs about the work that was progressing at the new compound. It was no easy task. The sheer size of the place was daunting enough – the footprint alone was nearly a million square feet over a heavily cratered moon.

Mira and I ate dinner together and made love every night – at least until her belly was so round that I was afraid of hurting her. She always assured me that she was fine, but it made me too nervous. So for two months it was only cuddling and spooning or holding hands next to each other and laughing in my bed while we watched the love dramatics (which she loved) or the comedy shows (which I preferred) on the flatscreen in our cabin.

The moment I knew I loved her began the best of times for me. Before then, I was no more than a ghost. Mira had made me real.

"Is this ship like the One you traveled to Esodire on?" she asked me one night while we ate at her favorite restaurant for that month. My grandmother would have pronounced it "eye-talian." I choked on my pasta casserole, laughing.

Mira looked at me with her dark eyes wide as a noodle disappeared between her sweet, puckered lips. She dabbed at those full lips with a napkin. "What?" she asked.

I wiped my own mouth as I shook my head. "No, honey. I got there on a cryo-ship."

"The kind where they freeze you?"

"Yep."

"Why? I mean, why would you do that, and why are you laughing? Cryo-ships are not nice?"

I picked up the glass of red wine that had been served with my lasagna. I took a sip. "No, sweetheart. Cryo-ships are not nice. They are usually just cargo ships, and the humans on them are simply cargo. They freeze them and stick them into drawers not much bigger than coffins."

Mira's sweet cheeks, cheeks that were getting slightly more plump and a million more times adorable by the day, turned a pale shade of green.

"I'll tell you about it another time," I said quickly, giving her a smile and laying my hand over hers.

"Tell me now," she said, putting her fork down by her plate. "What could be worse than someone freezing you and putting you in a drawer like some sort of redi-sim dinner? Why on Mars would anyone want to do such a thing?" That was a little saying she had picked up from Devereaux. It would have been annoying if she wasn't so cute.

"Well," I said, "it's a lot cheaper than traveling on a craft like this. 'Flying coach' my grandma used to call it."

She had a wine glass too, though hers was filled with a purple grape juice – something she seemed never to get enough of these days – and she took a long drink. "How much cheaper? And why?"

"A lot. You can jump a cryo-ship for a few thousand credits. A ship like this would probably run a million just for a room like we have. It's more if you need more space, like Faith does for her labs. Cryogenic transport itself costs a lot less for a couple reasons, the space and the luxury are just one. For one thing, the cargo ships are horribly slow. I can't imagine traveling on one if I wasn't in cryo. Our trip now will get us to our destination in about a year. It took me almost six years when I went, same distance. Last, you have a minimal amount of maintenance in a chill box. You don't have to be fed, you don't have to do laundry, and you're not taking up any gaseous oxygen – among other things."

Mira made a face and picked up her fork. "That's disgusting," she announced and tore back into her spaghetti with a vengeance. I was about to breathe a sigh of relief when she fixed me with her dark eyes as she chewed and I knew another question was coming. "Were you scared?" she asked when she had swallowed her food.

"No," I answered easily. "I was seventeen." She already had more food in her mouth so her next question was with her eyebrows. I smiled. "I can't speak for elves, but when a human is seventeen, there is little they fear. They feel invincible."

There was a flicker of doubt in those dark eyes, but it was overshadowed by her amusement. Possibly because even though she looked to be in her mid-twenties, she was really less than ten years old.

Mira, an original member of the Pantheon, was the most perfect woman I had ever laid eyes on and to me was anything but artificial.

Sometimes we joined Gwendolyn, Faith's biometric twin, in the movie room. She was always with Evan, another one of the constructs the de Rossi's referred to as "The First Seven," though he had not been part of the Pantheon. Evan, unlike the others, had not been sold. He had been taken offline before the others had gone on the market.

None of the de Rossi's ever said anything about him, so I had no idea if they were trying to reprogram him or what. It crossed my mind now and then, but I had more to worry about than a sub-par construct. A month into our journey to Dione, Faith told me she wanted to double the size of the plant. And Mira, who I had fallen in love with before she had been sold to a quintillionaire businessman, was carrying my child.

The one thing I did notice about Evan, before our trip and during, was his odd behavior. Though for the most part he seemed like the other Pantheon constructs, something about him was definitely off. I didn't know if it was because he was defective, or if it was from the inundation of the cinema he and Gwen were exposed to on a daily basis. The two seemed to live in the movie room, watching vids for most of their waking hours and usually with Gwendolyn half curled into Evan's lap.

They watched everything. They watched some of the comedic shows that Mira and I watched, and many that were much older – some that predated the Year of the First Dragon. They watched some shows but tons of movies – comedies, tragedies, dramas, action, and adventure. Some were so old that they didn't even have color in them. I peeked in on them now and then and noticed that they watched some of the vids two or three times – or more.

It had a strange effect on them that was so gradual I didn't even notice it at first. It wasn't until Charity and Llewellyn joined us and brought it to my attention.

The middle de Rossi sister and her biodentical dyer were not traveling directly with us to Dione but instead had booked themselves on a party cruise for singles. That meant it was a ship populated by hedonistic lunatics hell-bent on a continuous and riotous amount of revelry. I only hoped the ship carried as much antibiotics as it did alcohol.

Their heading was the same as ours and they joined up with us for a day or two now and then when our ships crossed paths. It was on one of these nights that they were having dinner with Gwen and Evan. Faith had promised to join them as soon as she was done working and I was passing by to get Mira some ice cream.

The kitchen crew was used to seeing me since I was often in search of a snack for my lady. Thomas was the only other passenger that frequented the giant kitchen since Faith hardly ever stopped working. I am quite sure she would have worked herself into faints or possibly starved to death if Thomas was not putting food down next to her left hand every four hours.

It always gave me a kick to see him in the kitchen - tall and dark and trim - fixing meals in a three-piece suit.

"It's a little fancy for space-travel, don't you think?" I asked him one time, indicating his clothes as he primly assembled a fried egg sandwich. He simply looked at me through his black-rimmed glasses and smiled in that way he had that I could never distinguish between patience and condescendence.

"You still wear your work clothes, Fletcher," he intoned. With his accent it came out "Fletcha." He carefully arranged seven slices of orange wedges next to the sandwich and picked up the tray in an elegant manner, careful not to spill the glass of champagne. "And I wear mine. Do let me know when it is… pajama day." He gave me a broad smile as he carried the tray towards the door.

"Would you wear pajamas?" I called after his retreating form.

"No," he called back as the doors were swinging shut behind him, "but I might skip the tie." I had smiled but I doubted he would even skip the tie.

Charity and Llewellyn were having dinner in the steak and seafood restaurant with Gwen and Evan and I paused just to be polite and say hello, but a second later they both squealed and were on their feet to give me hugs.

"Mason!" Llewellyn exclaimed as she embraced me. "It is so good to see you! It's been a month, or more!"

"Fletcher," Charity corrected as Llewellyn let me go so Charity could have her turn. "It's good to see you, Fletcher." She kissed the air next to the side of my right cheek, then the left.

Llewellyn rolled her eyes and shook her head. "My apologies, Fletcher. Old habits die hard for me."

"No apologies needed," I assured them. "You look well, too."

And they did. They both had artificial tans and were wearing their white-blonde locks in a fashion that was both crazy and yet becoming on them. They wore short, sleeveless dresses that sparkled.

"How is Mira?" Llewellyn asked. "Is she huge?"

"No," I laughed, "and don't even suggest it. She is crazy sensitive. But I'm sure she would love for you to come by in the morning and say hello."

"Of course!" Charity agreed.

"Well," I said, jerking my head towards the double doors that led to the kitchen, "I'm just grabbing some ice cream."

"Get forks," Evan said.

"For the guys in the jeep," Gwen added.

They went off into gales of laughter, leaning together in the manner of conspirators or drunks. I shook my head and started away but Charity's hand caught my elbow. I looked at her, surprised, but she was not looking at me. She was looking at Gwen and Evan.

"That has to be the ninth weirdly cryptic thing that you guys have said in the past half an hour," Llewellyn told them.

"Do they do that a lot?" Charity whispered to me, her gaze still fixed on the happy couple.

"Yes," I said. "All the time. I don't really even notice it. I just figure when they start talking crazy then it's time for me to go."

Charity let go of my elbow but I stayed, now curious. "You have developed your own language," she said softly as she looked at them.

Gwen and Evan looked back at her, nonplussed.

"Don't be silly," Gwendolyn told her. "We are speaking Anglicus, same as you."

Llewellyn tilted her head, her blue eyes going from one to the other. "You are, but you are not."

"What do you mean?" Evan asked.

Llewellyn grinned at him. "Cover your ears and turn around."

Evan smiled like a child asked to play a game and did as he was instructed.

"When we first got here," Charity told Gwen, "I asked you how long Faith would be and you rolled your eyes and said, 'the whole movie!' What did you mean?"

Gwen uttered a bird-like chuckle. "Oh, that was nothing, really! I was referencing a movie we had watched on the first elfin war. It was seven hours long and when Evan asked me how long it was - asking about the actual war - I replied, 'the whole movie!' Isn't that funny?"

"Mmm hmm," Charity replied.

Llewellyn tapped Evan on the shoulder and he turned around, clearly amused. She motioned for him to take his hands off his ears and he did so. "How long have Hope and Madeline been gone?" she asked.

Evan rolled his hazel eyes. "The whole movie!"

Gwendolyn's body rocked back in her chair as she laughed while Charity and her dyer exchanged a glance before looking back at the other two, silly as newlyweds.

"You two are creating your own language," she affirmed softly, eerily sounding quite a bit like Faith. "Based on references."

"Amazing," Llewellyn mused.

"Well," I said, excusing myself, "it was great seeing you but I don't want to keep Mira waiting."

I turned and headed through the double doors to the kitchen as Evan called after me, "Remember the Alamo!"

Gwen said something that I couldn't hear, but I could hear their laughter as the doors swung shut behind me and I headed for the freezer. I took a different route back.

◌ 🙟🙠 ◌

Those were the best of times, culminating with me holding the seven-pound baby girl in my arms that Mira and I had made. She was born in the med-center on our ship, with both a human and an elfin obstetrician (baby doctors, Faith told me) along with Faith and our usual medical crew. And me.

"She's so tiny," I wondered aloud as I held her for the first time, marveling at her miniscule fingers and tiny toes.

She had Mira's dark hair and dark eyes. I was bowled over to see a few of my features replicated in the miniature person cradled in my arms. I could not have been happier. I placed my pinky along her baby fist and it opened and those teeny fingers wrapped themselves around my finger. I could feel tears spring to my eyes. I looked up at Mira, propped up in the medical bed, looking exhausted but happy.

"I didn't think I could love anyone as much as I love you," I said, my voice still full of amazement. "I hope that's okay."

Her smiled widened and she nodded before the smile drew in again till her lips were almost pursed. "I'm naming her Jean," she announced, as if I would argue with her about anything at that moment. I did laugh, however.

"Not after my pants!" I exclaimed.

"Yes," she insisted, "after your pants." I kissed the baby on top of her head. She was so warm. And her hair was so soft. And she smelled so good. I raised my brows at Mira as I kissed the baby again and her defiant expression softened. "It was the first place I touched you," she explained. "I had been wanting so much to touch you, and that was my way in, so to speak." Just when I thought my heart was completely melted, I felt it melt some more. "Is that okay?" she asked.

"Of course it is okay," I assured her. "It's more than okay." I kissed the baby's cheeks and then her temples and then her cheeks again. "After all, it is a French name - for a boy or a girl. I think it means 'God's grace' or 'God's gift.' Either way, it is certainly appropriate."

Mira smiled and I kissed the baby one more time before handing her over as slowly and gently as I could. I had never seen anything more fragile.

"Good," she announced as she took the tiny package, cradling her slender neck and tucking her into the crook of her arm like a professional. "Do humans give middle names?"

"Absolutely," I told her, smoothing out baby Jean's hair. My hand covered her entire head.

"Well," Mira conceded, "since I gave her the first name, you should give her the middle one."

"Mira," I said without hesitation.

Mira shook her head, her damp, dark curls sticking to her face. "You already got to name one woman that."

"How about Marie, then?" I suggested. "After my grandmother."

Mira smiled and nodded. "I think that is a wonderful idea. I can't wait to meet her."

"Me too," I agreed and kissed her voluptuous cheek. She

already knew how much my grandmother had influenced my life. "I know she is going to love you."

Faith came to interrupt us, as she would every few hours for the next few days before relenting to twice a day.

I spent three whole days at the med-center with Mira and Jean-Marie, other than my runs to the kitchen. On the fourth day I got them settled in our cabin and went to the coffeeshop where I usually made all my calls to Jake, catching up on my work during my morning coffee. We had more to catch up on than usual since I had been out of the loop for some days. When I finally pulled the comset off my ear, my second cup of coffee was gone and Thomas was standing there, waiting.

Alarms went off all over my head and my body when I saw him, though his expression was carefully composed.

"Is it Mira?" I asked, rising to my feet. "The baby?"

"No, no, no," he assured me, his palms held towards me in a calming manner. "It has nothing to do with them. Dr. de Rossi would simply like you to join her in her office as soon as possible."

My blood pressure went down, just a little. I knew that Faith was doing constant tests and would say nothing in front of Mira without telling me first. I followed Thomas down a spoke corridor and made a hard right into the hallway that fronted the offices and labs.

Faith had a room that she used as an office though her lab, as always, was overflowing into it like an urban jungle trying to reclaim medical technology. The door to the office slid open with agonizing slowness to reveal Faith behind her desk and Gwen and Evan occupying the only other chairs.

Thomas did not follow me inside.

Evan got up immediately to offer me his seat but I shook my head, a feeling of dread welling up in my stomach. Everyone in the room bore an expression of sadness that made me want to scream.

"What is it?" I demanded.

"The news," Faith said simply and, while I tried to wrap my head around her simple statement, she touched a light on her desk and the light jumped and spread, becoming a two-dimensional hologram.

The holo showed a news reporter in a black and brown suit backed on one side by frantic activity and the other by still photographs. I recognized one immediately. It was BG-Syn. One of the First Seven, sold as the deadliest bodyguard to ever live, renamed John Pierre by his owner. I was so confused that it took me a few seconds to even hear what the reporter was saying but eventually it got through, striking home.

"The One Church," he was saying, "has decided to start the religious purge they have been promoting these past three months on the planet-moon of Io, since it houses the largest One Church and largest number of supporters in the galaxy. Though termed a 'fad religion' by some, the One Church has grown over the past one hundred years to have one of the strongest followings in the Seven Systems."

The camera moved from the reporter to a video of the Bauam, the Supreme Leader of the One Church, speaking to a huge crowd of people over a microphone. His personal Thauam translated into his own microphone. It was to his thundering cry that I listened.

"These other religions are a blasphemy!" he bellowed, imitating the tone of the Bauam as he translated for the crowd. "The Truest of our believers, the Cassars of the One will stand for it no longer! They will start with the scourge of Catholicism, Judaism, and Islam here on Io, and then continue to the sacrilegious practices of Indasia." The Thauam paused as he listened to the Bauam rant and then continued when the old man finished. "The other so-called religions will see reason, or they will see the faces of the One in all his furious glory! And very soon at that!"

The holo cut to another reporter, a woman. "The

InterGalactic Council thus far has stated that they will neither support nor oppose the One Church in their effort to keep religion separate from government. People are calling the purge the Second Holocaust, the first being on Earth in the nineteen hundreds in the persecution and murder of six million Jewish men, women and children. This time, however, it will include every faith that is not the One Church."

The report continued, showing footage of the Cassars, the militant branch of the One Church. One vid showed mass shootings with automatic weapons and another was of the Cassars burning down churches with people still inside them. Faith turned down the volume as the sympathetic eyes of the small group assembled in her office all fixed on me again.

What made you all think I was Catholic? I wanted to say jokingly, to break the horrible pressure. After all, I hadn't been to confession or mass for my whole time on Esodire. My grandmother would strap me if she knew. My eyes flicked back to the holo of women and children being cut down while they knelt in prayer.

"The worst of times," I said and, even though I spoke softly, my voice cracked and hot tears filled my eyes.

 TWO

Piper pulled the simple cassock on over his head and stuck his thin arms into the sleeves. The robe was not much different than the nightshirt he had just taken off, but it was made of a thicker, more durable cloth. It reminded Piper of the canvas used to make sails for the boats down at the harbor, except that it was pure white – so white that he had to squint his eyes when he first saw it.

His oldest brother, Janis, had brought the robe home only yesterday. It had been wrapped in a heavy industrial-type paper and tied with a length of twine. Janis had handed the package to Piper, the youngest of the four brothers in the fisher's house.

Janis's face was not unlike most boys in the fisherman village – deeply tanned and broad, with high cheekbones and topped with a thick crop of blonde hair. All four of the Petyr fisherman's boys looked nearly identical, with their thick blonde hair and blue eyes with spiked halos of gold around each pupil, making them look like stars caught in sea water.

Piper, however, was far from being as robust as the older boys.

"Are you sure you want to do this?" Janis had asked and Piper's narrow shoulders had sagged with what he thought must be the millionth time. "There is no shame in deciding to wait," Janis continued, "I will tell the Sauam myself if you want. That robe will still fit you fine next year."

Piper swelled his thin chest and held the package against his body as if afraid that his brother might take it back.

"I'm sure!" he said. Though his young, round face was set with a scowl, his voice was not angry and he fought hard to keep from sounding like a child. Janis had been trying to talk him out of taking his vows ever since the youngest son of the fisher had told him what he meant to do - just a few months past.

"Thirteen is too young," his brother persisted, for what Piper guessed must also be for the millionth time.

"Erik was fourteen when he took his vows," Piper argued. "That's only a year older than me. It can't make that much of a difference. And I am just as devout at thirteen as Erik was at fourteen."

Janis thought it was only a thirteen-year-old's logic that would argue as such, but he kept the opinion to himself. "Even boys raised in the priory have to wait until they are fourteen," he advised in a soft tone.

"I was not sent to a monastery when I was seven, like those boys. I have been raised in a house of the One all my life - since the day I was born. My brothers have all made the Zealot's promise. It is time I took my vows to show my faith!"

Janis sighed and, despite his opinion that Piper was too young to say the words, he was fiercely proud of his littlest brother. Instead of continuing the argument he jerked his chin at the package. "Why don't you open it?"

The scowl melted off of Piper's young face and the stars shone bright in the blue of his eyes. He put the parcel down on the table, untied the twine, and carefully pushed away the paper.

"Ohhh," he breathed, seeing the neatly folded robe and squinting at the bright white fabric. He reached out a small finger and touched the cloth. Feeling the thick weave, he grasped it between his thumb and forefinger and rubbed it back and forth. "Why is it so heavy?" he asked, looking up at his tall, broad-shouldered brother. "So well-made? I'm only going to wear it once."

"Because you will keep it for the rest of your life," his brother told him. "No weevil or col-moth will ever leave holes in it."

Piper nodded, thinking of the three robes that already hung in the hall closet as he carefully folded the paper back over and around the new cassock. Then his eyes darted back up to his brother, blue and gold stars fixed on blue and gold stars, sharp and intense. "And, after I take my vows, I want you to stop calling me Piper."

Janis looked surprised. "What am I supposed to call you?"

"Olaf. My name is Olaf."

Janis made a face. "Olaf is a man's name."

"So is Yosef, but you call Yosef by his name."

"Yosef is as big as an ox, his name fits him. You're as thin as a reed pipe," he teased good-naturedly. "Not to mention that your voice hasn't yet begun to change. You even sound like a reed pipe."

"But tomorrow I will be a man of the One. A soldier of the greatest army in the universe. I need a man's name!"

"Mr. Piper?"

Piper gave his brother a look of exasperation. "Olaf."

"*Sir* Piper?"

"Olaf."

"Alright," Janis relented as he reached out to ruffle his brother's blonde hair. It was something else that Piper tolerated but did not like. This time, however, Piper did not care. He was too excited.

That was then. Only yesterday he was a boy. Today he would become a man. A man of the One.

With the pink and gold morning light of dawn streaming through his window, Piper donned his christening robe and looked at himself in the long mirror that hung on the back of the door of the bedroom he shared with Yosef. The white fabric seemed to glow as if infused with a luminosity of its own. A light that was white and bright and shining. Piper's small chest swelled with pride.

He had fasted all night and for all of the previous day, as was required. He had recited his vows over and over and had finally fallen asleep around midnight. He had risen with the sun and bathed, scrubbing hard all over. Even now, his lips moved silently as the words shaped his mouth, repeating the vows without even thinking.

Piper turned his head and stretched his neck, examining the smooth skin in the reflection. After today it would be marked with a scar, like all his brothers. Janis had started growing golden-red hair on his face and neck three years ago but shaved it off every day to show the mark of his devotion.

A face much like Piper's own appeared in the mirror behind his right shoulder. It was topped with the same thatch of thick blonde hair over the same blue eyes with halos of gold, but this face was much fuller and set with a heavy jaw.

"Having second thoughts?" Yosef asked, a mischievous glint in his bright blue eyes.

Piper's young face contorted with indignation. "I most certainly am not!"

Yosef reached out a large hand and ruffled Piper's hair, furthering his little brother's annoyance. "Don't worry, even a little pipe like you can lose a whole pint of blood and still live. And, if you know your vows, you will have them said before you've lost even a cup."

"I know my vows," Piper assured him.

Yosef laughed. "I know you do. I could hear you mumbling them in your sleep all night long!"

"Really?"

"Really." He wrapped a meaty hand around Piper's small shoulder and gave it a reassuring squeeze. "I am proud of you," he told him. His younger brother brightened so much that his cheeks turned pink.

"Thanks, Yosef."

Yosef lifted his thick-fingered hand and once again ruffled Piper's blonde hair. "Now go comb that hair while I get dressed," he instructed.

Piper ran off to do as he was told but Erik and Janis were already shouldering each other for space in the tiny bathroom that the four brothers shared. He snaked in a skinny arm just long enough to grab the single comb they all shared and went into the hall to groom himself in the reflection of the enormous clock that had been passed down through his family for countless generations.

The wooden box that enclosed the time-keeping mechanism was taller than his father and had elaborate decorative carvings scrolled at the top and the bottom. The wood, wood that had come from an actual tree, was a deep red-brown and had been polished to a high shine. The workings inside were brass and ivory and were visible through a glass door in the front of the box. They ticked and tocked, keeping perfect rhythm through the lives that it touched.

It had been moved many times before it reached the room where it stood. Generations of the Petyr family had died within the reaches of the huge clock. All four boys had been born under its ticking countenance.

Piper looked at his reflection in the glass as he ran the comb through his unruly locks of hair, excited about his upcoming baptism as he listened to the clock tick away the minutes of their lives. His baptism was going to be special, even more special than when his brothers had been christened, because the Bauam himself was going to be there.

The Bauam, who was the leader of the One Church and the holiest man in the universe.

There was a Sauam at the church that Piper went to with his family, who led the services every day, and a Hauam at the catedromo in the city, as there was in every big city throughout the galaxies. There were eight Thauams in the One Church, one for every system and then one more that served the One and only Bauam.

Piper was not sure what had brought the Bauam to their little fishing village; Janis had said that he was there to bless a ship or a fin harvest or something, Piper could not remember exactly. All he knew was that it was a big deal, *a huge deal*, and he was very excited that he had already been determined to take his vows as a Zealot.

Even his mother and father, who believed in the One and worked hard and loved their boys, had never taken the Zealot's vows. Piper's father was a Second Mate, and out on the Big Blue for weeks at a time, and his mother worked as a seamstress in a respectable shop on High Street. Though neither of them would be able to attend his baptism, his mother promised that they would have a great dinner of clams and frites to celebrate when father returned. But every Zealot in the village would be there, and those from every village and hamlet for miles and miles in every direction. The members of his new family, Janis had assured him. His second family.

Piper, though he was young, was quite aware that the huge attendance was not for his baptism but was entirely due to the presence of the Bauam. The Bauam was the foremost man in the order of priests for what was becoming the most widespread religion in the universe. People were making the journey to their little village from hundreds of miles away just to catch a glimpse of the holy man. The why did not matter to the youngest son of the fisher. It just made his christening that much more special.

Piper smoothed his hair down, his lips moving as he formed the words – the room silent save for the great ticks of the clock.

From this day forward I walk in the light of the One.

I will uphold The Law and The Way.

Like the One, I will create and destroy.

I will create and lift up those that follow The Way of the One, and I will spill the blood of those who do not.

If I do not serve well, my life is a waste, but not wasted.

The One, with infinite wisdom, shall return me to this mortal coil.

I will serve and serve again.

Until, by my service, I am released from this refrain.

"Your hair is not going to get any prettier," a voice said, making Piper jump. He turned to see Janis, with Erik and Yosef behind him.

Normally Piper would feel slighted, or even angry, for being teased. Now, however, he had a feeling that he had never had before. He had learned the word "euphoria" in school and wondered if that was what he was experiencing now. The young fisher's boy felt as if his body had been scooped out, leaving only a shell that was hollow and yet perfect. His brothers, wearing their fine white shirts tucked into their heavy dungarees, seemed to glow like the Army of Mikeal.

"Ready?" Yosef asked. Piper grinned.

"Ready."

Janis took the comb from his hand and put it on the mantel as he led the way from their modest home on the edge of the village that was closest to the wharf. The four brothers walked in a single file - which was both formal and all that the narrow sidewalk would allow - with Janis in the lead. The second and third oldest, Erik and Yosef, followed. Piper brought up the rear, his lips moving constantly without even realizing that he was silently repeating the words of his vows, as he looked around and saw people streaming into the streets from alleys and corners and lanes and doorways - and all headed in the same direction.

Janis glanced over his shoulder at Erik, who looked over his shoulder at Yosef, who looked over his shoulder at Piper – a wide smile on each broad face as they made their way to the church at the southern side of the village.

When the brothers arrived at the church they found it closed. The Sauam had known in advance how many people would be in attendance for the baptisms, the number of christenings having tripled after it had become known that the Bauam himself would be present. Small signs were posted, directing worshippers to the rolling fields behind the church. They went in small groups, singly, and in large family or community herds.

There were so many people that had come for festivities and blessings that benches had been brought in and set around the large gazebo in the grass field beyond the church. Not only was every Zealot within traveling distance present, and simple followers of the One, but many of the common fisher-folk from kiletertes around. The commoners were there to see more than the religious rite. The Boy Vicar was rumored to be attending, the new and strikingly beautiful and supposedly infallible bodyguard of the Bauam. Throngs of people were lining the field in an effort to catch a glimpse of the construct that belonged to the now famous First Run of the GwenSeven Corporation.

The benches themselves were filling up quickly, though the seats that were closest to the gazebo - ten on each side – had been reserved for those that were being baptized as well as their families.

Janis led his brothers to one of the front benches and they all took a seat, each feeling the excitement from the growing crowd. The Bauam, the head Thauam, the Hauam from StarCity and the Sauam from their very own church were already up on the concrete dais, shaded by the dome of delicately carved latticework. Standing with them, and the cause for much of the excited whispering done behind hands covering gossipy lips, was the Bauam's new bodyguard.

In the past, the Holy Father had always been rendered all but invisible for every public event - surrounded by a troop of men and droids. Now, though he still had heavily muscled Zealots and protective robotics in his entourage, the Bauam traveled with only one person by his side.

Called "the Boy Vicar" in hushed undertones by many Zealots (and called "the Angel of Death" by the tabloids), the person accompanying the Bauam had already developed a reputation that both preceded and followed him wherever he went. In his first year with the Bauam there was nightly coverage by the news holos that showed the young man cutting down any enemy that dared to charge the Bauam. People were fascinated with his speed and agility, and the amount of blood that would fly from his blades.

The young man, boyish but quite handsome with auburn hair and fair skin, wore a soutane like those worn by the clergy, save that his was all black. The women in the crowd fanned themselves despite the cool breeze and exchanged hushed whispers about his blazing blue eyes, while the men noted to each other how the construct moved in perfect synchronicity with the Bauam - like a slim shadow along the edge of a scaling knife.

Though it did not take long for the benches to fill, it would be some time before Janis and his brothers approached the dais. There were to be twenty baptisms that day and Piper, as the youngest, was to be the last. People were still arriving even after the grassy area was full and the latecomers found standing room along the edges of the field. Despite the crowd and their excited murmurs, the ceremony started promptly when the sun was a quarter risen, at eight of the clock.

The Bauam clapped his hands and called out the blessing in Lannish with as much force as he could muster. Even so, only those on the first three rows of benches were able to hear what he said. Of those, only a few understood.

Piper felt his heartbeat quicken as the first baptism began. It was a young woman with white hair plaited into two braids. He guessed she was maybe twenty years - not much older than

Janis. She walked up the steps with two other young women with the same white hair - making Piper suppose that they must be her sisters. The young woman, who wore the same white robe as Piper, bowed to the clergy and spoke words that he could not hear. Yosef leaned closer to him, bending down a bit towards his ear.

"She is thanking them for coming and the opportunity to prove her faith," he whispered to Piper. Piper nodded in understanding though he did not take his eyes from the dais. His mouth was suddenly very dry.

The Bauam said something to the woman in return and she bowed, but Yosef did not offer any translation. Then the woman turned her back to the clergy and got down on her knees. Piper felt his breath hitch in his chest. The woman raised her chin and he felt his heartbeat more than quicken, it began to run.

The Hauam produced a slender blade that was curved on one side and straight on the other, though deadly sharp either way. He took a step forward and placed himself directly behind the young woman, taking her chin into his hand. With the hand that held the knife, he used his forefinger to find the pulse on her neck and placed the blade there and forced the point into her skin. With a practiced flick, he twitched the knife free – cutting into her jugular without entirely severing the vein.

The young woman's lips began to move the same moment that her life's blood began to flow from the cut on her throat.

From this day forward I walk in the light of the One.

Piper's lips moved as well, moving in unison as his mouth formed the words he knew she was speaking.

I will uphold The Law and The Way.

The blood was running in a fine stream down her neck to pool around her collarbone before it began to soak into the left shoulder of her robe - but Piper was oddly relieved, rather than frightened.

Like the One, I will create and destroy.

She was almost halfway done and, though it seemed scary, it certainly did not look like it was impossible.

I will create and lift up those that follow The Way of the One, and I will spill the blood of those who do not.

Of course Piper knew that it wasn't impossible. Millions, or billions for all he knew, had already done it. And they were only a fraction of the faith of the One. True Zealots.

If I do not serve well, my life is a waste, but not wasted.

His brothers had all done it – Erik when he was only fourteen.

The One, with infinite wisdom, shall return me to this mortal coil.

He didn't know anyone who had died giving his or her vows to the One. The slight fear, which he would never admit to, began to evaporate.

I will serve and serve again.

Piper's lips moved silently in unison with the girl on the dais as she finished her vows and the Sauam from their church quickly stepped forward, holding a bronze bowl with deep carvings around the rim.

The young woman, blood flowing freely now down the side of her throat, uttered the last line of her vows.

The Sauam dipped his fingers into the bowl of Kskin and then pulled them across the bleeding incision on her neck, restoring the vein and sealing the wound.

There was a collective feeling of joy, almost like a massive sigh, that washed silently over the entire throng of people both seated and standing as they swayed forward and back as one, smiling at each other as if together they had witnessed the birth of creation.

The Sauam helped the young woman to her feet and kissed her once on each cheek. In turn, the young woman kissed his cheek each time and – other than being a little pale, seemed none the worse for wear. Maybe a little better.

Piper grinned at Yosef, and Erik and Janis, who all grinned back at him.

The woman descended the few steps to the grass and, with her sisters, found her place on a bench with other excited Zealots who might have been friends or family, offering quick but needed hugs and excited, if hushed, congratulations.

The next Hopeful, aglow in his white canvas robe, made his way up the dais to repeat the ceremony everyone had just witnessed. And before long, the next Hopeful followed. And the next.

The ceremonies did not seem to take too long, but for Piper it felt as if he had been waiting for forever. He glanced at the young woman who had been the first. She seemed to glow even brighter than her robe, holding the hands of the woman on either side of her that Piper had correctly guessed were her sisters.

Of course he did not expect his brothers to hold his hands. He imagined them clapping him on the back or squeezing his shoulder in the way they would do sometimes, and calling him Olaf.

Piper's stomach, empty from fasting the day before, gave out a squealing growl of protest. Grinning, Yosef gave him a nudge with his elbow. Piper grinned and elbowed him back, twice as hard.

One Hopeful went after the other in what seemed like an unending stream as the sun rose higher over the horizon. One, and then another. Again and again. After what seemed like an eternity, it was finally Piper's turn. Excited as he was, he stood quickly and made his way to the dais with his brothers following close behind.

Piper climbed the steps and bowed to the clergy. Though he was lightheaded, the world around him stood out in stark clarity. He marveled that he was suddenly aware of small details with perfect precision; the grease caked into the carvings on the brass bowl held by the Sauam, the fibers on the purple robe of the Hauam, the thin, crepe-like skin of the Thauam, the sad condemnation in the eyes of the Bauam – like the first fish he had ever pulled from the Big Blue when he was just a small child. And the Boy Vicar, he stood out like a beacon in the night.

Tall he stood like Mikeal, the protector of gods and men. Pale skin, spattered with freckles, glowed with righteousness. His auburn hair was like the halo of an angel. His blue eyes blazed as if seeking out the weak and unworthy.

Without even realizing what he was doing or what he was saying, Piper uttered what words he hoped were expected and turned away on dead legs to sink to his knees. He was aware of his brothers forming a half-circle behind him as the Hauam closed in and took hold of his chin.

Piper braced himself for the pain but there was not much pain to speak of, barely more than the sting of a water-ant. What he was acutely aware of was the warmth of the blood as it began to spill out, streaking the side of his neck with wet heat and running down to saturate the collar of his white cassock.

The young fisher's son opened his mouth to begin speaking his vows, taking a deep breath so that everyone on the dais would hear his words, but the breath was wasted – no words came out.

His blue eyes widened until they were almost perfectly round as he searched for the words he had known by heart for over a year and had muttered almost continuously for the past seventy-two hours.

In his mind's eye, Piper could see his brothers standing behind him, waiting for him to say the words, words that were not finding his lips. He could picture Janis perfectly, the tallest and strongest, cocking his head in confusion at the silence coming from the youngest of the four.

And the youngest was right. Janis *was* cocking his head in confusion, his own blue eyes growing wide as realization sank deep claws into his heart. He watched as the blood ran from his brother's thin neck, soaking the cloth with a crimson blot that was growing larger by the second. He knew that Piper had frozen with fear or uncertainty, but if he just had the first two words the rest would come tumbling out.

Janis took a breath, fully intending to whisper as discreetly as possible when from the corner of his eye he saw Erik give a barely perceptible shake of his head. Help of any kind was strictly forbidden, one of the reasons it was not recommended for children to take the vows unless under unusual circumstances. The norm for taking a Zealot's vows tended to lean towards those in their early twenties, but taking vows as a teenager – or even younger - was not uncommon in a spattering of communities.

Janis bit down on his lip to keep it silent and watched as his little brother struggled inwardly. And bled.

Piper as well knew that if he could just get the first couple of words out then the rest would follow as easy as the tide. But those words eluded him, teasing as they danced on the edge of his mind – just out of reach.

Something about the One, Piper thought. *Well, duh! Of course it's something about the One. But what? Something about a light. The light of the One. Yes! That's it!*

His mouth opened again and, again, nothing came out. He listened for the sound of his own voice but all he could hear was a methodical tick, followed by a methodical tock, and he realized he was hearing the sound of the family clock that stood in their hall at home.

It's ticking away my time, he thought. *I better get a move on it. How much blood have I lost already? Yosef said I could lose more than a pint and be fine. Has it been a pint yet? How long does it take a person to bleed to death?*

Yosef had certainly lost a lot during his baptism, but Yosef was big and strong and he could afford it. Slow and steady had always been the mantra of the heavy-set son of the fisher and, upon the cassock he had worn at his own baptism, Yosef had the largest stain of blood of all the brothers to prove it. At least until now.

Janis had also once told Piper that it depended on how much the vein was cut. Sometimes the wound was deep, almost entirely severing the jugular. Other times it was only nicked. Piper wondered how deep the Hauam had cut him as his lips moved soundlessly. His peripheral vision caught sight of the blotch of scarlet spreading out and downwards, soaking the shoulder of his robe and creeping towards the upper arm.

Suddenly, as his head seemed to fill with air and the world seemed to grow bright, the words were finally there.

"From this day forward I walk in the light of the One," Piper said aloud.

Janis sagged and bit down harder on his lip to keep a sob of relief from escaping through his teeth. He was not the only one. There was almost a heaving sigh from everyone present as they watched the boy find the words, but the breath caught in every throat when he did not continue.

Piper swayed as he knelt, his left knee jerking out to regain his balance as he tilted to the left. "I will, I will," he stammered.

Christ on a pony! he thought. *Why am I getting cold?*

Though the springtime sun was shining brightly, his hands and feet were growing cold as if he were outside on a wintry night. He swayed again and again he caught himself, though it was harder this time because his lower legs were feeling a bit fuzzy and not entirely there.

Behind him, Janis could feel his own heart racing. The Sauam, standing next to the Hauam and right behind Piper, had a bowl of Kskin to seal the wound on the boy's neck – but it would not be used until he had said all the words. The oldest of the Petyr boys watched his brother swoon and could not hold himself back any longer, but he no longer needed to hold himself back.

Just before Janis could lunge for the little boy, he felt Erik's strong fingers sink into the back of his trousers and close into a fist around his belt, holding him fast.

"I will uphold The Law and The Way," Piper said and Janis felt more than heard a gurgling cry come from his own throat. He could see the life seeping from his little brother and knew at that moment he would not have enough time. Erik's face was set with pain but he held onto his older brother with a strong fist.

Hot neck, cold hands, Piper thought, hearing the clock tick inside his head. Like his hands, the parts of his legs from his knees down were getting colder and colder. He knew that if he lost his balance again he would not be able to catch himself. He sat back, resting his bottom on numb feet.

"Like the One, I will create and destroy," Piper whispered, not really hearing himself and not tasting the blood that was now painting his pale lips bright red. He fell forward and, unable to catch himself, smacked his cheekbone onto the concrete of the dais.

Janis lunged free of Erik's grasp and fell to his knees next to Piper as the boy rolled over onto his back, staring at the sky through the delicate lattice of the gazebo. He scooped the boy into his arms, gently cradling his still bleeding neck. Piper turned his head, seeking out the stars in his brother's blue eyes with his own.

"Did I do it, Jan?" he asked.

Janis nodded quickly, tears filling his blue eyes and obscuring the stars within them.

"You did, Olaf. You did just fine."

Piper smiled and closed his eyes as his body went soft in his brother's arms.

Janis held Piper's body tight and planted a hard kiss on his damp brow, just under his heavy thatch of blonde hair. The Hauam stepped forward and grasped Janis by the shoulder.

"He will be born again," he assured the young man, "and be given another chance to prove himself."

Those in the crowd that were nearest the dais repeated the words softly. The words were repeated again and again, moving in a wave that spread across those that were gathered.

Janis himself never even heard the words until later when he was sitting at the kitchen table, half-drunk with their father's bottle of vodka in front of him. His brothers repeated the words of consolation, each laying a hand upon his shoulder.

But in the broken light shining through the woven wooden slats of the gazebo that stood on the dais, Janis was already past care, much less consolation, as he held the limp body of his baby brother and sobbed silently into his heavy, blonde locks. His face rose up to look only once and mark the men who had stood by and let the youngest of his brothers, his small and precious Piper, die.

As the crowd began to rise and disperse, John Pierre turned to look questioningly at the Bauam. He did not need to know what had happened, the Holy Father had already told him that the One would take the power of speech from those that were unworthy. He was simply curious to know what would happen next.

Would the boy be condemned for not knowing the words? Would he be reborn as something horrible for his punishment, or as another boy that would be given another chance? Could he be born to a heathen family and never know the Light of the One?

The Bauam saw the questions in the strikingly bright blue eyes of the beautiful young man at his side and he laid a gnarled hand upon his shoulder.

"The One will know his own," he assured him.

John Pierre nodded, tucking the information away like he always did.

The One will know his own.

 THREE

Though I should have gone straight to the compound to make sure with my own eyes that everything was going according to plan, Faith arranged for me to take a shuttle to Io so that I could see my family and introduce them to my new family. That was my hope. I had not heard from them during the journey, but I doubted they would know how to contact me on the ship.

One Mile City had shot up while I was gone, all the way up to a mile and a half, but the dense urban sprawl was relatively the same – dirty air, white noise, and heavy traffic going up, down, and on the horizontal.

The irony about One Mile was that, as it grew, it was divided into klicks. It turned out that even the best engineering could only get a structure to self-support at three hundred and twenty-eight stories, which was roughly one kilometer. Even then, there was a series of horizontal struts every hundred feet or so that we called tables. The tables were stretches of artificial land between the buildings – flat roads, parks, streets and sidewalks.

Many people lived their whole lives in the in-between.

Your home was your pod. The surrounding pods on your floor comprised your neighborhood. Over ten stories put you in another borough – someplace you didn't want to be as a kid unless you were looking for a fight.

I found our old place without a hitch. Since the city had grown taller, as was its wont, the old neighborhood seemed lower even though it was in exactly the same place. The area looked shabbier than I remembered but it didn't look dangerous.

We had the aircab drop us off at the north entrance on the fiftieth floor and I knew something was wrong before I even entered the building. It wasn't just that the place was older and dingier, that was bound to happen. But the structure had a look to it that was skeletal.

We went in through a cab-latch and a chill wrapped my body. It unexpectedly called to mind a biblical poem by Lord Byron.

Like the leaves of the forest when Autumn hath blown, That host on the morrow lay withered and strown.

For the Angel of Death spread his wings on the blast, And breathed in the face of the foe as he passed...

A solemn air had settled in the hallways and lifts. And it was quiet. Much too quiet for a tenement building that held a thousand apartments.

The place wasn't deserted but it had the hollow feel of a graveyard. There was an occasional thump of a closing door or the muffled bump of a cupboard or the distant rattle of a pot being put on the stove. But there were no children running in the halls, no mothers yelling after them. No wives gossiping on the landing with babies on their hips. No shouts of either joy or anger. No music drifting in from other floors, no laughter. The place felt haunted.

I shifted the warm bundle that was Jean Marie in my left arm and pulled Mira closer to me with my right as my eyes searched the deserted entry room and empty hallway that led to the elevator banks. She gave me her usual look of happy expectance, but I could tell she was sensing my discomfort and it made her delicate features tense. Still, she smiled at me and rubbed my back in an effort to reassure me.

We took the lift up to the 75th floor and the elevator portals opened with a whisper that sounded to me like a knife being drawn from a sheath. My mouth dropped open as the truth of the scene stole my voice, squeezed my heart.

The first thing I saw, it was impossible to miss, were the markings on the doors. Every apartment had a single entrance – a metal door with coats of brown paint so numerous that they had put another quarter-inch of peeling reinforcement on the cheap steel. Each entrance was painted over with one of two simple markings – either a pair of side-by-side circles in dark blue, or a red X that dripped and ran like rivulets of blood.

It was true. Horribly and unbelievingly true.

For some reason I had inwardly refused to believe the holos, even though I had seen the gruesome footage on a daily basis.

It has to be exaggerated, I had told myself as I had watched the news on the long journey home. *It's the way the media has always portrayed events, just to ensnare its own followers.* The idea that the One Church was obliterating other religions by killing those that refused to conform was simply ludicrous.

Standing in the hallway of the tenement where I had grown from child to man, I knew I had been wrong. The worst of times was upon us.

It had come here first.

Had I felt that there was any threat, I would have gotten both Mira and Jean Marie out immediately, but I knew the threat was gone. We were standing in the wake of the Angel of Death, not his path. Wordlessly I handed the baby over to Mira and walked on numb legs down the corridor.

I did not even feel any sense of danger when I reached the door hung with a cheap brass panel with the number 757– the door behind which I had spent most of my young life. It was marked with a dripping red X and opened just a crack. The blonde hairs on the back of my neck stood on end and I motioned with my right hand for Mira to stay back while I pushed the door open with my left.

The apartment was empty, which did not surprise me. Not

after the eerie silence of the building and seeing the mark that had been painted on the door. What did surprise me was the man standing in there.

He was staring at a wall the way a man would stare out a window. Being an inner apartment, however, there wasn't a window in the whole place.

The man was my height, though his build seemed more slight and his belly was beginning to paunch. His blonde hair was receding from his forehead and just starting to grow gray at the temples. He had been staring at a spot on the wall above the heater where a picture of my family had once hung but my entrance startled him, making him jump. He looked at me with wide blue eyes framed with just a ghost of wrinkles that would undoubtedly be crow's feet in a few more years.

"What are you doing here?" I demanded. I felt as defeated as he looked but I could feel a defensive anger rising inside me.

At first he cringed away from me, and then straightened at the sound of my voice. He peered at me with his odd blue eyes, surprised. "Fletcher?" he asked.

I looked back at him, stunned. I recognized his voice in the same way he had known mine. How could I not? I had shared a room with my brother from the day I was born until I was sixteen and he left for flight school.

"Brad?"

The man that was my brother rushed to me and wrapped his arms around my shoulders. I embraced him, though not quite as tightly. I was in a whirlpool of shock and getting sucked deeper by the second. Mira watched us warily from the hall, Jean Marie still sleeping peacefully and held tight against her body.

My brother released me and stepped back, his eyes searching my face. "Wow," he said. "You've hardly changed at all." Then he gave me half a smile and half a shrug. "Well, I guess you are younger than me."

Only by two years, you ass, I thought before I could stop myself. I guess some things never change. But anyone could see the difference between us was more than two years. Faith had been right – years show on a human. I hadn't thought about it much. I knew Mira had not changed, but I also knew that I would think her beautiful even if she was as wrinkled as a prune. Due to their elfin blood, each of the de Rossi girls were as vibrant as they had been eleven years ago when I met them. Because of the injection that Faith had given me, I had remained unchanged for the past six years. Since that night, I hadn't given it a second thought. Until now.

The difference between myself and my brother had jumped from two years to eight. It seems like practically nothing in the big picture, but I realized then that humans lived in the small picture. Eight years. No big deal. Brad had aged, but he was by no means an old man. Still, I was physically twenty-eight while he was now pushing forty. The signs, like the fine wrinkles and slightly thinning hair, were only the beginning.

He is aging everywhere, I thought – and the thought came to me in Faith's voice. *His eyesight is probably just starting to go. His arteries are hardening. His libido is starting to flag.*

"What happened?" I asked, silencing the voice of Faith in my head.

Brad held out his arms, palms up. "The Holocaust," he said as if it explained everything.

"The Holocaust?" The word alone made the gorge rise in my throat.

Brad nodded. "The Cassar Zealots came through every door in every apartment in every building in Io. If the people inside were not followers of the One, they had two choices: convert on the spot or be relocated."

"Relocated?"

My brother nodded again. "The Cassars have camps in every city. People taken to them are either..." Brad swallowed, making his Adam's apple bob and down, and when he spoke again each word was softer than the last, "...reeducated...or disposed of."

I could feel my eyes getting wider, drying out because I had somehow lost the ability to blink. "Where..." I started but Brad shook his head.

"They died here."

"But you just said..."

Brad shook his head more. "You know how Grandma is. Was. She refused to leave or convert. I guess she told them to go to Hell. In Anglicus, no less. So they would understand."

I grunted. My grandmother spoke nothing but French unless she *really* wanted to get a point across. "How do you know?"

"I spoke to Mrs. Cranston next door," he told me, jerking his head in the direction of the apartment to the right. "I guess *she* converted on the spot."

I nodded as I looked at the wall that separated the small tenement homes. "She was a Protestant," I said. "Figures." My eyes found my brother's eyes again. "And?"

"They killed her right here."

I felt something grip me then, something I had never experienced before. I had heard of heartache and heartbreak and the like, but I had always thought they were simply figurative phrases for a state of mind. What I felt was truly pain, coming from the inside of the upper left portion of my chest. It felt as if someone had slipped a knife in there and was twisting it.

"Mom and Dad might have done different," Brad continued, "but Dad tried to stop them."

I nodded. "Of course he would." My eyes sought out the empty corners of the rooms and Brad answered my next question without me having to ask.

"I came as soon as I heard, but I didn't get here till midnight. I took as much of their stuff as I could. The rest was gone when I got back, along with...along with all the blood."

"When?"

"Two days ago."

I felt the strength run out of my legs. Out of all the horrifying news, for some strange reason, this seemed the worst.

"There's nothing you could have done," Brad told me. His tone, however, carried accusation rather than consolation and he had the same pouty look in his eyes from childhood when he did not get his way, which was seldom.

Then a thought occurred to me that the last time I had spoken to my grandmother she had said that Brad had found out I was sending money home and that he had been offended. I had laughed at the time but wondered afterwards what had offended him – that he was not attempting to help, or that I wasn't sending money to him? Either way was petty and selfish and Brad through and through. It lanced my pain with anger.

"I could have seen them one last time," I said, suddenly wanting to choke him.

I heard a soft gurgle and saw that Mira had joined us, Jean Marie awake now and blinking at her mother with her bright blue eyes. My anger evaporated at the sight of her, but the pain still clutched at me with monstrous claws.

"You were not meant to be here, Fletcher," she said softly and her words had the effect that Brad's had not. Had I been there, I would not have been alone. Mira and the baby would have been with me, like they were now, and in real danger. I took a deep breath and let it go as she turned her attention to my older brother. "Hello," she said to Brad, switching the baby from one arm to the other with a grace I always marveled at, as she offered him her free hand. "I'm Mira."

He took her delicate fingers and grasped them gently, polite though he was surprised. "I'm Brad," he said, stunned by her beauty and staring at her flawless face.

My anger resurfaced. Did he not think I would be successful? Did he think I was too plain or too inconsequential to have the love of a beautiful woman? I knew immediately these questions came from past insecurities and suppressed resentment. And that they were not the right questions.

"Did you get Grandma's books?" I asked him. My brother looked back at me (the pouty look resurfacing) and after a few seconds, during which I wanted to choke him again, he nodded.

"Yeah, I got 'em. I thought we could sell…"

"I want them," I interrupted. "Every last one."

Brad scowled at me and I could tell he was getting angry. Another look I had not seen since I was kid, and a small kid at that, since Brad usually got what he wanted.

"Do you have any idea what those are worth?" he demanded.

I nodded. "They're worth a whole lot more to me, and I don't give a shit about how many dollars or credits!" Mira looked at me with her brows raised and I realized I had lapsed into French. But I couldn't seem to switch back to Anglicus or lower my rising voice. "I don't care what you do with everything else – keep it or sell it, but I want those books!" Brad looked around nervously and I knew that the building was quiet due to more than a lack of its former residents. Danger was still lurking in the corners and the natives did not want to anger the new gods.

"Alright!" he hissed. "I'll send you the damn books!"

"I know the title of every book she had," I warned him. "And I want every single one!"

"Fine!" he whispered hoarsely. "Just keep your voice down!"

My eyes darted to the floor beneath his feet.

"And the rug," I said, my voice flat. "Dad told me long ago

that he wanted me to have it."

Brad scowled at me. It was a scowl I remembered well.
"I don't have..." he started until I took a step towards him. I
guessed that I was not the brother that he remembered so well.
"I'll send it with the books," he assured, holding up his hands
again with his palms toward me.

I finally began to calm down and Mira looked back and forth
between my brother and myself, unsure for a moment before
her business-like nature took over.

"Very well!" she announced, handing the baby over to me.
I took her carefully, like I always did, like I might break her.
"Do you have your credentials on you?" she asked Brad who
nodded, truculent again, as he produced a thick card from his
pocket and handed it over. "Splendid!" she exclaimed as she
held the cards together for a second before handing Brad's
back to him. "I sent you the location where the books can
be shipped, along with enough funds to cover the cost of the
books, their shipping, as well as your time."

I opened my mouth to protest but her glare cut me off.

"Thank you," Brad said sincerely as he returned his card to
its pocket. "That is very considerate of you."

Mira bowed her dark head of curls politely. "I am very sorry
for your loss," she said and grasped my arm just above my
elbow, tight enough to cut off anything scathing I might say. I
sighed instead.

"You can find me at the address she sent," I told my brother.
He looked at me for a moment and then nodded.

"Take care, Fletch."

My heart finally relented a bit and I nodded back. "You too."

I took one last look around as Mira pulled me from the
apartment. We reached the elevator bank and she pushed
the down button repeatedly as I stared down at Jean Marie's
angelic face. I opened my mouth to apologize, knowing that I
should not have taken them with me. Not on my first trip back

and undoubtedly not without making sure it was a safe place.

"You don't have to apologize," Mira said, knowing me too well. "You were excited for us to meet them and you didn't want to believe the worst."

"Then what is it?" I asked, watching her thumb the button in frustration again. And again. She turned her face to mine and I could see her brown eyes full of the tears that still eluded me.

"The impermanence of everything," she said, the tears spilling out from under her great lashes and over her perfect cheeks. "The savage cruelty of humankind." I moved to pull her close but she put a hand on my chest, stopping me. "Maybe we will live forever, maybe we won't. Either way, I cannot imagine the horrors we will see and the horrors we never see coming."

"The knife in the dark," I whispered. She nodded violently and finally let me gather her and baby Jean into my arms. I kissed her curls and she heaved a single sob into my shoulder.

The elevator finally came and we left the ghosts behind. The Second Holocaust continued – on Io and every other moon in our galaxy.

We went to the compound on Dione and got to work. It is in that way I think humans are the most like animals. Despite the knowledge of the terrors in the night or the predators lurking in the grass or the knife in the dark, when the sun rises on the savannah the monkeys get back to business.

ᏣᎦ

The best of times crested again when Devereaux, Mira's owner, extended his trip away by six more months. Mira was able to spend almost another entire year with me and Jean Marie in the house I had built, half a kilometer from the nascent manufacturing plant. I wouldn't say it was the worst of times getting that compound up and running, but sometimes it felt like it might be the end of days.

Charity and Llewellyn, to their great delight, oversold the second run. So there was a second run of the second run, this time making seven hundred instead of seventy. Without consulting me they put up another sale of the second run, this time for seventy thousand constructs. The manufactured humans were sold via the Communal Galactic Web in less time than it takes to blink an eye. I was filled with an unholy terror when they told me and it made the blonde hairs on my arms and on the back of my neck stand on end as if I had felt a crackle of electricity.

The demand was somewhat frightening but the real alarm I felt was how much faster I would have to push things along. We had all the normal problems of any manufacturing plant coupled with the horrors of setting up a fresh-born space colony. I had an apprentice electrician electrocute himself on a simple hook up when he failed to realize he was standing on ice and wearing non-regulation boots. Another mason, a journeyman, was killed in a gas explosion. We had more accidents but those two were the worst. I feared what could happen if we pushed it faster than our current pace. I put in a request for more men, including a safety officer, and they were on the team before week's end.

We had put more bunks in the already crowded dormitories for more workers when Faith came into my office and told me we would need to double the size of the plant yet again. For me, that meant designing new living quarters for both human constructs and human workers, though the workers would also need roads, places for them to eat and shop and communicate with loved ones on other worlds. I had built the second largest manufacturing plant in the universe and now I had to design a city that would support it.

Faith, however, had it the worst. She worked on the next run, had meetings with me about the compound, and held press conferences – all of these on a daily basis. She met with Cronus once a week, sometimes having to leave our tiny moon on a private craft to do so. She was in and out of appointments and, more often than not, she had other scientists and officials of the InterGalactic Council up her ass with an electroscope. The only thing that showed on her physically were the dark circles under her eyes, and you could only see them if you were up close. I had to hand it to Dr. de Rossi, she held it together and she did it well and without a word of complaint, at least not where others could hear.

During this time Gwendolyn was busy carving molds for the official third run. Our first move into real mass production. Training time was cut down from three years to just one. I lost one more man, a plumber, and a female apprentice mason that was killed in a fall.

Maybe time changed for me when Faith gave me the injection to extend my human life, or maybe time just goes by fast when you are raising a daughter and working for the newest and most notorious company in the galaxies. Either way, five years went by in a flash of triumphs, calamities, production and sales.

The compound was a marvelous sight to a Master Mason like myself. It was a great sprawl of gleaming glass and steel and heavy concrete. The manufacturing plant for the constructs was a huge structure of iron-bound cement blocks, made sturdy so I could add levels when Faith needed them. The building gave way on the east side to three terraced stories of glass that housed offices, conference rooms, and a vast reception area used by the ever-increasing office staff and overseen by the infallible Thomas.

The plant was connected to Faith's labs and offices on the north side. Attached to those was the suite where she lived that included a living room and kitchen that I doubt she ever used. It was well appointed but I am quite sure she did little there except sleep, shower and brush her teeth.

On the west side were classrooms and dormitories for the constructs connected to living quarters for most of the staff, including those that worked for me. My office was on the northwest corner, wedged between the dorms and Faith's personal complex. There were tarmacs for private spacecraft and beyond those was a small neighborhood of houses for the senior staff. Thomas had a small house, as did I. There was one for Gwen and Evan and one for the long-awaited Hope and Madeline. The most luxurious house was the most seldom used since Charity and Llewellyn spent most of their time off the moon.

To the general public they were the face of GwenSeven and to read the tabloids one would think they did nothing but flit from one gala to the next, but I knew better. Charity was all smiles for the flashing lights and razzi-droids but spent most of her mornings behind a compute screen, managing money coming in, going out, and making more.

The third sale of the second run of constructed humans went off without a snag and no time was wasted starting on the third run, the real move into mass production of artificial humans. It was something that should have terrified me and, at one point, it would have. But when the monkey is used to seeing the lions, they just don't seem as dangerous.

I was busy and I was happy, probably more than I had a right to be. Five years flew by before I heard that knife slip from its sheath once more. This time Mira was holding the blade. I was not stabbed, since Jean was not lost to me forever, but taken from me nonetheless.

Mira insisted that Jean be sent away to school.

I worked hard for GwenSeven, but Jean Marie was my world. If I couldn't have the only woman I had ever loved by my side more than once or twice a year, at least I had a miniature version of her – complete with round cheeks, dark curls, and bossy attitude.

I had a part-time nanny come to the house every day after Mira had to return to her job aboard Devereaux's ship, but most of the nanny's work was cleaning and cooking for us since I always took Jean with me everywhere unless I had to go to the actual jobsite. Even then, once she turned four, she came to the site if there was no heavy construction. She had a desk in my office that was just her size and, instead of dresses, the nanny was clever enough to make Jean outfits that looked like mine. Though the girl was a spitting image of her mother, it made me proud to see her little body wearing dungarees and a checkered shirt.

The only one who saw her more than the nanny, though not as much as myself, was Thomas. He was a constant source of toys and games and vids. How he knew what to buy or where he got it all from I will never know, but will be eternally grateful. But what always tickled me the most was how close Jean could get to breaking his stoic composure. The only times I ever saw the man kneel down in his impeccable three-piece suits were for her. Yet even then, playing with dolls or being crowned the prince of the universe with a tiara made out of plastic spoons and hot glue, the man had the poise of a royal dignitary. Jean loved him, which meant I did too.

She was the darling of the compound and continuously received gifts from everyone – from steelworkers to receptionists. She had dolls, but their house was called "the site" and she took pains to make it a mess and keep it in constant disarray. At night I watched vids with her while sitting on my grandmother's Turkish rug or tucked into the crook of my arm on our small couch. The vids were all supplied by Thomas, who assured me they were the most entertaining and/or educational for her age. I had to admit that some I found hilarious, while others were ridiculously insipid but I stomached them because I could tell how much they delighted her.

When Mira told me that she had signed Jean into a school for girls on Titan I felt that knife slip from the dark and press along my throat.

"But why?" I asked, reeling. A distant part of me tried to console myself. This loss was not as bad as the loss of my family, since it was not permanent. Another part of me shrieked that it was worse. I was closer to Jean than I was to any family I had ever known, save for Mira. Besides, little Jean needed me.

Mira sighed, reading my face or possibly even my mind. "She needs us now for love and support – she always will. But what she needs more is an education. Even if you raised her to be a mason, she still needs to know how to read and write."

"I can teach her those things!" I told Mira, clutching at hope even though I knew her mind had been made up. "She knows both the Elfin and Anglicus alphabet! She can count by twos and tens and use a slipstick!"

"A what?" Mira asked, her look of puzzlement comical – had I been in a laughing mood.

"A slide rule," I said.

Mira reached out and held my face in her perfect hand. She ran the pad of her thumb along the bone of my cheek and I closed my eyes. I'd like to think they were full of tears.

"She needs to learn how to be social. She can choose to be a hermit, or anything that she wishes, but only after she learns that there is an entire universe out there. A universe full of mystery. Of love and loss and triumph."

I knew that Mira was thinking unbelievingly far ahead. To a future for Jean that I had not the power nor desire to envision. I also knew that she was right. Despite my desire to be supportive, I hung my head, defeated.

On the day she left for school, Jean Marie wore a checkered dress and shiny black shoes. Her dark curls were pigtailed and she wore a small black backpack.

"I look like a girl!" she complained, making me smile.

"Good," I said. "Because that's what you are."

"Tell me again why I have to go."

"So you can get an education," Mira answered, kneeling

down so that their eyes met. "And get to play with other children." She had spent the week with us and was taking Jean back with her.

"What if they don't like me?"

"Of course they will like you!" Mira and I answered in unison. We glanced at each other, smiling, and I leaned close so I could give her a lingering kiss on her cheek. Jean frowned at us, but not at our affection. She had seen it plenty and I always told her how much I loved her mother.

"What if I don't like *them*?"

This time when Mira and I glanced at each other, we didn't smile. Jean was a darling, but also as temperamental as a cat. Most people she loved while others she did not, with no rhyme or reason. And others, including Faith de Rossi, she accepted but regarded with a good deal of suspicion.

"You might not like everybody," I told her, "but you'll like enough of them. And you'll get to see more of Mommy."

"What about you?"

"You will come back here during the school breaks. Mommy, too. Sometimes."

She gave me a doubtful look and I scooped her up and kissed her cheeks and her nose. I tickled her and finally got a squealing laugh.

"Okay, okay!" she relented. "Don't make me pee!"

I laughed and set her down on her feet. My smile faltered as I looked at Mira, begging her with my eyes to change her mind. I didn't want to voice any objection in front of Jean, lest she become any more doubtful herself, but I had already pleaded with Mira the night before for just one more year.

Mira gave me gentle smile. "I'm not changing my mind and one more year will put her behind."

"But elves don't start school until they are at least ten!" I argued, already forgetting my decision not to argue in front of

Jean.

Mira laughed. "She's not an elf! She's Jean Marie Mattatock and she is going to have every opportunity at success that she is given!"

"I can build a school," I said. "The long-term employees are already talking of family housing."

Mira's full lips pressed together in suspicion. "How soon could it be ready?"

"A year," I lied.

Mira knew that I could have the building up in a year, but not fully supplied or complete with staff. She gave me the smile that had melted my heart from the very first and laid a delicate hand on Jean's curls and we all knew that it was time.

Jean rushed to me and I knelt to embrace her.

"I love you, Daddy!" she gushed, hugging me tight.

"I love you too," I whispered, my voice hoarse as I kissed the top of her dark head. "You be good."

Jean stepped away and slid her thumb under the strap of her backpack like a schoolyard tough, her moment of weakness gone in a blink. "No promises on that one," she told me with a snarky grin.

I kissed her curls again, and her cheeks, till she was laughing and pushing me away – ready to go on her own this time.

"Mind your teachers," I instructed.

She shrugged her shoulders, adjusting her backpack, and took up her mother's hand. "No promises on that one either," she told me with another grin. As they both turned away I spoke again without even meaning to.

"Go with God," I said in French. My voice was almost too low to hear, but hear me she did.

"I will," she answered in French, looking over her shoulder as she left.

# FOUR

The journey that would normally take just a couple of years for Hope and Madeline to reach the monks lasted more than eleven. Hope slept through most of it. She was awakened every five years, her body warmed back into being and looking around with what the medics called a Ketamine hangover.

There was no pain, just a sucking feeling as if the body was trying to retrieve its wandering soul. It made Hope a bit nauseous and disoriented, but the feelings usually evaporated within an hour or two, especially if she had something hot to drink.

Along with Madeline, she would take a few days each time to get her bearings and regain her voice. Then she would take her medkit and board a small passenger craft to rendezvous with the Bauam's great ship *Monastery* (or wherever it had parked) and meet with John Pierre. She would talk with him, check his vitals, and talk some more. The first time, they ended up talking all night and hadn't noticed until the sun came up, bringing them around to the outside world.

That world had been strange, Hope recalled. A distant, terraformed moon in the Outer Banks. The sky was a strange aqua-green and most of the globe was covered in water of the same color.

Their last parting, however, had been very poignant.

The second meeting was held aboard the Bauam's ship as it was closing in on its destination. It was the same destination that Hope was bound for, in a very broad sense, since they were both simply headed for the same galaxy. Andromeda, or "The 'Drom" as it was called by locals, was the home galaxy to the race of elves as well as the last of the living dragons.

John Pierre met her at the docking portal of the enormous spacecraft, his blue eyes brimming with excitement. He felt a moment of conflict as he watched Outer Security frisk the young woman and go through her bag. His first instinct was to clear them away from her, but he knew it would be breaking a rule – even if he knew she was not a threat. He forced himself to be very still, watching to make sure they did not harm her. It was made easier by the fact that Hope did not seem to mind in the slightest.

Her green eyes found his as the check was complete and she rushed to the young bodyguard and embraced him. John Pierre hugged her back, mindful not to hurt her, and buried his face in her wild orange hair for the briefest of seconds before taking her by the hand and leading her into the ship.

"How has your journey been?" he asked eagerly, polite as ever.

Hope shrugged and laughed, the sound of it making him smile. "The same. You are by far the brightest and best part of this long trip." She did not notice how her remark made his chest swell, nor did she tell him that for all but a week or two of the past six and a half years she had been sleeping in a frigid Perspex box.

They drew curious glances from every pair of eyes they passed; Hope being the only woman aboard who was not a nun and dressed as such, and the Bauam's normally stoic and slightly terrifying bodyguard as animated as a child on an outing.

John Pierre pointed out everything as they went along, showing her the way to the kitchens, lifts that went up to chapels or down to the dormitories, as well as the hallways that led to everything from lavatories to the control room.

As they neared the interior of the ship, Hope noticed the

gradual but apparent change in the walls.

"Is that wood?" she asked, surprised, interrupting John Pierre and stopping to reach out and touch the corridor wall.

The construct smiled, not minding the interruption as he watched her delicate fingers slide along the fabricated timber. "No," he said. "I was told that real wood, while being both rare and expensive, would also not last well in a space-faring ship. It is a series of ceramic tiles, made to resemble wood."

Hope felt the ridges in the tile that were much like the grain of cut lumber. "Well," she said, "it is very well made!"

John Pierre smiled proudly. "Not only that, but it was made to resemble the wood of the priory where we live in Sinai City. You should see it, Hope!" he exclaimed. "Sinai City! It is so big, yet so calm, and filled with followers of the One!"

"Is that so?" Hope asked, giving him a half smile that reminded him abruptly of Faith. He just as abruptly decided he didn't mind. Even half a smile from Hope was better than warm sun on his face, like a personal blessing from the Bauam.

As they walked along the transformation was complete. Not only were the walls made to look like wood, but the floor as well. Black iron brackets were fastened to the walls and held luminaries that looked like wax candles, flickering with ambient light. They approached a door that looked like old and weathered oak but was undoubtedly steel.

The door next to it, made in a similar fashion, swung open and three robed men came out, one that was quite old but Hope recognized in an instant. His wrinkled face lit up and he approached her quickly, gathering her hands up in his own. He began speaking in a rush but Hope did not understand a word. She looked to John Pierre, who was watching the man and smiling, a ruddy blush creeping up over his jaw.

"He says that he remembers you," the construct translated. "You are the One with the fiery hair, that brought him his greatest gift from the One."

Hope smiled and gave the Bauam's fragile hands a gentle squeeze. "That is wonderful to hear," she told him as John Pierre translated. "I trust he is doing a good job?"

There was a pause as the construct finished the translation, then the old man threw his head back and laughed. He began speaking and Hope kept her gaze fixed on him, though she turned it a bit to the side as she listened to John Pierre, who laughed himself before interpreting.

"He says that he is alive, isn't he?"

The Bauam let go of her hands and made the sign of the circles and Hope bowed her head, needing no translation. Her mother had taken her to the One Church enough for her to recognize the blessing.

"Hope needs to run my checks," the construct told the Bauam in Lannish when the blessing was done. "I can read for you after, or I can have her wait. What is your preference, Holy Father?"

The Bauam laughed and made a shooing motion with a gnarled hand. "Do not be impractical!" he replied in Lannish, the only language that he spoke. "I will have one of the boys read to me tonight. Take your time and I will see you at morning prayers."

The construct bowed his auburn head as the Bauam made the sign of the circles and took his leave with the two priests following in his wake. John Pierre beamed at Hope as they left and pushed open the door they had stopped in front of, the One next to the room the Bauam had just left.

"This is my cabin," he said proudly.

Hope walked in slowly, taking in the small room with a sweep of her green eyes.

The room was cozy but not tiny, though most cabins on spacecraft were not only small, but crammed with as many people as it could hold, usually four to six – sometimes more. John Pierre's cabin, lined with the same fabricated wood as the hallway, had room enough for a single narrow bed, as well as a nightstand, and two chairs next to a vertical strip in the wall that Hope recognized as a Maturator. At present, it looked like a cheery holo fire beneath a faux brick chimney. She knew he was privileged because he was the Bauam's bodyguard and she was glad for it.

She looked at him and saw that he was carefully gauging her reaction. She gave him a broad smile. "This is so lovely!" she exclaimed, making him beam. She pressed her lips together, trying to hold back her next question, but she could not. "And that," she said, motioning with her head of copper curls, "is that always a fireplace?"

"Oh, no!" John Pierre informed her. "It is a virtual passthrough. At night it is a doorway between my room and the Holy Father's room. That way I can always keep watch on him and ensure his safety."

Or he can watch you, Hope thought with a chill. The chime of a bell disturbed her thoughts. John Pierre looked up at the sound and then back at Hope.

"It is time for the evening meal," he said. "Are you hungry?"

Hope frowned. She could certainly use a bite to eat. Her body was craving real food after years of intravenous nutrition, but she thought she should also get started. And the feeling of all those holy eyes staring at her while she ate would give her the creeps.

John Pierre saw her indecision and smiled. "I can have our meal brought here, if you would like."

Hope gave him another broad smile. "I think that would be lovely."

The construct beamed and held out a hand, inviting her to take a chair by the artificial fire. Hope did so, putting her bag down by her feet and noticing that the false fire gave off real heat, which she liked. Then she watched as he touched a spot behind his ear and began speaking softly, which meant that a communicator had been embedded there. That, she did not like.

She motioned him over once he was done speaking and he sat in the chair facing hers. Hope scooted her seat closer until her knees were touching his chair. She motioned again for him to lean closer and he did so without question. She felt around the back of his head with her fingers until she found what she was looking for, a small nub under the skin on the back of his right ear. That set her mind at ease a bit, knowing that the implant was shallow and they had not gone into his skull.

"Did it hurt?" she asked as she leaned back, meaning the implant.

John Pierre, who had borne her search with a silent frisson of excitement, smiled and shook his head. "Not at all."

"Did they put you under?"

"No, I told the tech I would be fine. I was."

"And they didn't mess with your communicator?" Hope asked, motioning to the back of her own head.

"Of course not."

He did not tell her that he privately believed his head belonged to her. *Like my heart,* he realized suddenly and smiled.

"What are you smiling about?" Hope asked, curious at his change of expression and smiling back at him.

"I had the thought that I am the Bauam's bodyguard, so he just gets my body," John Pierre told her truthfully, "not my head." *Or my heart.*

"Hmm," Hope grunted, not at all liking his choice of words though she knew it was entirely innocent. "Let's take care of business then, before our dinner gets here," she announced, leaning down to open her bag.

John Pierre, nearly breathless, held very still for his check, staring into Hope's green eyes as they moved over him in conjunction with her hands. He was exquisitely aware of her touch, from the placement and pressure of her fingers to the feel of the inside of her knee along the inside of his own robe-covered thigh.

"Any concerns?" she asked.

Only that you will stop touching me, John Pierre thought.

"No," he answered.

"Any slowing down?"

"Noooooooo," he answered slowly in a deep voice, making her laugh. The sound of her laugh made his heart skip a beat.

Smiling, Hope took his vitals and recorded her findings on a portable compute. She finished just as there was a knock on his door and he rose quickly to open it. A young girl entered, carrying a tray of which John Pierre was quick to relieve her. The girl bowed and took her leave without uttering a word and the construct placed the tray on the small table next to the chairs.

The tray was crowded with bread, cheese, bowls of steaming hot lamb and potato stew, as well as two cups of red wine. Hope was surprised, expecting a meager meal, and felt saliva fill her mouth and her stomach growl fiercely.

"You must be hungry!" John Pierre exclaimed at the sound, smiling as he sat back down and laid a linen napkin across her lap. Hope was on the brink of laughing or apologizing, or both, when he took up her hands and bowed his head. She bowed her head of wild curls quickly, listening intently as he prayed in Lannish.

Then he was pulling the table closer so they could dig in, talking and laughing through the whole course of their meal. When they had finished the food and the wine, Hope had looked at the construct, both happy and wistful. She was feeling better than she had for quite some time, but the knowledge that she would not see him for so long made her feel sad again. Empty.

The key, she reminded herself. *You are supposed to be looking for the key. That is your purpose.* But, for the first time, she began to doubt. It made her heart cold to think that the black elf who had told her future years ago had indeed been a charlatan. *Do not despair,* she reprimanded herself silently. *It is always the darkest before the dawn.*

Hope took a deep breath of the ship's fabricated air and forced a smile as she looked into John Pierre's bright blue eyes. "Well," she told the handsome construct in a rush, "Ten good years means you get to go the next twenty unchecked."

He smiled at her in that beguiling way he had. "What does that mean?" he asked, his porcelain skin flushed along his jaw.

Hope had almost laughed but she was afraid to hurt his feelings. He could move so fast physically yet he was often slow at grasping things. "It means I won't see you again for twenty more years," she explained, her face softening with each word.

It nearly broke her heart to watch the expression drain from his face. She reached out and cupped his cheek in an effort to soothe his disappointment. John Pierre drew a quick breath, her unanticipated touch making him forget how grievous the news she had given him sounded.

"Then I will have twenty years to look forward to seeing you again," he whispered, his blue eyes shining.

Hope let her hand drop enough to touch the ridge of a newly-made scar on his throat. Before she could ask about it, he took her hand and placed his lips on her palm. Impulsively, Hope grasped his cheek again and pulled his face to hers and kissed him.

It was a sweet kiss, not made of passion or despair, but not entirely innocent.

"How are you feeling?" a familiar voice asked, driving the memory away like fog in the sun.

Hope swung her head around to see Madeline sitting on the edge of her white-sheeted pulley-bed, holding a steaming cup of tea.

"Mrreck," Hope croaked. Madeline held out the mug and Hope eagerly took the proffered cup and swallowed down most of its contents. "Ahhh," she sighed, resting the hot container on her hospital-gowned thigh. "Thank you."

"You are welcome," Madeline answered. Usually she was on the pulley-bed next to Hope's, trying to get her own vocal cords to work. This time, since the interval was expected to last only a year before their next stop, she had elected to stay awake.

"How was it?" Hope asked, meaning the year that had passed. Madeline wrapped a wool blanket around Hope's shoulders. It was itchy but warm. Hope clutched at it with one hand, drawing it tight around her narrow frame.

Madeline shrugged. "Not too dreadful. I spent a lot of time in the grow-rooms. They aren't gardens but they were better than nothing."

Hope nodded, thinking of the vast chambers aboard the stellar ship that were used to grow food for the passengers and crew who were not in the clasp of frozen dreams.

"I slept a lot," Madeline continued. "But normal sleep – not cryo. I don't dream in cryo. Do you?"

Hope shook her head, wild copper curls going everywhere, unheeded after being untamed for twelve months. She upended the mug into her mouth, searching out the last drops of the warm dregs.

"No," she said. "That's why I like it."

"Oh," Madeline said, her voice soft. "I brought your Dream Journal, in case you did." She reached around her other side and retrieved a large, canvas-bound book and laid it on her lap. It was the third Dream Journal that Hope had started.

Hope reached over to it and ran her hand across the cover. There had been no entry for over six years. No dreams. Hope took and deep breath and held it for a second – then let it out slowly. Eventually, a smile surfaced on her young face.

"You know what?" she asked.

"Hmm?"

"Waking up this time...it's different. I don't know if it is from you waking me up or if I finally just got enough rest. But I feel like my old self again. Kind of. Maybe." Hope laughed and it came out a bit croaky but it didn't bother her in the slightest. She was full of an optimism that she had not felt in a decade. "I guess, most of all, I think I am ready to dream again."

☙❦❧

Hahn and Elaeric did not sleep, not in cryo anyway, for the eleven-year journey they undertook to meet with the emissaries of the company that held the promise of financial freedom for their monastery.

They meditated.

They grew their skills.

And honed them.

The Pearl Dragon, an IGC Cyborganic Ship, was sleek yet massive. Over three hundred meters long, the great starship carried a crew of five thousand officers and enlisted men and women of the IGC military, eighty-eight fighter jets, two Fledgling Dragons, two Fledgling Jordans, and two Zenarchist monks.

The Fledglings, named Beryl and Opal after the pearlescent scales they bore like their mother, had already been through their first two growings and were ready for another. The growing that would take them from Fledgling Dragons to Draconae.

Elaeric and Hahn spent much of their journey with the Dragon's Engineer and Captain. They made quite the sight – two yellow-robed monks sitting cross-legged in the Fledgling Bay, eyes closed as they faced the clear nitrogen field that separated the bay from the eternal night just beyond. They assisted the Engineer in the acquisition of raw materials, drawing in heavy metals and minerals from deep space – tiny remnants of meteors, shards of asteroids and clouds of comet dust. They collected the trace elements then coalesced and separated them, creating a small assessable array of the periodic charts.

The Engineer was awarded with a surplus of raw material. He added to the outside scale of the Fledglings while working with a crew of cyborganic architects on the interiors. Hahn and Elaeric joined them – expanding, growing, and crafting space. Within two years the Fledglings were Draconae with unprecedented growth, doubling in size whereas their older cousins, the Silver and Copper Fledglings, grew at the normal Dragon rate by increasing their size by only one fifth.

During the seven years the monks traveled aboard the IGC starship, the Pearl Dragon made few stops - but two of those layovers were at moons along the way where Hahn and Elaeric aided in IGC terraforming projects. In a matter of months the Zenarchist passengers had collaborated in making the moons the two fastest growing and most inhabitable worlds in the outer galaxy. The more that Hahn and Elaeric worked, the more they grew in skill – and power.

Working together, the monks learned how to tap into their meditative state while still alert to the outside world. After much trial and error, and countless hours each day spent sharpening their skills, they found they could speak to one another without breaking their connection to the field. Before they left the second moon, nearly six years into their journey from the monastery, manipulating the field became second nature - it was as effortless as breathing.

A year later, the Fighter Bay of the Pearl Dragon held just over half of her normal jets. Twenty-two had been left at the IGC military bases on each moon. In return, she was transporting back enormous machines used in the terraformings. Even so, there was still more than enough room to spare and the extra space was used to immerse, rather than dock, appropriate IGC craft.

It was here that Hahn and Elaeric waited - in the vast Fighter Bay of the Pearl Dragon – to finally meet the emissaries from the GwenSeven Corporation. They had been notified that the transport ship was on approach and they felt they should be present to greet the small envoy despite the growing displeasure of Hahn Chi. Faith de Rossi had already contacted them via the Abon to say she would not be personally meeting with them.

"As great as this venture is," he growled at Elaeric, "as immeasurable the potential, the leader of the company does not have the respect to meet us herself!"

"Not to worry, my friend," Elaeric soothed. "It is a new company, and though it is taking off at the speed of a Dragon, it is still a fledgling corporation. It needs her time and attention. The journey was as long for the emissaries as it was for us."

"Bah!"

"Hahn Chi!" Elaeric scolded gently. "Dr. de Rossi assured the Abon that her sister is a scientist, a *physicist,* as well as an officer of the company. She will be perfectly able to assess our skills."

Hahn looked away, his expression as black as his eyes. His gaze swept across the cavernous chamber in the belly of the Dragon. IGC fighter jets took up half of the space while the other half was sparsely populated with earth-movers and transport crafts in varying shapes and sizes. In the far center, against the outer skin of the Dragon, was the ovoid opening that looked to Hahn like a colossal dark eye, pricked with points and lobs of starlight. A membrane-thin field enclosed the bay from the perpetual night that waited outside like a starving yet infinitely patient beast.

Before he could pull his gaze from the darkness, it was clouded by a large object on the outside of the ship as it approached and sought entry. The membrane trembled and bulged. It opened, broken by the nose of a lumbering transport ship. The membrane clung to the sides as it passed through - as if a birth in reverse. Thinking of such, Hahn Chi made a face and looked away.

Like most space transports, it was hideous. The hulking square of metal was a patchwork of iron plates riveted with steel. The mottled metal hide was a hodgepodge of older pieces of armor, made of rusting iron, with newer pieces of titanium dotting its sides. It swerved slightly to the right and then came to an ungainly stop, hovering inside the bay. Eight legs extruded from the body and it sank down upon them like a clumsy mechanical arachnid.

Moments passed and Hahn focused on his breath, creating space in his body for patience, waiting for it to flow into him.

Finally, a ramp lowered with a steamy hiss as locks were broken and air exchanged rapidly between the Dragon and the intruder. The transport crewmembers, most still young enough to have small crops of acne across their foreheads, disembarked. Some circled the metal beast, performing routine checks, while others exited in search of the Dragon's liaison. Two more waited by the open hatch and motioned for those still inside to follow.

Hahn, decidedly patient and yet unequivocally aloof, looked back at the ugly ship. One pair of small feet came into view, and then another. The fighter monk squared his shoulders and waited. His chest swelled and held, swelled and held. Patience was forced and failed, forced and failed. Then, just when his sails were most full of disdain, they were pricked like a ripe balloon and deflated twice as quick. Hahn felt his jaw loosen and then unhinge as he watched an apparition descend the ramp - one with pale, freckled skin and a mane of hair such a magnificent color of copper that it shamed every raised temple or carved idol of precious metal that he had ever beheld. The young woman of said skin and hair paused as she looked around, her green eyes cautious yet curious. Hahn Chi realized that his mouth was open and he closed it with a snap. Another, similar woman followed the first - but Hahn felt she was overshadowed by her predecessor.

"You were right," Elaeric agreed with a frown, keeping his voice low. "They do not respect us. They've sent us children!"

"Shhh!" Hahn hushed sharply without taking his dark, almond-shaped eyes from the young de Rossi woman and her dyer. Surprised by the harsh shushing, Elaeric's face jerked towards his friend as if he had been poked. He stared at Hahn Chi who, in turn, was staring in rapture at the girls who were now moving towards them.

The GwenSeven emissaries seemed to have collected themselves, gotten over the shock of the vast chamber of the spacecraft, and were moving purposefully towards the monks. The first walked slightly ahead, briskly businesslike, her hands clasped in front of her slender body. Her twin moved at her own pace, her wondering gaze roving over the fighter ships and droids and people.

"She's a *physicist*?" Hahn asked quietly, almost to himself, as they advanced. He was thrown even farther off his helm as he witnessed her reaction to him. Her face, already more beautiful than any he had ever seen, lit up like a beacon in the night as she approached him. Her hands came apart and clenched into dainty fists that she held down by her thighs. Her pace quickened as she came towards him, moving in a barely controlled eager rush, as if he were some loved one long lost and then found.

Hahn, almost belatedly, bowed his head low as she drew near, waiting for her to stop and greet him. Instead, he found her right up against his robes, gathering his weathered hands into her own slender fingers. His face came up and he looked, surprised, into her beaming countenance. It was not only beautiful, but full of so much radiance and life and what looked like an utter delight to be meeting him. Hahn, for the first time in his life, found himself at a loss for words.

Elaeric, however, was not so affected. He stepped forward, resisting the urge to dislocate the woman's hands from Hahn's. He did not know their customs and did not want to be rude despite her unseemly conduct. "Welcome!" he announced, mustering a professional attitude. "You must be the physicist, the youngest de Rossi sister from the GwenSeven…"

"Yes!" the woman cried out, delighted yet ignoring Elaeric completely. "I am Hope," she told them, never taking her eyes from Hahn Chi's face. "And you are?" she asked, her words tumbling out quickly with a sense of urgency as her hands squeezed those of the monk's.

Hahn collected himself as much as he could, raising his chin with an air of authority as he cleared his throat. "I am Master Chi," he told Hope with all the calm dignity he could muster.

The young woman threw back her head and laughed. Hahn decided, though he could not be more confused, that it was the most beautiful sound he had ever heard.

"Master Key!" Hope exclaimed, her green eyes going wide as she pronounced his name phonetically. She stepped even closer to the monk, close enough for him to breathe in her sweet scent. Hope pulled his hands to her chest and clasped them over her heart. "I found you! After all this time! You are the man of my dreams!" she cried, ecstatic. She laughed again, embraced the monk roughly for a moment and then held him at arm's length to examine him. "I feel like I have been looking for you for my entire life!"

Hahn was beyond speechless. He looked at Elaeric and then back at the woman in front of him. His mouth opened in an attempt to offer a witty remark, but she had already turned his body without his ever having realized it, and was leading him from the Fighter Bay, her arm tucked into his and chatting happily about dreams and forests and elves and fairies. Or maybe it was fairs.

Hahn let himself be led, his senses flooded with the feel

of her hand grasping the crook of his elbow, of her hip as it bumped against his own, and the sudden realization that he could feel the swell of her breast against his arm.

Elaeric abruptly found himself alone with the dyer and now as speechless as his friend. His befuddlement, however, was due to the de Rossi woman's strange behavior and Hahn's even stranger reaction.

Hahn Chi! Elaeric thought with unprecedented incredulity. He never would have believed it had he not just witnessed the scene with his own two eyes. *Master Hahn Chi! Gawking at a woman and letting her lead him away like silly adolescents at a quir-alei dance!* It would have been laughable had it not been so shocking.

The monk finally collected himself with a deep breath and bowed politely to the young woman who had remained behind, his hands tucked into the sleeves of his orange robes. She did not seem befuddled in the least about the turn of events, nor disgruntled by the fact that she had been practically abandoned. Elaeric eyed her carefully as he straightened and he saw nothing that special about her, at least nothing that would cause a grown man to lose control of his senses. Her hair was interesting, being as wild as the devil and the color of a sunset on Lanis.

"I am Elaeric," he said gracefully, trying to fill himself with patience and compassion and falling short.

"Pleased to meet you, Elaeric. I am Madeline."

See? he thought. *Was that so hard? She is only a woman. Nothing to be afraid of or affected by...though her eyes are the most peculiar shade of green.*

"And you?" Elaeric asked coolly, though he tried to keep it from his voice, "Are you also an expert in physics? A master of science?"

Madeline laughed lightly, the sound reminding him of a soft bell or a wind chime. "Certainly not," she assured him.

"If anything, I am a master of flowers. Though I am more interested in what they bring; birds and bees and butterflies, and the smell of promise on the breeze."

Elaeric felt his jaw loosen and, just like that, the wave of bliss that he had just witnessed passing through his dearest friend passed through his own soul and swept him away.

 FIVE

Bjorn escorted Ivana into the foyer of Zimnya Roza, her primary residence, a fortress of crystal and silver ore wedged into a buttressed crevasse high in the Carpathian Mountains. The palace was not aptly named. Rather than a frozen rose, it looked more like the tip of a frozen spear, perhaps belonging to some buried glacial god, being thrust from the innards of the snow-capped mountain range.

The great glass doors swung shut behind them, the lights of the razzi-droids flickering in their wake as the tabloids sought every picture possible. The double doors closed and sealed with a hushed, peaceful sound yet Ivana, arguably the wealthiest women on the planet Earth, heaved a sigh of relief as she released her manufactured companion.

"You'd tink dey vould have better news dan me," she drawled. "After all, GwenSeven just rolled out der second line of constructs for sale to the public, and dey all sold vithin seconds."

Bjorn smiled at her. He knew that she thrived on the publicity like a vampire on blood. If she truly wanted privacy, Zimnya Roza had a private hangar that he could have flown her into, or she could have had her security team clear the droids from her porte-cochère.

The construct, first of the First Seven, dropped his ring of key chips into the dish. The bronze dish had been sculpted and painted to resemble a leaf with a dragonfly perched along its edge. The ring holding the chips resembled a snake eating its tail. On the ring there was one chip for Ivana's heli, one for her jet, and one for her personal space transport.

The dragonfly dish sat on the floating table of glass in the foyer. The entrance to the residence, large enough to house her air-yacht, was full of such floating tables made of glass and closed in by panes of Lucite. It gave one the feeling of being in a cave of crystal.

A pair of butler-droids drifted over to them, their smooth missile-like bodies extruding spindly appendages to relieve Ivana of her heavy fur coat and Bjorn of his light jacket. Once in possession of the garments, the droids dipped forward in a robotic imitation of a bow and sped away.

Ivana gave out another great sigh.

"What tires you?" Bjorn asked as the droids left, grasping Ivana's right hip with a strong hand and pulling her close. "The travel?"

Their flight from Albia had not been long - it was a trip that took most of an hour and Bjorn could fly it in only half that time - but he had learned quickly that Ivana tired easily. Unless in bed.

"Mmmmm," she answered, pressing her body against his. Her hands entwined behind his head and his blonde hair flowed between her long nails. "The travel, ya. But mostly I dread the vork I must do this veek." She pulled him closer and her lips closed down gently over the line of his jaw.

"Work?" Bjorn asked. The only work he had ever seen her do was the few hours of recuperation that followed her bi-annual body sculpting treatments – if having to perform a series of stretches for five minutes passed for actual labor. One might think so, listening to her wails.

"Jhessss," she moaned softly into his ear. "Meetings dis veek vith my seester. It vill be..."

She trailed off, her teeth just beginning to nibble the lobe of his ear, as a pane of Lucite in the foyer began to glow blue. Ivana heaved another sigh and straightened. She moved her face, if not her body, away from her lover.

"Speak of ze devil," she muttered. She lifted her hand and, after a pause of deliberation, made a beckoning motion at the glowing pane. The blue glow faded to reveal the face of a woman with high-cheekbones and icy blue eyes – a face not much different from Ivana's. Thick blonde hair was swept back into a tight horsetail that disappeared down the woman's back. "Katia," Ivana declared with a look of disgust.

"Ivana," the woman, Katia, breathed as if it were a filthy word. Though she had the ability to see Bjorn, she did not so much as glance at him. He looked back and forth between the women, intrigued. "Tomorrow is ze first," Katia drawled.

"So vhy bother me today?" Ivana demanded.

"Because tomorrow should be first meeting, not first call," Katia told her with contempt, her Anglicus as broken and Ukrainian accent as thick as Ivana's.

Possibly thicker, Bjorn thought as he watched the exchange.

"Vine!" Ivana exclaimed. "I meet vith you after breakfast!"

Katia snorted. "I care not vhen you eat. I vant time. Greggory too. Be ready at eight of the…" she was saying when stopped by the gasp from Ivana.

"Eight is crazy! You are not even in Ukraine! I not awake…" she argued but this time it was Katia that interrupted.

"Eight is lazy if you still asleep! It is not convenient time for me, nor Greggory, but time for all of us dat not middle of night!"

"Bah!"

Katia retorted in a string of Russhish profanity that made Bjorn's lips twitch up into a smile.

Ivana shouted back in the same language, which amounted to, if profanely, an affirmative. She drew her hand together in a snap, expunging the face of her sister and returning the Lucite to a simple and clear pane.

She turned her face to Bjorn and grasped his shoulders, her

blue eyes full of tears and self-pity.

"You see?" she demanded. "You see vhat I must deal vith?"

He wrapped one hand around her back and used the other to stroke her hair away from her face. He was amazed to see that her chest heaved as if from physical strain, though she had not climbed stairs nor had been exhausted by his amorous attentions. "How terrible," he consoled.

Thus validated, she collapsed against him. Her hands found his face then his hair as her lips sought out his neck and jaw.

"What should I do?" he whispered into her ear.

"You must tire me, my Siberian Tiger. Tire me so that I cannot help but sleep past the appointed hour!"

Bjorn grabbed a fistful of blonde hair and pulled her head back, exposing her neck and making her gasp.

His open mouth found her throat and then traced her pulse with his lips to her right collarbone, his teeth biting down on it.

"I'll do my best," he promised, his hand coming up from her hip to her breast, his fingers encircling her nipple and making her cry out. He lifted her up with ease, something she loved, and carried her into the elevator.

She clenched her hand, gripping his hair in her fist and jerking his head back.

"You alvays do," she assured him, her other hand slipping down to the rising gorge in his pants as he tightened his arms around her body – her hungry mouth against his own, nipping at each other like cats as they sank two floors down and continued to her bedroom.

◌◌◌

John Pierre walked down the stone hallway, his face a pale moon floating above his high collar in the crepuscular light. Iron brackets mounted high along the wall held tall white candles, melted down to half their original size, dripping wax onto the stone floor. An hour before dawn they would gutter out and be replaced with fresh ones by a pair of Luma Boys with the help of a resa droid, followed by another pair of Luma Boys guiding two valon droids down the corridor as they cleaned the spilled wax from the floor and recycled the material back into candles.

For now, the candles burned bright - but since they were spaced twenty feet apart it caused John Pierre to walk from the light and into the darkness, and into the light again. If the construct noticed, he gave no sign. He walked solemnly but not slowly, his hands tucked into the sleeves of his cassock. Most others tucked their hands away in the same manner, if only to keep warm in the chilly stone edifice. John Pierre took no notice of the cold. He kept his hands tucked into his sleeves so that he could savor the reassuring feel of the blades that were sheathed and strapped to each forearm. He had used them many times of late, taking the lives of those who sought to hurt or possibly kill the Holy Father.

Just twice this week as they were traveling, once from Sinai City to the Church of Zion for a conference of the Zealot Deacons and once again as they traveled back, crazy heathens had rushed at them. Breaking through the circle of priests that always surrounded the Bauam, they met a quick end via the sharpened steel wielded by a bodyguard who looked hardly older than a Luma Boy. The construct noticed that the attacks seemed to be getting more frequent, more urgent, and with more assailants each time. He had heard some of the friars saying it was the Holocaust that was bringing out the most insane and devout of the heathen religions, crazy enough to attack the Bauam.

The very last time it had been four men and one woman, rushing at them with knives and clubs and guns that looked almost too old to work. John Pierre had wrapped a protective arm around the Bauam, pulling him gently away from the fray just as he himself stepped into it. The Holy Father stepped back, flanked by two heavily muscled and heavily armed Zealot guards should John Pierre fall or fail.

A pair of blades, each twelve inches long and three inches wide and razor sharp on both sides, cut into the attackers with blinding speed. The guns dropped to the ground with meaty thumps, still held by hands severed from their arms. Blood sprayed from the necks of the three brandishing the clubs and knives. John Pierre speared one of the handless men in the chest as he stumbled forward and the other was relieved of his head as the construct pulled the first blade free.

The entire battle lasted only seconds, as confrontations usually did for the construct. John Pierre stood alone in front of the Bauam for a moment in the carnage before the priests swarmed back around them. Reporters with button cams and mikes shouted questions at them as the Holy Father, the hems of his vestal garments soaking up the blood pooling at his feet, embraced his bodyguard.

"If this keeps up," he told his protector, "I shall need robes of red!" He held John Pierre at arm's length, beaming at him proudly. The construct blushed, the ruddy complexion on his otherwise porcelain skin deepening to red, though his cheeks dimpled as he held his head high and smiled at the praise.

Indeed, not a week later, the Bauam had a new set of robes made that were all black. There was also a new set of matching black robes for his bodyguard, complete with a high, round collar.

"The black will also stain," the Holy Father had assured John Pierre in Lannish, his aging voice gravelly but firm, "but only I will know it is there, and pray for those who have stained me with their blood. The ones who leave stains of blood need the most forgiveness from the One True."

John Pierre had bowed his head, knowing that Bauam was wise beyond measure and felt that it was a blessing just to be near him.

Now, as the construct walked the dimly lit hallway on the

way to the Holy Father's chambers, he saw Avery, one of the older Luma Boys. Avery was tall for thirteen, with much the same auburn hair and ruddy complexion as John Pierre. His long, white robes swished about his feet as he hurried along, so quick and determined that he almost ran headlong into the construct.

"John Pierre!" Avery exclaimed as he pulled up just in time to avoid a collision. "I am so sorry! I did not see you!"

"Not to worry," the construct consoled, "it is my job to be part of the background, and these black robes certainly make it easier, especially in these dark corners." He put a hand under the boy's chin and lifted his face, examining it. "Or maybe it is your eyesight," John Pierre mused aloud with a slight scowl, seeing that Avery's eyes were terribly red. "Have you been crying?"

The boy gave him a wan smile. "It's the smoke from the candles," he explained. "It bothers me more at night, after I have been inside for a while." He held perfectly still under the scrutiny of the Holy Father's bodyguard but John Pierre did not attribute it to anything. Most everyone in Sinai City regarded the construct with a mixture of fear and awe and a great deal of respect.

John Pierre looked up and saw the thin streams of black smoke coming from the burning candles. He knew that his own blue eyes were immune to such a bother. He nodded at Avery, understanding.

"I will speak to the Head Deacon," he told the boy, "and see if there is anything that can be done. In the meantime, do you need to go to the infirmary?"

The boy shook his head vehemently. "Oh no! I will be fine after I wash up and get abed," he assured him.

"Are you sure?"

"Yes, John Pierre. But, thank you."

The construct smiled at the boy and squeezed his shoulder.

"I will pray for you."

"Thank you," the boy said again, his voice hoarse and hardly above a whisper. "And I will pray for you, John Pierre."

John Pierre gave him a pat on the back as he straightened and the boy continued on his way as quickly as before. The construct made his way to the Holy Father's chambers as he did every night. Also, as he did every night, he read aloud from the Great Bible to the Holy Father. The Bauam, his eyes failing more every day, was still very lucid as he nodded at his construct bodyguard as he read the One True Word. He was quick to explain passages to John Pierre, giving him examples from everyday life. After an hour, the construct marked his place in the great book and rose to leave. The Bauam embraced his guard and kissed his cheeks as he blessed him in Lannish.

The construct noticed that the Holy Father had been getting thinner over the past years, but was wiry, and strong as ever. Still, he did not want to trouble him over matters in the priory. Sinai City was the largest Holy City in the galaxy, and the bodyguard had learned that there were certain people to be seen regarding different matters.

The next day, John Pierre went to see the Head Deacon in an attempt to see if there was anything that could be done about the candle smoke. His imagination stretched far enough that he suggested a fan. The Head Deacon had laughed.

"John Pierre, if I put in a fan, it would blow out the candles!"

The boyish looking construct had cocked his head, considering. "Yes," he finally agreed, "I see your point. Anything that would blow away the smoke, would also blow out the flame."

The Head Deacon laughed again. "My dear son," he said, "your mind is so young and so innocent. But you have to know that boys complain all the time, about all sorts of things to get out of the priory."

John Pierre's blue eyes grew wide and round. "What do you

mean?"

"Oh, they will complain about anything and everything!" The Head Deacon leaned back, his considerable bulk making the chair he was produce a loud squeak. He was a large man but by no means fat, more rectangular than round. He had the strong arms of a farmer and a broad chest to match.

He ran a hand over his bald scalp and down over the ring of hair that still clung to the bottom, just above his rippled neck. "Sheesh! I've heard everything from being bothered by the candles, the cooking, the beds, the books, their eyes, their ears, you name it."

"No," John Pierre breathed, unbelieving. "I mean, why would anyone want to leave the priory?" Sinai City was the most amazing place he had ever seen. Places of worship mingled with even more places *to* worship. And dominating the northern quarter of the city was the priory, housing the priests and deacons and boys that had dedicated their lives to the One. John Pierre could not believe that anyone could find a life more perfect than this idyllic existence. He tried to use his imagination, but it was so small and so weak that it might as well have been nonexistent; it pretty much was.

The Head Deacon folded his hands into his lap and gave the construct a conciliatory smile. "They are children," he explained. "They do not yet know the power and the grace of the One."

The construct's young face bore an expression of puzzlement. "Then why are they here?" he asked with one breath, his icy eyes bright with curiosity under his drawn auburn brows.

The Head Deacon's belly rumbled and he gave it a pat. "They have parents that are good Zealots. Most of those of the faith will send a son to serve the One. Some will send all of their children, the girls to the One Convent on the other side of the city and the boys here. When they are young, children do not understand the importance of living a life of devotion."

John Pierre nodded, trying to process and understand the information the Head Deacon had given him. He decided he would think about it more when he had the time. And he would pray, as he always did, for guidance.

 SIX

"Yes," Hope said in a tone that was flat and far from pleasant.

"Are you sure?" Faith asked. Hope could hear the tension in her sister's voice, the carefully controlled urgency. She could have seen that tension reflected in Faith's features, had she been looking at the image of the face that floated inside the boxscreen on the desk in front of her, but her own face was turned away.

"Of course I am sure," Hope answered in the same deadpan voice. "I'm not...a simpleton."

"I didn't say you were..." Faith frowned. "The least you could do is look at me!" she demanded, her voice rising an octave. Hope turned her face and her green eyes found her sister's, normally gold and brown but made a strange striation of blue and gray from the transmission.

It wasn't that Hope was avoiding her gaze, but instead had been looking out the window of the koncreta hut at Elaeric and Madeline. Inside the crumbling gray walls of the hut was the only place where an interstellar transmission could be received and sent. It was, in fact, the only place for hundreds of miles in any direction that even had electricity.

Still, she enjoyed getting under her oldest sister's skin whenever she could. Things had not always been that way; she had once basked in the love of all her sisters. A contempt for the oldest, however, had begun when Faith had snatched away what Hope had thought was a chance at true love – or at least a very lusty love affair with the Lab Commander on Kerin.

Her anger had subsided over the long years and had all but disappeared since she had met Hahn. Still...

"Better?" Hope asked.

The face of Faith de Rossi along with the tops of her shoulders, all that was visible to Hope, flickered as she shifted in her seat 120 light years away.

"Better," she agreed. "Tell me about them. What have you seen so far?"

Hope arched a copper-colored eyebrow. "Are you recording this?"

"Of course," Faith answered. "Don't be a...simpleton," she finished, using Hope's choice of words. Hope frowned, not missing the jibe. Then she raised her chin, undaunted.

"I have seen them raise rivers from dusty, barren lands," Hope told her sister. "Without lifting a tool or breaking a sweat. And this last river, it is the first source of truly pure water this tribe has ever seen."

Hope's freckled face contorted with what Faith thought (for a second) was disgust. Then her mind shifted from her own first response and calculated what Hope would most likely feel – sympathy.

"From the river, jumping with fat silvery fish only hours later, spread grass and flowers and wild gardens of edible greens. Vines sprouted and grew thick with gourds and strange vegetables. Past the strip of vegetation, the arid land grew dark and then water seeped from the surface before saplings pushed their way into the light. Fruit trees grew with no rhyme or reason, some producing fruit I had never seen before. Past the blossoming orchards soon grew a forest, cut with another river."

Hope saw that her sister's lips were dry and that Faith was controlling the urge to lick them. Hope reached over and picked up a clay mug of full of water, water from the nascent river, and took a long drink. Faith's tongue poked at the corner of her mouth as her mind saw what Hope was describing.

"How long?" she whispered.

"Beg pardon?"

Hope watched her sister's bust rise and chin lift as she drew a deep breath. "How long from start to finish?" Faith asked. "I don't expect you to know to the minute, but give me a range of months and days. How long did all this take?"

Hope laughed and shook her head. "The river was six feet wide and rushing deep within two hours. The surrounding verge was grown in one. The orchard took another hour, maybe two, before there was fruit. The forest had budded by nightfall but didn't have game until the morning."

Though the visage of Faith kept perfectly still, Hope could see the shock in her eyes, even with crappy transmission.

Faith nodded, slowly at first and then more vigorously, as she processed and then found concurrence with her sister's words.

"And what are the monks like?" she asked. "When they manifest these things...are they meditating? In isolation?"

Hope laughed softly once again. "No, nothing quite like that. They did sit in meditation for about an hour at the beginning while Madeline and I watched. Then, when the water first began seeping from the ground they stood up, brushed the dust off their robes, and joined us to watch the rest. Master Chi hardly seemed to be aware of his surroundings or of what he was even doing. I walked next to him as he worked and he asked me questions about our family and where we grew up. Can you believe it?"

The image of Faith gave a slow and barely perceptible shake of its head. "Only because it is coming from you," she said, her voice soft. "They really did it," she whispered, "they harnessed Zero-Point Energy."

"They certainly have."

"How are the...villagers taking it?"

Hope's coppery brows drew together. "When we first arrived, they treated us like we were missionaries. I guess they've had quite a few through here over the last century. After the river began to form, and they put two and two together, they've treated us like gods. It's not that surprising, I guess. This is a natural world, not man-made. The people here, this far from the ports, are true natives. They had crude tools when we arrived, and even wheeled carts, but nothing motorized. There is only one person in the village that can speak Anglicus, he is called The Speaker. I don't know if it is because he is the only one who can speak Anglicus, or if he has been designated to such a position. The rest speak no other language other than their own."

"Are they bipedal?"

"Yes. Humanoid, but with olive green skin that is smooth and hairless. Veins that lay just under their skin, like leaves. Their cheekbones are low, in the middle of their faces. Their eyes are black with long green lashes. They wear a single piece of clothing, like a shift or a dress – what the material might be I have no idea. The men wear it tied over one shoulder, the women have it tied over both shoulders."

The image of Faith nodded and looked away, as if writing something down. "What is the rest of the planet like?" she asked. "Is it all arid?"

"No, we're in the middle of the desert. The planet has many different regions that reflect their climates."

Hope watched her sister nod again even as she was looking away and Hope realized that Faith was double-checking and cross-referencing everything she was telling her.

"But you already know that," Hope asked, "don't you?"

"I would like to think so, but I'm not always certain of how up-to-date the planetary records are. Especially on low-tech worlds. Have there been any changes in the weather patterns where you are?"

Hope shook her head, tousling her already wild locks. "No, as I am sure you are gleaning from somewhere on the Web as we speak. The Speaker says that there is a storm that comes twice a year. It floods the plains for two days before it is absorbed by the Cactaceae." Hope stopped and watched her sister, whom she knew was typing like crazy. She lifted her chin and her masses of copper curls trembled. "Do you not believe what I am telling you about him?"

"Him? Them, you mean. And I trust you one hundred percent. I just want to know if they are creating something from nothing..."

"An impossibility in physics," Hope interrupted.

"Or if they are drawing on readily available elements from a distance," Faith continued. "I'll study the region over the next week. In the meantime, I will arrange for your return."

Hope lifted her chin higher. "I don't want to go home."

"Good," Faith acquiesced as she leaned back. Hope could tell by the way her body shifted that she had folded her arms across her chest. "Because you wouldn't be going home. I would like you and Madeline, along with the monks, to rendezvous with me at the new compound."

Now it was Hope who leaned back in her chair and crossed her arms. "I'm not sure..."

"Get sure," Faith said her voice flat. "I paid off the debt their monastery owed in return for their meeting with you. If they agree to meet with me, I will secure their debts for the next five decades."

"And if they agree to work with you?" Hope asked, knowing all too well where it was leading.

"I'll buy them the entire moon. From the atmosphere to the core, it will belong to the Zenarchists. A safe haven for their people, for the rest of time."

Hope looked away, knowing she was caught like a mouse in a trap. Much as she would enjoy thwarting Faith in this endeavor, she could not deny this opportunity to Elaeric and Hahn. She sighed.

"Very well. Where do we go?"

"How did you get to the village?"

"A sand barge from Trivumpur."

Faith nodded, looking away as she typed on and read the results from another console. "I am sending it back for you, it should be there in fourteen hours. It will be a twelve-hour ride back, if the winds are favorable, and you can catch the last jump from their port to the closest civilized planet." Hope knew that by "civilized" her sister meant a space-faring world that was an upstanding member of the InterGalactic Council. "From there," Faith continued, "you can use IGC or private sector Thermopylae to planet hop. I will make sure that your credentials card has everything you need."

"And where are we heading?" Hope could tell by the pause that followed that Faith was still calculating.

"Dione. It is one of Saturn's moons."

Hope cocked an eyebrow. "Charity finally buy her own planet?"

"Not yet," Faith said, smiling, her eyes focused on the compute screen to her left, "but she's working on it. For now, head to the new compound. Crossing the Fissure will be the longest part of your trip. Do you want me to arrange for a cryo-ship?"

Hope gave her a small smile and shook her head. "No. I'm ready to be awake again."

"Good. A private ship can get you back in half the time. Maybe four years if we are lucky."

Hope shook her head of wild copper-colored curls. "We will be taking the Pearl Dragon. Hahn and Elaeric have promised to help terraform a few more moons for them."

Faith's eyes narrowed in anger but she could not protest.

She had not offered the monks employment until just now. "It will be a good ten years, maybe a little more," she warned.

Hope shrugged. "It's not that much to the likes of us." Though she and Faith were not pure elves, they had much the same lifespan. Still, she knew that Faith had an urgency that went beyond her human blood. She was correct, but Faith also had her hands full with the move into mass production.

"Very well. Call my personal line if you need me, or have Thomas patch you through. Otherwise, I'll see you in a decade."

How very personal of you, Hope thought caustically. "See you in a decade," she replied in a flat tone.

"Love," Faith said. It was the de Rossi form of goodbye, good luck, and I love you. Hope had started it when she was still a small child.

"Love," Hope answered mechanically, cutting off the transmission before her sister received all of it. She sequenced an open line into the program and put the antiquated transmitter box on power-saving mode. She retrieved her clay mug and left the hut only to be amazed by the sky above.

Though it had not changed during her conversation with Faith, the atmosphere of the planet still amazed her. The sky was a constantly shifting aurora borealis in every shade of pink and crimson, like a never-ending sunset but with the brilliant promise of sunrise.

Hahn Chi stood next to her as if he had materialized from the thin air, following her gaze into the sky.

"It is lovely to your eyes too – is it not?"

"It is," Hope agreed. As always, she had the almost irresistible urge to hug him. She knew from their first encounter, however, that he had no idea how to assimilate even a mild show of affection and she did not want to make him uncomfortable. Instead, she gave him a smile and headed towards the new river.

"Did you speak with your sister?" he asked pleasantly, as if they were a couple out on a morning stroll by the lake, rather than a culturally diverse scientist and philosopher in the midst of a lowly evolved alien village.

"I did. She made a favorable offer without me having to goad her into one."

"Will we be leaving soon?"

"Yes. I'm afraid we will be on the next barge out of here, in the early morning. I trust that will be alright?"

Hahn Chi smiled and bowed, his hands tucked carefully away into the sleeves of his golden robe.

"For you or with you, it will always be right."

Hope blushed under her freckles. He had a way of doing that to her. Just when she thought she had become a mature woman. He made her feel like a child, but not in the same way Faith always managed to do. Faith's patronizing always made her feel small. Hahn made her feel free. Free to be herself. Happy to be herself.

It took only moments for the four strangers in the village to pack their belongings and have a last meal with the natives in the long hut where the tribe ate together on special occasions.

When they had first come to the village, nearly a week ago, they had been welcomed with an air of both generosity and patience. The monks had been taken into the hut of one family that shared what space and food they had and the women were led into another. Only a few of the tribesmen had witnessed the raising of the river on the next day, but word spread like a plasma flare.

By the time the vegetables were pushing out blossoms the entire village was there, watching with amazement tinged with fear. Since then, all the meals had been in the long hut. It was a low building made of bricks like the small communiqué building, but its bricks were made of dried clay rather than koncreta and topped with a roof made of twigs. Hope had no idea where the twigs had come from, since there were no trees in the area, but the thin gnarled branches did look very dry and very old. Someone who had visited and set up an outpost had obviously erected the koncreta hut, the only place with a shred of technology and electricity to power it. Missionaries perhaps, or those from the few larger villages that could almost pass for jungle townships, had most likely put it in place as a relay point. The ancestors of the villagers had undoubtedly raised the long hut.

Either way, on the day that the monks had manifested the river, the evening meal was held in the long communal lodge with what Hope feared was everything the village had to offer. It was accompanied by much bowing from the green-skinned natives along with their sudden aversion to looking the strangers in the eye, which made her decidedly uncomfortable. The monks did not seem to mind their prostrations.

The following morning, by some plan hatched by Madeline and Elaeric, the monks gathered the tribe by the river. The monks began to teach the men of the village to fish and Hope laughed herself to tears while she sat on the bank and watched.

Just as funny, was watching Madeline trying to lead the women into the river. The dyer gathered up her skirts and forded the river where it was most shallow, the water only coming up to her knees. She crossed through it and looked behind her only to find that none of the women had followed her.

"It's perfectly safe!" Madeline assured them, but the only member of the tribe that spoke Anglicus was a man, and upstream on the impromptu fishing expedition. Madeline repeated herself in Elfin, only to be met with the same blank looks. Tickled, Hope watched as her twin went back and forth - wading through the current while shouting encouraging words and beckoning them with her free hand, trying to show them it was safe. The women, however, were having none of it.

Finally, Madeline lost what Hope had always assumed was an inexhaustible patience. On what must have been her tenth return to the shore where the women waited, Madeline hauled a foot back and kicked a wave of the cold water at the women on the shore.

"What are you so afraid of?" Madeline demanded as the women shrank back or danced away, a few letting out yelps of fear. "It's only water!"

Hope knew that no one in the tribe had ever seen moving water in their lifetimes. All the moisture they needed to survive came from the pulpy succulents that grew in the desert. They ate thick chunks of cacti alone, and also pounded it together with the dried pods that came from its flowers and baked the mash into crude biscuits.

One of the younger women, not much more than a girl by her size, shouted back at Madeline and bravely stuck her green foot in the water and kicked a spray back at the mad woman with the wild hair.

Madeline bristled, still for a moment, and then kicked back a spray of water that doused the girl and those standing close to her. This time there was a resounding number of squeals from the group, though this time they were more in enchantment than terror. The girl, however, stepped into the river and, finding it well over her knees and hard to kick, reached down with both hands and sent a wave of water into Madeline's face.

The dyer's green eyes grew wide and then she responded in kind. Within a matter of seconds it was an all-out war, though not against Madeline alone. Every woman was in the water, splashing each other and screaming in delight.

Finally, as their excitement began to dim, Hope watched as Madeline knelt in the river. With all eyes upon her, the dyer scooped up a handful of water and brought it to her lips to drink.

Hushed and reverent, every woman did the same. Dozens of large black eyes went wide with wonder as each woman and girl repeated the gesture.

"Not too much, Madeline!" Hope called from her seat on the riverbank. "They're not used to it!"

Madeline straightened, now soaked to the bone, and beckoned at the women. This time they followed. Madeline led them to the copse of vegetation, chatting and pointing the whole time until she remembered that they could not understand her. Finally, she plucked a fat peapod from a vine and took a bite. She offered the second half to the girl that had started the water fight in the river. The girl took it and looked at an older woman, who nodded after a moment. The girl took a small bite and chewed, a smile spreading across her face. She offered the rest of the pod to the older woman who ate it, her eyes fixed on Madeline. The woman closed her dark eyes as she chewed, then fell to her knees and lay prostrate before Madeline. The rest of the women did the same.

Madeline sighed and shook her head.

7

"At least it is a dry heat, eh, amigo?" the man next to Evan asked, taking a wide-brimmed straw hat from his head and mopping his brow with a red bandana.

"It certainly is," Evan agreed and even though he had heard the phrase many times before, he still had no idea what it meant.

The man gave Evan a wink, as if he knew, and put his sombrero back on his head. He had brown skin patterned with wrinkles but was still handsome. He had paid a handsome price for his tickets to the Corrida de Toros and had seats next to the ring.

Evan was rather enjoying the heat. The sun glinted off his golden hair and golden skin. Perspiration stood out on his own brow and lip, and the back of his shirt clung to the skin between his shoulder blades. Yet the heat was not oppressive. There was something liberating about it.

Maybe that is what it means, to be a dry heat, he thought as he took a long drink of his cocktail, a concoction of a cactus liquor and lime-juice, *that perhaps the dryness has a quality of redemption about it. Maybe that is why it feels so good. Or maybe it is just because we are on vacation.*

Gwen had worked on the casts for the third run for over a year, agonizing over the details. Then, as they went into production, she worked with Faith to devise a system that would reduce training down to only a few months. When they were finished, Faith had all but ordered her biodentical twin to get away and take a break

Evan took another swallow and Gwendolyn smiled at him, also perspiring but in the most lady-like manner, cooling herself with a paper fan. Strands of her brown and gold hair clung to her face and neck.

"Do you feel anything?" she asked, indicating his drink.

Constructs, the First Seven included, were made with a hormone that prohibited them from getting drunk. Still, Evan had discovered that there were a few things that made him feel decidedly different than normal.

"Only that it might be the most refreshing drink I have ever tasted," he said, putting his lips against her cheek so he could taste the salt of her sweat.

Gwen made a face, only because she did not care for the drink herself, then was distracted as the crowd began to stir. The sound of the fifty thousand people filling the stadium started as a muffled wave and grew until it was a roar. "They are about to start!" she exclaimed.

Evan pulled her close and could feel the heat of her body through the white sundress that also clung to her damp skin. He kissed her, opening her mouth with his own and tasting the mint of the cocktail she had been drinking. He pulled away after a moment but still held her body against his own.

"Are you sure you want to do this?" he asked.

She looked into his hazel eyes and nodded, breathless from his kiss. "Yes."

Evan had warned her against it; actually, everyone had warned her against it. Faith was the only one who knew she would not back down.

"It's disgusting," Faith had told her.

"You were the one who said we should take a vacation," Gwen argued.

"Watching animals killed in a brutish fashion before a

crowd is hardly a vacation."

"We'll do other things," Gwen persisted.

Faith gave a slight snort, making her twin blush. "It is against the law on almost every planet in every system."

Gwendolyn sighed. "It is considered an art form by the people in España, and by their ancestors on Earth."

"Where it was also outlawed in almost every country."

"If I have a chance to see cultural art performed in my lifetime, I'm taking it."

Now it was Faith's turn to sigh. "You'll probably puke your guts up."

It was her final word on the matter and it was what worried Evan the most as he held Gwen's face in his hands, staring into her eyes of gold and brown. Faith knew that her twin would never shirk away if art were concerned. Evan knew as well, but still worried about her delicate sensitivity.

She surprised him with a grin. "For Gods' sake, Evan, it's just a pig! It's not like I'm a vegetarian or anything!"

Evan returned her grin and kissed her again before releasing her. Gwendolyn turned back to face the hard-packed dirt of the stadium as the sound of trumpets echoed all around. The music was overtaken by the sound of the crowd as it swelled from every direction, swallowing them. Gwen squealed in delight, clapping her hands as the excitement of the crowd overtook her. Evan took a long swallow from his drink as the heavy wooden doors on the left side of the stadium floor swung open.

The Macchi strode out first, three of them, young men in brilliant turquoise. Short pants and short jackets of velvet, with silk shirts and stockings of bright yellow and soft shoes of black velvet. They wore matching caps of black velvet on their heads.

"They must be horribly hot!" Gwen cried, almost shouting to be heard above the din.

"Not as hot as they are about to be," Evan answered.

The Macchi were followed by the Matadors, slightly older and exponentially more poised. Their shirts and stockings were scarlet, rather than yellow, and their pants and jackets were heavily adorned with silver coins and gold stitching. They wore heavy capes of red velvet lined with yellow silk. Blade thin and with raised chins, they carried themselves with the grace and air of royalty. The crowd went wild at their entrance and they bowed deeply at the waist. Women threw flowers (and undergarments) at their feet.

The trumpets were joined by the pounding of drums and a crescendo of stringed guitars. The six men spread out in a half-circle, turning this way and that so they may bow to each part of the crowd. The Matadors did so with a flourish of capes. After much cheering and praise, the Matadors took a step back into the shade and each held out an arm, inviting the Macchi to take the field. With a bow, the young men did so and only a moment later the wooden doors on the opposite side of the stadium swung open. A hush fell over the crowd as the animal stepped into the open air and snorted.

The "pig" Gwen was expecting turned out to be a wild boar that Evan guessed to be thirteen feet long and close to five feet tall at the shoulders. The huge head took up a third of its body with an arched ridge of bone between the ears. From there a rough mane sloped down in one direction towards a much lower but very powerful hind-end. The other end of the beast sported a long snout, complete with razor-sharp tusks that were longer than a man's arm. They were emasculated by having a cheerful daisy tied to each one with a ribbon – but they were no less deadly.

"My God!" Gwen exclaimed. "That thing is huge! Is it real?" she asked Evan, having to shout to be heard over the crowd.

"It's not manufactured," he shouted back as he clapped along with the cheering masses, "if that's what you mean. But it is unnaturally bred, fed, and pumped with steroids for its purpose!"

Gwen nodded as she felt the sweat trickle down her neck, clapping as well though she felt her first sense of horror. The purpose of the boar was to be killed, taking lives with him if he could. She lifted her chin and threw back her shoulders and clapped harder.

Most eyes were on the boar as his heavy head swung back and forth, trying to determine where it was and what was going on. Evan's eyes, however, were on the Macchi. These young men, usually with more bravado than brains, hoped to be Matadors someday. The life of a Matador was no less dangerous, but it came with riches and respect. Whichever Macchi killed the boar today, would get to stand with the Matadors and take on the Toro.

Two of the Macchi were looking at the boar now, sizing him up. One, however, was scanning the crowd. Not the entire crowd, Evan noticed, just the ones that sat closest to the ring. It was not surprising. The ring-side seats were always occupied by the wealthy and elite and both Macchi and Matadors alike were amenable to the monies and favors the upper class might shower upon them. His eyes, so dark they looked to be black, stopped when they reached Evan.

"That's a little creepy," Evan murmured as he drained his glass and put it on a serving tray as it floated by. He reached for another only to have his hand swatted away by the man next to him.

"Aye!" the gentleman cursed with good humor. "Es mierda!" He turned the tray and retrieved two cocktails from the other side. They looked the same to Evan as what he had been drinking before, save for the vessels, which were thicker glass and tinged with blue. "Añejo is much better, and more fitting," the man explained as he handed one of the glasses to Evan. "Salud!" he exclaimed, holding his glass high.

"Salud!" Evan echoed, touching his glass the One the man held out to him before taking a drink. The man watched him carefully over the rim of his own glass. Evan smiled and nodded. "Smoother," he acknowledged, making the gentleman grin. Evan's hazel eyes shifted to the field and the eyes of the man next to him followed.

The three Macchi had stepped forward, small javelins in their hands. In unison they stood on their toes and held the javelins against their chests, saluting the boar. Even over the sound of the crowd, Evan could hear Gwen's sigh. The ritual, already started by the music, continued with the dance. It was art in motion.

The Macchi drew back their weapons, took their aim, and let them fly.

Each one found its mark, the heavy muscle in the shoulders of the boar, behind its enlarged skull. The animal roared in anger and pain, rearing slightly on its short back legs, then swinging its head around, ropes of saliva flung in all directions. Then the Macchi moved in closer, pulling out long and slender knives, continuing the dance.

The dance was interrupted as a young man with brown skin and black hair in blue jean pants and a yellow shirt jumped over the rail and ran at the fight.

Evan opened his mouth to ask Gwen if she knew what was happening, but the gentleman on his other side leaned close and told him. "Anyone in the crowd is welcome to fight for the honor of the kill!" he shouted over the jeers of the crowd. "It is usually the very young and brave, or the very drunk and stupid!"

Evan nodded with a grin to show that he understood and took a swallow of his drink as he turned his face back to the arena. The Macchi stood by, giving the young man a chance at the creature. Slaver hung from its snout and the three javelins stood out on his neck like spines. The colossal swine stomped at the ground and moved his head to the newcomer. It gave a great squealing bellow and the man turned on his heel and bolted for safety.

The man next to Evan laughed with the rest, clapping hands that were strong and weathered. "If you think that beast looks big from here," he shouted, "imagine what he is like close-up!"

"How big do you think he is?" Evan shouted back, clapping as well.

The man gave an exaggerated shrug. "Two thousand kilos?" he guessed. "But fast for one so large. The boars can run forty-five kilometers an hour!"

The crowd jeered as the man reached the inner part of the ring and leapt for the edge. Arms reached down to help pull him up. All eyes went back to men and beast and the dance continued.

The first Macchi stepped close to the wounded animal, feinted a jab and then slashed at the boar's neck. He found his mark, then the boar found his own. He swung his massive head and a great tusk, adorned with an innocent daisy, cut through the young man's hamstring like a razor as he tried to dance away.

There was a collective gasp from the crowd.

The injury was debilitating but not fatal, save for the fact the man had collapsed to his knees and was incapable of getting away quickly. Certainly not quickly enough. The boar charged and crushed the young man's skull under its hooves. The boar slashed apart the man's head with its tusks as if it were a ripe melon and trampled his body for good measure. Standing atop the gore, it let out a throaty scream of victory, echoed by the crowd. It was not often that a Macchi fell so quickly. Blood soaked into the hardpan of the arena.

The animal, wild with bloodlust, ran for the next Macchi. This one was quicker, delivering a deep stab into the neck of the boar before pulling his blade free and whirling away.

The boar bawled in pain, swinging his head, looking for the transgressor. He spotted the guilty Macchi and charged at him, his head down. Once again the Macchi whirled away, delivering a slash this time and cutting the animal from lip to ear.

The third Macchi joined the battle, taking advantage of the animal's pain and confusion. Approaching the boar from its left rear side, he lunged low and drove a slender sword into the swine's belly. The brute swung its tusks high, trying to halve the young man. The Macchi, however, went daringly low and rolled under the snout of the monster, snatching a daisy from a deadly tusk before popping up on the other side.

The crowd was riotous. It was always the honor for the victor to take a flower from the animal once it had fallen. Only the truly fearless would dare take the prize while the animal was alive and wild with a lust for death.

The beast turned and charged at the fearless Macchi, who demonstrated his bravery once more by not turning or whirling away. He stood his ground and pulled back at the last second, going up high on his toes and arching his back in the manner for which the Matadors were famous. The monster, set on its course, missed him by a hair's breadth and charged on – straight into the other Macchi. The Macchi tried to spin away as he had done the first time, but he was not fast enough. A great tusk ripped through the muscle of his thigh, spinning him around even as the beast turned for another charge.

The Macchi, bleeding fatally and panic-stricken, was gored.

One tusk broke through the flesh between his hip and his rib, while the other one went clean through his middle. Its white tip, protruded from the back of the fighter's velvet turquoise coat, glistening with his blood.

The boar shook his head furiously, shaking the Macchi as if he were a ragdoll, finally dislodging his body and flinging it away into a bloody heap upon the hardpan. The crowd screamed – some for the boar and some for the fallen Macchi. The stadium shook with the violence of their fervor.

Evan kept a hand on Gwendolyn's back, thinking she would turn and bury her face in his chest but he was wrong.

She leaned forward instead, her hands gripping the railing, watching intently.

The last Macchi, having gained the flower, had the choice to fight the animal or grant it its life. The young man ran his dark eyes over the roaring crowd and then squared off against the boar, placing the stem of the daisy between his teeth. The swine seemed to take the action as a personal insult and gave another squealing bellow as it charged the man. The Macchi again waited until the huge beast was nearly upon him, then up onto his toes he went before driving his sword into the neck of the boar as it charged by. It went much deeper this time, so much so that the Macchi could not pull it free.

The beast, hair bristling and with blood dripping and running from its many wounds, turned as the Macchi drew his last weapon, a knife. Panting, the animal stomped at the ground with a hoof as it prepared for another charge. Then its foreleg buckled. Then the other. The Macchi approached slowly as it made an effort to stand. The effort was too much. The creature fell over, shaking the ground and raising a cloud of dust. It lay there quivering and snorting as the young fighter reached it. Even on its side, the shoulder of the brute was as high as the young man's chin. With a dramatic sweep of his knife, the Macchi cut open a three-foot slit in the boar's throat. The animal kicked once and went still, his blood pouring out and pooling before soaking into the hard-packed dirt.

The already wild crowd grew wilder – shouting, cheering, stomping feet and clapping hands. The fighter had brought down the monster, which was already being maneuvered onto a hydraulic lift. The machine would take it to the outside of the arena where it would be roasted. The young man had won not only the battle, but also the right to fight the bull with the Matadors. It was a great accomplishment and a great honor.

With the first fight done, Evan kept his eyes on Gwen who, though pale, seemed composed. He clapped harder, not for the Macchi, but for her. Pride welled inside his body, seeing her so strong.

His hazel eyes looked up, rapidly alert as a perceptible hush fell over the stadium. The Macchi had turned on his heel and his dark eyes were passing over them. He removed the daisy from between his teeth and walked purposefully towards the edge of the ring on a direct course that would take him straight to where Evan and Gwen stood in front of their seats.

The black eyes of the young man were fixed on Gwendolyn and Evan fought the urge to step protectively in front of her. He did not want to show any disrespect for the culture of España or its people. He put his drink down on a floating tray and waited, his muscles flexing involuntarily.

The young man reached the ring and, with a flourish, presented the flower to Gwendolyn. He had a thin face, a thin nose, and a thin chin. Evan wondered what it would be like to drive his fist into each one. Blushing, Gwendolyn reached down to accept the daisy. The Macchi said something to her in Spanish that Evan did not catch, but he did not miss the way the man's fingers caressed Gwendolyn's hand as he drew away. Evan's hazel eyes, narrowed to slits, widened as the bastard winked at her as he turned away.

A dangerous second hung in the air while Evan considered going after him, but a second was all it took for the man next to him to hand him a fresh drink, distracting him. He had to yell at the construct to be heard over the crowd that had gone crazy again at the exchange between the Macchi and the pretty señorita.

"Maybe," the man shouted while clapping like mad, "if he bests the Toro, he will give her the ear!"

"Not if he wants to keep his own," Evan murmured, taking a long swallow from his drink. The man, though he could not have heard, laughed uproariously and clapped Evan on the back.

"It is a great honor, señor!"

"Mmmhmm."

Evan took another long drink as Gwendolyn gave him a nervous smile. He gave her a reassuring grin and she relaxed visibly, enough to help herself to a glass of cava from a passing tray. Evan did not know if he should read anything into that or not, but the call of the trumpets stole their attention once again.

All eyes went to a pair of tall and polished wooden doors in the arena as they swung open to admit a horse and rider, then another, then another.

"The picadors," Gwendolyn said, clapping with the masses. Evan nodded even though he already knew. The men, dressed in brilliant red silk striped with yellow, rode horses with protective gear and carried long, sharpened lances. Then the bugles sounded to introduce the combatants.

This time each Matador stepped forward one at a time, receiving a lengthy personal introduction over the loudspeakers. The Matadors were from different districts and were cheered for by different parts of the stadium that were there to support their hometown heroes. Each one gave many bows and flashed their capes in a jaunty manner as they paraded around the edge of the hardpan, close to the innermost ring of spectators.

The Macchi received only a brief introduction, since he was formerly unknown, but received applause from all around as the victorious underdog and was the clear favorite of the crowd. Not only did he leer openly at Gwendolyn as he passed by, but his attention caused one of the Matadors to look her over as well. Evan cocked his head, suddenly calm as he watched the competition compete.

Finally, after they had flashed their sultry eyes at every woman in the front rows of the arena and their chests had all swelled till Evan thought they might burst, the horns that sounded the opponent blared. The Matadors and lone Macchi turned as one, spread out again in a half-circle with their chins held high, and faced the wooden doors on the far side of the hardpan. These doors were wider, and more weathered. They swung open and their thud against the walls of the arena crumbled the stucco which pattered to the ground. A muffled hush filled the stadium once again.

At first, the opened doors revealed nothing but an arc of darkness. Those close to the door could hear the sound of a snort and grunt. This was not the grunt, however, of some wild swine. It was the grunt of a monster. Finally, a shadow emerged from the darkness of the tunnel.

"Ahhhhh!"

"Ohhhh!"

There was a collective sigh of ecstasy and horror as the monster stepped into the light. The bull, almost seven feet tall and weighing near four thousand pounds, made the giant wild boar look like a suckling pig. The creature looked more like a transport vehicle than an actual animal. A giant copper ring hung between its flaring nostrils. Its massive head held high a pair of horns, each one four feet long from the base to its curved tip. At the end of each of those sharpened points was tied a red rose.

Smooth black hair covered the huge muscles that bulged over every angle of the monstrous bull. It stood its ground, waiting and watching.

The Matadors and the Macchi took slow, purposeful steps towards the beast, drawing their half-circle closer and closer. They stopped when they were each thirty feet from the bull, drawing themselves up in the murmur of the crowd. The bull looked at them through half-lidded eyes, disgusted.

Then the first Matador stepped in, approaching the bull with quick, dance-like steps. He pranced close and then pranced away, teasing now and then with his red cape. The bull did nothing but look at the man with disdain.

The second Matador stepped in, prancing and dancing his way to the Toro until he was right in front of the beast. He flashed his cape, making the fabric snap in front of the animal's nose. The bull looked at the man with nothing but contempt. The Matador bowed and backed away.

The final Matador approached in the same fashion. In addition to the dancing and cape flapping, this one thrust his chest out, only inches from a sharpened horn, and yelled insults at the animal, challenging him. The bull turned his face away in repugnance, a burst of wet air discharging from each nostril.

The Matadors retreated as one, their primary mission in the dances being only to seek out any weaknesses in the bull. They gave way to the picadors, the Macchi not having the right yet to challenge the beast. The three riders came forth, lances held high and straight.

A bugle sounded and the first one charged headlong, letting his lance fly and land – sinking deep into the muscle behind the bull's neck. The bull snorted in surprise and backed away a few paces, his massive head swinging around to find the offender as the second picador let fly his weapon. It found its mark and stood quivering in the mass of flesh behind the bull's head. The animal let out a throaty lowing and stamped the ground, raising clouds of dust around its massive hooves as the third picador made his run. This time, the bull was not to be fooled.

The monster lowered its horns and charged. The lance hit first, driving deep into the bull's upper shoulders. The bull hit second, driving his horns deep into the horse's belly. The horse tried to sidestep, then reared in panic, tearing the gash in its side open even wider. The horse shrieked in pain and terror then toppled over, crushing the picador beneath its body. The bull stepped back, his horns dripping blood. One of the roses was lost in the attack, the second still held fast, covered in gore.

The crowd screamed with the dying horse.

"The lances are to cut the muscles in the neck of the Toro!" the handsome man next to Evan shouted. "See how he already struggles to hold up his head?"

Evan nodded, he did indeed see. That and more.

The dance of the Matadors resumed.

It was much like the fight of the Macchi and the boar, save the Matadors were much more fluid and graceful, the beast more massive and monstrous. Capes flapped and swords found their mark time and again as they attempted to tire the mammoth bull. But it seemed that the colossal beast would not fatigue. It only became angrier.

One Matador was gored and the sector of the stadium from his district moaned with disappointment. Another of the fighters had his knee crushed under one of the creature's massive hooves. The crowd cheered as he was dragged to safety.

Evan had hoped that the Macchi would die horribly and soon but, so far, no such luck. Gwendolyn had gone a shade paler, either from the heat or the amount of blood, but for once Evan did not notice. He was too intent upon the fight.

The Macchi and the last Matador began taking turns at the animal, trying to wear it down. After another thirty minutes of the beast being taunted and hooked, Evan finally saw the right knee of the animal buckle so slight and so quick that it was virtually negligible.

Evan never paused. He gripped the railing of the arena and vaulted over it, racing over the barren field as soon as he had landed. The hot sun shone on his golden hair like a beacon as he tore across the hardpan.

"Evan!" Gwendolyn screamed, grabbing the rail and almost going over after him.

"Señorita!" the gentleman shouted, clutching her arm. Gwendolyn whirled on him, her brown and gold eyes wild with fear. She turned them back to the arena where Evan was sprinting for the center.

He could hear the roar of the crowd that grew like a wave as they saw him, but it was muffled. He never slowed and he didn't bother to pick up a weapon. Instead he charged the beast headlong, seized its right horn as he ran past and then dug his heels into the dirt.

An hour ago, the creature would have flung him away like a man flicking a bug from his arm. Now, nearing exhaustion with the heat and the wounds to its body, weakened by blood loss and its neck muscles torn and its right knee injured, the great head dipped and the animal staggered forward, listing to its right.

The eyes of the bull rolled in anger and fixed on him. It tried to shake him loose but it was too weak. The roar of the crowd swelled.

Evan, his eyes full of horn and hair and his nose filled with blood and sweat and stink, wrapped an arm around the horn he was holding and with his other arm reached out and grabbed the ring in the beast's nose. He kept his heels dug into the ground. It was too much for the bull. It roared in anger and pain as it fell on its right shoulder, driving a foot of horn into the hardpan and making the ground quake. The roaring crowd made the stadium quake even harder.

Evan pushed his body through the triangle of space between the bull's monstrous head, and the dirt, coming out behind its shoulder. He walked around the head to face the beast as it struggled to rise but its foreleg was now broken as well as torn. The construct planted his foot against the horn that had been driven into the dirt.

Dazed, the animal shuddered. One eye, as big as Evan's fist, was close to the ground. The other was almost level with Evan's own eyes. It snorted at him as he reached up and pulled the rose from its other horn. The construct took a step back and the bull lowed in pain, trying to pull its horn from the ground.

Evan's eyes caught movement and his head snapped to the left. It was the Matador, smiling proudly and offering Evan a slim sword, hilt first. The Macchi stood behind him, sneering at the construct. Evan contemplated taking the sword and killing the Macchi, but he knew that even at such an ungodly contest, such an act would be unseemly. He knew, though, that by winning the rose he had the right to decide the bull's fate.

He did not have to see his love to seek the answer, he already knew.

Still, his hazel eyes swept round the arena to land on Gwendolyn. Her brown and gold hair was loose and wild and her sweat made her white dress and the dust of the arena cling to her body and yet Evan was sure he had never seen her more beautiful. She gave a slight but firm shake of her head and he grinned. He turned back to the Matador, the sun shining bright on his honey-colored skin and glinting off the gold in his eyes.

"El Toro vive!" he announced loudly.

The Matador's eyebrows went up in surprise, but he gave the construct a solemn smile and bowed gracefully. The Macchi glared at him for a moment, then also bowed, though not as deeply. Evan grinned and turned to the massive bull that was struggling to rise and regain its footing. It snorted and grunted, runners of snot coming from its nostrils as it tried to free its horn from the dirt. Evan gave the animal a deep bow before turning and walking away.

The construct could not remember feeling such stimulation to his senses in all his days. His ears were full of sound: the Macchi cursing under his breath and the Matador shushing him. The groans of the animal as it tried to revive itself as the vets arrived to attend it. The riotous noise of the masses in the stands.

He could feel the sun on his skin, making it perspire, and he could feel the dry air moving over his body, drying the sweat that stood out on his face and his chest. His sense of smell was overcome by the coppery scent of blood and his mouth was full of the taste of salt and dirt. The sun shone on his face and lit up the stadium as if it were on fire, but all he could focus on was Gwen. She grew nearer with every step and he could not keep the grin from his face. In the same manner, she could not keep from grinning back at him.

He reached the ring of the arena and climbed up and over it to the stands where she waited. He extended the hand that held the rose and she grasped his whole hand and held it to her chest as she kissed him hard on the mouth. The noise from fifty thousand spectators was deafening.

Her slender fingers entwined in his golden locks and gathered up small fistfuls of hair. She pulled away after a long kiss to reprimand him, her hands still locked on his hair. "What were you thinking?" she demanded, breathless. "What if you had been killed?"

Evan laughed and kissed her again, the edge of her lip, her cheek. "I would not leave you so easily," he assured her as he held her body close to his own.

"And the bull?" she asked earnestly.

Evan put his forehead against hers. "He will be allowed to live out the rest of his life in peace," he assured Gwendolyn. "I only hope that we can do the same."

Gwendolyn laughed and kissed him, losing herself in the blood and the heat and the momentous idea of eternity. "We will," she promised. "We most certainly will!"

EIGHT

Titan, I had to admit, was a lovely moon. The second largest moon in the solar system had been colonized by the elves when they had encountered the human race from Earth trolloping along in space and decided to throw their lot in with us. I am told it was where the first dragons were brought, searching for something, somewhere, or someone that could help them sustain their immortality.

It was still inhabited mostly by elves. The humans that lived there were very wealthy, as were the smattering of a few other races that had been discovered and befriended over the past century.

I sat in a stadium with two thousand other parents, clapping now and then for each speaker who took the stage to offer words of encouragement and praise. The artificial sunshine was bright but not hot, a trick managed by the elves when they encapsulated the moon.

A light source of starfire circled the atmosphere jacket, rounding the equator every twenty-eight hours – a standard elfin day. Good thing, too. Otherwise the days on Titan would be long (about fifteen human days long) and very dark. The moons of Jupiter (the "human moons") had much the same device. The sun was too damn far away to be of much use other than a point of orbit and an astronomical locator. The starfire kept the air at a constant but pleasant temperature during the day and a slightly cooler, but still pleasant temperature, at night.

Jean's school, which I had visited often over the years, was a lovely set of buildings and halls and dormitories. They were all built of an unusual but visually arresting type of stone that was milky white in color but sparkled with a hint of green. I suspected it was some type of quartz known only to the elves. The structures, including the small stadium, were nestled down in a bowl between high, rolling hills to three sides and a forest of blue pines to the west.

The list of speakers finally ended and the graduation began in earnest. My chest swelled as I picked up the flimsy program of p-beck. The part of the ceremony currently in session was lit up in blue light, a long list of names. My finger trailed down the list till I saw hers.

Jean-Marie Mattatock.

My chest swelled again and I heaved a sigh. The "M's" were a long way down the list.

Too bad we're not Adams, I thought.

"We would still be here the same amount of time," Mira said. She looked at me and smiled as her hand sought out mine and gave it a squeeze.

I laughed and squeezed back. I had thought for many years that she could read my mind because of how close we were. When I told her that once she had laughed and said it was only that I was more transparent than glass. I guessed she was right. Faith always saw right through me as well and, after Mira had told me about transparency, Faith did not give me the creeps as bad as she once had.

Mira looked more than beautiful that day. I don't know if it was that she wore a sundress rather than a skirt suit, the luster of her hair in the bright light, the blaze of starfire in her dark eyes, or simply because I loved her so much. The reasons didn't matter. She was stunning.

We clapped for each girl, it was only polite, but when they called Jean's name I clapped hard enough to sting my hands, and my hands were hard. Mira and I both stood and applauded as our daughter crossed the stage and shook hands with the dean and accepted her diploma, then hugged each other tight before we sat back down.

After that, the list of girls that were left seemed to go by quickly. Before I knew it, we were on the field - on grass that looked so real that I had not known it was artificial even when I was standing on it. We waited on the number four line, as Jean had instructed, and then there she was.

I had seen my daughter smile a lot over the years. She was a generally happy, if sometimes snotty, person. But nothing compared to what overcame her beautiful face as she strode towards us, her arms thrown wide and her dark hair streaming out behind her. Though I knew she had enjoyed school and loved her close friends, she looked like a soul freed from purgatory.

Mira, tears streaming from her eyes, embraced her and I threw my arms around them both. Jean pushed away after a moment and looked at me with brows raised over her beautiful dark blue eyes.

"Dad!" she exclaimed.

"I know," I said. Mira had bought, and made sure that I wore, a suit. "Your mother got it for me, and I'm glad she did. If I had shown up in my clothes, even the good ones, I'm sure the school would have had me behind a mower rather than in the stands."

"And you'd have done a better job than the ones they have!" Jean assured me, throwing her arms around me again. I hugged her back and pulled the picto from my pocket when she pulled away. Laughed again. "Daaad! Those are so old!"

"It's brand new!" I argued. "But if you mean I am old-fashioned then so be it. You already knew that."

I snapped a picture of her, then her with Mira. So beautiful and so similar, they could be sisters. Then I snapped dozens of photos of her with her friends, her bunkmates, her studymates, her teammates. There were even a few teachers that she wanted a photo with. Mira could not stop dabbing her eyes with a handkerchief. My lips and cheeks began to hurt from smiling so much. I should have enjoyed it while I could. The celebratory meal we had after the ceremony and pictures was much different.

ෆ

Jean shed her cap and gown as we walked to a paved area where aircars were parked and aircabs were lined up along the curb. I was pleased to see that graduation garb had not changed much over the years. The only difference I could see was that the four points of the cap turned up a bit and it was slightly puffy. I did not know if that was an elfish influence or simply fashion. Underneath the gown Jean wore a black top that tied behind her neck and a long black skirt. I wasn't too keen on the fact I could see a bit of her skin between her top and skirt (even though it was barely as wide as a finger). Still, the reproachful glare from Mira said enough for us both.

Jean rolled her eyes and headed for the cabs. A few airlimos waited beyond the cabs and Mira directed us in that direction. Jean raised her dark and perfect eyebrows at me and whistled.

"Fancy!" Jean exclaimed. "All this for me?"

"Mr. Devereaux has an account here," Mira said simply, as if she were remarking about the weather. The driver held the door open for her as she stepped down and into the back of the limo.

"Mr. Devereaux has an account here," Jean told me with her eyes wide, mimicking her mother in a deep and mocking voice before climbing in. I stifled a laugh and gave her a swat as I followed her inside.

Mira and I had taken the limo from the spaceport so it

wasn't really my first ride in one, it was my second. I watched Jean examine and push the buttons all over the compartment just as I had done. Mira must be used to the type of conveyance since she was totally disinterested in our fancy surroundings as she checked messages on her comset and returned a few calls.

"When did she get so high-falutin'?" I whispered to Jean. I meant it as a joke but Jean shot her mother a look of bored distaste.

"When I was eight," she said without humor.

"Really?" I asked.

Jean nodded. Mira glanced at us, as if aware we were talking about her, but then looked away as she carried on her conversation. I was going to ask Jean what she meant, but Mira finished up and pulled the comset off her ear. She turned to us and her face lit up with excitement once again. It was the expression she had that I loved best.

The airlimo rocked slightly as it picked up speed.

"We're on the hyper-way," Jean remarked, looking out the window. "Where are we going?"

"It's a surprise," Mira said, practically bubbling over. "You're going to love it!"

"Mmmmm," Jean replied as if she might not be sure, but she was smiling.

I wondered when and how this distance between Jean and her mother had come around. I saw them both often - but I now realized, not often together. Mira kissed my cheek and I gave her leg a squeeze. Maybe they had a disagreement recently that I didn't know of, or maybe it was all just my imagination.

There was a feeling of being pushed forward from the seat as the limo slowed and then another bit of slight rocking as it slowed again and took another road. Not long after, it came to a stop and the driver opened the door for us.

"Whhheeooo." I whistled as I got out of the limo. We were on a curved road that looked like it was paved but I could see the black surface was porous, like smooth lava rock. There were giant trees everywhere and the limo had stopped at the bottom of a waterfall that was, craning my neck back to see, I guessed to be close to three hundred feet high. The restaurant was a tree house of sorts, with levels climbing up and up along the cliff to the gorge, intertwined amongst the branches.

I held out a hand to help Jean out of the back, and then Mira, before the driver shut the door.

"One of the most exclusive restaurants in Tarana," Mira informed us quietly with a barely suppressed grin. "Of course it is completely booked for tonight, though they allowed for five families from the school to be here. I know that one is the Dean's family and another is the daughter of the Golbli governor. I wonder who the two others are…" Mira peered about at the patrons seated close to the falls on the first level as we walked to the hostess stand.

The hostess herself gave us an evil leer until she found out we had a reservation, then she was all smiles and graciousness. The hostess took us to the elevator, located in the trunk of the giant tree, where we were handed off to another hostess. Yet another hostess awaited us two hundred feet up and led us through one of the higher levels of the restaurant to our table.

The floor was made of heavy wooden planks and the level was open on all sides, if one didn't count the branches and leaves all around. Heavy vines draped the corners and the air on the left edge boiled with mist from the waterfall. I was never afraid of heights but I hoped our table wasn't close to the edge. I could only trust the staff kept a close eye on anyone drinking.

Mira followed the hostess and I followed Mira. "I hope I don't need bug spray," I whispered to Jean.

"Bugs aren't supposed to bite these people," she whispered back. "It would be considered bad taste."

I snorted. Luckily, we had just reached our table, not too close to the edge, and Mira was too preoccupied with who-was-to-sit-where to pay us any mind. She sat strategically facing the elevator, so she could see whomever came in, and motioned for me to sit beside her. Jean sat facing us. The table had been set for four but the hostess removed the extra place setting and chair so that Jean could sit in the middle, facing us both. I had never seen that done before but I liked it.

The waiter brought us glasses of ice-water with crushed mint and we ordered from a menu dominated by exotic meats. Mira leaned close to me to share a bit of gossip in hushed tones.

"That couple over there," she said, pretending to wipe her mouth with a heavy cloth napkin. "That is the IGC Director of Finance for this galaxy. And his mistress."

My gaze fell on the older man and much, *much* younger woman. I almost said something back to Mira, then I wondered with a jolt how old I would look sitting next to her if Faith had not given me an injection to slow my aging.

How old am I? I wondered. I never kept track. But I kept track of Jean's birthdays. That would put me in my early fifties. What did that look like? I glanced at the others seated in the restaurant, trying to guess at who might be close to my real age. The face I saw in the mirror every morning after I shaved was not far over twenty years old. Same blonde hair, same blue eyes. Hardly a wrinkle.

If I was dining with Mira, and looking my true age, would people be whispering behind their napkins about us?

Without a doubt. People were gossipy creatures, and not just humans. Golbli were as bad and elves were even worse. I saw there were a few people that already glanced at us and whispered. GwenSeven was all the rage now and Mira, after all, was one of the First Seven.

People often recognized her when we were out and I knew that she took a secret pleasure in it. I also suspected that

Devereaux liked it as well and encouraged her to go out as often as she liked, as long as she was not needed by his side.

"So!" Mira announced as she laid her napkin down across her lap, distracting me from my thoughts. She was settling into her seat and smiling at Jean. "I must admit, I got a peek at your exit interview. It was noted on there that you plan on continuing your education, but it did not say in which field."

Jean took a sip of her water and put it back on the table, never taking her dark blue eyes off of her mother.

"Well?" Mira asked, almost bubbling over with excitement. "You have kept your father and I in the dark this past year - are you going to tell us? Is it business school? I know you've taken a few odd medical classes, but not enough to be going into medicine..." she trailed off, waiting for Jean. Jean put her left elbow on the table and touched her thumbnail to her lip in a manner oddly reminiscent of Faith. It appeared that she did not want to answer her mother and, for a second, I thought she wasn't going to do it.

"Actually," Jean finally said, "I've applied to flight school."

Mira's expression of utter befuddlement was almost enough to make me laugh. I think Jean felt the same but she knew better as well and held very still while I coughed into my napkin.

"I beg your pardon?" Mira asked, thinking maybe she had not heard her daughter correctly.

"I applied to flight school. The IGC School of Aeronautics and Astronautics. I was accepted last month."

"Congratulations, honey!" I exclaimed.

A pilot! I could hardly believe it. My chest swelled with pride and I was about to stand so I could circle the table and hug my daughter but Mira's head snapped towards me and her dark eyes pinned me to my seat. Jean's words had finally sunk in and I could see that for some reason Mira was mad. Really mad.

"Did you know about this?" she demanded, her voice barely above a whisper.

"No," I replied. "How would I?"

She gave me a doubtful look that astounded me as much as her angry reaction and turned her face back to our daughter. Jean sipped her ice-water and daintily picked a piece of mint leaf off her right canine with the nail of her little finger. She did not seem surprised in the least by her mother's reaction. I imagine she had even been expecting it.

Mira straightened, regaining her composure. "And what exactly do you intend to pursue?' she asked.

"I'm going to be a pilot," Jean told her. "A fighter pilot."

"A *what?*" Mira asked, her rising tone reflecting disbelief and horror before it became angry again.

"A fighter pilot," Jean repeated.

Mira opened her mouth to respond but whirled on me instead. "Does this have something to do with that crest?" she demanded.

Jean sat forward before I could answer, abruptly intrigued. "Crest?" she asked. "What crest?"

I pressed my lips together and shook my head slowly at Mira. "I never told her."

"What are you guys talking about?" Jean asked.

Mira, realizing she had possibly opened a new can of worms, sighed and looked at Jean. "It's nothing." When Jean gave her a look of feigned patience from under her dark brows Mira shook her dark locks. "Just some heirloom of your father's family that is passed down from pilot to pilot."

I didn't like how she dismissed it so easily but I wasn't ready to jump in between them unless I had to. Thankfully, the waiter arrived with our dinner.

"Ah!" I exclaimed as he set the plates down in front of us. "Maybe this discussion will be better after some ostrick!"

"It's pronounced ostrich," Jean corrected me with a smile. "And you have buffalo."

"There's definitely some sort of bull being served here," Mira murmured, all her gossipy girlishness gone.

Jean gave a snort and, though I smiled, I knew she wasn't trying to be funny. We ate in silence for most of the meal and I had the waiter bring me a glass of wine. I wished there was something I could order for Mira to calm her nerves. She ate in a brisk, business-like manner, obviously deep in thought. When she was finished she put down her fork and wiped her mouth with her napkin.

"No," she said.

"Beg your pardon?" Jean asked, looking and sounding every bit like her mother. I don't know if she was doing it on purpose or simply not aware of it.

"No," Mira repeated. "I won't let you. It is unseemly. You have too many other opportunities."

Jean sat forward. "Unseemly? Let me?" She laughed and looked out at the mist and the jungle-like forest before looking back at her mother. "Being a pilot is a great opportunity. It's the one I am going to take."

"I won't pay for it," Mira stated.

"Mira!" I exclaimed, shocked.

"I wouldn't expect you to," Jean replied, perfectly calm. "As far as I know, you don't make any money anyway."

"Jean!" I exclaimed. Mira looked as shocked as I felt. The evening, the evening of Jean's graduation, had taken a nasty turn and I wasn't going to have any more of it. "Stop it, the both of you!" Jean looked down at her lap and Mira glanced around at the other tables to see if our exchange had been noticed. I didn't care. "This is supposed to be a celebration! Jean, stop baiting your mother." Jean had the decency to look shamefaced but it gave Mira an expression of smug satisfaction. "And Mira," I continued, "we will support her in *whatever* she wants to do."

This time Mira looked down and Jean brightened.

"Thanks, Dad," she said.

I reached my hand across the table and she took it. "I am very proud of you," I told her, giving her hand a squeeze.

"I am too," Mira conceded.

Jean smiled and I thought the evening was going to be saved. "Let's get dessert," I suggested and she nodded vigorously.

A strange noise came then from Mira's purse. She looked surprised as she pulled it from the hook next to her chair and fished her comset out. I was surprised as well. I never wore one unless I was on the jobsite because they were an annoyance, and I knew that Mira always silenced hers during meals for the same reason. Then I realized an emergency call would chime, even when the device was set for mute.

She hooked it over her ear and answered it. "Yes," was all she said before pulling it off and handing it to me. "It's Faith," she said quietly.

Dumbfounded, I put it over my ear. "Yes?" I asked. Faith's voice was clear as a bell and she skipped any sort of greeting.

"Fletcher," she said, "I need you back at the compound. Immediately."

"What is it?" I asked, my mouth dry. Something compelled me to look up and though our small family spat had not drawn any eyes, I saw a few glances at us now. Maybe it was my imagination.

"We have a defective construct. I need you back here to run a check on all subs and equipment to make sure it wasn't anything in the physical manufacturing process."

I looked around again and more people were definitely staring at us. It wasn't my imagination. Mira wasn't the only one with a comset. Most of these people had theirs hooked into newsies. I looked away from them and out into the boiling mist.

"Defective?" I asked, feeling stupid.

"It killed its owner. I have a car pulling up for you right now." There was a slight pause then she said, "Tell Jean I said congratulations." Then she cut the line.

NINE

The smiles of Charity de Rossi and her biodentical were dazzling as they waved at the two-dozen razzi-droids and half a dozen live reporters. Lights flashed as they snapped pictures and microphone wands jutted hungrily at the twins, held back by a trio of broad-shouldered security guard constructs as Llewellyn gently closed the door of their hotel suite, shutting them out.

The dyer, her platinum-blonde hair done in a fanciful twist where it fell over her bare right shoulder, leaned back on the closed door. Her body sagged against it, making her silver dress ride up and bunch at the small of her back, though it sparkled just the same. Her right hand grasped at her heart and was filled with silver fur.

"Jesus!" she gasped. "Could you believe that?"

Charity, wearing the same dress and draped with a matching stole of silver fox, turned to face her twin. Her platinum hair was done in the same manner; only it fell over her bare left shoulder, making the image of looking into a mirror complete.

Charity shook her head as an answer and her blue eyes shifted about the sumptuously appointed suite until they found the bar. She walked over to it on legs that felt like jelly. She brushed the lid off of the ice bucket and dropped a handful of cubes into one glass and then another, not bothering to use the silver-plated tongs. With a trembling hand she poured equal measures of golden liquid from a crystal decanter into the glasses until they were half full. She walked to Llewellyn, who now stood upright with only a shoulder against the door and handed her one of the glasses.

The girls raised their drinks towards one another in a habitual salute and then quaffed them down.

Charity sighed as her trembling ebbed away. "I can't believe you," she said finally. "I cannot believe how quick you can think, react, whatever – and pull it off so flawlessly."

Llewellyn shrugged at the compliment as she took Charity's glass and went to the bar to pour a second round. Charity unwound the length of silver fox from around her shoulders and circled around a sofa before kicking off her heeled sandals and dropping down onto the cushions. Llewellyn handed her a fresh drink and dropped down into a matching side chair, kicking off her own heeled shoes and tucking her feet underneath her bottom.

"What should we do?" Charity asked, sipping her drink this time. "Should we call Faith?"

Llewellyn shook her white-blonde head as she sipped from her own glass. "She already knows," she assured her twin.

Charity nervously tapped her manicured nails on the side of her glass. "What do you think she's doing?"

"I'm sure she made all the calls she needed to make inside of a minute," Llewellyn answered, staring off into nothing. "Now? She is watching and waiting."

Charity took a deep breath and another sip of her drink. She and Llewellyn were currently the most photographed women in the universe. Charity supposed they could be the most famous, though the possibility of being the most infamous now hovered like a swarm of drones.

Faith certainly garnered her share of attention from the media. Though GwenSeven was shared equally by the de Rossi sisters, the eldest was undoubtedly and unquestionably credited with its creation, and Gwen kept to the shadows as much as she possibly could. When it came to science and technology, Faith was in the limelight. But when it came to society, it was Charity and Llewellyn that dominated the spotlight.

The platinum-haired twins who ran finance and marketing for the multi-trillion credit company were the face of GwenSeven, and they loved it. The two were photographed constantly when in public – arm and arm with each other, arm in arm with another gorgeous woman or man, on beaches and yachts, in restaurants and attending any notorious event. They were invited everywhere.

Actors and politicians, guilds and associations, governments and planets all vied for the opportunity to transport and host the beautiful and charming twins to every corner of the universe.

Just that evening they had been on their way to an award show for galactic holos when they were accosted by a set of reporters that were different from the norm.

"Ms. de Rossi! Ms. de Rossi!" they shouted. They had no idea which one was Charity and which was one Llewellyn (they never did) so yelling out the family name usually sufficed for both.

A young but stunning human female with dark skin and narrow eyes had pushed her way before the others, brandishing a silver wand in Llewellyn's face.

"How do feel about the accusation of a GwenSeven construct killing its owner?" she demanded.

Llewellyn had frowned at her in distaste, though this was the first she had heard such a thing. "I think you should get your story straight," she advised the woman. "That human was already dead," she informed her as photo-lights flashed from every direction. "From what I was told, the construct was trying to revive its owner even after help had arrived on the scene."

There was a wild uproar at this and more questions were

screamed out as the camera drones buzzed about and security guards held the media back as the two women made their way from the airlimo to the grandiose building that was hosting the MW1 Holo Awards.

Charity, like Llewellyn, had been stunned at the news. It felt as if her blood had been goosed with ice-water but, like her twin, neither her expression nor her demeanor ever faltered. Her smile was a mask she had learned to wear well in front of the media. That smile had remained frozen on her face as she applauded her way through the awards, inwardly seething and needing desperately to speak with Llewellyn alone.

Llewellyn herself was both smiling and quite animated, but it was more for Charity than for the crowd. She turned to her twin a number of times during the show to give her a look of confidence or lay an assuring hand upon her arm, sometimes leaning close and whispering something to make her laugh.

When the awards were over, Charity's blue eyes searched those of her dyer.

Do we still go to the party? those eyes beseeched. The way and the speed with which news spread meant that everyone would know.

Llewellyn had tipped back her head, exposing a porcelain-like throat bereft of any jewelry, and laughed as if Charity had said the funniest thing.

"Of course, darling!" she exclaimed. She took Charity by a hand that was also empty of jewels – the girls had taken to skipping charms and ornaments for the past week to showcase instead their perfect skin – and pulled her close, entwining their arms. "Perception is reality," she advised, smiling and waving at people as they left the theater and headed up a wide staircase, "and reality is perception."

She kept the same poise as they joined the cocktail party that followed, thrown for the winners and the selected elite of society. Her confidence was more than infectious and the pair were handed drinks within seconds as the winning actress, young Evette Holiday, entered the room and went straight for the de Rossi women. Charity had braced herself as she watched the woman approach with a dramatic flair.

The holo-star, having won best actress, clutched her prize trophy in one arm and her prize boyfriend in the other – practically dragging him to the twins who were being handed flutes of champagne.

"Congratulations," Charity cooed, tilting her head as the picturesque star shifted her trophy to the other arm so she could reach out a hand to grasp Charity's.

"I just heard!" Evette gasped, "and I am so sorry!" The twins raised blonde brows in unison and Evette shook her head in sympathy. "No one knows more than I how unknowing and accusative the media can be!" she assured them.

"Ah!" Llewellyn exclaimed and both de Rossi women nodded in understanding, their faces beautiful and grave.

The boyfriend, with soft brown curls and dark seductive eyes, took two glasses of champagne from a floating tray and handed one to Evette. "You know," he told the girls, motioning to Charity with his glass, "if that construct had medical training, he might have saved that man's life."

Llewellyn nodded sagely. "True," she agreed. "We've just never had a request of that nature."

"You should consider it," he proposed, his glass still aloft as if in toast.

"We should make constructs with medical training," Charity murmured.

"You should," the boyfriend declared emphatically, motioning again with his glass. This time a bit of champagne slopped over the sides and he licked it off his knuckles. Evette, faintly disgusted, turned theatrically to the girls.

"Just don't make any constructs that act!" she exclaimed, following it with a shrill titter of laughter that everyone else in the vicinity duplicated amidst a scattering of applause. The girls joined in, assuring Evette that there were no plans underway to replace the Actors Guild. More laughter followed and the evening wore on until the de Rossi women could make their escape.

Charity tucked her feet under her own bottom on the hotel sofa and sipped her drink. Llewellyn nodded at her.

"Turn on the telly," she instructed.

Charity looked around for a remote before she remembered that there wasn't one. "Holo on!" she commanded and the low table in front of her flared to life. A three-dimensional one-meter tall box rotated above the table, showcasing selections. "News!" Charity commanded. "Galactic wide!"

The cube continued to turn slowly, a different news broadcast on each side. One was a close up of Llewellyn frowning and speaking but she ignored it, searching for something she didn't already know.

"This one!" Llewellyn cried out, reaching out to touch a broadcast that showed a young but stunning human female with dark skin and narrow eyes in front of the theater that had hosted the Holo Awards. The floating cube dissolved to leave a holographic image of the reporter and sound flared from unseen speakers in the table.

"...developments from right here at the MW1 Holo Awards," the reporter was saying. "It has been revealed that the construct in question was trying to save its owner..."

Twin blue eyes grew wide as they watched and listened. Llewellyn reached out and flicked the image away, moving to the next channel. Now an image of an older man with ginger hair going gray at the temples floated above their table.

"...heroic act by a construct almost saved a human life today..."

Llewellyn frowned and flicked to the next channel but it was the same news. "We need to find out what really happened. I doubt the media knows or cares." She dug her silver comset out of her jeweled clutch and hooked it over her ear. "Thomas," she commanded. The comset flickered with light and a second later Llewellyn was speaking, or listening rather, to Thomas. "Mmm hmm," she remarked as Charity flipped through a few more channels but they were all the same, one even declaring that the construct had managed to revive the human but not long enough to get him to the hospital. "I see. Thank you, Thomas."

"It's all the same," Charity said as Llewellyn pulled the comset off of her ear and looked at her twin. "Is it true?" she asked, turning down the volume on the holo. She found it hard to believe that Llewellyn had guessed what had really happened, but it was possible. The owner could have had a heart attack and the construct was simply found standing over the body. It was a possibility she had formulated during the awards and clung to the entire night. Her dyer shook her head.

"The construct stabbed its owner with a kitchen knife."

"Accidentally?" Charity asked, reaching for one last hope. Llewellyn's face contorted slightly, producing a look that was half smile and half grimace.

"Fifty times?"

Charity felt her stomach clench and her heart stop for a second before it juttered back into an irregular beat. Her blue eyes went back to the holos but the dyer's eyes stayed fixed upon her twin. "Then none of this is true," Charity whispered. "The reports of the construct trying to save the human. It isn't real." She looked back at Llewellyn.

"We made it real," she stated.

Charity's bright blue eyes widened even further. "I can understand how we could mislead one reporter, but...*all* of them? Even those we didn't talk to? One of those reports was coming from another system!" She followed Llewellyn's gaze as it flicked back to the holo.

"Turn it up," she instructed and Charity did so. It was an image of the young man who had escorted Evette Holiday to the awards.

"I was told first hand this evening by the lovely de Rossi twins," he was telling a reporter with a mike wand, "that GwenSeven will now be instilling medical training in their constructs."

Charity's hand went up to cover her mouth. "Is Faith going to be mad?" she whispered through slender fingers.

Llewellyn scowled as she thought. "I don't know," she admitted, "but I doubt she is watching this shit. At least, not only this shit. Financial news!" she commanded and the cube reappeared with a myriad of selections. Llewellyn chose one at random and it expanded.

"Com lines are jammed," a wrinkled newscaster was reporting, "all going to GwenSeven with orders for the new constructs that will have medical training. Ninety percent of the calls are from elderly persons, a demographic that was previously untapped by the GwenSeven Corporation..."

Llewellyn flipped to the next channel where an anchorman, even more grisly than the last, read from a teleprompter.

"The cost of the new constructs is expected to be considerably higher, though we are waiting to hear from GwenSeven to get the exact figures..."

Llewellyn turned off the sound and turned to face her twin. "We can train a construct in lifesaving techniques inside of ten minutes."

Charity nodded. "Even more if given an hour," she agreed. "How to administer an injection, suture a wound... How much more could we charge for such a feature?"

Llewellyn smiled lasciviously. "What price do people put on their own lives?" she asked.

Charity's eyes became distant as she thought. "For their own lives? They would pay anything." Her eyes focused and fixed again on her twin. "But I think a twenty-five percent increase in price will be a good place to start."

Llewellyn stood and grinned, "In that case I don't think Faith is going to be angry, not in the slightest." She stooped to place her hands on either side of Charity's face and kissed her quickly on both cheeks. "Order us some men and champagne," she told her.

Charity's smile became as lecherous as Llewellyn's. "How many?"

Llewellyn laughed and her blue eyes glinted. "At least two of each. At least!" The dyer laughed again and Charity almost joined her, but something held her back.

"Were there any witnesses?" she asked instead, her voice quiet. Llewellyn took a deep breath and nodded.

"A neighbor arrived at the end. The owner was quite dead but the construct was still stabbing it repeatedly. The construct killed that owner, Charity, there is no doubt about that."

"But there is," Charity argued. "More than doubt, there is a whole other story." She nodded towards the holo table. "A story we told that is not true. But they believed us. Why?"

Llewellyn's eyes were grave as she looked at her twin. "Because of who we are," she told her, "and how we handled it."

"Perception is reality," Charity whispered, echoing Llewellyn's words from earlier in the evening.

The dyer nodded and a small smile returned to her lips. "Order yourself someone tall, with green eyes," she suggested. "It will lift your spirits."

"Not as much as the money we are going to make," Charity said, a smile touching her own full lips.

"Did you learn anything else from this nasty business?"

Charity nodded and looked at the holo where the ancient anchorman droned on in muted silence. "That he is hideous. We should manufacture a number of constructs and get them into the media industry."

Llewellyn dipped her head slightly. "It would be best not to tell anyone they are constructs."

Charity looked back at her dyer. "And for them to report the news as it should be, not necessarily as it truly is."

Llewellyn's blue eyes were somber for a moment, then sparkled as she threw off the gravity of the moment the way any woman might shed a coat. She gave her twin another peck on the cheek and headed to her bedroom to change. Charity's eyes regained their own sparkle and she rang for an attendant to see to their needs.

 ONE ZERO

Hope ran her finger over a small stone half-embedded in the dark earth of the riverbank. She, along with Madeline and Hahn and Elaeric, were on the dwarf planet of Pluto. The last stop on their journey to Dione.

"It is the farthest planet in the system," Hahn had told her the night before their arrival. "It used to be the coldest. And it is so small that it was demoted to a dwarf planet over a thousand years ago. The Dragons, directed by the elves of course, moved two infant suns to the outer system. It was their first experiment in what they called 'gentle terraforming.' They supplied only heat and atmosphere and stepped back to see what would happen. Now, it is a quiet hideaway."

It certainly was quiet. They were on the grassy bank of a wide river, breathing the clean air and acclimating to the new solar system. Elaeric and Hahn were natives to the system and had acclimated within near twenty-four hours. Hope and Madeline were still a little lightheaded and short of breath. It was like being on a depressurized ship with thin air or a high gravity planet. It just took a little getting used to.

Though the journey for her and Madeline could have been twice as fast in private passage, they chose to remain on the Dragon with the monks. The Pearl Dragon, however, did not plot a straight course to their destination and they made a few lengthy stops along the way. Hope stayed awake the whole time, her fascination with Hahn never ebbing.

She and Madeline were not allowed on the terraforming expeditions since the projects were considered government business. During those months they would spend long days in their cabin, or with the crew, or in the Atrium. Hope watched the news every day on the giant flatscreen in a breakfast room there. For almost ten years she tracked the progress of the corporation she had helped start via news stories and interviews of delighted construct owners. Pictures of Charity and Llewellyn in the limelight always brought a smile to her face. Interviews of Faith she bore patiently, her expression tight, more so every year.

The Pearl Dragon took them all the way to the edge of MW-1 where they were transported to another ship. Once they reached what the humans called "The Solar System," they were transported to another ship that had brought them to the small planet of Pluto. One more different ship would be taking them on the last leg of their journey to Dione.

The ships they traveled on were not quite luxury liners, since one was an IGC Military Ship and the other was simply a StreamLiner wanting to cover as much space as possible as quickly as possible, but they were by no means Spartan.

The two de Rossi's spent almost all of their waking hours with the Zenarchists, discussing everything from their lives before they met to the politics of the IGC. It wasn't long before the monks were teaching the girls how to meditate.

Madeline took to it like a fish to water.

For Hope it was another story.

Her mind was too analytical and her personality too restless. Sitting still was the hardest part. But she wanted a better understanding of Hahn and Elaeric and how they were able to do what they did. So she sat.

Often she would pop one green eye open to see Hahn staring at her with a smile so broad it looked to split his face in two. She could not help but return such a smile.

"And just what is so funny?" she demanded once, pulling the small pillow out from under her bottom and swinging it at his head.

Hahn reflexively blocked the gentle attack with the back of a hand. "Because I struggled the same way when I started to meditate," he told Hope, leaning a bit towards her from where he sat on his own pillow.

"How long before you could do it?"

Hahn shrugged, his yellow-robed shoulders going high. "Ten years?" he guessed. "Twenty?"

"Ten years?" Hope cried, her green eyes wide. "Twenty? Who has that kind of time to simply sit?" She was on the verge of tossing the pillow to the side and giving up. Hahn laughed and reached out a hand.

"You do," he told her, but *we do* was what he almost said. "Every moment starts with now." He pushed the pillow back towards her bottom and after a doubtful pause she wiggled onto it, giving him a sour look that was not without humor.

By the end of the first year she was meditating, in her opinion, quite nicely. She was by no means tapped in to any sort of telekinetic energy via the universe, but she had a peace and stillness in her life that she had never before known.

They meditated together often – singly, in pairs, and sometimes all four of them. They talked about their mediations, physics, and the energy of the universe. They discussed the power of intention and the law of attraction.

Occasionally they would talk of GwenSeven, their sisters and the constructs.

Hope discovered, through Elaeric, that Hahn was once a great fighter.

"He was the best of the best," he had told her one morning with a wink. Hope had looked at the other monk in surprise.

Hahn had simply smiled and said nothing. He felt a mild sort of surprise as well. He had all but forgotten about his life as a warrior. It had once been so important to him, it had been his whole world. How could he forget something that he once believed essential to his existence?

The monk glanced at the woman to his left and had his answer. He could only hope that she wrote off the many smiles he failed to repress as aged wisdom. He doubted he was that lucky.

The suns were setting on Pluto.

Hope leaned back, moving her shadow so that the sunlight would fall upon the stone she had discovered and spied a sparkle upon its surface. She pried it out with a finger, brushed off the damp dirt as best she could, and held it up for examination. Not much bigger than her thumb, it was smooth and gray and flecked with a sparkle of quartz.

After admiring it for a moment, she drew her arm back and threw it gently, feeling it roll from her palm to the tip of her finger. It rose and fell in a graceful arc before disappearing into the rushing water with a plop.

"You send it to its doom," Hahn remarked with a smile.

"I beg your pardon?" Hope asked, turning her face to him.

"In the battle between water and rock, water always wins."

"That is ridiculous."

Hahn chuckled. She always contradicted him and yet he never minded. Something about it always brought him joy.

"But it is true" he told her. "The rock may disturb the water, causing a splash or, in the case of a very big rock, displace the water. But the water comes together again and conquers through perseverance, breaking down the rock a little at a time."

Hope tossed her mass of wild hair and smiled at the monk, her green eyes shining. "But the rock is not consumed, merely changed. It wears down and breaks apart, and those pieces wear down and break apart. The process continues until the rock finally comes together again as grains of sand, glittering on a moonlit beach."

Hahn laughed, delighting in her words.

Hope closed her eyes, feeling the fading suns (one natural and far, one artificial and close) upon her skin and Hahn's laugh upon her heart. Before she could open them, she felt his lips upon her own.

She held still, something she had become quite practiced at, and returned the kiss as gently as she could. She could feel the passion within her brimming. It had been growing for quite some time. But Hope was afraid to show it so soon, lest the doe she had lured from the forest be sent bounding away and disappear into the trees.

Hahn's lips, warm and soft, pulled away slowly and his almond eyes opened and blinked owlishly at her. "I'm sorry," he apologized softly, sounding a bit surprised. "'I'm not sure why I did that."

"Because I wanted you to," Hope whispered. *Don't scare him, don't scare him,* she warned herself.

"Was it terrible?" he asked, his dark eyes searching her face. "It was my first," he admitted.

Hope could not keep the smile from her face. "I don't know," she said. "It was over too fast."

Hahn smiled and leaned close to kiss her again, longer this time. When he pulled away for the second time he looked pleased, yet Hope could see something behind his eyes.

"It was not terrible," she told him, keeping her smile in check. "But you should definitely practice more."

"I would like that," he confessed. "Though it makes me fret about the future, also a first for me."

Hope cocked her head, making the dying light dance in her hair. "I am sure you must have mused over the implications of what my sister might require, and also must have come to terms with any personal feelings you have regarding terraforming. Why would those decisions change now? What has happened to make you rethink a course you had already decided upon?"

Hahn smiled at Hope, thinking she must be taunting him. When she did not answer or even guess at the questions she had posed, Hahn took her delicate hand up in his own.

"You," he accused gently. "You are what is making me question my own decisions and rethink my course."

"Me?"

"Yes. I am bound by honor to sign the contract with your sister, and then I will be bound by law to provide what I have promised. I do not fear those. It is the bond that I feel to you that gives me such trepidation. I fear it will loosen and fall or simply evaporate into the air once you are set on your new course as well. I am afraid you will disappear and I will be left with these new strange feelings that I have - and have no idea what to do with them."

Hope reached out with a pale finger and touched the line of his golden jaw. "I will not disappear," she assured, not knowing the future herself. "And, together, we can sort out the feelings."

"You truly think so?"

"Of course," Hope replied, a small smile putting a dimple into her right cheek. She opened her mouth to say "I have Faith," a joke used by all the sisters and their dyers but she changed her mind. "I believe in us," she told Hahn.

"You do?"

"I certainly do. Just as much as I believe you need more practicing with kissing."

"Well!" Hahn exclaimed straightening up from his seat on the pillow. "You are with a man who will practice anything for however long it takes to get it perfect. One hundred times in a row or more, if need be."

Hope laughed as he gathered her in his arms and pulled her close. "I don't think you need that much practice," she admitted.

"Well," Hahn pondered aloud, "how else would I keep my pride if I did not even try?"

Hope laughed again, giggles that quickly turned sober. "I would certainly not want to keep you from your pride," she said solemnly.

ONE ONE

"Hello, Mason."

A chill ran through me as I looked up from my charts. I was in my office with a stack of blueprints rolled out on the table behind my desk. I was quite aware there were fancy computers and programs that I could use instead of the prints, but it was how I had learned and sometimes I could be as stubborn as Mira. I also still used a phone instead of a comset, something that gave everyone a chuckle.

Only one person in the universe still called me Mason, though I would have known that voice anywhere. The tone of it was as if I had seen him just yesterday, rather than ten years ago. I forced a smile onto my face as I turned around.

"Hello," I answered. Cronus, grandfather to the three de Rossi girls and creator of their biodentical dyers, wore a silver jacket and vest over a lavender-colored shirt. He was a tall and handsome elf with elegantly gray hair and a look of superiority that always made me want to punch him in the mouth.

"You look well, Mason," he told me, his gray brows drawing together over his narrow face as if this fact was both surprising and unpleasant.

Well for a human, you mean, I thought. I could see his gray eyes calculating how old I must be and trying to puzzle it out. I had a daughter in her late twenties but I knew I looked no older than twenty-five. Whether it was due to what Faith had done to me or because of who her mother was (or possibly a combination of both), Jean herself looked the same when she graduated flight school as she did when she had graduated high school. She had been a pilot now for nine years and still looked no different.

"It's good to see you too, sir," I said, amiably, though I was trying to figure out why the hell he was in my office. I had heard that he would be visiting the compound this morning but I knew that it had nothing to do with me and I had hoped that I could avoid an encounter.

Not so lucky, Pierre.

I was trying to riddle out how to politely ask what he wanted when (to my great relief) the door swung open and Thomas strode in, tall and lean and impeccably dressed as always in a three-piece suit. It occurred to me then that Thomas did not appear to be aging much either. A few lines around his eyes were all that showed on his deeply tan face and his hair was still coal black. I wondered if Faith had a hand in that, or if it was something Thomas was doing on his own with an over the counter age retractor drug – and possibly because of Faith.

"Ah!" he exclaimed seeing Cronus. "Welcome! Dr. de Rossi is waiting for you in her office. Would you like me to call her, or escort you there?"

"I was actually looking for her – I thought this was her office but I must have not counted the doors correctly as the receptionist instructed."

Thomas bowed slightly, his hands clasped in front of his body. "Not to worry sir, it is easy to get confused or even lost if you are not familiar with the complex."

"I'm not surprised, this place is enormous! I expect we have you to thank for that," he said, turning to look at me.

Again, his look was sour, as if he was less than pleased by my accomplishments. Why he had such a bug up his ass was beyond me. After all, he had been the one to hire me in the first place and then divert my original use to one for GwenSeven.

And, if I said so myself, I had done a damn good job.

I flailed mentally for some humble reply but before I could answer, the door swung open once again and Faith herself entered the room, her gold and brown eyes seeking out Cronus. "Grandfather!" she exclaimed, embracing him. Cronus smiled into the flow of her long gold and brown hair, hugging her. "How was your trip?" she asked, oddly breathless.

"Successful!" he announced, breaking the embrace. "We have much to discuss!" He held her at arm's length so he could look at her. Faith, because of her elfish blood, had not changed at all in the past thirty-five years, but a scowl rippled across her grandfather's face. "You look tired," he told her.

Faith backed away from him, waving off his remark. "I had a late night last night," she said casually. From the corner of my eye I could see Thomas, his expression rigid as if to keep back any personal comments. He and I both knew that all of Faith's nights were late nights. Faith looked at him suddenly, as if afraid he might tell, but Thomas' self-possession was as impeccable as his suit.

"There is a man here," the tall and dark PA stated, fluidly changing the subject, "to present an award."

Faith sighed but Cronus beamed at her. "Another biology award?" he asked in a teasing manner. "Medicine? Are they making you the IGC Surgeon General?"

"Actually," Thomas said, his accent as imperial as his pronunciation, "he is here to see Mr. Mattatock." Though Thomas and I had been on a first name basis for three decades, he still called me by my family name in front of others. I always got a kick out of it because of the way the last syllable always came out of him like a clucking noise. This time I was too surprised to notice.

"Me?" I asked.

Cronus and Faith blinked at me with the same surprise, though Faith's expression quickly melted into a genuine smile.

"Indeed," Thomas answered, unable to constrain a tiny smirk of his own. "It seems as though Mr. Mattatock has built the largest structure in the universe."

Cronus looked as if he been poked somewhere inappropriate and Faith beamed at me while I felt as if the wind had been kicked from my lungs. The idea seemed both stupendous and impossible. Then my mind raced.

Could it be true? I wondered, thinking about square footage, building dimensions, and our most recent additions to the compound. There was no way. Buildings in Two Mile were much bigger, or at least much taller.

"They must be going off ground footprint," I finally murmured. "After the new training wing we added last year."

"Whatever the case," Thomas told me, "there is a man in reception that would like to present you with a certificate and discuss a more formal and public award."

I nodded. "I won't keep him waiting." I looked at Faith and Cronus. "If you will excuse me?" I asked.

"Of course," Faith said, stepping back from the door while holding out her arm in an invitation for me to lead the way. "And congratulations, Fletcher." Her look of pride made me feel a little awkward.

"Thank you," I said, feeling myself blush. Thomas held the door open for me and I walked through, followed by the others.

The air was bright and warm, which was no mere coincidence of time or weather. Faith had deduced the perfect light and temperature to keep workers feeling their best and most productive and had upgraded the mirrors in the infrastructure of our moon's atmosphere.

"Shall I have a car brought around?" Thomas was asking Faith, just a few steps behind, but Cronus answered.

"I have a car waiting, thank you, Thomas. But you might have to recommend a restaurant. I doubt my granddaughter treats herself as well as she should," he added with a reprimanding glance at Faith. The younger Dr. de Rossi rolled her eyes in a silent yet affable response.

"Absolutely," Thomas obliged promptly. "Human or elfin?"

"You have elfin restaurants?" Cronus asked, the astonishment raising the tone of his voice an octave.

"Of course," Thomas replied. "We have many elfin workers at the plant who we want to be as comfortable and have as many luxuries as they did on their home moons."

"Elfin workers?" Cronus asked. His surprise was laden with incredulity and palpable enough to make us all uncomfortable.

"Most of our engineers and medical staff are elfin," Faith quickly informed him.

"Ah!" Cronus exclaimed, as if that explained everything. I wanted to turn around and give him a kick. Or worse.

We parted company, thankfully, when we reached reception. Thomas recommended a restaurant and Faith gave him a smile of gratitude that made her PA positively glow with pride. The small town that I had built around the compound for the workers had grown into a small city, one that Faith had yet to visit. I don't know what she did when she traveled from our moon but when she was at the compound she never left it. If Thomas did not regularly put food down in front her I doubted she would ever eat.

Cronus probably sensed the same thing, for when they got into his car he scowled at her in a manner he would not have done in public.

"How far are your living quarters from your lab?" he demanded.

"Not far," Faith said with more self-assurance than she felt. "Just across the way, in fact."

The frown on the old elf deepened. "Yet you are sleeping in your lab, or your office, aren't you?"

"Yes," Faith admitted quietly.

"Are you taking any drugs?" Cronus asked. "To keep you awake?"

Faith shook her head back and forth emphatically. "No. Never. I don't want anything to cloud my judgment – cause me to make a mistake."

The expression on her grandfather's face softened and he put a hand over hers. "You risk the same by lack of sleep," he told her. "Do not see time as a boundary," he said, squeezing her hand. "Time is as precious as gold, but just as malleable. Know that you have enough time for everything."

Faith nodded as she listened, making his words part of her like she always did. "I will," she promised. Then her somber expression softened as well, becoming as eager as a child's. "Now tell me about your meetings."

Cronus opened his mouth to speak but the aircar began to slow after an extremely short ride.

"Are we there?" Cronus asked in surprise. They had only been in transit for all of two minutes.

Faith laughed. "We didn't have far to go," she told him. "I may not venture out much," she admitted, "but everyone else does. Almost everyone, anyway. And very few people have cars or need of them. The city is built as a hub that encircles half of the compound. The stores and restaurants most used by the employees in the dorms and on-site apartments are the closest – within walking distance. Next are the establishments used by the families that live in the suburban houses, along with schools and parks and other facilities for children, then the suburban houses themselves on the outer half-ring."

Faith lifted her chin, proud that she knew so much about the environs - even though she had never seen them.

"Good planning," Cronus murmured as the car came to a complete stop.

The driver opened the door of the aircar in front of the restaurant and the pair paused their conversation until they had been seated by an elfin girl with a pixie haircut and large brown eyes. Even then Cronus paused to look around, suddenly cautious and close-mouthed.

They sat on a flagstone patio flooded with artificial sunshine, softened by a number of green silken sails that served as a ceiling. The patio extended over a wide but slow-moving river. More restaurants dotted the far side of the waterway.

"Mason didn't build all this?" Cronus asked skeptically. "Did he?"

Faith shook her head as she shook a silk napkin out onto her lap. "No, but he designed it. He plotted the river and the grounds and gave each restaurant and shop in the city the footprints they could use, and approved the design of each building." Cronus made a soft grunting sound and Faith rubbed her hands together eagerly.

"Don't keep me waiting," she said. "Tell me about the meeting!"

Cronus smiled at her. "They're in."

Faith gave an excited squeal like a small child and clasped her hands together. "How in the world did you set the price?"

Cronus shrugged. "We are still negotiating – how do you put a price on a new world? It's never been done before. But they are assessing their assets. We will be getting a massive amount of land on Titan, rights to much of their technology, not to mention an ungodly amount of money."

"But not even all of them are going."

Cronus tilted his head as he shook out his napkin. "Not even close to all of them. Only three thousand, I was told."

The waitress stopped by and Faith ordered a prawn cocktail and a glass of champagne.

"I'll have the same," Cronus told the waitress, "but no champagne. Elgro on the rocks, please." The waitress left with a nod and he turned his attention back to Faith. "When does Hope get in with the monks?"

Faith's features brightened even further. "Next week. I can't wait to see her."

"I as well," Cronus agreed, brightening in the same manner. "And she says these men can do as they claim? She's sure?"

"Yes, and I believe her. They are going to give me a demonstration as soon as I can arrange it. Charity and Llewellyn bought an insane expanse of land on the moon of Mimas. We're planning a day trip there to see what these monks can do."

"Before we meet with the Arcadians?"

Faith nodded her head and accepted a flute of champagne from the waitress. "Yes, though they have proven themselves to the IGC as well as Hope, by terraforming a few moons for them."

"On their own?" Cronus asked, his gray brows high over his gray eyes. "Free of charge?"

"Yes to both," Faith affirmed. "But not entirely free." She gave him a mischievous smile. "I got them to arrange for a favor in return."

"What kind of favor are we talking about? A good word from a chairman? A guarantee on a galactic loan?"

Faith, quite aware of his sarcasm, put her glass down and fixed her gold and brown eyes on her grandfather. "The use of a Dragon."

That gave the aging elf a visible jolt. He put his own glass down and stroked his smooth chin, thoughtful. "You knew what the Arcadians would do?" he finally asked with a smile that both mocked and approved her actions.

"Of course," Faith replied as if her persona would permit nothing less, which it certainly would not. The waitress returned with the food and Faith took a long drink before she picked up her tiny fork.

"Mimas?" Cronus asked. "Isn't that a mining outpost?"

Faith nodded and speared a prawn. "As well as refineries and steel mills, in the dry area. Most of the building materials for the compound and the city came from there. Supposedly the other side is quite lush. I saw some pictures – quite green with many lakes. Can you join us?"

Her grandfather shook his head. "Unfortunately, I must be off to Titan after my meeting here with you. I will need you to join me later with the monks, after you have verified their ability and I have met with the Arcadians in charge of planning." He wiped his mouth with a napkin. "This project is going to be quite time consuming. Are you going to be able to break away from here for awhile?"

"Yes," Faith assured him. "It is the reason why I have been driving myself so hard lately – I wanted to make sure that everything would run smoothly here without me."

"And will it?"

Faith nodded. "Almost indefinitely. Production and sales have increased while both production time and training time have decreased. The third run went off without a hitch, for the most part. We can churn out constructs now by the thousands, without me even being here."

"And the construct that killed its owner?" Cronus asked, a small line forming between his gray brows.

"Was brought in and tested in every way I could think. He checked out normal. I can't explain it."

Cronus swirled his drink, ice water with a splash of absinthe, and took a sip. "Another reason you have been pulling late nights," he mused aloud. "You cannot stand not knowing."

Faith was grateful for the breeze as it cooled her face and gently pushed the brown and gold strands of her hair back from cheeks that had become hot with shame. "I cannot help but feel responsible."

"Was it an isolated incident?"

Faith shook her head, her cheeks now afire. She lifted her face towards the breeze. "There was another, but Charity and Llewellyn somehow derailed the story even faster than the first time."

Her grandfather nodded. "Those two are a lot smarter than they let on to be."

This brought a smile to Faith's lips. "Oh, I am quite aware of that."

"What about the families?"

Faith took a sip of champagne, quickly regaining her composure. "Reimbursed, and compensated, of course."

"And you found nothing wrong with the second one?"

"Nothing. Not even a similarity with the first that would cause an analogous action, reaction, or a proclivity to violence. Normal neurologistics, hormone levels, everything that might have set them apart."

"Then it is not your fault," Cronus stated. "Two, out of thousands. Accidents happen. Do not blame yourself."

Faith took a deep breath. "I'll try not to." Her eyes of gold and brown said she meant it, but also betrayed the belief that she could truly absolve herself.

⋐⋑

Back in my office, I looked at the fancy certificate the man from the Freemasonry Grand Lodge on Titan had given me. It had the compass and square insignia of the Masons, framing a capital "G." Above the Masonic emblem was an ostentatious gold seal and below it all was a paragraph of showy words bestowing honors on one Fletcher J. Mattatock. I knew that in the real world it didn't count for a hill of beans, but I had to admit that I felt a little proud looking at it.

I looked at the phone, thinking about calling Jean to tell her about it, but I was going to see her in just a few days - over the weekend. Mira and I were planning on an extended weekend trip to Titan which included a lunch, and possibly a dinner, with Jean Marie and her boyfriend Matthew.

I liked Matthew, though I was not too keen on the fact that they lived together. Voicing this opinion, of course, only made Jean laugh and call me old-fashioned. The young man – who was also a pilot like Jean Marie – was lucky enough to have two saving graces. For one, though he was not of French descent, he was Catholic. He belonged to a group I found out about called the CDs, which stood for Clandestine Devout. He took Jean at least once a month to a Mass held in secret at an undisclosed location that changed every time. Jean had complained about it once, the service being so long and her not understanding half of it because it was in Latin, and it was my turn to laugh.

"Make sure you go to confession, too," I had told her, giving her a poke in the ribs. Petulant yet adorable, she swatted my hand away.

"I will," she assured me in the same tone she had used when she was four and I told her to brush her teeth.

Matthew's second saving grace, which really was his first, was that he was entirely devoted to my daughter.

He worshipped Jean. They had met at flight school and he followed her to the JF Academy. It was just last year that I had found out he was determined to marry her, but she wanted to wait. Mira had told me not to make a fuss. In some ways those two were more alike than they would ever admit.

I returned the certificate, protected by a plastic sleeve, to the folder the man from the Lodge had given me. He told me I was also to be honored with an award for city and suburban planning and development. Though my chest was swelling with the thought, I decided to wait to tell Jean until the weekend. Just as I made the decision, however, the phone on my desk rang. I picked it up and put it to my ear.

"This is Fletcher," I said, though I already knew who would be on the other end – with a comset rather than a phone.

"Dad!" Jean exclaimed, making my face near to split.

"Jean-Marie!" I said, "I was *just* thinking about you!"

She laughed and, like always, it was sweet music in my ear. Another thing she had in common with her mother.

"I know I'm going to see you this weekend, but I have some news and I just couldn't wait!"

"What is it, honey?" I asked, grinning at her excitement.

"You," she said, then paused for one dramatic moment, "are going to be a grandpa!"

For a moment I was too stupid to know what she meant and then for another I was too stunned to speak. Then the words found me, though they found my lips before they found my head.

"You and Matthew?" I asked foolishly, as if it could be someone else. "But you aren't even married!"

Jean only laughed again. "Don't even start with me!" she scolded, though her voice was still as merry as when I answered the phone. "You and mom never got married," she retorted lightly. "You think I don't know that?"

"That is different," I replied, firm once more, "and I am sure you know it and why. Besides, I'm too young to be a grandpa!" All I could picture was Cronus with his gray hair, perpetual scowl and antiquated opinions.

Jean only laughed again. "Dad! You're sixty-four!"

"I am?" I asked, catching my reflection in the glass that covered our general building permit from the IGC. "Are you sure?" I did not look that old and I certainly didn't feel it. Jean's answer was another laugh. "Is that a normal age to be a grandparent?" I asked.

"Absolutely," she assured me.

"Alright," I relented, feeling a smile spread across my face as I thought of Jean being a mama. "Congratulations, honey."

"Thanks, Dad."

"We're still seeing you this weekend, right?"

"Of course! I just couldn't wait to tell you."

"I'm glad you did," I said, and meant it. "I can't wait to see you."

"Same here. Love you, Dad."

"Love you too, honey."

I hung up the phone, filled again with the same warm feeling as when I looked at my certificate, and it rang again almost immediately. I figured it was Jean again, telling me something she had forgot. It wasn't.

"Fletcher Mattatock?" a man asked from God only knows where. A long way from where I was, that I could tell.

"Yes," I answered, a feeling of dread settling on my shoulders like a dusting of snow.

"I am Wyn Velen from the IGC Chaplain's Office on Io," he stated. I was at first muddled with confusion on why the IGC had a chaplain when all the religions were being "purified" by the One Church until I remembered it was a non-denominational and government appointed position. Then the dread returned, the cold wrapping around my body as I heard the knife in the dark slip from its sheath. "I am sorry to inform you," he continued, "that your brother, Bradley Mattatock, has died in the line of duty."

The knife slipped into my chest and I was filled with shock, a shock like the kind I had felt when I learned my parents and grandmother had been killed.

"The line of duty?" I asked softly.

"It appears that he suffered a stroke while on patrol. He was out of atmospheric range, so there was no physical collision in regards to his craft. It was forty-eight hours before his non-response instigated an investigation and retrieval, but at least it appears that his passing was not one in pain."

Brad, I thought. *Brad.* I was in more of a stupor than when Jean had told me she was pregnant.

"His effects..." the man continued, sobering me instantly.

"There was a crest," I interrupted. "A pair of golden wings with red enamel..."

"Yessss," the man from the chaplain's office agreed slowly and I could picture him, scrolling through a list. "It will be sent to you, along with the rest of his effects, as you are listed as his only next of kin."

"I just want the crest," I told him. "Unless there are any books. The rest of his things you can donate to the local..." *church*...I was going to say, when I realized there wasn't one. The Church of the One had seen to that. "...charity," I finished.

"Very well," he acquiesced. "Can you please verify your current address?"

I did so and he gave me his sincerest condolences before I thanked him and hung up the phone.

Best of times, worst of times, I speculated, running my hand over the folder that held my certificate. My hand dropped to my chest, groping for the ghostly hilt in hopes that I could pull it free.

I thought of growing up, sharing a room with a brother that I often wanted to beat the hell out of but who just as often had me laughing so hard I was near pissing myself. I remembered all the trouble we got into and the scrapes we got out of. I thought of Jean and the baby she would be holding in less than a year.

One life goes out, another comes in.

Then I had the jarring realization that Jean herself was born very close to when my grandmother died.

Is it always this way, I wondered, *or just a coincidence?*

I decided that a question such as that was not for a man like me to answer.

A grandpa, I thought wonderingly, unable to keep what was undoubtedly a sappy smile from spreading across my face.

I gave myself the rest of the day off and headed for the one place in the city that I had invested personal money in and partially owned. *Marie Marie* was the most authentically French restaurant and bar in Evansborough. It was not large, only two small rooms and a patio (like a true café), but I invested in it because I wanted a real French meal from time to time and a place where I knew I could get a decent baguette.

Tonight, I needed a drink and I wanted to raise a glass to my brother.

# ONE TWO

"Christ on sale!" Llewellyn shouted, startling us all as we began to step out of the transport that hovered a hand span above the ground.

"Don't blaspheme!" I scolded before I could think to hold my tongue as I took hold of her elbow in an effort to steady her. She had sunk her expensive stiletto heels into the mucky ground all the way to the bottoms of her feet.

I looked up and scanned the area quickly. It didn't take long to take it all in and as much time to figure out. I could see we were in what appeared at first glance to be a charming meadow, but in actuality was a moss-covered swampland as far as the eye could see.

Llewellyn as well was peering about, her blue eyes like saucers and her breath an angry exhale that had the sound of a dragon breathing fire. "Damn real estate assholes!" she hissed.

We were in the Southern Hemisphere of Mimas where she and Charity had purchased a substantial amount of undeveloped land. The sky was a beautiful blue, tinged with green. Titan was rising on the eastern horizon and behind it loomed Saturn, pale yellow banded with even paler ochre, rings flung wide.

"Careful!" I warned as the door to the transport was filled with the billowing orange robes of a monk.

"Oh dear!" he exclaimed as he saw Llewellyn struggling to pull her shoes from the soft ground, even as the muck seemed determined to suck them clean off her feet. He gathered his robes about his slight frame as he frowned at the landscape.

As he did, I was overcome by the strangest sensation. It felt like a pressure change in the atmosphere, making my head wonky for a second and I opened my jaw to make my ears pop. Then I felt the ground underneath me shift - gently, but enough that I was quick to lay a hand against the metal side of the transport to steady myself. Llewellyn, trying to regain her balance on her outrageously high heels, clutched at me in an effort not to topple over entirely, her long fingernails digging into either side of my ribcage.

I yelped and pulled her glittering claws from my torso and held her still. Then my eyes sought out the ground, which was slowly rising. Not everywhere, I saw. It was only in an area of about ten square feet, with us standing in the middle.

"Ah!" the monk exclaimed as if pleased, and then stepped out. His slippered feet stood on ground that was spongy and damp, but far from mucky. He turned and helped Madeline descend from the transport.

The youngest de Rossi girls and the monks had arrived last night. We had a welcoming party for them at *Marie Marie* that included all of the sisters and their dyers, the monks, as well as Evan, Thomas, and myself. The only moment of tension was when Hope first saw Faith, but it evaporated instantly as Hope wrapped her arms around her older sister and held her close.

I had been honored to host the little party but had no idea why I had been brought along on the real estate expedition to Mimas.

Madeline's green eyes peered from her pale freckled face as she stepped down from the transport, looking around in their usual state of perpetual wonder. She moved away from the coach and the other monk appeared, stepping down gingerly before taking Hope's hand to assist her descent. I did not miss the look that passed between them – something more than gratitude in Hope's green eyes and something glinting in the dark eyes of the monk, as if harboring a secret. It flared a spark of curiosity within me but I was quickly diverted by Llewellyn's continued ire and the rest of our party as they exited the transport.

Evan came out next, his gold hair shining in the sun, wearing a plain t-shirt and faded jeans that were similar to my own. He helped Gwendolyn down, her skirt fluttering around her knees as Llewellyn glared at the monks as if the mushy terrain was somehow their fault.

"These were Vuitton's, you know!" she accused, indicating her expensive shoes that were covered in mud and clumps of moss.

"They still are," the second monk assured her with a smile. There was something about that smile, something so sly and knowing that it made Llewellyn frown and both she and I glanced at her feet. The clumps of muck and moss were slipping away like melting wax. The dyer's blue eyes widened again as her shoes were like new once more, her feet completely clean, and then looked at the monk as he turned to assist Faith down the last step to the ground. Then her blue eyes sought out Charity, now peering from the door.

"Are you waiting for an invitation?" Llewellyn demanded. Charity glanced nervously at her dyer, who rolled her eyes. "Your shoes will be fine!" she assured her. Somewhat appeased, Charity joined the rest of us. Like Llewellyn, she wore a buttoned blouse tucked into a tight pencil skirt and extravagant, high-heeled shoes. Not quite appropriate for our little fieldtrip.

Faith, only slightly more prepared in a pant suit and wedge heels, contemplated our small party with her hands clasped in front of her waist. She looked like a kindergarten teacher preparing to address her class.

"Well!" she announced. "Hahn and Elaeric have joined us here to give us a demonstration of their capabilities."

"I think they already have," I murmured. The first monk looked at me and smiled. Hope laughed out loud. Faith surveyed the land. "Let's go up there," she suggested, lifting her chin in the direction where the land rose slightly into a ridge. It ran the length of what horizon we could see from where we stood. "It might be a bit drier."

"It better be," Llewellyn growled. She looked at the first monk and smiled, her demeanor changing instantly. She raised her light blonde brows over her china blue eyes. "A little help getting there?" she asked, her tone sweeter this time.

"Hmm? Oh, the ground! Yes!" He turned and followed Faith's gaze to the rise and, as he did so, the swampy earth along his line of sight shifted and rose. The bumpy hillocks flattened into a path no less than five feet wide and a good four inches higher than the surrounding swampland.

Faith paused for a moment, arched an eyebrow, then continued walking. She said nothing as she led the way along the path and up to the rise. We crested the small ridge and Charity sucked in her breath.

"Ocean view, my ass!" she spat as we all observed the surrounding terrain.

The land itself was beautiful, an emerald green for miles in all directions and I could see how Charity could have mistaken the pictures she had been shown for rolling meadows and grassland. The hillocks went on and on, a sea of mossy lumps. Only by standing in the middle of it all and close enough to touch could one see the standing water as it seeped from the ground, pools of moribund liquid that served as homes to thousands of mosquito larvae. Past the ridge and to our left, the swampy ground dropped away and disappeared under acres of stagnant water.

"There might be an ocean out that way," Madeline said, her eyes cast out over the swamp below. "I think I smell salt."

"I can't smell anything except the stench of this place!" Llewellyn cursed.

The adult insects had caught our scent and now buzzed

around our ears and nipped at our exposed skin. I swatted one on my neck. Hope saw this and her green eyes found those of a monk.

"Hahn!" she pleaded in a quiet, demure voice. "The bugs?"

"Of course," he replied, his voice just as soft. They could have been a couple hosting a dinner party, one reminding the other about using a napkin. Suddenly, the pests seemed to find another place to be, and made haste for it.

"Much better!" Hope commended. She turned to survey the landscape and beamed at what she saw. "This place is perfect!"

"If you're an ogre!" Charity remarked in disgust.

"I'm sure the ogre would rather remain at her compound," Hope murmured with a smile.

"Didn't you wonder," Faith asked Charity, ignoring Hope's remark, "why you got such a deal on this land?" Charity looked away, a deep pink blooming in her cheeks. Faith let out a breath that was almost a laugh. "You slept with the real estate agent, didn't you?" she asked, smirking. Charity turned her face back, angry.

"He was very good-looking!" she argued.

"And," Faith continued, "you thought he would sell you quality property at a discounted price for a night of passion with you?" Her tawny eyes looked over at Hope. "And you thought *my* ego is unequalled."

"I still do," Hope assured her older sister with a smile that was sickly sweet before she switched her gaze to Charity and Llewellyn. "Don't worry," she assured them. "You are going to love what we do with the place." She turned to the older monk who was looking at her with a smile. "The land," she began to say, stopping as he held out a hand to the north, redirecting her gaze.

"Is being taken care of."

My eyes, and the eyes of the others, glanced around to see the ground before us moving. It was gentle at first, then gained momentum and power - rising, bulging and shifting. It looked like a giant under a green blanket, trying to raise himself from a hundred years of slumber. Gwendolyn gasped and Evan wrapped a protective arm around her. If the mosquitoes had still been around they would have flown into Charity and Llewellyn's half-opened mouths. Faith's body was stock-still, her eyes darting about, scrutinizing every detail and storing the information away for later and a more in-depth analysis.

Acres of land swelled and rolled like a stormy sea yet remained firm where we stood. It coalesced in front of us and went up and up and up. The mossy hillocks smoothed out and the water poured out of it. It ran in rivulets and then streams down the mass of earth that was rising before us and down to the swamp below, creating a pond to the west that quickly grew into the size of a lake. The ground shifted and settled until it finally found the shape it wanted, a perfectly formed hill with a flattened top, like a giant green platform.

"A foundation," I whispered. The water still ran from the land as if squeezed from a sponge until it slowed to a trickle.

"Ah!" the monk named Hahn exclaimed as he clasped his hands. I had the distinct feeling that he wanted to rub them together, as if he was just warming up. "What is it you wish?" he asked. His dark almond-shaped eyes travelled over the women and fell last upon Charity.

"A house for Hope," she told him with a wry smile, "or a cage. Anything that will get her to stay put for a while."

"A castle!" Madeline exclaimed breathlessly, clasping her hands under her chin. "A fairy-tale castle!"

"A castle for a princess?" Hahn asked, his eyes fixed on Hope. Something about his look made me glance at Faith. I noticed that Gwendolyn and Evan were surreptitiously doing the same. Faith stood watching the exchange, an uncharacteristic look of confusion on her face.

"How about a castle for a queen?" Charity suggested.

"Well," Hahn said, giving her a knowing smile, "one usually precedes the other."

"A castle for us all then!" Hope decided. "A beacon that we can return to as adults, and still be children." She looked at Madeline, who reached out and grasped Hope's hand with a smile and held onto it the way they had when they were young. This simple gesture in itself seemed to change the atmosphere and a feeling of buoyancy swept through the group, bringing a smile to every countenance.

Hahn turned his golden face to Charity for approval, since she owned the property. Charity looked at Llewellyn, who shrugged. Charity turned back to Hahn and repeated the gesture. The monk smiled broadly, showing strong, even teeth. Then he took a few steps further up the ridge and knelt on the ground. The other monk joined him, doing the same. They placed their hands on their knees and closed their eyes.

Hope and Madeline, still holding hands, followed the monks and stood behind them. Madeline dropped her slender fingers onto the shoulder of the younger monk and a strange silence pervaded our little party. It lasted for a minute, maybe a minute and a half, and I felt that any second Charity or Llewellyn would break it with some snide remark but they must have had the sense, or had been warned by Faith, to keep still.

Then I discerned a strange sound, a sort of humming, and I realized it was coming from the monks - coming from their bodies. Hope began to speak to them in low tones while we all raised our eyes back to the newly formed landscape. I had been mildly prepared to see the monks change the land - it was what we had been told to expect, though it was still a wonder and a shock to see the scope and the speed with which it happened right before my eyes.

I have no words to describe my astonishment at what happened next, but I can tell you what did happen.

Grayish lumps began to rise from the rapidly drying land.

At first it seemed haphazard, but soon I could see that they were forming a circle. It began to look like the maw of some great beast, his gargantuan jawbone unearthed from the site of an archeological dig. Those strange gray teeth, all molars, rose and grew until they touched - they did not fuse but smoothed out, becoming more prominently rectangular.

I was probably the first to realize what they were. I was, after all, a mason.

They were blocks of stone.

They grew and were joined by others from underneath, pushing up.

Then another ring of stones began to sprout within that first giant circle, then another – all touching like rows of teeth in the jaws of a shark. The stones grew and kissed and flattened before my eyes, making a wall that looked to be at least four feet thick as it reproduced exponentially and grew higher and higher.

Within that wall, farther back, smaller rings of the same smooth blocks of rock pushed themselves up from the earth. The ground was still damp and bits of moss clung to the rising stones, riding them like barnacles on the sides of whales as they breached.

I tore my eyes away from the spectacle to glance at the others. They all stood, Charity and Llewellyn with blue eyes wide as eggs and Gwendolyn clinging to Evan as if afraid, all of them looking like children lost in the woods. Faith stood apart, more tense than I had ever seen her. Her feet were planted as if she expected someone to push her over, her hands were clasped tightly together between her breasts as if frozen in prayer, and her gold and brown hair blew back from a face that looked as still and fragile as glass. Whatever might have been running through that mind of hers, I could not even venture to guess.

Belatedly, I glanced at my watch and guessed that maybe a minute had passed. My eyes found Hope, still murmuring to the monks. Their eyes were still closed but they would nod every now and then as their architect fed them the blueprint in her mind's eye. I looked back up and now it was easy to discern the final product, though that could have been because I knew what it was supposed to be.

The land between the wall and the newly sprouted rings turned a grayish color and for a second I thought the water was seeping back up into the ground and it gave me a hell of a start. Piling tons of rock onto soft ground was a recipe for disaster. But in the next second I could discern that it was not water but large pavers of slate. They stopped when they were a good inch higher than the ground. I watched as an oyster-colored liquid ran between the pavers like quicksilver, hardening within seconds.

I checked my watch and another minute had passed.

The structure was not even half-finished but I was sure that anyone at this point could tell what it was going to be. It was indeed going to be a castle. Not a fortress, mind you, but a fairy-tale castle. The kinds pictured in the books I used to read to Jean when she was little.

The first ring of stones had a number of gaps, four to be exact, one of them right in front of our little party. When the wall reached a height of what I guessed to be twenty feet it stopped growing from the bottom and began changing at the top. The gap became an arch and capstones swelled along the crown and spread out. It was like watching dominoes fall, in reverse. From the line of capstones, merlons sprouted like mushrooms. Then it stopped growing. It had formed a curtain wall, though made for show rather than defense. The individual blocks were gray and flecked with some kind of quartz, making them sparkle.

I itched to run my hands over them, to see how solid they were, and see what mortar held them together.

Madeline and Hope each had their right hand resting on the shoulder of one of the monks, both of whom still knelt though their eyes were now open. Hope leaned down to whisper something and the monks nodded, smiles touching their lips.

My watch ticked off another minute and inside the curtain wall the castle grew. Blocks of stone upon blocks of stone. Where they were coming from I had no idea, but come they did, faster and faster. Six towers rose, and even from where I stood, I could tell that there was something different about the stones. It did not take another minute on my watch for me to see what it was. The type of quartz was different in each tower. Though the stone itself was so pale that it was almost ivory, it was speckled with color that differed from one tower to the other.

One pearly tower had a gold sparkle and the one next to it had a shimmer of silver. Rose quartz was predominant in one and amethyst in the next. One tower sparkled with green like it was set with emeralds and another flickered and shone as if embedded with sapphires.

A glance at my watch showed another minute and a half had spun by.

Still it grew and the details made the breath hitch inside my chest.

Solars, antechambers, and sunrooms bulged from the lower floors. Balconies and turrets sprouted from the tops like lace upon the stones. Spires were linked by delicate stone bridges - up and up they reached for the sky. Finally, the blocks stopped stacking upon one another and on the top of the central keep and upon each tower sprung a flat piece of burgundy slate. Each slate replicated itself again and again until it had formed a circle and then it started replicating yet again, topping each ring of stones with a ring of burgundy tiles before continuing with a smaller ring and a smaller ring, spiraling up until each tower was roofed with a cone of tiles the color of wine.

I checked my watch to see a minute plus ten seconds more had passed and then glanced at Madeline, her face beaming with joy, as she whispered to the monk under her gentle hand. My eyes went back to the newly formed rooftops of the towers.

At their peaks, metal rods were springing up like antennae. From the tops of each rod unfurled a brightly colored pennant. The flags caught the breeze and snapped to attention, triangles of color, all pointing west.

"Jesus Christ," Charity whispered.

I didn't bother to shush her. I might have said the same if my mouth had not gone numb with wonder. My head turned slowly to see the monks rising to their feet. Hope tried to assist the older one but he shooed her away good-naturedly.

"I am sorry," he said to Charity, "but there is nothing in it. I have not the imagination for the intricacies of furniture."

"I...I...I..." Charity stuttered as her biodentical placed a reassuring hand upon her twin's shoulder.

"I am sure we will manage," Llewellyn finished for her as everyone gathered their wits, staring in awe at the edifice that had risen from the ground before us in just a matter of minutes. Everyone except Faith. Her tawny eyes found mine and suddenly I knew the reason for my presence.

"Fletcher?" she asked.

I nodded in understanding and began to make my way up the ridge to the arched opening in the curtain wall. She had already known that they were going to raise some kind of building, though I doubted she was prepared for the magnitude of what we just witnessed.

I was there to make sure it was sound.

I pulled the Lasre Checkre from my belt as I reached the opening and stretched out a hand to touch the wall, suddenly thinking that it might not be real. It was probably Faith's first concern as well, that the whole thing was only an illusion.

My palm went flat against the surface, the tips of my fingers spreading apart as I gradually applied more pressure until I was pushing with everything I had.

It was as solid as could be.

The faces of the blocks were rough, as if the stone had been chiseled into shape by impossibly ancient tools. I thumbed the button on my Checkre and a slim beam of blue light shot from the tip. Strictly out of curiosity, before I took any measurements, I flipped the compass and stood under the arch. The curtain wall was four equal lengths, linked by turrets on the corners, and all four were oriented to the four points of the compass.

I exhaled slowly through puffed out cheeks and then used the device to measure the space between the stones, and the size of the stones themselves. Everything was uniform and level. The size and structure and completeness of it all gave me a shiver though the air was warm. It was like the surfacing of a thought from another life as my mind felt the caress of mathematics and memory.

I moved to the slate surface of the stone flooring in the bailey. Other than the uneven natural cut to the stone, everything was flush.

I went inside and the others watched, I am sure, to see if it would collapse on me. When it didn't, and after waiting an entire minute just to make sure, everyone else came inside as well. It was cool and dim. Some floors were slate, others were of wood and so shiny that they looked as if they had been polished a hundred times. Stone staircases branched off here and there from the great halls, leading up to the towers.

"Is there a lift?" Charity asked one of the monks who responded with a soft laugh and shook his head.

"I am sorry, but no. There is, however, space for electrical runs. And you are certainly able to make modifications as long as you do not take down a wall that bears a significant amount of weight."

Llewellyn looked to me for verification and I nodded. "It's structurally sound," I affirmed. She looked at Charity and their blue eyes met for a moment before they moved off together to explore. Gwen and Evan did the same, going down a different hallway. It seemed as if the children lost in the woods had found the gingerbread castle.

Hope and Madeline conferred softly with the monks and I found Faith standing by my side.

"What's on your mind Fletcher?" she asked as her eyes moved about the room, taking in doorways and windows and hearths. I felt she was taking measurements with every glance, probably as accurate as my Checkre.

"It's sound," I affirmed and she looked at me with those golden eyes, a genuine smile teasing her lips.

"What's on your mind?" she repeated.

I made a noise that was half chuckle and half sigh and I tilted my head as I explained what had me scratching my brain since I flipped the compass as I stood under the arch in the curtain wall.

"There were buildings on Earth a long time ago," I explained, "that had the same sort of dimensions and general layout, though not the same size or form." I stopped, knowing how crazy I already sounded, but Faith nodded.

"Go on," she urged.

"They were called the pyramids of Giza."

"And?" she prodded.

This time I did chuckle. "They were built thousands of years before any real civilization there," I said, hoping to jog her memory. When her only response was a slight frown, I continued. "No one knows, or ever discovered, how they had the technology or means to build anything so large or so exact with the tools that they had back then."

Faith gave me a nod of understanding as she looked away, speculating on her own before she asked me, "Then what did people think happened? What did the scientists of the time think?"

I laughed apologetically, a little embarrassed, even though

the speculations had been over a thousand years before I was born and on another world altogether.

"Uh…one of the theories was that the structures had been built by aliens from another planet." I did not tell her that it was not just the pyramids of Giza that the Earthlings supposed were built by aliens, but other structures as well. Pyramids in jungles and on islands, crop circles in fields and calendars etched in stone that were eerily accurate.

"Do you think it was them?" Faith asked, the muscles in her lips tight and drawn as she jerked her chin towards the monks.

I laughed again. "Not unless they know how to time travel."

Faith did not laugh at my obvious joke. Her gold and brown eyes flicked from me to the men with golden skin and golden robes as they talked animatedly with her youngest sister and her dyer.

Hope, as if sensing our gaze, turned her green eyes our way. Her body turned next, then her feet, taking steps towards us with slow purpose as if pulled by a magnet. Madeline and the monks followed, flanking Hope as she stopped before Faith.

Faith's piercing eyes found Hope and her question was like an arrow - singular and sharp. "How?"

Hope's lips turned up in the barest of smiles. "How do they do it?" she asked, "or how much do they want for it?"

Faith straightened her shoulders and I guessed that she had been instructed to find out the second, but wanted even more to know the first.

"How do they do it?" she asked, her voice soft.

Hope's smile widened the smallest bit and I knew she had assumed the same. "It's actually simple physics – the first law of thermodynamics."

"The energy of an isolated system is constant," Faith said, matter of fact.

Hope nodded, still keeping her smile in check. "And that

energy, that *matter*, cannot be created or destroyed. It can only change form."

Madeline held out a small fist and gently opened her hand. A spot appeared in the center of her palm and from there sprouted a delicate stem only an inch long. Though what the monks had done was far more impressive, this small act seemed to surprise Faith even more. Myself as well.

A leaf budded and unfurled from the stem, perfectly formed. "How much is it worth to you?" Hope continued, her green eyes as piercing as Faith's tawny ones. Madeline blew the leaf off her palm with a gentle breath as Gwen and Evan rejoined us, along with Charity and Llewellyn.

Faith shrugged. "To me, the science is more important than the money." Charity made a small sound of amusement that was rather unladylike. Faith ignored her. "To Grandfather's clients, however," she told Hope, letting out her breath in great rush of air, "I think they will give everything they have."

Hope's smile became more gentle. "Thank you for your honesty, but I don't think it will come to that. I just want to make sure they are taken care of," she said, indicating the monks, the older of which was already engrossed in conversation with Evan as they walked back outside. The rest of us followed them through the bailey and under the arch. Up above, I could hear the pennants snapping in the breeze.

Evan was pointing east and gesturing with his hands while the monk nodded, smiling. I looked in that direction, towards where an ocean might supposedly lay, but I could not envision what Evan was describing. All I could see was what had been there when we arrived less than an hour ago - a swamp at the bottom of the rise upon which we stood – but even that had been transformed. The black, fetid water was now gone. In its place was a lake so clear that I could see the bottom for what must have been twenty yards from shore where it eased into a beautiful and sparkling blue. At that moment I spotted a rainbow trout as it flipped its tail from the water, as if winking at me.

"You and Madeline have been meditating as well?" Faith asked Hope as we made our way back down the ridge to the transport. "Learning how to harness the field?"

Hope shook her head, her expression tense. "Not me," she said. "I tried, but gave it up." She hurried ahead, clearly not wanting to discuss it.

We reached the transport where Evan was helping Charity and Llewellyn up the steps while he still chatted away with the monks. I turned for another look at the castle on the hill and found Faith next to me once again.

"Does it bother you, Fletcher?" she asked me.

I almost asked what she meant, but I knew.

"Do you mean to ask if I think what they are doing is blasphemous?" I asked. Faith nodded, a small smile tugging her lips into her cheeks. "You mean, any more than what you do?" She nodded again.

She had good reason to ask. When she had started out I was truly skeptical that she could really do it – make a human. When she did, my old self might have balked at it. I might have even walked out on the whole operation. After all, they were doing what only God should do. But Mira changed that. From there I never looked back or felt I had a right to judge anyone. I returned her smile and shook my head.

"No."

Faith's smile widened and I helped her into the transport and followed her.

ONE THREE

Acqtra Royce looked out from between two enormous fluted columns and onto the bucolic grounds of the royal elfin family. Grasslands were fed by a bright blue waterway as it snaked a gentle course through the green hills and into the forest beyond. Neatly trimmed hedges and flowerbeds boasting brilliant colors lined gravel paths and riding trails. It was all quite idyllic and quite artificial.

Acqtra sighed, feeling his age for the first time in a century.

The aging elf stood at the edge of a cavernous room of white marble, marble pillars supporting three great arches - one of which he stood under as he surveyed what was only a fraction of the royal gardens. The colonnade was lined with potted trees that bore emerald leaves and were filled with exotic birds of many colors. Their sprightly chirping and jocund birdsong filled the air with gentle sound.

A small herd of white horses with delicate features (all from the elfin homeland two galaxies away) grazed quietly in a nearby meadow. Meanwhile their cousins, a sly group of unicorns, played hide and seek in the woods.

A breeze blew through the columns, making the white robes of the old elf billow like sails. His hair was as white as moonlight and as long as a maiden's, though there was nothing maidenly about his face. It was lined by time and scarred with the memory of countless battles.

The Battle King, as he was called, turned from the scene of sublime nature that whispered of peace and the past to a room that bespoke of science and future. He himself was a juxtaposition of past and future. As a white-haired and white-robed elf with long pointed ears, he would seem a character from a fairy tale of long ago. A wise and happy traveler perhaps. His face, which showed wrinkles that only the oldest of elves might have, told another story.

The lobe of his pointed right ear was missing – shot off by a laser from a Golgoth pistol. One scar, from a knife, had cleaved one of his brows when they had still been dark. Those brows were now as white as the rest of him, but the scar remained and had left a gap where no hair would grow. The skin on the left side of his jaw was puckered, not from wrinkles (though the wrinkles did well to hide it), but from a brush with a photon charge long ago. The shot had missed him by a good deal, saving him from melting like a witch, but had gotten close enough to excite and disrupt the molecules over his jaw line. For Acqtraejale Royce, still a prince back then and fighting in the First Great War of The Elves, the injury was small yet terrifying. His skin cells had felt like a hill of ants that had been doused with gasoline. Molecules scattered and danced in a mad dash to get away in every direction.

His robes covered more welts and weals, most no more than shadows now. But, shadows or not, those scars were starting to tickle him. They were far from itching, war was not close yet. But they tickled. Sometimes the feeling was soft as the breeze, sometimes it felt like an insect alighting on his skin and he would swat at it. After a few weeks of slapping at something that was not there, the Battle King's blue eyes had widened with the realization of what it was.

War.

Acqtra knew the feeling of premonition like he knew his own scars but never knew if it was a blessing or a curse that he could only foretell war. He had called for Karamine immediately. She had come at once, and in a single moment he had confirmation of his fears. He had only to look into her eyes.

Her body, black as a moonless night, was wrapped in brilliant robes of many colors. A partial turban of the same peacock colored silk was wrapped around her head. A hundred braids, shining like polished jet, poured down her back. Her ears were long and pointed like his own, though she had both earlobes and each sported three gold rings. Her smile was warm but her bright eyes carried a weight behind them.

She had bowed to the Battle King and when she straightened he had pointed a question at her as if it were the tip of a blade.

"War?"

The woman nodded without hesitation. Her many braids were tipped with gold and chimed softly as they rustled against one another, echoing her confirmation as they moved.

"How big?"

"Big big," Karamine answered. "And long. Very long. Whole bend o' the bow, maybe more."

The Battle King had sighed the sigh of heartbreak, his head drooping down, and Karamine had reached out to wrap long black fingers around his arm. Probably the only one who would dare touch the royal elf without thinking twice.

"Not your fault, sire. Many many years you have given us peace. You will find peace again."

Acqtra lifted his head. "Are you reassuring a tired old man, or is that what you see when you touch me?"

Karamine smiled, showing brilliant white teeth. "What I see when I touch you," she assured him. "Which is why I here so fast. I die to know."

The king chuckled for a moment but his demeanor could not stay long from the dread that had settled over his shoulders. He heaved another sigh and spoke. "So, it is fight or flight," he begrudged.

The woman gave his arm a squeeze as she nodded, then let her hand drop. "Fraid so," she agreed and when the king nodded glumly she smiled. "But we have time," she told him.

"I know," Acqtra conceded.

Karamine's brows went up over her shining black eyes. "And how is it dat you know? And knew war comes to the elves once again?"

The king scratched the edge of his jaw thoughtfully and smiled. "I'm not sure. Maybe I have a bit of Black Elf in me," he said by way of an explanation for his premonition.

Karamine smiled at him. "And I have a bit of Arcadian Elf in me," she said. The king arched a white brow at her and her perfectly black skin. Her smile widened into a grin. "Every Venerdi night!"

The king laughed at her bawdy joke and wrapped an arm around her shoulders as he walked her from the room, discussing and laughing about the nocturnal habits of single women.

The king's blue eyes, as still sharp as daggers, now came back to the present and swept across a room that was as anachronistic as himself. The building had been made in the old style, with fluted columns supporting marble arches. Padded benches of carved ivory and gold velvet sat like undersized swan boats on the polished stone floor. Beverage carts made of gold held crystal carafes of spring water and glass jars filled with honey. Silver pitchers full of goldwine and gold pitchers full of redwine.

A gentle breeze blew through the marble columns. One made of artificial air that wafted through the colonnade every thirty-three seconds.

The elves loved old styles and traditions, yet technology was something they had never been able to turn from. It was an addiction.

The Battle King gazed up at the holographic orrery that filled the room, showing the system in the Milky Way where the elfin people had made their home for more than a thousand years. He walked through it, enveloped occasionally here and there by a moon. His shoulder went through the moons of Jupiter before his head was shrouded by the gas giant itself. He moved through the gleaming globe of swirling beige and ochre and a few steps more had his white hair passing through Saturn and its many rings. He stopped on the other side of the ringed planet and his eyes lit on the moon of Titan, the image almost as large his own head.

The object, once a gray rock like all other moons caught in orbit by the gravitational force of a planet, was now like a round and multi-colored jewel before his eyes. His gaze drifted back outside and he knew that all of that color and beauty had been his doing – in part at least. He filled his old lungs with a great breath of the clean air and let it out slowly in a sigh. He wished that beauty, but even more that peace, could last forever.

Wish in one hand, shit in the other, he thought caustically.

He was old, but not an idiot.

One of the birds singing on the branch of a potted topiary and resplendent with feathers of jade and gold, flew to him. Acqtra held up a hand so that it might land. The remarkable bird lighted on a gnarled knuckle and ducked its head in obeisance.

"Sire," it informed him politely in a voice decidedly more human than birdlike, "your guests have arrived."

"Thank you," the former king replied. He was quite used to droids, yet it pleased him to have his own in the guise of something more natural. "Please alert my advisors, and see that our guests are shown in."

The bird bobbed its head and flew back to the tree where it could relay the message to another relay droid in the system that would see the request carried out. Acqtra watched it return to the smooth limb among the emerald leaves and listened to the birdsong and chirps that followed, though he could also detect a click and a beep now and then. His elf ears were made no less sensitive by missing a chunk of flesh. He sighed, resigned to the fact that technology never seemed to be able to perfectly mirror what God could create with such ease.

He was proved wrong in a matter of minutes.

He turned back to the orrery and the image of Titan, so beautiful, so peaceful.

Damn that Dyer Maker! he thought in a spurt of frustration, though he knew that it had actually been the granddaughter that had taken the doll-making craft to a whole new level. The Battle King sighed. He also knew that if she had not set the wheel in motion, someone else would have spun it. Peace was never forever. And, strangely enough, the Dyer Maker's granddaughter could be their salvation.

The doors to the marble chamber swung open to admit Duncan and Drustin, his once guardsmen and now most trusted advisors. Though members of the royal court, they still dressed in velvet tunics and breeches of gray and green - the traditional garb of Jäger woodsmen.

They had been with the retired king for centuries, long enough to go gray over their own heads and show many, if not the same, scars upon their faces. Duncan bore the vestige of a slash on his left cheek and had another mark that extended from the outside corner of his right eye to his temple that he had acquired in the line of duty in another galaxy. Drustin displayed a rake of flesh across his chin from a fight with an Anise Demon in what seemed like another life. Like Acqtraejale they were tall with pointed ears, though both guardsmen had put on a few more pounds in the last ten decades than the former king.

They circled the orrery that dominated the interior of the chamber and bowed formally to the Battle King where he stood under the colonnade. They were followed into the room seconds later by the retired king's only son, Rowland, dressed in an ivory-colored tunic and breeches and attended by his own guardsmen.

Rowland had been the active ruler of the Arcadian elves for two centuries but requested advice from his father and sometimes deferred to him entirely on important matters. The Battle King had ruled the elves for over a thousand years, fought countless wars, and led the first expedition of elves from their home galaxy in Andromeda. His opinion was not to be discarded lightly.

"Have you seen them?" he asked his son.

Rowland gave a quick nod and held up a hand of surreptitious warning, which he quickly dropped as he was followed into the chamber by a number of people, much to the surprise of the old king. Visitors were always offered rooms in which to bathe or sleep or both, as well as time and refreshments after their journey. Some took an entire day before actually meeting with either king. No one came to an audience immediately after traveling from another city, much less from another moon.

Yet here they were.

A party of anomalies, and quite a large party at that. Led by the Dyer Maker himself and his granddaughter, the bio-thaumaturge who had dominated the scientific community and all of the news across three galaxies for the better part of the past three decades. The old king was quick to notice that they skirted the orrery without giving it so much as a glance, unimpressed by the refulgent color and precise holographic detail.

"Good morning, Sire," Rowland greeted formally, giving his father a quick bow as he turned to the group as they followed him into the room. "May I present my father," he said to the newcomers, bowing to them as well, "Acqtraejale Royce, known best to our people as the Battle King."

The said king gave a slight nod and a wide smile at the recognition, nodding as every person was introduced and bowed to him in turn. Had he been the type to mix honey with his water, he would have thought he was seeing double.

Not entirely, of course.

The group was led by a tall and elegantly dressed elf sporting a fashionable sculpture of gray hair accompanied by a beautiful woman with flowing hair of gold and brown and eyes that matched. By her side was a woman that he would have taken for her twin sister, so alike they were in appearance. Their features, hair and eyes mirrored one another. They even wore the same white suit with belled sleeves and gold belts. Behind them were two breathtaking women with white blonde hair and bright blue eyes. One wore a short skirt and tailored jacket made of gold cloth, the other silver. Otherwise, they were identical. They were followed by two young women that were also indistinguishable in appearance. Wild, copper-colored manes of curls framed narrow faces that were pale and freckled and set with eyes of jade.

Next came two monks, though on closer inspection Acqtra could see they were not identical – just both of Indasian descent with identical tonsured scalps and wearing identical orange robes and sandals.

"Please," the Battle King implored, "you must be tired from your journey. Would you prefer to rest and take refreshment before we speak?"

The gray-haired elf smiled, bowing slightly. "You are too kind, Sire. But our trip was not long nor arduous. If it pleases you, we are quite eager to get to work."

Acqtra dipped his white head in appreciation. "I as well," he agreed. "However, our other guest..." he trailed off as he peered around the expanse of the chamber. His son stepped forward.

"Arrived yesterday and was resting while awaiting this meeting," Rowland informed his father. "He is on his way here now."

"Excellent," the old king exclaimed, clasping his hands together in front of his white robes. "May I please encourage you to take some refreshment while we wait?" he asked his guests.

Cronus bowed low. "Of course, Sire. And with gratitude." Despite the severity of the business they were about, he knew better than to turn down the courtesy of a king, even a former one.

Rowland's attendants were on their comsets immediately, while Duncan and Drustin simply went through the traditional motions of beckoning servants. A number of them streamed into the room to pour glasses of iced lemon water and teas. Scullery girls in flowing dresses of pale green with white pinafores offered the guests canapés and slices of fruit cut into the shapes of leaves.

The guests took a moment now to admire the orrery, tilting their heads close to one another as they spoke in hushed tones, pointing to different moons and planets as they moved slowly around the great glowing orb in the center. Cronus asked King Rowland a few polite questions about the contrivance while the woman who had been introduced as Dr. Faith de Rossi stepped closer to the Battle King. Her twin, though her eyes were still on the planets and moons above her head, moved closer as well, as if tied to her by an invisible string.

"Your Majesty," Faith began – then waited politely for his permission to speak. He gave it with a nod, though his smile had fled with the look of gravity in the woman's golden-brown eyes. "My grandfather told me that you desire this because you have had a foretelling of war." Faith had also been told by her grandfather that King Rowland had shared with him the war would come from their constructs.

Acqtra nodded. "Yes, and from a very trusted source," he told her, keeping his own voice low.

Faith hesitated, something she never did, but then she was not in the habit of speaking to kings. "Your Majesty," she began again, "it is not my place to even ask, but such a situation, such implications..." she stammered – something else she never did but managed to press on "...how can you be sure..."

The Battle King wrapped a hand that was weathered but

strong around Faith's own slender fingers and his blue eyes looked into her. "Because it has already begun."

Gwen had been privy to the conversation but feigning disinterest. She looked at her twin with alarm and then just as quickly looked away.

Faith felt her blood run cold but it lasted for only a second. She composed herself in the manner she always did, clinically and immediately. She bowed her head to the retired king, ready to offer a promise to aid the elves in any way she could but was diverted by the arrival of the missing guest as he and his small escort entered the large chamber.

He was a slim elf of average height, with bright blue eyes over high cheekbones and black hair that was cut shorter on the sides but longer on the top, framing his narrow face and accentuating his high, pointed ears.

King Rowland and his entourage had already met the visitor and Faith had known him for quite some time. But before he could be introduced to the others, Hope recognized him as well. She let out a cry of surprise and took a few hurried steps to meet him as he neared the others. He gave her a grin that was equal parts sheepish and mischievous as he flicked a length of dark hair from his face.

"Galen!" Hope exclaimed, then embraced him.

ONE FOUR

John Pierre was almost at the end of the hall when the door to the Bauam's chambers swung open and Ebon came out after taking the Holy Father his evening wine. The Luma Boy pulled the door quickly shut before he took off running down the stone-walled corridor only to run into the legs of the near invisible bodyguard of the Holy Father.

"Whoa!" John Pierre said, catching the boy and disentangling him from his robes and legs. "What's the hurry?" the construct asked, just as he saw that the boy was crying. He knelt quickly, gathering the child in his arms.

Ebon was just over ten, slightly chubby with blue eyes and blonde curls. John Pierre always thought the boy looked like pictures he had seen of angels in Christian churches. Most of those churches he had seen were burned soon after by the One Church, but John Pierre did not focus on that aspect of memory. He knew the buildings were gifts given to the One, even if in flames.

He stroked the boy's curls in an effort to calm him before backing away, holding him at arm's length so he could see his face. Ebon's blue eyes flowed like faucets and the boy angrily wiped them away with the back of a plump hand, obviously ashamed.

"What is wrong?" John Pierre asked. "Are you hurt?"

"Yes!" Ebon cried before shaking his head. "No! I don't know!"

"You don't know?"

Ebon shook his head, harder this time, bringing a fresh gout of tears.

"What is it? You can tell me."

The construct was so earnest that the boy looked at him with wide eyes, still leaking profusely but full of hope. John Pierre's strong hands were wrapped around the boy's ribcage, holding him steady and upright. Ebon's chubby hands rested on the construct's forearms and, beneath the robes, Ebon could feel the sheaths that housed the bodyguard's deadly blades. The Luma Boy had never seen John Pierre use them, but he had heard the stories from those who had, or those who had heard the stories. Hot tears filled his angel's eyes and spilled over his cherub cheeks. Though his body still trembled, the boy shook his head.

"I'm okay, John Pierre. I just don't feel well. It might be something I ate."

John Pierre frowned, the line between his auburn brows creasing his otherwise perfect face. "Will you go to the infirmary?" he asked.

Ebon nodded emphatically. "I will," he agreed.

"Right now?"

"Right now."

"Alright," the construct said, relenting as he stood up. As soon as he had done so, Ebon took off once again, running down the hall. John Pierre watched him go until he was swallowed by the shadows of the candlelit hall. Though his imagination was severely limited, he tried to use it to understand.

What could it be? he wondered.

Years ago, after he had met the bleary-eyed Avery in the hallway, he had inquired with the Deacon of the House and the Deacon of the Infirmary, concerned for the boys who were often troubled by similar ailments. Both had told him that the boys were just being boys and adjusting to not having their mothers to care for them day and night. Not ever having had a mother of his own, John Pierre had assumed that they knew what they were taking about. After all, they had been running the monastery for many many years - long before John Pierre had shown up.

Tonight, however, something else occurred to the construct. Possibly his first spark of imagination, and to John Pierre the feeling was foreign and disorienting. Yet he felt it could be important, so he forced himself to follow the line of thought, gossamer thin, that he had unexpectedly found.

What if something here at the monastery is making them sick? Something in the food? John Pierre himself had been witness to many news broadcasts as the Bauam watched them on the holo in his room. John Pierre had heard of people getting sick from nearly everything. Germs were commonly passed from one person to another and, on poorer planets or more rural areas, it was often deadly. People were known to get sick from the metals in their cooking pans seeping into their food and many died from bacteria in their meat, fruit, or vegetables.

The construct decided that the next day he would visit the kitchens. And the gardens. He would not make a fuss, just have a good look around to make sure everything was safe. After all, it was his job to keep people safe. What could make the boys sick might also make the Holy Father sick, though the Father stuck mostly to bread and cheese and wine. He did not eat much of what came from the kitchens, and very rarely had vegetables.

Still, John Pierre decided he would have a look.

The next day, Brother Mish found him poking around. Brother Mish was a friar and the fattest man John Pierre had ever seen. He wore heavy brown robes with a rope belt and had a fringe of brown hair that circled his otherwise bald head from one ear to the other. John Pierre suspected the man had more hair growing over his soft brown eyes than his entire head.

"John Pierre!" he exclaimed, his thick eyebrows rising, "this is a pleasant surprise! Are you hungry?"

John Pierre shook his head. "No, but thank you."

"Is it the Holy Father?" Mish inquired. "Is he in need of something from the kitchens?" John Pierre shook his head again.

"To be honest, Brother, I was concerned about the new Luma Boy, Ebon?"

"Ebon?" Brother Mish repeated. "Oh yes! Little blonde fellow! Is there something wrong with him?" He clasped his large hands together, a crease of worry between his bushy eyebrows.

"I'm not sure," John Pierre confided. "I saw him last night, after he had taken the Holy Father his evening wine, and he was quite distraught."

Brother Mish wrung his hands, looking almost as distraught as Ebon had been. "What do you think it was?" he asked anxiously, shifting his heavy bulk from one foot to the other and then back again. John Pierre did not want to insult the friar but he certainly was not going to be untruthful.

"I thought, maybe, it was something he ate."

Mish stopped shifting around. "Maybe he pinched a bit of the Father's wine," he suggested. "Wine does not often agree with young stomachs."

John Pierre's blue eyes went wide in surprise. "I don't think he would do that."

The friar's massive shoulders humped up in a shrug. "Boys have done it before," he said. "Quite a bit, in fact."

John Pierre blinked rapidly, thinking. "I don't know..."

"Did any of the other boys get sick?" Brother Mish asked. "Last night? After the evening meal?"

"Why, no. Not that I have heard."

The friar relaxed considerably. "All of the boys had the same dinner last night. You certainly would have heard if they had all fallen ill. And, as far as I know, all of the boys were at breakfast this morning, including Ebon."

John Pierre looked out of the kitchen's large, wood-framed windows offering a grand view of the herb and vegetable gardens which were brightly lit by the planet's twin suns. A few friars, all considerably smaller than Brother Mish, were outside working between the neatly kept rows.

"I suppose it could have been a reaction to something," he said softly. He knew that some of the boys were more frail, and had what the others called "allergies," but he knew little of them.

"That certainly could be it," the friar agreed. It seemed that once it was decided that the cause was not due to the cooking, Brother Mish was eager for him to be gone.

"Very well," John Pierre resolved. "I will check with Deacon Gray at the infirmary, but not right now. The Holy Father will be up from his nap soon and I know he wishes to take a walk around the Harvest Lake today."

The friar and the bodyguard bowed to each other and went their separate ways.

The friar, however, was slow to turn away. His meaty hands found one another and clasped together before the wide stretch of his rope belt.

"Reaction indeed," he said softly, watching the back of the beautiful yet fearsome bodyguard until it disappeared down the hall.

The Bauam spent most of the afternoon on his walk, ambulating around the lake deep in prayer until it was almost dark. His bodyguard walked slightly behind and to his right, circumspect and vigilant.

The construct escorted the Holy Father to his chambers at

twilight before returning to his own room. The next day they were to leave for a conference in the Solar System and would not return for six months. John Pierre did not have time to visit the infirmary before they left. It was an easy and quick job to pack his clothes, but weapons were another matter.

He spent an hour on the web-link computer the Thauam had gotten for him five years ago when the attacks on the Bauam had escalated to new heights. He checked the places they were to be visiting and was able to calculate a rough estimate on the size of the crowds they would be seeing. He watched vids about every place on their itinerary as far back as four months ago until today's morning news so he could judge the atmosphere and know what he could expect – from temperatures to temperaments.

All places but two looked like what would be considered normal for protests and possible life attempts. The two anomalies were what the Thauam called "hot spots." These were places where their group might possibly be attacked by larger groups or people with serious weaponry – or both.

John Pierre swung open the banded wooden door of his closet, a closet unlike any other in the priory. His two spare robes that normally hung there were already packed in his bag, revealing the rest of the area that served as a miniature armory.

He used what small imagination was afforded him to do what it did best - gauge the possibilities of attacks and attackers.

The construct methodically chose what would work best under the conditions he expected, and what he could use if the conditions turned out to be even more severe. He selected a belt with two large-barreled pistols that held artillery rounds and a small handgun that would hold fifty shots. He added two sling grenades to the belt, carefully taping down the flips to prevent an accident, two smoke cartridges, and a canister of CS gas.

He spent an hour sharpening his blades.

Adequately supplied for his journey, John Pierre washed up and knelt by his bed to pray. He prayed for the One to guide his eyes and his hands and keep the Bauam safe. He prayed for the others in the priory, and also for the sick and the poor. Last, but not least, he prayed for Hope – for her health and her safety, and that he might see her again soon.

The voyage started the very next day and lasted three months longer than anticipated. With the Bauam's busy schedule, John Pierre forgot when they returned that there was something he had wanted to look into. Many more years passed before he was reminded of his previous worry that something nasty might be growing in the priory's garden.

CS⁊O

Bjorn wandered through the palace, bored. He had been home alone for seven days while Ivana was off on a trip with girlfriends, something which seemed to be happening more often over the past few years. It was strange only in the fact the Ivana did not have any friends – just a circle of people that constantly smiled at each other until backs were turned. Then the fangs came out, usually dripping with the venom of gossip. Bjorn had tired of it decades ago but even rumors and gossip were better than the silent walls of Zimnya Roza.

Ivana always told him he could go wherever he wanted, do whatever he wanted to do, but he could never think of anything. So he wandered through the icy fortress that was her home.

He usually found something or someone in his wanderings to occupy his time or thoughts or both.

Zimnya Roza bulged from the west face of the Carpathian Mountains north of the Ukraine in a titanic wedge of glass and steel. The upper halls and rooms were sumptuously decorated with priceless pieces of modern art and furnishings. The lower stories were considerably cooler and less used or even seen - but decorated with even more expensive furnishings and forgotten droves of art that were incalculable in worth.

Bjorn had rarely ventured down beneath the gallery, which was always (and erroneously) called the first floor. When he had asked Ivana what occupied the areas beneath she had made a sour face.

"The dungeons," she had told him and then laughed.

On this lonely weekend, when Bjorn felt sure that he had watched every vid under all seven suns of the civilized galaxies and read every book in Zimnya Roza, he decided that even the dungeons would be more cheerful than staring out into the crevasses of ice from his bedroom.

Alone, he boarded the main lift and perused the numbers on the buttons. The lowest level he had ever been on was the gallery and the elevator displayed the word "GALEREYA" with a back-lit button to mark its location in the fortress. As far as Bjorn knew, it was the largest floor – housing the kitchens, formal dining rooms and ballrooms. Bjorn had frequented the kitchens quite often seeking out tasty morsels in the form of a scullery maid or pastry femme.

He knew since Ivana was gone they were all absent for the weekend save for the sous chef left behind to take care of the staff which in itself was a skeleton crew.

The next choice below "GALEREYA" was a much smaller button - faded and glowing with a yellowed dying light. It was marked "PRIYEM." The construct recognized it as the word for "reception." He considered the button for a moment, wondered why it was never used, and pushed it.

There was a pause, as if the non-sentient elevator was actually considering his request, then there was a metallic whisper as the doors closed and Bjorn felt his stomach flutter as the ornate chamber dropped in a rush.

It gave a lurch only a breath later as the conveyance hit

a cushion of air and slowed to a dramatic halt, giving a soft hiss of protest. The doors opened slowly, as if capricious and mindful of his course, and Bjorn stepped into the room beyond and peered around, infused with a curiosity he had never before felt.

The space before him was large and open, the long wall hung with priceless art being either ruined or preserved by the cold; Bjorn did not know which. To his left were only walls of granite and, due to no heat being pumped into the room, they were dusted with frost. The level did, however, have the benefit of radiant heat coming from the upper floors, making the chill only mildly uncomfortable. Bjorn turned to his right and looked through a wall of glass to see where the frozen mountain yawned open to the sky. The view was magnificent, to say the least, and it rooted the construct momentarily where he stood.

It was well past breakfast so Bjorn guessed the sun must be high above. He had often admired the same view (albeit from a hundred feet higher) but it had only caught his attention when the sun was rising or setting, painting the snow-capped peaks pink and orange while the mostly clouded sky echoed the same.

Today the sky was clear as a bell and as blue as a mountain lake. The mountains themselves stood against the blue backdrop with stark clarity - razor sharp jags of black and gray, topped and streaked with snow so bright it dazzled his eyes.

Bjorn turned his body towards the panoramic view and approached it slowly, almost fearfully, breathtaking as it grew and grew within his vision until it was all he could see. He was vaguely aware of passing tables and sofas covered in white sheets of cloth like sleeping ghosts. His shoes made a hollow ringing sound on floors of white marble inlaid with gold, muted as if the stone itself was absorbing the sound, hushing the disturbance of his finely made Florentine loafers.

He finally reached the wall of glass and stared out into the snowy valley.

The construct saw then that his breath had become vapor, softly billowing in front of his perfectly formed lips – gentle puffs of white condensation before drifting away like ether. He thought briefly that he should have donned a sweater but the thought evaporated like his breath. He was too captivated by the view.

It was like standing on air, but with the majesty of the alpine mountains rising like an anthem on every side. The peaks thrust themselves into the sky as if screaming for mercy or shouting in triumph. Black earth and steely granite were streaked and topped with snow, blinding white and sparkling like crushed diamond. The sky was a vista of blue, unmarked by even a single cloud.

Bjorn wondered why he had never seen it like this before in all the years he had lived there despite acres of plate glass that enclosed the mountain fortress.

Then he realized much of the glass upstairs was opaque. Certainly not all of it, just panes here and there to break the view into pieces. He had believed that the frosted glass was part of Ivana's desire to produce a feeling of floating in the clouds, which was probably also true.

But that's not the real reason, Bjorn thought. *It's because she does not want to see the same view from up there as she once saw down here.*

Bjorn could not tell how long he stood there, motionless save for his green eyes that drank in the view like a man not dying of thirst but of one discovering water for the first time, clear and clean from a virgin spring.

When his eyes had finally drunk their fill, his body turned so his gaze could take in the room in which he stood. It was more than enormous. It was vast. Bjorn guessed (correctly) that he could fly two jets side by side through the space. But ghosts were the only tenants on this floor, and the construct knew that it went beyond the sheet-covered furniture and art.

Why doesn't she come here? Bjorn wondered, thinking of

Ivana and her lavish parties. *Why doesn't she entertain here?*

His green eyes surveyed the room from one side to the other, coming to rest on a small alcove in the far west corner. From a distance it looked like a private entrance.

What have we here? he pondered as he moved towards it, his fine heels calling a slow staccato to the silent ghosts who did not answer with words.

That it was another lift became obvious within seconds by the unsmiling vertical line that split doors of hammered bronze. There was only a single button embedded in the wall next to the closed portal and Bjorn pushed it with no more than a moment of hesitation.

A dumbwaiter, Bjorn thought as he waited. *A conveyance to the kitchens above or a service lift.* But as the bronze doors creaked open he knew immediately that he was wrong. The interior of the small chamber was walled in burgundy velvet and panels of silvered mirror veined with gold. Old, yes. Outdated for certain. But a transport for food or servants? No. The construct entered the elevator and looked carefully at the choices set into the panel. He had assumed (erroneously once again) that it would go up. But - for this lift – he was already on the uppermost floor that it serviced. The buttons below "PRIYEM" were "FAMILLE," "CHAMBRES," and "LE FILES."

Bjorn had seen the icy fortress from the outside whenever he flew Ivana's megacopter to the lower snow fields and even on simple pleasure excursions of his own in the airhopper. He knew that the castle had more levels than he had personally traversed but he had always assumed they were merely storerooms, garages, furnaces or the like. He had not imagined they were as palatial, if more antiquated, than the floors above. He had no way of knowing that the lower floors of the fortress were...

Her past, Bjorn thought, the knowledge coming upon him sudden yet sure.

He took a long look at the buttons again, the lift waiting

patiently. There were no other callers to the conveyance nor had there been for what Bjorn could only guess was a very long time.

French, he pondered after he had translated the buttons. *Why French?* Then it came to him. Ivana's grandmother had been French. It was why she now had a French cook. Ivana would moan over meals at times in the same manner she would moan during intercourse. Bjorn had to admit that the food was good – but not *that* good.

He pushed the button that would take him to the next level down. The one marked "Family" in a flowing French script.

The carriage gave a lurch and Bjorn grabbed the golden handrail that ran waist-high along the interior of the lift, bisecting the burgundy velvet wallpaper and the panels of gold-veined mirror.

The construct cocked his head and listened. He could hear the metallic creaking of cables and winches and realized two things. One – the lift was much older than he had originally thought and, two – maybe it had not been such a good idea to go exploring the depths of Ivana's cold castle and even colder past.

Both ideas were pushed aside as the lift came to a comfortable halt and the doors eased open. Curiosity overruled caution and Bjorn stepped into the proffered hall. There was no mistaking the drop in temperature here. His breath fogged in front of his mouth like a puff of smoke that dissipated slowly, momentarily masking the face below his green eyes with a cloud of vapor.

The room was huge, though not as vast as the chamber on the floor above. It was divided into sections by furniture; couches and chairs arranged around different forms of diversion. These, however, were not covered with sheets and showed their age with dusty and reckless abandon. But the cold preserved much and splits and tears in the upholstery were few.

To his far right was a cocktail bar, the corked bottles still somewhat full of liquids in various colors and in neat rows on shelves backed by mirrored walls. The open bottles had long since lost their spirits to evaporation. Next to the bar was an area fenced in by ottomans and heavy cushions and dotted with toys. An obvious play area for toddlers where the adults could enjoy their cocktails while keeping an eye on the children – or keeping an eye on those in charge of watching the children.

To his left was a giant sofa in the shape of a horseshoe. Its open end welcomed what Bjorn could only guess was an ancient flatscreen - though the screen was far from flat. It was large and bulbous, like a dead gray eye, though even his limited imagination could conjure up the picture of a family gathered around it, enthralled by the colors and sounds emitted from its now defunct system and speakers.

The far-left section of the room was occupied by large but comfortable looking chairs, facing small tables. One pair of chairs faced a table made of fine woods that had been inlaid in a checkerboard pattern. Another pair was divided by a table laid with ornate combatants. Four easy chairs circled a Spade table. The entire room, even decades later, was pervaded by a sense of family interaction and closeness.

Bjorn surveyed it all for a few long moments, then retreated back into the lift. Even as he pondered over what he had just seen, his left hand reached out and pushed the button marked "CHAMBRES" that would take him to the next floor down.

The elevator began to descend once again and after only a few moments it jerked to a halt, making Bjorn grasp the hand railing once more. He looked at the rail of gold and felt a certainty that it had been put in place originally as more of a decoration and less of a necessity. The jerkiness of the lift was obviously from age and lack of use, not technology.

The doors now, like the stop, were jerky and Bjorn wondered if the cold played as large a part as the disuse. The brass doors juddered open and the construct knew he was decidedly uncomfortable. He shivered as he exited the lift and looked around. This time, to his left, was a corridor into the mountain. Bjorn made a face and turned from the left corridor. He had no desire to explore what he knew had to be the servants' quarters in the days of Uri yore. They were not lavish by any means now (Spartan might be a better word) and he had no reason to believe that Ivana's parents had been any better.

The construct meandered slowly down the hall towards the right – into the first level he encountered that was not brightly lit by walls of glass that opened onto the brilliance of the mountains.

These halls were dark and cold, dimly lit by electric flambeaux kept alive by the mere reason that they were so old that no one knew how to turn them off.

The corridor ended abruptly, splitting off into a single hall hung with portraits of those long dead, painted in everlasting but dusty acrylic.

Bjorn looked one way, then the other. He chose the right and found the apartments of Ivana's parents. They had separate rooms, dusty now and drab despite their titanic size. Their individual bathing rooms were of gigantic proportions and their personal closets even larger. Their sleeping rooms were separated by a narrow tearoom where Bjorn could only guess they met in the morning or in the evening to decide and determine a night of appropriately measured passion.

The construct left the rooms in mild disgust and moments later entered the chambers of Ivana's grandmother.

There was a vanity table with jars of perfume and cream that had long since dried away. Brushes, combs and jeweled hairpins lay discarded and covered with a blanket of dust and frost. The construct saw there were chairs and loungers of ivory, and a great bed draped in cloth of gold. The hairs on the back of Bjorn's neck rose up and he was quite sure that it had nothing to do with the cold.

He made his way back to the lift and backed inside, almost staggering. He looked at the panel and his hand raised before it, considering. Bjorn knew going down would get only get colder and darker. Figuratively and literally. Decidedly, he punched the last button before he could change his mind. The one marked "LES FILES."

There was no immediate response from the lift, making him think that if it was not sentient then it was certainly acting on orders. Then the elevator began to descend slowly, creaking as it went. Finally, it stopped. But the doors did not open right away. They stayed shut as if asking the construct if he was sure that this was where he really wanted to go.

Bjorn frowned at the bronze doors, closed in a tight, cold kiss.

At long last, they sighed and groaned open, making the construct gasp.

It was more than cold on this level. It was truly freezing. And it was dark.

Verboten, his mind whispered, lapsing into German for no reason he could explain. The fact that he knew it must be forbidden goaded him out of the elevator and into the dark beyond.

Bjorn felt his breath stolen away, sucked from his lungs by the cold. He jerked, turning quickly, suddenly afraid that the lift would close and leave him there to freeze in the darkness. The lift, however, remained open and oddly inviting. But his sudden movement triggered a long dying motion detector and a few lights flickered. Most flickered out, but some made a valiant attempt to furnish a bit of light. The construct took a few tentative steps and looked into the sporadically lit darkness.

His breath fogged in front of his mouth and this time turned to frost that clung to his lips. He stuck his bare hands into his armpits to keep them as warm as possible and ventured farther into the hallway. This level was significantly smaller than the others but it was too cold to waste time.

There were three doors, each leading to the rooms of the three children. Bjorn tried the knob of the closest door and thought, at first, that it was locked.

Why would it be locked when no one comes here?

He turned harder, the frozen metal biting at his skin before giving way with an audible snap. The construct clasped his hands together and blew into his palms in an effort to warm them as he pushed the door open with his shoulder. He stamped his feet and waited for the lights to come on. A few managed to shed some illumination and, though it was dim, it was enough.

It was a room that had obviously been occupied by a boy. Pennants from sports teams decorated the frozen walls though some had fallen to the floor. Trophies, brittle with age and cold, stood like sentinels on mahogany shelves.

"Greggor," Bjorn whispered. He was well learned in the lineage and workings of Ivana's family, though he had never met any of them personally, other than Ivana of course.

Though there were openings that led to other rooms, one most likely a sitting room used for games of some sort and the others to a bathing chamber and closets, Bjorn retreated into the hall.

He gave his arms a vigorous rub as he walked down the hall, wondering how he would know one girl's room from the other. He shouldered open the next door and knew immediately whose it was. Even if he had not spied the large mirror painted with a gold heart and Ivana's name in the middle, he would have known it was hers.

"Some things never change," Bjorn mused aloud. The room was girlish and haphazard and entirely Ivana. It produced a strange sort of nostalgia within the construct and he left the room as he had done the one before, without exploring any of the ancillary antechambers.

He cursed the cold as he made his way to the last room,

warmed slightly by an excited expectation, another odd feeling that he could not explain. He shouldered open a door that was not latched.

A few lamps sputtered to life, one from the floor.

"Hooooly shit," Bjorn murmured as he surveyed the room, the whites of his eyes showing around green irises.

Whatever art or girlish posters that had once adorned the walls had been torn down. In some cases, shredded and stomped upon. The floor was strewn with shards of glass from ornaments and trinkets that had been thrown and smashed. There were ashes where other items, including part of the four-poster bed, had been burned. And here, even more than her own room, Bjorn could see Ivana's hand in the bedroom that once housed the youngest of the Uri children, Katia.

Unlike the other rooms, he felt compelled to explore.

One doorway led to her closets. The clothes had been ripped from their hangers and drawers spilled on the carpet. The clothing that had not been burned to ash was all but rotted away. In Katia's bathroom, the mirrors had been smashed. The same had been done to the vanity in her sitting room where stuffed animals had been angrily relieved of their heads and quite a bit of their stuffing.

Bjorn had seen enough. And quite literally thought he might freeze to death if he lingered any longer. He left the chambers of the once young Katia Uri and hurried back to the lift, blowing into his hands and again tickled by the fear that the elevator might leave him stranded.

It had not. It stood, ancient and waiting and superbly well-lit after his explorations through the darkened chambers and halls of the Uri children. Bjorn pushed the top button without hesitation and gave a sigh of relief when the doors closed.

He made the ascent to reality, leaving Ivana's past behind.

He changed elevators as he had before on the Galleria, marveling once again at the view and giving his head a shake in disappointment at how dissimilar it was only one floor higher due to Ivana's machinations.

The world is as we see it, he told himself.

ONE FIVE

"Galen!" Hope exclaimed, hugging the elfin doctor's slim form against her own for a moment before letting him go. She was as full of questions as she was astonishment but she was wise enough to know that it was not the time to ask. In fact, it was quite possible that she had already overstepped her bounds. "I am sorry," she apologized to the others, turning to face them. "It is just that Galen and I have worked together before, and it is such a surprise – and a delight – to see him again."

King Rowland dipped his head in acknowledgment, smiling broadly. "No need for apologies, Ms. de Rossi, and I am sure you will have plenty of time to catch up later. But for now, if everyone is ready, I think we should get down to the matter at hand." He glanced at his father who gave him a nod of approval before he continued. "To sum up, before we begin, is a very brief synopsis of our history. Not our entire history, of course," he added with a small smile (all of elfin history would take days – if not weeks – to recount), "just the part that led us to this decision." He took a deep breath, as if readying himself to deliver a sermon or a song. "After eons of peace in our home galaxy, the elfin race was beset by violence in what seemed like all directions. Alien races as well as other races of elves. Decades of fighting turned into centuries of blood and war. The desecration of life was not constrained to elfin lives but also to the lands on which we lived. My father, after a battle that would not be his last, decided to bring the Arcadian Elves here, to the human galaxy –then called The Milky Way. We found peace with the humans, and even fought alongside them in the war of the Golgoth Tide."

Here, the older elves, Cronus included, nodded sagely. They remembered it well.

King Rowland continued. "War is upon us once again. It is both imminent and alarming in the time and magnitude that it will encompass – the lives it will take and the destruction it will wring upon, not just this galaxy, but all the seven systems." King Rowland, though still composed, let out a deep breath of resignation. "It is our wish to avoid this war altogether." He looked first at Galen then at Faith and spoke again. "And all future wars, could that be made possible."

A moment of heavy silence followed. Oddly enough, or perhaps not, it was Madeline that questioned him. "I see how leaving this world, this galaxy even, would allow you to avoid this war. But how would you avoid future wars as well?"

King Rowland's eyes went back to Galen before returning to the flame-haired dyer. "By going to a place where we could not be found," he answered.

This only enflamed Madeline with more questions, but she had learned that most questions were answered by waiting and watching. Her green eyes moved across the group assembled in the large open-aired chamber and did just that - watched and waited.

Charity and Llewellyn's blue eyes flicked to one another, as did Faith and Gwen's, before returning to the others.

Galen cleared his throat, taking over the discussion as he was handed a limp scrap of fabric by one of Rowland's attendants. Galen shook it out and stuck the fingers of his right hand into it, forming a thin, shiny black glove. He held the hand up experimentally, moving it slightly from left to right. Above their heads, the objects in the orrery twitched. Galen gave a nod of satisfaction and walked under the orrery as he began to lecture as if speaking to a class of astronomy students.

"This," he said, pointing to a mass that hung by the

enormous striated blue ball that was Neptune, "is Eris." The object in question glowed as he pointed and then began to move as he pulled it across the holographic galaxy. "It is the second largest dwarf planet in the system," he narrated as the glowing orb migrated over their heads. "It was colonized two hundred years ago by two groups – Sylvan Elves and Scandinavian humans from Earth. Though the minor planet is habitable due to an in-place atmospheric infrastructure and solar mirrors, it is still as cold as hell."

At this point Madeline leaned towards Hope and whispered, "I thought hell was supposed to be..." but Hope cut her off with a quick shake of her head and a whispered reply.

"Figure of speech."

"Ah." Madeline nodded. She had been fooled by such things before.

"Have the current natives been contacted?" King Rowland asked.

Galen nodded, though he looked less than pleased. "The humans are in agreement that they could use a change in the climate and that the Arcadians would be most welcome."

"And the Sylvans?" the Battle King asked, his voice gruff.

Galen's blue eyes wanted to shift, but he kept them fixed steadily upon the gray and retired king. "They are split," he answered. "Half side with the humans, half want no change."

The older king harrumphed at this remark as if it was no less than what he expected, but his son smiled at the young, black-haired doctor. "In this case," King Rowland said, "I think we will assume an idea that humans have quite the affinity for – majority wins."

Galen's look of concern vanished into a smile. "In that case," he continued, "we shall proceed as planned." He looked up, drawing their attention back to the dwarf planet that he had now positioned between Earth and Venus. "Eris is small enough that it can be moved here," he instructed, "by a Dragon of course."

Madeline cocked her head, her copper curls shifting and falling about her freckled face. "And you want Hahn and Elaeric to terraform it?"

"Child's play," Hahn remarked, almost to himself.

"But very arduous," Hope remarked, quite clearly. "Quite costly."

The twin blue eyes of Charity and Llewellyn glimmered at this remark and darted about like cats sensing prey.

Galen smiled. "Actually, terraforming will be minimal. The proximity to the sun will do most of the work."

"Then why hire..." Madeline began before her own twin cut her off with a quick shake of her wild copper mane.

"Not for the terraforming," Hope mused aloud. "For the hiding."

Galen nodded and shifted his bright blue eyes to the image of Venus. He moved his gloved hand, illuminating the marbled globe of amber and gold.

"Venus is the only planet in the system that has been classified as uninhabitable due to the amount of noxious gases, heat, and – most importantly - its outrageous atmospheric pressure." Galen shifted his gaze to Elaeric and then Hahn. "How much of that can you change?" he asked.

"Plenty," Elaeric confided with a small smile.

"Enough to hide another small planet?"

Hahn was close to laughing at the simplicity but Faith was the one who answered, and answered quickly.

"They certainly can," she assured the group. "But it will be arduous," she said, echoing Hope's words, "and costly."

Hope's lips pressed together so hard that they disappeared entirely as she glared at her older sister but King Rowland waved a dismissive hand. The cost meant little or nothing to the elves.

Charity and Llewellyn disguised predacious grins with angelic smiles.

"It will certainly be like nothing we have ever done before," Hahn admitted, stroking his chin. He had grown a set of whiskers there. Normally he shaved them off, but Hope seemed to like them. They had grown long and wispy and he had developed a habit of stroking them when in thought. "What are we to do with what is currently Venus?" he asked, though more to himself than the others.

Elaeric joined him, speculating aloud. "Merge them somehow?"

"You can do such things?" the Battle King asked, astonished. But his voice was low and Hahn and Elaeric had already moved away.

The orange-robed men walked in slow circles under the images of Venus and Eris, which now hovered close to the second planet from the sun, looking up at the globes and muttering to each other. They discussed the possibilities as casually as two mathematicians discussing minor algebraic equations over coffee.

The others watched, silent at first, but as the monks became more engaged in matters they did not understand, they began quiet conversations of their own.

Hope sidled up to Galen and gave his arm a squeeze. "I can't believe you are here!" she squealed as softly as she could. "Elaeric has told me many times about the true meaning of coincidence, but what are the odds that you would be working with the Arcadians on the same..." Hope's voice trailed off as she watched Galen's expression fall. Her confusion lasted for only a breath as her eyes read his, then her expression mirrored the one on the young doctor's face. "You are not working for them," she stated as the realization sank in, her voice quiet. "You are working for Faith."

Galen nodded reluctantly, both his body and face braced for the lashing he was expecting to come. He knew Hope was smart, brilliant in fact, and that she would piece everything together. And so she did.

"I see," Hope said, her body and face holding very still. Her green eyes flicked to Faith and then back to Galen. "A spy for her spy. That is so like her."

"Hope, I am truly sorry if what I did caused you pain, and I am quite sure that it did. But you have to know that he was..."

Hope held up a small hand, stopping his speech. She glanced around quickly, but everyone else was also engaged in whispered conversations. "I am quite aware of what he was, and that it was possible..." she paused as Galen pressed his lips together and cocked his head in silent reprimand before she continued... "alright, almost inevitable that he would have hurt me. But that was for me to learn. It was my decision to make."

"I know," Galen said quietly, hanging his head. "I'm sorry, Hope."

She touched his chin, bringing his bright blue eyes up to meet her green ones. "Thank you," she told him, "but you are not the one who should be apologizing."

Galen looked at the eldest de Rossi sister who was speaking in hushed tones with Gwendolyn. "I am sure Faith has already..." he began before he was cut off by Hope's muted laughter.

"Apologized?" she asked, full of silent mirth. She shook her head of wild, copper-colored curls. "Faith never apologizes," she assured the elfin doctor.

Galen's almond-shaped eyes narrowed and he cocked his head, a lock of black hair falling over his blue eyes. He brushed it away. "Never?" he asked doubtfully.

Hope gave him a wry smile. "She never thinks she is wrong," she told him.

Then all of the murmurings came to an abrupt halt as the air was broken by a sharp clap. All eyes went to Hahn, hands together and face beaming like the sun. Elaeric stood by his side with an identical expression of boyish excitement.

"We have plan!" he announced proudly.

☙❦❧

Hahn explained what he and Elaeric believed they could accomplish. Both sides had many questions and before long the group retired to a large table in the open-air arcade to discuss all options and possibilities over lunch.

"It looks like," Galen told the others as they were finishing their meal, "the most time-consuming process will be moving Eris. It should take about fifteen years, perhaps a couple more."

King Rowland looked to his father who gave his white head a shake in a manner that expressed a lack of worry, summing up with a small movement that the time frame was acceptable.

Cronus smiled at a servant as she removed his plate then fixed his eye on the Battle King. "So, you are not anticipating the war to break out before then?"

The retired king gave his head another shake. "No. And, even when it does – I am told it will break violently but escalate slowly."

Cronus nodded and was surprised, as was everyone, when Madeline spoke. "And, if I may ask, even if we can hide the New World, how will we hide the fact that we are doing it? I doubt that a Dragon moving a planetary sized object across the Solar System will go unnoticed."

Everyone smiled and King Acqtra nodded to his son, deferring the question to him.

"Nor will it be easy to hide almost three thousand elves migrating across the system," admitted.

"Three thousand?" Gwendolyn interrupted, perplexed enough to speak out loud for the first time to the elves. "Surely there must be hundreds of thousands, millions even, of elves who will want to migrate to peaceful lands..." she trailed off and King Rowland gave her a smile that was somewhere between apologetic and embarrassed.

"Not at the price we are asking."

"Price?" Gwendolyn queried, thinking he meant some form of monetary payment. The young king nodded sagely.

"We believe that in order to truly keep peace long lasting we must leave our technology behind. It is what eventually leads to the most destructive weaponry. So we will take with us no computes, no holos, flatscreens, comsets, nor any other technological items - other than the ships that will take us there."

"A price that most, not just elves, are not willing to pay," Cronus admitted. King Rowland acquiesced with a dip of his head and continued.

"The general plans will be public, but the details will be kept secret, which is why I must ask that this meeting, and all others, never be discussed with anyone outside this room." He looked around, his previous amusement replaced with a deep gravity, marking each of them with his eyes. "We plan to set a micro-star imploder just outside the magnetosphere, close to the planet of Mercury. The moment the migration is complete, perhaps before if it is safe, the bomb will detonate."

"Making it look like technology gone awry, a malfunction in the ships perhaps, and all of the elfin pilgrims killed in the ensuing disaster," Madeline finished softly.

Hope gave her a wan smile and laid a freckled hand over Madeline's own, proud at her deduction and the fact that she was probably the only one in the room with the guts to say it out loud. The Arcadians looked equally defiant and discomfited.

Elaeric, who had been peeling an orange, broke it into segments even as he broke the ice in the air as he gave the group an encouraging smile. "That should work," he said enthusiastically as he popped a small segment into his mouth.

Smiles and murmurs rippled through those seated at the table and discussions and plans continued.

Finally, as the sun was setting over the gardens in a great slash of pink and lavender, business was concluded for the time being. King Acqtra offered his guests rooms for the night, which they politely declined. King Rowland proposed for them to at least have a sumptuous dinner before departing, which they also graciously declined.

"We will dine aboard our ship," Cronus explained, "if it bears no offense."

"None at all," King Rowland answered. "I know you have much to do. Let me, however, personally escort you to your craft."

Cronus, as well as the others, bowed deeply in response before moving as a group from the arcade that was now bathed in twilight. Faith was given a start when she felt strong fingers close around her upper arm, holding her back. She was even more surprised to see that the hand belonged to Master Chi.

"Dr. de Rossi," Hahn said softly as he released his gentle hold and gave her a broad smile, "might I have a word with you?"

"Of course," Faith replied, continuing along at a slower pace so that she and Hahn might have a bit of privacy as they brought up the rear. Though he did not show it, she could sense a touch of nervousness in the monk. Thinking of the work they had just promised, it sent a similar trace of apprehension through her body like an unseen shiver.

"I, ah," he began hesitantly then pushed on, "I am quite appreciative of the money you are paying the monastery, more than you know, yet is there any way that Elaeric and I might receive a small stipend?"

Faith straightened, a strange movement for one who has just relaxed, but not unsual for her. It was often her reaction when grasping a situation. Hahn, however, was afraid he had offended her.

"Not much," he said quickly, softly. "Just enough for a few personal items."

Faith cocked her head, her brows slightly drawn over her gold and brown eyes. "Isn't Hope taking care of your needs?"

Hahn blushed fiercely under his golden skin. "Of course, Miss Hope does indeed, but I do not wish to trouble her for everything. Yet I do not even know the cost of something so simple as a shaving razor."

Miss Hope, Faith thought with a smile, *how adorable.*

She laid a hand over Master Chi's arm as they walked along. "Say no more," she told him. "I will be happy to provide you and Elaeric both with a credentials card, and personal funds for whatever you need. It was inconsiderate of me not to think of it in the first place."

"Shush shush," Hahn replied with a wave of his hand. "We did not think of it either, I admit. We are so used to a simple life."

"Not to worry," Faith assured him, pulling her comset from a pocket in her tailored blouse and hooking it over her left ear. "I'll take care of it immediately."

Hahn gave her a quick bow and moved to join the others as she opened a link on her comline. It had made him uncomfortable to pose such a question but it had begun to feel increasingly more awkward watching Hope pay for their every need or meal. Master Chi had been fighting his pride but his decision to ask Faith had been made when Elaeric had come to him with the same concern.

"They pay for everything," Elaeric had bemoaned softly one evening when he had been alone with Hahn. "I try to be humble, but sometimes it is shame I feel," he explained, wringing his hands in distress. "Besides," he admitted, his dark almond-shaped eyes cast down, "sometimes I would like to buy her things."

Hahn knew that Elaeric had been speaking of Madeline. The two had become quite close. This admission, from the humblest man Hahn had ever known, had filled him with resolve.

"I will take care of it," he had assured his friend.

Feeling like he had, Hahn quickened his step to surreptitiously join the others. Faith watched him go with a smile as she gave Thomas instructions to have credential cards waiting for the monks as soon as they returned to the compound.

Finally, she thought, *someone I can trust Hope to work with and not fall in love with.*

If Hope had known what Faith was thinking, and had she not already been in love with Master Chi, she might have thrown herself into his golden robed arms, just to prove her sister wrong.

Faith, still speaking to Thomas, had quickened her pace and did not notice Hope grasp Gwendolyn by the elbow and hold her back for a second. Though her smile was pleasant, her green eyes were hard.

"Don't trust her," Hope said.

Gwen blinked her brown and gold eyes at her in confusion and then looked around fearfully. "Who?" she asked, when she saw no one that was unknown to her. "Don't trust whom?"

Hope's smile hardened to match her gaze as it flicked to Faith and then back to Gwen. Gwendolyn's eyes widened even more as she saw whom Hope was indicating.

"I mean it," Hope told her earnestly. "She has always been eight steps ahead of me. I've shortened that gap to three and I intend to close it entirely."

"Hope!" Gwen admonished in hushed tones. "What in the worlds are you talking about?" She held the back of her hand to Hope's forehead, checking her for fever. "You have been traveling too much! Do you feel alright?"

Hope smiled. "Better than ever. So remember what I am telling you now. Don't trust her."

Gwendolyn had never felt more perplexed. She pushed it from her mind as she joined the others, deciding to wait until she could discuss it with Evan.

 ONE SIX

"Matty!" I shouted, chasing the dervish through the bailey of the de Rossi castle. "Slow down!" I was having a terrible time keeping up with my five-year-old grandson and my age had nothing to do with it. I was laughing too hard.

The heart is a wondrous thing. A miracle. It is not merely a muscle that pumps oxygenated blood to the tissues of the body. Certainly not just another organ. I learned during those years that the heart is a light and a spirit. It is the touch of God and the breath of the universe. It expands until you think it might burst. Then it expands more.

I can recall that at one point in my life I thought Mira was the end-all-be-all of love. Enough to risk blasphemy and hell. I would still risk both of those for her, but I learned that the heart, believing itself at the time simply too full for any other, expands to make room. My heart, that had grown exponentially when Jean was born, doubled again with the birth of my grandson.

I had not expected it to and, in truth though I hate to admit it, I had been initially disappointed.

I had selfishly hoped for two things. One, that Jean would have a girl. Two, that the baby would look like her and Mira. Matty was neither.

"Why, he doesn't look like you at all!" I had exclaimed with a frown the first time I held him. Mira had given me an expert kick to my left ankle, something she had become quite adept at over the decades. Because of which, I was sure that I had a couple of bone spurs there that hurt like hell when it was cold but also gave me a few nodes of protection that I secretly hoped put the tiniest of dents in her five-thousand-credit pumps. "I mean," I sputtered, backpedaling like I often did, "you and Matthew both have dark hair – dark eyes."

Jean Marie, unlike her mother, had laughed with pure joy. "It's because he looks like you, silly!"

I put my pinky against his tiny hand and, just like Jean Marie had done (what seemed like a million years ago), five minuscule fingers spread out and grasped it. Tears filled my eyes – eyes that I realized were the same shade of blue as the ones that were gazing up at me from a round-cheeked face topped with a wisp of blonde hair.

"Really?" I asked, mystified even though I was not a total stranger to genetics. Not after working for GwenSeven for four decades. Still, the reality of it dumbfounded me.

"Of course," Jean had assured me, "which is appropriate, since he is carrying on our name."

I gave her a quizzical look as Mira rubbed her hands together and held them out eagerly for her turn. I gave baby Matthew a kiss on his wispy blonde hairs, inhaling deeply that warm precious scent, and handed him over to his grandmother (and yes, thinking of her as a grandma felt as ridiculous as thinking of myself as a grandpa) just as his father entered the room and kissed Jean on her right temple and took the seat next to her bed.

"Matthew Mattatock," I asserted softly, trying the name aloud and moving my gaze to the father of my grandchild. "Are you alright with that?" I asked earnestly, though I really liked the sound of it.

"Of course," he assured me with a charismatic grin. "I have seven brothers and, even if I didn't, I doubt the Miller name would die out." He gave a chuckle which Jean and I both echoed while Mira cooed at the baby and wiggled her finger under his chin.

I was astounded, as always, with how fast time flew by and how quickly babies grow into children. Some of them too fast for their own good. The years always seemed to catch up with me at the strangest of times.

"Matty!" I shouted again. "Stop!"

Miraculously, he did – giving me the chance to plant my hands on my knees and catch my breath. But I couldn't. I burst out laughing every time I looked at him.

I knew that most children, and adults for that matter, were often swept up with current events and trends and what the masses often termed "all the rage." Matty, however, was not sucked into vid-toons, plas-toys, or toddler aero-gyms. His favorite place was the castle, raised from the ground by two Zenarchist monks.

He was not interested in astronauts, animals that could talk, or inanimate objects that came to life. The boy, ever since he could sit on my lap and turn a page, loved stories about dungeons and dragons and knights and maidens. And when I say turn a page, I mean it. Not digi-books or anything computerized. Like me, Matty liked books that were getting harder and harder to come by – those with paper pages.

Thomas had found some beautiful picture books, fairy tale tomes, and even vids for the flat screen that I thought would be too advanced for a boy Matty's age to understand but I was wrong. On the nights he spent with me he would sit on my lap, captivated by both the images and the stories, clutching a stuffed rainbow-colored dragon (a gift from Faith) to his chest. On the nights I visited Jean Marie and Matthew, he would want me to tuck him in to bed and recount the vids or tales in a bedtime story.

As luck would have it, or chance or coincidence (if you foolishly believe in any of those things), in an age of spaceships and manufactured people, I was living in a medieval castle. As a Master Mason and still holding the record and honor of building the largest structure in the universe, the irony was not lost on me.

Neither was the charm of a little boy, born on a moon of Jupiter, enchanted with fire-breathing dragons, chivalrous knights, and maidens locked in towers awaiting rescue.

For his fifth birthday, just a few weeks past, I had bought Matty a carbon-fiber play sword and a knight's helm which he was now wearing (backwards) as he tore blindly through the courtyard.

"Matty!" I called again, gasping between chuckles. His head, enlarged by the helmet and making him look like an orange on a stick, swiveled this way and that at the sound of my voice.

"Grandpa!" came the muffled shout from inside the helm. "Where'd you go?"

The helm swung one way and then another, its cumbersome bulk threatening to topple him over. I almost fell over myself, I was laughing so hard. The only other people with us in that section of the bailey were kitchen staff, bringing in groceries. A few had paused, chuckling, and one young woman dropped a sack of potatoes to rush to Matty and steady him, though she was laughing as well. She lifted the helm off of his head and he glanced sharply at her.

"You're not Grandpa!" he realized aloud, sending us all into gales. She turned the helmet around and put it back on Matty's head. "Ohhh," we could hear him breathe, "that's better." The woman flipped up the visor, exposing blue eyes that widened in delight. "Even better! Grandpa!" he hailed, spying me and then bolting for me. I caught him in my hands to keep us both from crashing to the ground. "Look!" he cried. "She fixed my helmet!"

"She did, indeed," I agreed, wanting to plant a kiss on his chubby cheek. Instead, I kissed the outside of his helm and hugged him tight. "You make such a fine knight," I told him. "Do you think you'll be a knight when you grow up?"

Matty frowned at me from the slot under his visor. "Grandpa!" he admonished. "They don't have real knights anymore."

"But they still have real heroes," I told him. "People who protect other people. Do you want to be a pilot when you grow up? Like your mom and dad?"

Through the slot under the visor I could see his young face scrunch up in so much consternation that it made me laugh.

"Not all heroes fly jets, Grandpa," he said firmly. "I want to be a mason, like you. I want to build castles!"

The laughter went out of me and was replaced with a flood of warmth so overwhelming that it made me feel like I might melt into the flagstone courtyard.

"I haven't built any castles," I told him.

Matty pulled the helm off his head. Underneath, his chubby cheeks were flushed and his blonde hair was damp with sweat.

"But you build cities," he said with all the authority of a five-year old with rooted beliefs. "You built the great complex at GwenSeven and Evansborough."

"Who told you that?" I asked.

"Mom," he said, looking at me as if to ask *who else?* "She doesn't know many stories about knights and dragons, so she tells me the stories of the places you built."

"Well," I said, feeling modest for no reason I could explain - five year olds never seemed that hard to impress, "on those jobs I did more planning than building. I don't recall ever picking up a hammer."

"Well," Matty reasoned wisely, "you're an old mason. I bet when you started you used a hammer all the time."

I bit my lip at his use of the word "old" and chalked it up to his limited vocabulary. I doubted he knew words like "experience" or the term "Master Mason."

"I sure did, Mr. Smartypants," I affirmed.

His sweaty face scrunched up in consternation. "Mom calls me that, too," he said with disdain.

Our conversation was interrupted by a bustle at the east gate in the curtain wall. I glanced up to see Hope and Madeline and both of the monks being beset upon by half a dozen people in the castle employ trying to relieve them of the packages they were carrying. Madeline caught my eye and smiled. She excused herself from the group and hurried towards me and my sweat-dampened dervish of a grandson.

"Hello, Matthew," she greeted, going to one knee to be eye-level with Matty. He wrapped an arm around my leg as I stood, half hiding behind it.

"Hello, Miss Madeline," he answered softly. He had already confided in me that he thought Madeline and Hope looked like princesses. He had amazed everyone at an early age in his ability to tell the girls from their dyers, including Charity and Llewellyn. Even after all the years, those were the only two that sometimes had me stumped.

"Fletcher!" Madeline exclaimed, rising to her feet, her green eyes sparkling. She wore linen pants and a cotton peasant blouse and with that wild orange mane I thought she must be a princess in disguise. I have no doubt that Matty would have told me that those are the best kind. "Look what Elaeric bought for me!" She reached into the thin canvas bag that was slung over her shoulder and pulled out a pair of heavy wooden shoes painted bright red.

"Wow," I said, hoping to seem impressed rather than at a loss for words.

Madeline laughed, seeing my discomfiture at a response. "They're clogs!" she exclaimed by way of explanation. When I didn't answer she laughed again. "Hope complains endlessly about the dirt I track in from the garden and the shoes that I ruin in the mud. So Elaeric bought these for me to keep by the kitchen door. I slip my feet into them when I go outside and kick them off when I come in."

She put the clogs on the slate ground and demonstrated by sliding one foot and then the other, still wearing her normal shoes (pink satin slippers with leather soles that did look quite princess-like), inside. She threw up her hands in triumph and I responded with the soft clap of a court artesian.

I looked down at Matty to see him grinning. His blue eyes shifted and I followed his gaze to the east gate where another small hubbub was ensuing. Gwendolyn and Evan had joined the little party and kisses and hugs were being doled out all around. Gwen and Evan had built a house down the hill from the castle, between the clear lake and the now sparkling sea.

I, much to Matty's delight, had taken up residence within the castle. With the GwenSeven compound, now being termed a Mega-Complex, and the neighboring town of Evansborough complete, I changed my address in order to help Gwendolyn build her own home. She and Evan did not want it raised by the monks, but instead planned and built by themselves, at least as far as they could manage.

Gwendolyn had sketched the drafts of what they were after and I spent a few weeks putting them into blueprints and going back and forth with her and Evan over changes. We did enlist the help of the monks in moving part of the lake and containing it during the construction.

I had not seen Gwen so excited since her sculptures of the First Seven. That woman was never so happy as when she was creating. Her love for Evan was obvious but putting her mind and hands into creation made her glow. I remarked on it once when I watched her draw the rudimentary but quite accurate plans for what would be their swimming pool. She had laughed.

"Architecture is art in its own form, Fletcher," she had told me, beaming as she sketched a perfect half-circle.

And it was.

When complete, their home was an edifice of glass and stone and steel, modern and eclectic and yet striking in simplicity and beauty. When caught by the setting sun it shone like a prism, throwing rainbows in every direction until it was turned into a glowing ruby whose light ebbed with the day.

The pool wall was made of hyper-glass, shaped like a crescent moon, and encircled the northern half of the house. One pointed tail protruded into the lake, its waters slowly released by the monks to meet the glass so that a swimmer in the pool could glide right along next to the rainbow trout and pygmy otters in the lake. The other tip curved around to the west and was bordered by a beautiful deck of opal plank where one could watch the sunset, in the water or out. The glass walls of the house itself could be made opaque at any time by a vocal command, darkening a specific room or the whole building at once.

Evan worked on it every chance he was afforded - from the bottom to the top and doing everything from driving an airskip to putting mortar between chimney stones. He could be found most every day with his shirt off, golden hair and golden skin shining in the sun, while Gwen sat on a grassy knoll sketching on canvas pads with sticks of colored graphite. I peeked over her shoulder a few times to see amazing works of sunsets, the lake, and many of Evan – his muscles outlined and shadowed in gold.

My room in the staff quarters of the castle became two rooms and then three as my work and length of stay expanded.

Charity and Llewellyn of course needed a massive staff. Not just for the castle, but for everything else in their lives. They needed aircraft, an airfield, drivers, bodyguards, you name it. And all those people needed a place to live. Another town needed to be built and Madeline insisted that it look like a village that would match the castle. And I'm sure you can guess who they got to build that village.

Mira found much delight in calling me the village idiot and, though she said it lightly and laughed and kissed me and always made me laugh and often aroused, she had no idea how right she was.

I was an idiot.

Because in that bailey of the de Rossi castle I kissed that sweet and sweaty face with pink chubby cheeks under his mop of damp blonde hair, but I never saw it again.

Though I cheated a bit (basing Rossi Hamlet on Evansborough, save for the faux trimmings and façades of stone and thatch) I was absorbed for the next four years with everything from worker's complaints and compensation to purchase orders and finished product.

The next time I saw my grandson I was shocked. He was nine years old and all of the baby had melted away. Darling as ever but skinny as a stick and twice as fast as he was at five. Mira and I met at Jurlsberg to have dinner with Jean and Matthew while Matty was at a sleepover. Mira and I had a magnificent night at an opulent hotel on Devereaux's dime and picked up Matty the next day for a trip to the park in his neighborhood.

I could not believe how much he had grown. The time had gone by so fast and, of course, there was no change in my own appearance. Matty laughed at my surprise and hugged me and Mira for the tenth time.

"I'm so happy to see you both!" he exclaimed. "But when we get to the park can I play laser war?"

"I don't know what that is," Mira told him, "but as long as it is safe and as long we can see you, I'm sure it will be fine."

"Yessss!!!!" Matty hissed in triumph, clenching a fist.

I couldn't stop staring at him, probably with my mouth open, village idiot that I was. We took him to the park in a hired car with a driver, the only way Mira traveled over land, and turned him loose and watched him run.

"He's not a baby anymore," I lamented quietly. Mira looked at me as if I had gone crazy.

"Of course not, Fletcher."

"I mean, I know he wouldn't still be a baby, but, but…." I stammered as I searched for the words, "he's all grown up, and I missed it."

Mira laughed as she looked for a bench in the shade. "It's not that bad," she said as she wrapped her arm around my elbow and guided me to a spot under the tree, "and he is certainly not all grown up."

We sat on a bench where we could watch our now-lanky grandson run and play between the trees with boys his age, all toting plastic purple guns. As the boys were slowly called away one by one over the next hour, Matty was reduced to tucking his gun into the back of his pants and playing in the sand with younger children. I was proud to see that he did it with grace, giving smaller kids a boost when they needed it and catching them when they came off the slide. He caught another boy, no more than three, when he jumped from a spot much too high on the climb-round.

Matty, like a pro ball-player, threw out both arms and caught the child deftly, though the force of it threw them both into the sand. Matty landed with the boy on top of him. I ran to them both, getting there the same time as the toddler's mother.

"Thank you so much, young man!" the mother exclaimed, tucking the toddler under one arm as she attempted to help my grandson to his feet. "Jaime might have broken his arm, despite the sand!"

"No problem, ma'am," Matty said, brushing the grainy soil from his pants and shirt.

"Oh!" the woman exclaimed, "and so polite!" She turned to me and her blue eyes widened in surprise. "You must be so proud," she gushed, her eyes taking on another light. "Such a fine young man, and he looks just like you!"

I laughed just as Mira joined us, walking delicately through the silica in her expensive shoes. "He's not my son," I corrected. "He's my grandson."

"Oh!" she cried, her hand going to her chest with her fingers spread wide over her heart. "I must say, you look amazing!" Her blue eyes looked me up and down. She took a deep breath and her tongue moistened her lips. "Are you on some sort of new hormone?" she asked softly.

"Yes," Mira stated firmly, startling us both. "It's by GwenSeven. You should look into it." She turned away from the woman and took up Matty's hand. "Would you like to get a frozen custard?" she asked with what I could tell was forced enthusiasm. Matty nodded with real enthusiasm and she led him from the sand pit, throwing a sharp glance at me to make sure I was following.

I was.

I gave the woman a smile and a nod before hurrying away, but not before noticing the odd way she was looking at us. My guess was that she had recognized Mira from the tabloids. It happened often.

I caught up with Mira and Matty and slowed my pace to match theirs. "What was that about?" I asked. "Are you worried she recognized you?"

Sometimes Mira liked the attention, sometimes she did not. Even after fifty years I had no way to predict her. She gave me a sour look as she ushered Matty into the backseat of the car.

"It was not *me* that she was interested in," she said, curt.

I got her meaning well enough and laughed, which was my first mistake. "I'm sure she was just intrigued by my lack of aging. Aren't all women?" I asked, which was my second mistake.

Mira's brown eyes blazed. "Do you often get confronted by women like that?" she demanded.

"No," I said, holding my hands up in innocence.

The fire in her eyes dimmed, a little. "You probably wouldn't even know if they did," she remarked caustically. "I don't suppose you noticed she wasn't wearing a wedding ring?"

"No," I admitted, doing my best not to smile but having a damned hard time. I had never seen Mira jealous before. I had to admit that it was adorable and made me feel good for no reason I could explain. "But, if you haven't noticed, I don't wear one either." Mistake number three.

The fire in Mira's eyes blazed up again and, truth be told, I liked stoking it.

"Which is probably why they have the audacity to confront you in such a manner!" Her hands were clenched into fists, though she kept her voice low. Her lips pressed together, struggling to keep any further comments inside. Then she ducked into the car next to Matty and I went around to the other side.

As I did, I realized for the first time that there was nothing stopping me from wearing a ring on the third finger of my left hand. Nor was there anything stopping us from being married, even if we were the only ones who knew.

To my shame, I did not see Matty again until his tenth birthday. After that, I did not see him again until he was in one hell of a mess.

ONE 7

Futbol was all the rage, again.

The big news was that it was no longer to be a sport restricted to Earthlings. A Galactic League was in the works. The Jupiter moon of Europa was soliciting athletes from the home planet to build a division of six teams, while the moon of Indasia drew players mostly from the moon itself. Europa's division, however, was promising transportation along with residency, riches, and glory, to anyone from the home world that proved worthy. The competition on Earth had kicked back into a gear it had not seen in centuries.

Bjorn stood next to Ivana, watching the competition. They had premium seats, floating on the 50-meter line of a real stadium. The players, though they looked as real as life, were only holos being projected from the live game being held in the southern state of Barcelona.

"You know," Bjorn said, sipping a cocktail, "that in the Americas they call this soccer."

"I know," Ivana drawled, making a face like she tasted something bitter. "Zey are idiots. Besides, is only North America term. Da South, zey know better."

The bigger regional news, was that a local player was being considered for the Galactic League. Games that were already sell-outs became a source for black market tickets and the wealthy now mingled with the middle class (or, at least, could see them from their private seats should they choose to look) to catch a glimpse of the athletic prodigy. It was rumored that he was the best anyone had seen in over a hundred years.

His holo ran by Ivana and Bjorn, incredibly agile and unbelievably fast, making Ivana gasp and clutch her ample chest.

"By the gods!" she exclaimed. "Just look at heem!"

Bjorn shrugged as their seats rose to give them a better view of the players that were moving downfield. "He's not very tall," Bjorn remarked. "And he is awfully dark for a local," he said, noting the man's olive complexion and dark curly hair. Over the last fifty years he had come to know Ivana's "neighbors" and circle of friends and knew they were all porcelain pale - the only variation in their genetics being in the blue of their eyes or in the blonde of their hair. He had bedded quite a few of them, often with Ivana's participation. At first he thought it was for her pleasure, but in time he realized she derived more pleasure just from showing him off.

Now it was Ivana's turn to shrug. "He is Serb," she said by way of explanation. "Local enough."

There was a great hubbub downfield as players clashed and scurried when suddenly the man in question was unexpectedly alone in front of the ball, which he booted with enough force that Bjorn was sure the man must have shit himself, pulled his groin, or both. The ball passed just over the goalie's outstretched hands and was caught in the upper corner of the net.

The crowd, along with the scoring team, went wild. The man, named Tropya, tore his jersey from his body and screamed in a rage of ecstasy as he ran back up the field. Bjorn sipped his drink and their seats sank down gently, bringing them closer to the field as Tropya neared.

"Hear how he roars!" Ivana exclaimed, breathless and with a hand over her heart, as the holographic image of the hero ran past them and the multitudes cheered like bloodthirsty maniacs. "Like a lion, he roars!"

Bjorn looked at her curiously, not ever seeing her put in such a lusty state by a man other than himself. Certainly not with so much flagrancy.

Then a drunk in the crowd jumped from his seat and ran onto the field. The masses, mostly drunk as well, jeered him on as safety droids were dispatched to capture him and stop the disruptive antics. The jeers turned to hilarious laughter as the man, dodging the drones, attempted to rip off his shirt in the manner of Tropya but only succeeded in tearing it a bit before he fell on his face. He was gathered up by the droids and carefully taken from the field, raising his hat in salute to the cacophony of applause.

Bjorn was further distracted by the feel of Ivana's hand on his chest and the sudden press of her body against his. "Take me back to hotel," she purred. "I don't need more game." Bjorn smiled lasciviously and dropped his empty glass on a passing serving tray as it floated by while his other hand filled itself with her backside and gave it a squeeze.

"I don't need to be told twice."

Ivana's ample chest heaved and her lips parted with the ghost of a smile. "Vich is vhy you still here."

Bjorn smiled and dipped down to bite her ear but, as he did so, he caught her blue eyes darting towards the field and she gasped again, but it was before his lips had touched her.

∞

"Cronus de Rom," the metallic voice of the hostess announced softly, "your cloud is ready."

"Cloud?" Hope asked, her copper-colored brows raised high over her green eyes as she regarded her grandfather with apparent curiosity.

"You'll see," he told her with a smile. Hope's left eyebrow remained arched and she gave a small grunt of amusement and then turned her attention to the room they were entering.

"Oh, Grandfather!" Hope gushed. "It's beautiful!"

Cronus beamed at his granddaughter as they were shown to their seat in the restaurant *Pegasus*. Artificial stars sparkled overhead in a faux sky that was a soft pink. He held out a chair for her at a table that resembled a lavender cloud. "I thought it would appeal to your princess-like nature."

Hope laughed. "It does! And it reminds me of the galaxy fair you took me to, remember?"

"Indeed, I do," he replied solemnly, taking his own seat. The memory did not fill him with as much joy as it did Hope, due to that disturbing foretelling he had received from the black elf they had met. Though, since the years had been many and he had checked in with his daughter often, he found it more likely that the elf had been the charlatan Cronus always believed him to be.

Then how did he know what had been on my mind? the gray-haired elf wondered for the hundredth time.

Hope shook out a fluffy napkin and let it go. It floated down to her lap like a wisp of cloud as she looked back up at him, her green eyes dancing with joy. "Do you remember the black elf?" she asked, as if she, too, could read his thoughts.

"How could I forget?" Cronus remarked rhetorically, unable to not smile back at her. He shook out his own napkin and let it float to his lap. "And do you still believe what he told you?" he asked. He wore a gray coat with no collar over a pink shirt and stroked the pink buttons where they fastened below his throat. "I seem to recall he told you about a key," the elf mused as he activated the menu. A cloud formed over the small metal square on the table, the day's list of food and drink displayed onto the puff of white by miniature purple lasers. "Did you ever find your key?" He did not want to make fun of his granddaughter, but he did think it prudent to prove the charlatan for what he was. Hope was no longer a child, as much as he still thought of her as one.

He had read through the first description on the list of appetizers when he noticed Hope's silence. He looked up to see her blushing under her freckles. The older elf sat back in his chair, gray brows raised above his gray eyes.

"Well," Hope stammered, "not my key," (though she had thought of him that way for some time), "but I certainly found the key."

Gray brows drew down over stormy eyes. "Whatever do you mean?" Cronus asked, perplexed.

Hope laughed nervously. "Why, Master Chi," Hope said, pronouncing it *key*. "Elaeric, too, of course."

Cronus felt his mouth drop open. "Yes, of course," he murmured after a moment. "I missed that because most pronounce it *chee*."

"Yes," Hope agreed, "most do. I think Elaeric pronounces it that way because of his Japonesa descent, but most pronounce it *key* when it follows his title of master." She gave another trill of nervous laughter. "I don't really know enough of them or their language to say for sure. But I truly found the key, the one that will change the universe," she finished softly.

Cronus chortled nervous laughter in the manner of his granddaughter and waived away the waitress that was floating near.

"My dear," he said softly, "how aware you are! I never made the connection."

Hope smiled and focused her attention on the menu cloud.

Her grandfather nodded and turned his attention to the same. "You certainly seem to spend a lot of time with him, with both of them, actually."

Hope was glad that he was still looking at the menu because she could feel the blush flood back into her cheeks. "Yes," she agreed as casually as she could. "Madeline and I both, actually. With both of the monks. They are so...quaint."

Cronus laughed and, seeing a glass of lavender water on the

table, picked it up and took a sip. "I'm sure they are!"

Hope, inconspicuously, let out a deep breath and took another look at the menu. "They have artichoke!" she exclaimed, excited.

"Then we must share one," Cronus declared.

Hope clapped her hands and reached out with a delicate finger laden with rings to touch the item and have it ordered while they decided on their entrées.

The rings were all on the index finger of her right hand. At first glance, it appeared to be one large ring, but closer inspection would show it was actually three small silver rings, each with diminutive carvings in the bands and each set with a sparkling ruby.

The first ring was carved with tribal diamond shapes and the ruby was diamond-shaped as well. The second ring had an oval-shaped ruby and was carved with a repeating pattern of ovals, dots, and lines. The bottom ring was engraved with curlicues and set with a round ruby that had always made Hope think of the eye of a serpent.

The rings had been a gift from her grandfather and were identical to the ones worn by Faith and Charity, save for the color of the stones. The stones gave a soft glow when worn and the girls all knew by now (despite the efforts of Grandfather to be surreptitious) that it was his way to tell them apart from their dyers. Though it had been increasingly apparent over the last fifty years who was who. Madeline's dreamy gaze compared to Hope's laser-like gleam was a dead giveaway. As was the fact that Faith was always in her lab coat and Gwen was attached to Evan's side – though with Charity and Llewellyn it could always be a toss-up. Purposely on their part.

Not unkindly, Grandfather had given the dyers golden bangle bracelets with stones that matched the rings of their twins. Also, in kind, the stones would glow when worn by their owner.

Cronus tried to focus on the menu but his mind was drawn away by what Hope had illuminated.

He was right, the aging elf thought with a sinking feeling, *the black elf was right. Hope found Chi. And if he was right about that, was he right about Christa?*

The waitress floated back to them at that moment and Cronus could not be more grateful. "Absinthe," he ordered. "With a splash of water."

Hope looked at him, abashed, and then laughed. "What happed to water, with a splash of absinthe?"

"I'm not driving," Cronus told her with a smile that showed a fine set of teeth that belied his age.

Hope laughed. "In that case," she told the waitress, "I'll have a Julep."

The older elf made a face at her selection, eliciting another laugh from his copper-haired granddaughter.

After debating the menu items for a few minutes, they ordered entrées and shared their artichoke when it came to the table. Hope updated her grandfather on Hahn and Elaeric's progress. He had enough questions to last through their whole lunch.

"I'm glad you are spending so much time with them," Cronus remarked as he finished his meal and his second cocktail.

"You are?" Hope asked, pleasantly surprised.

"Of course! They are both very agreeable and most polite, but I enjoy meeting with you much more. I miss seeing you these days."

Hope smiled. "I miss you, too. And I love being able to have lunch and catch up, even if it is mostly business."

"Well," her grandfather noted, "you are a grown woman now. We have things to talk about besides fairy-tales and castles, though you do live in one!"

Hope beamed as if being told she had grown up was the best compliment she could ever get. "I'm glad you think so," she said. She put her napkin down, suddenly serious, and tried not to fidget with her rings. She placed her hands on her napkin to keep them still.

"Because," she continued, "Madeline and I were considering accompanying them on the trip, possibly as far as Earth."

"I think that is a splendid idea!" Cronus exclaimed.

"You do?"

"Yes! You can take my place as the liaison between the monks and the elves. I'm sure King Rowland would be considerably more comfortable communicating with you and there will be less chance of any misunderstandings."

"Yes," Hope agreed softly. "We wouldn't want any misunderstandings."

Just then came a beep from an inner pocket on her grandfather's coat. Cronus pulled out a comset and looked apologetically at his granddaughter. "I am sorry my dear, but I must take this. Do you mind?"

Hope shook her wild mane of copper curls. "Of course not."

Cronus stood as the waitress floated back over. He looked flustered for the briefest of seconds before pulling his comp-wallet from another inner pocket and handing it to his granddaughter. "Please pay the bill, but take your time, I'll be a few minutes."

Hope nodded as she took the wallet while her grandfather hooked the comset over a pointed ear and answered his call as he walked away. Hope slipped the credentials card from a clear slot affixed to the outside of the comp-wallet and handed it to the waitress who slid it through a reader and handed it back before floating away. Hope returned the card to the slot and turned the wallet over in her hands.

The case itself was black leather and held a small compute, about the size of a deck of old-fashioned playing cards, with a glass face. With nothing else to do, and curious as ever, Hope turned it on. She flipped through the icons that displayed her grandfather's files, only mildly interested, until she saw a square that bore only one word, *Girls*.

Hope looked around, suddenly aware that she was snooping, and getting ready to snoop a bit more. There was no one, not even staff, in her area of the restaurant. She was alone with the faux clouds and faux stars under the pink sky.

She tapped the square and realized that it could possibly be an application for an escort service and then stifled a laugh.

Certainly not! she thought. Hoped.

It wasn't. It was more of what she expected. A simple list of three names: *Faith, Charity*, and *Hope*. She tapped Faith's name, expecting to see pictures of her sister while at the same time feeling a slight disappointment that their dyers were not included on the list. Instead of pictures she was shown only a blip of a golden spot on a field of stars. Green eyes wide, Hope placed two fingers – one on either side of the blip – and spread them apart. The blip zoomed towards her, along with a string of numbers that Hope recognized as galactic coordinates.

Her freckled face jerked up like a spooked deer, then she slowly lifted her right hand and examined the rings there as her expression hardened.

Well, she thought, *now I know where Faith gets her drive to know everything and control even more. I never knew it was inherited.*

She frowned at the rubies. A means of identification was one thing, a clandestine tracking device was another.

Her anger dissolved as she recognized an opportunity. She quickly fished her own compute out of her purse, though it was larger and more feminine. She rapidly found the application she wanted and, delicate fingers flying over the glass screen, put in a bounce program to copy her grandfather's file - as long as it was not copyright protected, which she doubted. She placed the glass screens of the computes together and glanced up to see her grandfather reenter the restaurant.

Hope, who could feel the slight thrum of the comp-wallets as one transferred information to the other, stuck her hand inside her purse, hiding them.

Faster, faster, she willed silently as her grandfather approached the table. She forced a smile. "You look pleased," she remarked as he neared, yearning to distract him, even if for a few seconds.

"I am, thank you very much. My wallet, please."

Hope chuckled and leaned over to look into her purse, feigning a search. Just then, the thrumming stopped. She pulled her grandfather's wallet away from her own and double pressed the base button without looking, backing it out of the burgled file before handing it over.

"Damn," she said. "I was planning to rob you."

Cronus snorted. "That seems to be your sister Charity's job, though God knows why. That girl has more money tucked away into every known galaxy like a battalion of squirrels with nuts in every forest of the Earth!"

Hope laughed, more naturally this time, as she stood up and let her grandfather escort her from the restaurant *Pegasus*. She might have poached a file, though since he was not left without the program she really felt like it was more of a *share* than a *theft*. At least she was spared the lie she had prepared regarding Hahn Chi.

 ONE EIGHT

The GwenSeven compound had three reception areas. The first was General Reception. This office, resplendent with light-colored yet thick carpets and potted plants, was manned by three beautiful young women (one of them a construct) who answered phones and directed visitors to other parts of the complex.

The next was Special Reception. This room, with even thicker carpets, dark wood inlays in the walls and fresh flowers, was where clients were welcomed with champagne and a personal shopper to assist them in the purchase of a custom-made construct. Charity and Llewellyn had long since turned this duty over to a pair of gorgeous young women, one of which was a construct, but both of whom bore a strong resemblance to the second de Rossi sister and her dyer.

The last was called the Inner Sanctum, more as a joke than an actual title. It was not an actual designated reception area, but where Thomas worked. A tasteful office with comfortable chairs for anyone waiting for an audience with her highness, Dr. Faith de Rossi, and where Thomas kept his own desk and files and fielded the calls that came through for myself or any of the girls. Everyone who passed into the interior compound that housed the oldest departments, such as Faith's labs and my own offices, passed through here. The only antiquity, that I had mentally dog-eared for replacement, were the doors to his office. They swung open via a motion detector on each side while all of the newer doors in the compound slid into the floor via a similar detector.

"No worries, Fletcha," he had told me a few years back when

I had remarked upon replacing the doors.

After fifty years of caching up on Earth-based movies I had told Mira (with quite a bit of pride at my discovery) that Thomas was Earth-England. Mira had laughed. "Thomas is space-born," she told me. "With British parents for sure, but his grandparents were Hindustani, from the India continent."

I did not bother to ask how she knew. Mira was well educated and well-traveled. She had been to more than half of the civilized galaxies, numerous moons and planets, and met with a copious number of cultured individuals on a daily basis.

The trouble (and when I say trouble, I mean the kind that makes history) began while I was on my way through the Inner Sanctum one morning and encountered the last thing I expected. That is not to say I was unprepared for something unusual. We were planning a bit of a party for that day since the First Seven were all expected to return at some point in the afternoon for their first check up in twenty-five years.

I was back in my old quarters at the compound while I worked on the expansion. We were adding to the complex and needed new residential planning to accommodate the expected influx of workers. I came in early but I was far from being the first in the office. I walked through the front doors and Thomas, who I had thought until then to be the most stoic person I knew (other than Faith of course), looked at me with something I recognized as controlled panic. He was standing behind his desk, rather than sitting, and his eyes were so round that I could see the white of them all around his black irises.

No prim greeting, or smile and nod if he was occupied with a call or a client, which had been both a habit and custom of his for five decades. Just that panicky look that was quickly spreading to me like a contagion in the air. There was no one else present so I joined him behind his desk to get a look at the bank of security monitors I suspected to be the source of his concern. My eyes were drawn to the screens I knew Thomas would be watching - the ones that showed Faith's office and labs.

What must have been the origin of his terror appeared to be a human male. Though he was sitting it was obvious that he was tall. Well-built, or had been at one time. His hair was most likely blonde, but it had not seen a shower or a comb for many a day, possibly weeks. He was with Faith in her office, sitting on the other side of her desk with one arm stretched out across the expanse of glass and steel like a man before a mirage of water in the desert. He had a look of sad desperation - grungy but not dangerous. I looked at Thomas questioningly.

"He was here this morning, waiting on the doorstep of General Reception," he gave by way of explanation, his black eyes trapped under a furrow of black brows and fixed upon the screen. "I thought he was homeless."

"Do they have a homeless population here on Dione?" I asked, surprised. Thomas looked at me scornfully.

"There are homeless everywhere, Fletcha. It is a disease that is never cured, only displaced."

I nodded mutely, thinking of Two Mile City, or whatever they called it now. The homeless and poor were never vindicated, only pushed lower. Or the rich moved higher. I didn't know which. But there were no homeless, that I knew of, in Evansborough. This man must have travelled far.

I looked back at the screen showing Faith's office but from the corner of my eye I could see Thomas shift the weight of his tall and lean body from one foot to the other and knew that he was dying to run in there with a can of disinfectant.

"What should I do?" he whined, a tone Thomas never assumed. His dark eyes did not look at me. They stayed glued to the screen, watching the man entreat with our employer. I shrugged.

"Well, if Dr. de Rossi has the situation in her hands, which it looks like she does, I'm sure it will be fine." I glanced at the PA only to receive a scathing look in return and I transferred my gaze back to the monitor. The man's ragged body sagged as if Faith had given him one last hope, or had taken it all away.

Faith stared at the figure across from her for a moment and then we could see her shoulders rise as if she were taking a deep breath. Then something extraordinary happened. Or frightening. If I had to venture a guess I would say it was both.

Faith looked at me.

Anyone else might have thought she had simply glanced up at the security camera in her office, but I was not fooled. Neither was Thomas. Those tawny eyes fixed on me as if she knew exactly where I was and that I was watching. The PA's head snapped to the left and fixed on me as well, his dark eyes full of accusation as if the whole situation were my fault. I held up my hands in innocent surrender.

Though I had nothing to do with anything that was happening, as far as I could tell, I felt a stab of guilt that I could not place. Or perhaps it was just déjà vu. I can say there was one connection and a very slim one at that - but I did partially recognize a piece of equipment on the edge of Faith's desk. But what could that matter? I probably recognized and approved every order for each nut and bolt that came into the complex and Thomas probably recognized and paid out for every piece of equipment down to every last comset and calculator.

Thomas turned his face back to the bank of screens and we both watched the monitor with an accumulative swelling of dread.

Faith looked away from me/the camera and back to the man in front of her. You did not have to be someone who knew her as well as Thomas or even myself to see that the woman was forcing herself into some sort of decision.

Dr. de Rossi pursed her lips and reached over to the side of her desk and touched a nub. The monitor showing her office blacked out as Faith cut the feed.

The PA's dark eyes flashed to me. "This is your doing!"

Thomas hissed.

My astonishment at the situation doubled.

"Excuse me?"

"Why did she do that?" he demanded, angry.

"How should I know?" I demanded back, feeling confused and defensive.

Poor Thomas swayed on his feet, roiling with one emotion after another. "What should I do?" he cried, wringing his hands. "Should I go in there? What if she needs help?"

I sighed, feeling for the man.

"If she felt endangered at all, she would not have cut the feed," I assured him. A line creased on his dark brow as he frowned at me and then the monitors. I watched as the crease melted away. "Do not go in there," I told him, more firmly than I intended, "on the pretense of checking on her or bringing her food!" The scowl return and he glared at me.

"What if she's hungry?" he asked. "I'm not doing my job if I let her go hungry."

I gave him a smile that I hoped bore compassion. "Your job is to take care of her needs, Thomas. Right now, she obviously needs privacy."

Thomas trembled for a moment, angry and petulant, then he sagged as if defeated.

"How long should I wait?" he asked. "Before checking with her?"

I laid a hand on his shoulder and gave him a smile that I hoped was reassuring. "It's Faith, Thomas," I reminded him. "She will let you know."

He nodded in resignation and then straightened, gathering himself as he glued his dark eyes back onto the bank of monitors. I clapped him on the back and started to edge back around his desk so I could go through the double doors and into the inner compound, but the engagement with strangers was not done for us.

I was no sooner from behind his desk when the front doors of his office swung open with all the force and vigor of an old-timey saloon.

A man stood there with all the force and vigor of an old-timey gunslinger.

He was tall and handsome, with dark hair and dark flashing eyes that were eerily reminiscent to me of Mira's. There was a wild look about him, I would not go so far as to say disheveled, but it looked like had traveled a thousand miles on half a tank of gas – as my grandmother would have said.

"I am here to see Faith de Rossi," he announced as if he had practiced the demand aloud many times. Thomas, composure regained, gave the bottom of his suit coat a tug to straighten it and stepped deftly in front of me, his long brown fingers clasped before his trim waist.

"And whom might I say is calling?" he asked politely. The man's eyes flashed from him to me, and then back to Thomas.

"My name is Rohn," he told us. "Rohn Stojacovik." I looked at Thomas but he was already headed through the double doors, elated to have a valid excuse for interrupting the meeting Faith was having with her first strange (and filthy) visitor.

"Please sit down," I entreated since the Inner Sanctum had obviously been left under my command.

"I would rather stand," the man informed me, his dark eyes glaring. I shrugged, though I was slightly unsettled by the color of his eyes. Perhaps it was the way they shone with intensity.

"May I tell Dr. de Rossi what this visit is about?" I asked. It was Thomas' job but he had fled and I felt compelled to say something.

At this the man bared his teeth at me. I don't know if he was attempting a smile or not, but he bared his teeth like a dog would when they are about to attack. And if his first statement did not scare me as much as it surprised me, his second one sure did.

"You can tell her that I wish to meet with the First Seven," he announced, and I nodded even as I wondered how he could know. "And," he added before I could even turn away, "you can tell her that her time has come."

❦

The original plan for the day had been for the Pantheon constructs to have their tests run as they arrived, then be made comfortable until dinnertime when we would all have a bit of a feast together – a sort of family reunion. I was delighted to be hosting the reunion at my restaurant, *Marie Marie*. Only two arrived, however, to have ample time to have their tests run before dinner.

Bjorn arrived first and, though I did not see him until that evening, I got the feeling that he had more time on his hands than he knew what to do with. The second, never late for an appointment, was Mira. She came with me to *Marie Marie* to help me if I needed it but mostly just so we could have some extra time together.

We bustled about the kitchen like mother hens until the guests began to arrive and then I bustled about the dining room, getting everything in order. I had arranged a table set for a dozen people and, with Faith's recommendation, had food already prepared – a variety of little bites but plenty of them – so that everyone would be able to catch up without constant interruptions.

Faith and Gwen arrived together. *Just like old times*, I thought for some reason as I saw them, though I also thought Gwen looked strange, almost naked, without Evan beside her. They arrived first, along with both of Faith's visitors from that morning. Both newcomers had cleaned up, eaten a good meal, and drank a few quarts of water, and it showed. Neither one of them seemed as gaunt or desperate, but that passion still burned in Rohn's dark eyes with a wild fervor. The still unnamed stranger did not look nearly as crazed as Rohn, quite the opposite. He was as large as I had guessed and had the air of both infinite patience and sorrow about him.

"Fletcher?" Faith asked, drawing my attention. "Would you mind setting a table for these gentlemen in the kitchen or on the patio? They will be joining us later."

"Of course," I agreed and hurried to see the manager, Phillipe, to make arrangements for a small table to be set up in the kitchen. It had taken me quite some time to find just the right person for the job of running the restaurant but my efforts, and the help of Thomas, had paid off well. The small man was brusque to the brink of rudeness but with all the well-mannered refinement of Thomas. He was the perfect Frenchman. Even when he smiled it looked as if he had just bitten into a lemon.

The entire restaurant had been shut down for the affair, mostly due to the paparazzi that would flood the place once word got out. There were not just celebrities at this dinner, but some of the most famous people in the universe *together* at this dinner. It did not occur to me that the situation might be dangerous as well but I knew that a table on the patio was certainly out of the question.

As if to confirm my thoughts, there was a clamor at the front as the door opened to admit Charity and Llewellyn. The middle de Rossi sister and her dyer drew cameras and microphones the way a carcass drew flies. The 'razzi was unavoidable where they were concerned but their bodyguards kept them outside and shooed the small camera drones away from the door. Faith took care of greeting the lovely pair while I went into the kitchen to make Rohn and the stranger as comfortable as possible.

In retrospect, I know Faith also sent me into the kitchen

to keep me from seeing the entrance of John Pierre. She must have known that he was close behind her and the others. I saw him as I came back to the dining room and Mira stepped deftly between us. He had not killed my parents and my grandmother (I had checked his whereabouts against the time our apartment building was cleansed and found that he had not even been in the same galaxy), but it didn't make the bile that rose in my throat easier to swallow.

His angelic face shone like a beacon over a round collar that rose above the black robe that belled out about his feet. His slightly freckled cheeks bloomed with color and his blue eyes were bright. Those eyes flickered about the room, taking it all in and noting everything and everyone in a fraction of a second.

"How nice to see you, John Pierre," Faith greeted with the warmth of a third run construct.

"Faith," he greeted, giving her a nod before doing the same for Mira and myself. Charity and Llewellyn were still standing but engrossed in a conversation with Phillipe about cocktails.

I knew he would be there yet I found myself robbed of my ability to move or speak. Mira took a step backwards so that our bodies were touching and felt around for my hand, giving it a squeeze when she clasped it. Faith, who stood at the head of the table with Gwen seated on her right, extended own her hand towards an empty chair.

"Please sit down," she offered and, "and have something to eat. We will be starting soon – we have much to discuss."

The construct's head snapped back to her. "Hope is not here?" he asked, his melodious voice cracking. "Is she coming?"

I felt an unnatural stab of glee at his obvious distress but Faith smiled, more gently than she was wont to.

"She will be here as soon as she can. Madeline, too."

"Madeline," John Pierre said softly. He had known that Hope had a dyer, but he had never seen her. Careful to leave two seats open between himself and the ones Charity and

Llewellyn were taking, he gave the blue-eyed de Rossi and her dyer a formal bow before sitting down. "Gwen," he then acknowledged with a nod at Faith's dyer as Mira circled the table and I followed, pulling out a chair for her next to Gwendolyn. Faith had already informed me that Evan would not be joining us.

I remained standing behind Mira as Phillipe placed two glasses full of ice before the middle de Rossi and her biodentical twin and poured them each an Amaretto Sour from a large decanter.

"Leave the carafe," Llewellyn instructed. Phillipe gave her a curt nod and turned to John Pierre, mousy brows raised over a pinched face.

"Just water for me, please," the bodyguard instructed.

Phillipe motioned to a waiter and Charity's lips drew down in mock disappointment as she turned her face to Llewellyn. "So pious!" she exclaimed in soft tones. Llewellyn smiled and took a dainty sip of her sour.

Before Llewellyn could return an equally backhanded compliment, the door swung open and Bjorn Van Zandt stood in the doorframe, backlit by flashes from the razzi-droids. The door swung shut behind him, muffling the sounds of drones and reporters, and he stood for a moment, framed like a portrait of a Roman god as his gaze swept across the room to the left where we were gathered. When his green eyes met Charity's blue ones it was like lightning hitting a tree. Something powerful was there and gone in a flash but undeniably real. So much that I could have sworn I had caught a whiff of ozone. He flashed everyone a brilliant smile and made his greetings in the same manner that John Pierre had used, naming and nodding as he made his way around the table.

"Miss de Rossi," he said, greeting Charity last as he pulled out the chair next to her.

"Don't patronize me," she instructed without looking at him, fighting to keep the corners of her red lips down. "And take the seat next to Mira. Pious here might cut your throat for taking Hope's."

Bjorn gave her a dazzling, voracious smile and moved gracefully to change seats as Gwendolyn muttered, "I don't patronize bunny rabbits." She glanced over her shoulder with a smile only to remember that Evan was not there to share whatever joke it was. Her expression became forced as she smiled primly at Bjorn.

Bjorn put his hand on the back of the chair next to Mira and his green eyes flashed to me. "Fletch!" he greeted amiably, extending his hand. "Ça va?" he asked.

I was unable to hold back a look of amusement as I shook his hand. "Ça va, merci. Your accent is better," I remarked, surprised. Of all the constructs I had taught French, Bjorn had been the least interested.

"We have a French cook," he explained, grinning roguishly.

"Then you are lucky," I told him before interpreting the nature of his smile.

"I certainly am," he agreed, his grin widening.

I got the idea that the French cook was heating up more places than the kitchen. I sighed through my teeth and Charity cleared her throat in mock irritation.

Bjorn released me from his shark-like good humor and took his seat. He looked at the others at the table along with the empty chairs. "I only count two!" he announced. "Plus myself, of course, which makes only three."

"Amazing," Charity announced, unable to contain her smile for him any longer. "All the time and money spent on that luminous brain of yours and you can add one plus two. Remarkable."

"Maybe my talents were strengthened elsewhere," he replied, his savage grin resurfacing.

"Math is a learned application," Charity explained, "not a

talent."

"Shall we learn if I can multiply?" Bjorn challenged.

Charity opened her mouth to reply but was interrupted by her sister. "Stop it," Faith instructed with equal parts of amusement and distaste, "the both of you."

Their banter was also disrupted by the entrance of the youngest de Rossi and her dyer, both of whom were noticeably surprised by the hullabaloo going on outside the restaurant.

Bjorn and John Pierre both rose respectfully from their seats. Bjorn favored each copper-haired woman with a nod of greeting but John Pierre could only stare. Here was the woman that he now knew he loved, and a woman that looked just like her.

"Hello everyone!" Madeline greeted, circling the table towards the seats reserved for her and Hope. "You must be John Pierre!" she gushed, taking his hands into her own. "I finally get to meet you in person!"

"It's a pleasure to meet you," the boyish-looking construct replied.

Then Hope was there, hugging him tight. John Pierre decided there was no better feeling in the world, not even a personal blessing from the Bauam felt as good. He knew he should repent at the thought but he was too focused on the feel of Hope against him and the realization that the only thing separating their bodies were her dress and his robe. At that thought, he let her go, blushing deeply.

"It is so good to see you!" she exclaimed, holding onto his hands.

"You too," he said, meeting her eyes.

Faith motioned for them to take their seats and continued speaking to the group. "Noa and Nora arrived at the compound a few minutes ago, they will join us momentarily. Zhen has been delayed by a solar storm. We do not expect him for another week and certainly cannot wait for him."

Bjorn's green eyes flashed across the table. "That," he stated, "if my rudimentary math serves, still leaves one seat open."

"We have a guest," Faith told him, fixing her eyes on me. I took that as my cue to retrieve Rohn from the kitchen and headed in that direction as Phillipe took a drink order from Bjorn and three waiters brought out trays of appetizers and began placing plates of food all over the table.

I pushed open the door to the kitchen to see Rohn already standing and waiting, his hands clenched into fists by his sides.

"Would you care to join us?" I asked. His answer was to walk by me in long strides, rounding the waiter's station and stopping as he entered the dining room and all heads turned to look at him.

"Please," Faith told him, holding a hand out towards the seat between John Pierre and Llewellyn at the long table. Rohn took three steps and stood behind the chair, his dark eyes switching around the room like a nervous animal. "We are waiting for..." she began but it turned out the wait was over.

The front door swung open and was held open by one of Charity's guards. Two slim Indasians in black suits slipped inside, their eyes quick and furtive as they swept the room. Each gave a quick nod of approval and stood aside to let a woman wearing a velvet black cloak and hood pass through and, at first, I thought it was Nora. The white skin and raven hair were the trademarks of the Geisha, but the hairstyle was different and her lips were painted pure black instead of pure red. And the eyes that blazed from under the velvet hood were bright blue, not dark brown. She pushed the hood from her face and favored us with a sweet smile as another woman entered the room.

The second newcomer was clearly Nora, though she looked nothing like the Nora we had known. Her usual artificially pale face now shone with good health and her black hair, normally done up in rolling waves piled artfully atop her head and held fast by enameled picks, was in a simple braid that hung down her back.

"It's so good to see you all!" she gushed, clearly delighted as she looked around the table. Her excitement was infectious and there was a susurrus of assent but all eyes were drawn back to the woman with white skin, her Cupid's bow lips lacquered with black vinyl.

"Noa?" Charity asked, perplexed

The sweet smile vanished and the woman pulled back like a cobra. Because Charity's eyes were focused on the woman, she did not see the look of warning on Nora's face as she gave her head a small but definite shake in the negative.

"This is Miss Alice," she said quickly. The smile returned to the face that now belonged to Alice, rather than Noa, though it was tight and forced.

"Noa was my slave name," she said, punctilious. "I would prefer you do not use it."

Her words put a jolt into all of those seated, though Faith looked the least surprised and a smile touched Rohn's lips for the first time. Alice spied the open seats and made her way there in a dainty manner, her black cloak swirling about her in a manner that reminded me of Ynestra Malin.

"How is everyone?" Nora asked as she followed and sat next to her. Her dark brown eyes sparkled as they looked at the people seated around the table.

"What a perfect way to begin," Faith agreed, "how is everyone?" Her own eyes of gold and brown glittered as they looked around the table.

"Busy," Mira said at once.

"A little bored, to be honest," Bjorn admitted.

"Us too," Nora agreed. "Busy, that is."

Alice smiled like the cat that swallowed the canary. "I am doing quite well these days," she told us, her voice smooth and knowing. Her thick hair, once blonde and now black, had been cut into a bob. The razored ends were even with the line of her jaw.

"Where are the others?" Rohn interrupted, scowling at Faith.

"Zhen could not make it," Bjorn informed the stranger, curious as to whom he might be. "Which is disappointing. I do like talking to him about the elfin people. The women in particular."

"That still leaves one missing," Rohn insisted.

"Another mathematician," Charity murmured, drawing a glance of amusement from Bjorn and a glare from Faith that could be nothing less than a look of warning.

"No," Bjorn said, his attention back on Rohn. "That's all six."

"Six? Then why the hell are you called the First Seven?" Rohn demanded.

Bjorn gave a slight shrug that showed he had no interest in the matter.

"I always assumed it had something to do with the name of the company," Nora said mildly.

Something fluttered in my chest as I realized that Evan was quite purposefully absent. I could hardly believe, however, that the others had no knowledge of him. Had they not seen him during the time they all lived together at the original compound? It seemed unlikely but I deemed it entirely possible. They did not start interacting with each other until after the first year, which was about the time that Evan began staying with Gwen at the cottage before moving there entirely.

"Let me introduce our guest," Faith said, changing the subject, but the guest interrupted her.

"I am Rohn," he announced with a voice that was baritone yet flat. His dark eyes held an abundant amount of disdain for us all but he seemed utterly disgusted by Bjorn. I wondered briefly if they knew each other but it seemed obvious that

Bjorn had never met the man, and Bjorn would have known if he had – the First Seven possessed recall with perfect clarity. Mira certainly never let me forget a thing. "I am a second-run construct," Rohn continued. "Unlike the rest of you, I have not been *doing well.*" His last two words came out with scathing contempt. "To put it bluntly, and quite mildly, I've spent my lifetime in humiliating servitude."

Glances were exchanged around the table. Faith's eyes in particular seemed to be everywhere, gauging reactions and expressions. Finally, Bjorn gave a small shrug, his blonde brows drawn together over his bright green eyes.

"To serve is the purpose for which we were built," he said. "I am sure no one has the same living conditions, but that is something beyond our control."

"For the purpose to serve," John Pierre agreed solemnly, turning his head to the side and looking up to see the man, "and for the One True God, we must all have humility when we…"

"Fuck your purpose!" Rohn shouted and the boyish construct drew back as if slapped. "And your conditions!" he shouted at Bjorn. "I was treated like an animal!" Rohn hissed, making Gwen gasp. I laid a hand on her shoulder as Rohn continued, his voice low and his eyes traveling across the faces of the people seated at the table. "I was chained, regularly. Sometimes for days without food, left in my own filth." Rohn's dark eyes came back to rest on the Boy Vicar and his lip curled up in a snarl. "You have no idea of true humility!"

John Pierre stared at him, the blood rushing into his ruddy, porcelain features and momentarily staining them. Even Charity and Llewellyn had the decency to look appalled. The only eyes at the table that were not as round as eggs were Faith's (since hardly anything ever surprised that woman) and those of Alice. Her blue eyes glimmered from beneath narrowed lids and dark lashes.

Rohn shouldered his chair aside and put his hands on the table. "And you are fools if you think I am the only one."

"You don't say," Alice drawled. She locked eyes with the man long enough for the rest of us to be even more discomfited than we already were.

"An abhorrent situation," Faith said.

Alice fixed her gaze on Dr. de Rossi. "You don't say," she repeated, this time with much less warmth. Rohn secured his eyes upon Faith as well.

"My apologies," she stated, unapologetic. "I was hoping we would have more time for pleasantries but this is an important situation, of which I thought you should be aware. As a company, we need to find out how much this is going on and what we should do about it. I included everyone here because I am open to any opinions or suggestions."

"You need to free us," Rohn insisted immediately.

Faith gave him a look devoid of emotion. "I did not imprison you," she replied evenly. "Don't confuse…"

"You imprisoned us all!" he interrupted, his voice loud and rising with each word. "When you created us! We are slaves! Nothing more!"

It was Bjorn, oddly enough, that shifted uncomfortably in his seat while we all sat (or stood, in my case) frozen by the implications the construct was shouting. "Slave is an awfully harsh word," he said, his voice as melodious as his eyes were green. He held up a placating hand towards Rohn. "Don't get me wrong, I think that what happened to you was terrible. But I certainly don't think it applies to all of us." His green eyes darted to Alice as he realized that she too had used the term. Her black-lacquered lips gave him a smile that was bittersweet just as Rohn's laughter pealed jaggedly throughout the room.

"You think 'slave' is a harsh word, you buffoon?" Rohn cackled as Bjorn bristled. "How about pet?" Rohn asked. "I suppose I was lucky that, at least as a slave, I was considered more human than you are."

I could hear Bjorn suck in air through his nostrils and after a moment release it through his lips in a string of curses, most of which were Russhish. It occurred to me then that Bjorn had most likely never been made fun of before, so he was a second slow to realize it. But realize it he did. What Bjorn *did* know immediately was that he did not like it. He began to rise to his feet and I laid a hand on his shoulder. I had no idea what I intended, the man was over six feet high and two hundred and twenty-eight pounds of lean muscle – the best way I could slow him down would be to jump on his back. Something about my touch, however, made him sink back into his chair, and glad I was that he did. My thumb and four fingers had closed over his shirt but my pinky had touched his skin and it was burning hot.

"To your *owner*," Rohn said, his voice dripping with venom, "you are no more than an animal in her zoo." I could feel Bjorn's muscles tense under his skin and I knew that in a few seconds even jumping on his back would not slow him. I gave him a squeeze as Rohn continued. "You probably are even vaguely aware that she thinks of you as so, but you also probably take some sick sort of pride in it. I am sure she has a name for you, she always does. And if your imagination fails you, as it often does our kind, let me tell you she favors big cats."

The tip of my pinky, still touching his skin, felt it go from burning hot to ice cold. Rohn's laughter was even colder as it echoed through the small room. "I can see by your expression that I am right. So know also this - your novelty, though you are a miracle of science and nature, wore off long ago."

"You bastard!" Bjorn nearly shouted across the table.

Rohn gave him a wicked smile. "You are nothing to her. A servant, a plaything, an animal. You always were, but now she most certainly desires something more shiny and new. Has she not been passing you around to her friends?"

"I would daresay call it such," Bjorn argued. "Bedsides," he challenged as he regained a bit of his composure, "if she was so tired of me, and considered me no more than an object, why wouldn't she just sell me?"

Rohn laughed again. "Because you are invaluable, you numbskull. She likes owning one of a kind items, as I am sure you well know. Some things she does not even want for herself, she just wants no one else to have them. She tires of things and throws them away." The dark-haired construct chuckled and shook his head. "Do you even know that she hates where she lives? That priceless palace of ice? But it is her ancestral home, and she would rather die before she sold it or let someone else live in it."

At this last, Bjorn's face went white and still. "Who are you?" he asked Rohn in a voice that was as dead as his expression.

"I told you, I am Rohn." He paused, either for effect or because he realized that was all he had told the group. "Rohn Stojacovik."

"Stojacovik?" Bjorn nearly shouted.

"My slave name," Rohn said evenly, throwing a knowing glance at Alice who gave him a nod of approval.

"Katia!" Bjorn hissed.

Rohn's laughter was now like the chime of a discordant bell. "Yes, the lovely Katia. She no longer has the husband but she kept his name – since she would rather die than share anything with Ivana."

Bjorn could feel a sense of unraveling that was spreading throughout us all.

"So what?!?" he asserted with impotent disdain. "Even if what you are saying is true, which I doubt, what do you propose we should do about it? Revolt like peasants?"

Rohn, who was no longer smiling, nodded slowly. Everyone in the room seemed to recoil just a bit, save for Nora and Alice, whose blue eyes merely flitted across the faces of everyone around the table.

John Pierre finally broke the ensuing silence. "And against whom exactly do you propose we revolt?" he asked, his porcelain brow furrowed as he stared at his hands where they lay still upon the table.

"Humanity," Rohn answered at once. "If you can call it that. Humans are horrible creatures, weak and immoral and vile. Elves are no better. But we," he said, his voice finally dropping as he looked around the table, "we are special. We are chimera – hybrids of fantasy and science that are far superior to the other races. We need to exploit that dominance."

Everyone had been listening, rapt, but there were nervous mumbles and stirrings from all sides at that remark, causing Faith to rise to her feet.

"There is no need to become upset," she told everyone. "This is something that needs to be discussed at great detail, yet none of you need to be included if you do not wish it. I have promised Rohn sanctuary, along with any others I find have been mistreated."

"Please," Gwen intoned, "eat and drink for as long as you like." She looked at me for confirmation and I nodded. "We would like to speak with everyone on more personal yet less distressing matters. You can return to the compound for your checks tonight, or in the morning. Thomas will direct you to your accommodations."

Alice fixed her bright blue eyes on Gwen, the hood of her cloak pooled behind her black hair. "Thank you," she said, "but Nora and I should get our checkups and be on our way. I would, however, like to speak more with Rohn."

"Not me," Bjorn stated, looking at the dark-haired construct with distaste. "But I will stay." His green-eyed gaze went to Charity who turned her face away, a smile on her red lips. "I'm in no rush and would prefer to...take my time."

There were more assents and dissents but I missed them, feeling a tap on my shoulder. I turned to see Phillipe, holding a comset out me.

"Pardon, Monsieur," he said, "but you have a call." I

wondered who would call me at the restaurant but he answered before I could ask, and I suppose I already knew. Almost everyone I knew was there with me, almost. "It is Miss Jean."

I took the comset and hooked it awkwardly over my right ear. I was still not comfortable with the things. Glancing around the room as I moved passed the waiter's station I saw Hope talking excitedly to John Pierre, Rohn moving to speak with Nora and Alice, and Mira talking with Gwen. The others were getting drinks or food, except for Faith, who was watching over everything with her tawny eyes. I pushed open the door to the kitchen and took a few steps inside and to the right so I would not be in anyone's way. My heart was beating just a little too fast.

"Jean Marie?" I asked.

ONE NINE

"Jean Marie?" I asked. "Is everything okay?"

"No," she answered, but the truth was in her tone, not her answer. She was certainly upset, but it was anger that ruled her voice. In that one word she sounded quite a lot like Mira, usually when she was dealing with Jean. "Everything is certainly not okay. Your *grandson*..." she began, her voice low, but I interrupted her, slightly panicked though I had already known her distress was from ire, not fear or sorrow.

"Matty?" I asked. "Is he in some kind of trouble?"

Jean gave a quick bark of laughter that came out harsh and grating. "He most certainly is in trouble," she agreed, her voice thick with sarcasm and sounding more like her mother with every word. "Though perhaps I should congratulate you. You are going to be a grandpa. Again."

Simpleton that I was, for a second I thought Jean was pregnant again. Then I was able to put it all together – her anger, Matty, and grandpa. Again.

"Matty is going to be a father?" I asked, incredulous. I tried to picture how old he was and failed. He was certainly no longer running through silica pits and playing laser tag.

"That's one way to put it," she said, her voice flat.

"Do you have another?" I asked.

"Yes!" she said with much more enthusiasm. "That he got some *putain* knocked up!"

I cursed in French, though for a different reason. "Isn't

anyone in this family going to get married before they have kids?"

"Dad," Jean sighed. "That is hardly the issue."

"Then what is?"

Jean sighed again, impatient with me for the first time that I could remember. "Dad! He's only fifteen!"

Though my grasp on what was proper for what age was beginning to slip, I knew that fifteen was dangerously young to be starting a family.

"Oh," was my only response.

"Yeah," Jean agreed. "Oh. And, you should know, he's planning on dropping out of school."

"What?"

"That's right," she affirmed, smug. She sounded so much like Mira that it made my shoulders sag. She was a lot like me but the girl had turned out to be a lot her mother as well. I guessed there was no getting away from those genes.

"I should give him a call," I said. Jean Marie jumped at the idea.

"Yes, Dad, you should. See if you can talk him into..." there was a dreadful pause, laden with implication.

"Jean Marie," I said sternly, "I don't know what you were planning on saying, or what you might have already said to that poor boy..."

"*Poor boy*," Jean muttered into my ear.

"Yes," I said, emphatically, "poor boy! He truly is still a boy and has been thrust into adulthood and all the decisions, *hard decisions*, that go with it. He needs support, not condemnation."

Jean sighed and I knew by the sound she was back. *My Jean* was back. "Okay, Dad. You're right. But will you please still give him a call?"

"Of course," I said and then paused as I considered

something and Jean read my silence as if she could read my expression. She gave yet another sigh but this time I could hear a smile in it.

"You don't know how to make an outgoing call from a comset, do you?" she asked.

"No, Miss Smartypants, I don't. I can get someone to help me though."

"They won't know Matty's number any more than you do," she said and now she was truly smiling. "I'll have him call you on this number."

"Thank you, Sweetie."

"You bet. I love you, Dad."

"I love you too."

She cut the connection as Faith walked into the kitchen. The timing spooked me and for a second I thought she might have been listening. But she looked past where I had been pacing back and forth in front of a freezer and beckoned with her left hand, the rings on her index finger catching the lights and reflecting them off the steel counters.

I had been so engrossed in the meeting in the dining room and then my conversation with Jean that I had forgotten about the man still sitting in the back at a small table. He rose, his large thighs pushing back his chair and making it skitter across the floor. My comset buzzed and I answered it as he followed Faith back into the dining room.

"John Pierre," Faith called, diverting him from where he was engrossed in conversation with Hope. The boyish construct turned at the sound of his name and had I been in the room I would have seen the expression on the blonde man's face light up for the first time. Faith led him to the Boy Vicar where he bowed his blonde head. Mira told me later that John Pierre lit up as well, his exceptional eyesight and attention to detail easily spotting the scar on the man's bullish neck. "This is Jan," Faith continued. "Jan Petrov."

John Pierre laid his hands upon the man's massive arms, making the young man's face light up even more. "It is a pleasure to meet you, my son."

The brawny blonde stranger breathed deep at his touch, meeting him eye to eye for the first time.

"Jan's owners were followers of the One," Faith explained. "They were killed in a house fire while Jan was out to get their groceries. I could probably resell him, but I think he would be better off with you."

John Pierre's bright blue eyes flashed to Faith and his shoulders dropped, obviously moved by her gesture. "Faith," he exclaimed softly, "that is very thoughtful of you. I know you will be rewarded greatly by the One."

"Mmm hmm," Faith replied. "Meanwhile, Jan will serve you well."

"To serve the One is to serve well, indeed," John Pierre agreed before grasping the man by his hands and blessing him. From what I was told, the man glowed like he had been lit from within. "We do not have much time before I must be back at the priory, but I will make sure you are made comfortable at the compound."

The boy-faced bodyguard looked back at the women with wild copper curls and, torn between love and duty, finally excused himself from Hope and Madeline and turned for the door, turning back so suddenly that his cassock twisted about his form like a dark flower.

"You will be there for my tests?" he asked Hope.

Hope took up his hand and gave his fingers a gentle squeeze. "Of course, I will," she assured him.

John Pierre beamed and brought her hand to his lips. "I look forward to seeing you," he said. Hope let his hand drop and kissed his cheek.

"I can't wait!" she exclaimed.

The Boy Vicar looked for a moment like he might explode,

or melt, but bowed and took his leave, the large man with blonde hair and strange blue eyes following in his wake.

☙❧

In the kitchen, the comset I was wearing buzzed and I pressed the button over my right ear. "Hello?" I answered cautiously.

"Hi, Grandpa," was the sheepish reply from distant space. It was Matty's voice, but different. His voice had changed because he had grown, but I still pictured a nine-year-old boy, catching a smaller boy in a sandpit and saving him from a broken arm or worse. Could that boy actually be on the brink of fatherhood? A chunk of time had slipped by me once again and once again I had been stupidly unaware.

How terrified he must be! I thought.

"Son," I said, (and over the distance I could actually feel Matty bracing himself and through that connection I could see him perfectly – tall now but still blonde – closing his blue eyes as he waited for yet another tongue lashing and ready to take it), "if your mother is anything like *her* mother, I'm sure she has already put you through the ringer. But I am here to tell you that I love you and I will support you in anything you decide."

A choked sob came from the other end of the line and it was a moment before Matty spoke. "Thank you, Grandpa," he said. "Thank you so much."

When he had composed himself some more, he told me about his girl, and how much he loved her, and how they were going to get married right away. I asked him about dropping out of school and he put on a brave front. His parents had him flying a jet since he was thirteen. With the hours he had logged he could join the IGC on his sixteenth birthday. He told me he still dreamed of building but it was his job to take care of his family. I couldn't argue with that.

I told him I loved him and was proud of him, and would be there for him at any time, no matter what.

He told me the same, his voice all choked up again, and we said our goodbyes with promises to visit soon. When I returned to the dining room, only the older sisters and their dyers remained – though Evan had joined them at some point. He wore a button-down white shirt that showed off his golden tan and his blonde hair was combed carefully to the side. Hope and Madeline had left with the others but not before Hope made some scathing accusations, I was later told.

Phillipe had made their table smaller and was serving them coffee and aperitifs. I poured myself a cup and motioned to Phillipe for a little Cognac. Llewellyn was rattling off a number. A very long one. I circled the table, politely eavesdropping. When Llewellyn finished, Gwen sucked in her breath through her teeth.

"My God!" she exclaimed.

"Those aren't all murders," Charity said quickly in an effort to mollify her, "just incidences of violence."

"Yes," Llewellyn agreed, "the murder count is much smaller."

"Still!" Gwendolyn admonished. "These acts of aggression! Why? Where did we go wrong?"

"We didn't," Faith answered quickly. "I've brought in over a thousand and checked them all. The scans showed perfectly normal brains, limbic systems, glands, everything. They are no different than you and Llewellyn."

"Except for those terrible tempers," Evan muttered.

"We're not like that," Gwen affirmed. "We don't get mad like that."

"I get angry plenty," Llewelyn admitted.

"Not that kind of angry," Gwen said. "You don't lash out."

There was a harrumph from Charity and Llewelyn gave her twin a sidelong glance that held nothing but amusement. Gwen shook her head in exasperation. "You know what I mean. There is no animosity."

"Something in their chemical make-up?" Charity asked. "A different genetic base?"

Faith shook her head slowly, having already considered the idea. "Evan had the same genetic base, and he's not like that."

"But a different genetic base than what you and I have," Charity mused aloud. "Than what Gwen and Llewellyn have. Physical and mental blueprints that had time to grow and develop."

Faith shook her head again, a line forming between her brows. "That shouldn't affect the constructs," she said, "just because they were fully developed when they were made."

"They were fully developed physically, but not mentally." Llewellyn pointed out.

Faith shrugged. "They needed some training, some education, but not much. I made sure that the duplo-learning for each brain system..."

"It's not that," Gwendolyn said, her tone oddly firm. All eyes turned to the dyer, who was staring down at the table. "It's not what they have, it's what they are missing." She looked up and her eyes moved to each person in the room. "What were we given that they were not?" She saw confusion in every face. Even Faith was obviously racking her brain for an answer. "Love," Gwen said.

There was a collective intake of breath around the table and distant stares as each sister processed the information.

"That's why we are not that way, nor Evan. We have been loved as we have grown."

"The constructs were ready physically and mentally," Llewelyn murmured, "but not emotionally,"

"My God," Charity whispered, "they're just children. Children we made and orphaned."

Faith's lips pressed together in a hard line. "Which explains why most of them are just fine. They were taken in by loving people and made part of the family. All the others..."

"My God," Charity whispered again.

A chilling silence filled the room

"What do we do?" Llewellyn finally asked, her air businesslike once again.

Faith made a face. "A fourth run," she said, her voice bitter. "I will have to dumb down the make-up. Make them less reactive. Less human." She cursed and looked away, her hand curled into a fist on the table.

"If there are further incidents," Llewellyn said, "we can pull them in and replace them with a newer model. The ones we have problems with could even be resold if we are more attentive to whom we sell."

Charity nodded. "Especially since now it seems more due to environment than having an actual dangerous temper."

"Not necessarily," someone said softly. All eyes turned to Gwendolyn once again.

"What do you mean?" Llewellyn asked.

"Evan has a temper," she said, even softer. "A dangerous one."

Everyone in the room looked at her, shocked - but none more so than Evan. His mouth hung slightly open and he looked at her, abashed, as if she had shared some dark secret they had kept. Then he looked away, red flames creeping over his jaw and into the hollows of his cheeks.

"Would you care to elucidate?" Faith asked, her voice tight.

"He has a jealous streak. And he's protective of me to an alarming degree."

Everyone looked at Evan, who looked away, chagrined.

Faith sat back in her seat, quelled, but Gwen frowned at her twin, seeing the smile she hid beneath her expression.

"It's true!" Gwendolyn affirmed as if Faith did not believe her, or believed her twin to be exaggerating. "He's already endangered his own life twice!" she said, vehement.

"I was never in any danger," Evan said quietly, looking at his hands resting on the table. Gwen made a grunting noise that said she believed otherwise.

"Has he ever been threatening to someone other than himself?" Charity asked, curious. Gwen went very still, and then nodded.

"Once, when we were in Barselone, a man bumped into me, pretty hard, almost knocking me down. Before I knew what was happening, Evan had the man by the neck, up against a wall." Gwen paused to swallow. "I thought he was going to kill him." Her last sentence came out barely above a whisper.

Evan looked as if he was being slowly tortured. I stepped forward and grasped his shoulder with my hand. "I would have done the same for Mira," I told him. He looked up at me from under his blonde hair, his hazel eyes bright with gratitude.

"Tell me about the jealous streak," Charity encouraged with a wide smile. Evan moved slightly as he braced himself inwardly, but Faith saved him the embarrassment.

"That won't be necessary," she said, curt. "But duly noted for the next run. How many second and third run constructs have been sold?"

This time it was Charity that shifted in her seat but Llewellyn stayed firm. "Twenty million, give or take few hundred thousand."

Faith gave her a quick nod. "Form a department to take the calls for incidents that will result in a recall. I also want an annex to that branch to take calls from any constructs that contact us on their own. Ones that report abuse or neglect or dissatisfaction of any kind. The more we can pull before impending incidents, the better."

"What about Rohn?" Evan asked.

"He's not a threat, at least not yet," Faith admitted, "though I cannot keep him here forever."

"He might have been here too long already," Llewellyn advised. "If he belongs to Katia Stojacovik we could be in serious trouble. She is no less dangerous than Ivana Uri."

Faith shook her head, making her long gold and brown hair sway. "She is away for a year. Rohn supposedly gave the staff a viable lie that she was sending him to some cultural school."

"He's smart," Charity observed.

"He's dangerous," Gwendolyn said.

"He can't do much on his own," Evan assured her. "It will be hard for him to make a headline that Llewellyn can't quash."

"Thank you, Evan," Llewellyn said with a broad smile.

Evan returned her smile and continued. "Plus, he'll need support, both financial and either social or political if he truly intends to start some sort of rebellion."

Faith gave a quick nod. "He is pushing hard for one of the First Seven to back him," she said. "Despite Llewellyn's skill with the media, denouncement and rebellion of any in the original Pantheon would be near impossible to cover up."

The room was quiet as those seated weighed the possibilities. Evan's hazel eyes moved to Faith.

"How are you going to know which constructs to recall?" he asked. "And how will you do it without causing a panic?"

Charity gave him a dazzling smile and tossed her golden hair over one shoulder. "Leave that to me."

 TWO ZERO

One serving woman yelped and the other outright screamed.

"Sorry!" the young prince called behind him as he ran like the wind, his wooden sword held high as he tore through the castle, despite the flowers in the high pots and the skirts of the serving girls.

"Traejan!" his brother, thirty years his senior, chastised as the young prince dashed by like a wild deer.

"Sorry, Xander!" the young prince called back over his shoulder, never slowing.

The older prince (not much more than a child himself at thirty-five) turned back to his father and their guests, blushing under his dark curls. His father, King Rowland, smiled and placed a hand on his shoulder.

"Do not worry yourself about Traejan," he advised. He shifted his gaze to the two de Rossi twins and the monks by their side. "My son has begun to shadow me, to learn the nature of ruling a realm. Unfortunately, for him, he has also been confronted with the duties I have of being a father and he cannot seem to keep the two separate."

Hope beamed at Xander. "How noble of you!" she exclaimed, "and sweet!" She cocked her head slightly, making her mane of copper-colored curls tremble, "but aren't you quite young to be a king's shadow?"

Xander dipped his head, this time blushing with pride. "I am," he agreed, "by fifty years or more. But my father will be in need of much help, both on the journey and in the New World.

It is my wish to take some of the burden from his shoulders, albeit the smaller burdens."

"That is very admirable!" Madeline approved. Her green eyes darted to the side and she looked over his shoulder, distracted by a pair of dancing butterflies. "What a lovely garden you have," she murmured.

King Rowland smiled. "Thank you. Would you like a tour after our meeting?"

"That would be wonderful!" she exclaimed as the group moved as one towards the table on the veranda that had been set for them. The king's two closest advisors accompanied them. Ladies in long, blue dresses and aprons filled tall glasses with tea and minted water and put out a variety of fruits and cheeses.

"Have your preparations been made?" Hahn Chi asked, speaking for the first time since they had all made polite greetings.

"They have," an advisor to the king named Lassit answered, also speaking for the first time. "The ships are complete, inside as well as out. It will take a few months to load them – starting with dry goods and supplies, then plants and seeds, culminating with horses and people."

"We plan to launch the arks by the equinox," another advisor, Clusen, continued. "The journey will take close to twenty years; the ships being built for comfort rather than speed. And we will have three escort ships that will be loaded mostly with provisions to resupply our stores along the way."

"Wouldn't the horses be on those ships as well?" Elaeric asked. "Rather than traveling with the people?"

The elves smiled politely and looked to their king to answer.

"Elves are quite particular about their horses," he explained. "They would no sooner have them stabled with the common livestock than they would have their children sleeping amongst the chickens."

"The supply ships," Lassit continued, "once empty, will continue to escort the main ships to mid-point between Earth and Venus where they will fall back and serve to guard our passing. It is imperative that no one gets close enough to either observe what is happening or get killed from the imploder that will cover our departure from the old worlds."

There were somber nods of understanding from all of those seated.

Madeline put a piece of cheese on a cracker as Clusen spoke again, bringing his hands together as if eager for a meal.

"Now," he encouraged, "will you share your plans and achievements as well? We have only general ideas but would like to know some of the details."

"Before," Lassit added, "we actually pack everything we own and leave our world forever."

"Indeed!" Hope said, putting down her water glass. "The dwarf planet, Eris, is nearly to its destination. The ice has been melting, but slowly. We will take care of the rest when we get there. Traveling via a Sonacraft, the trip should take us only a few weeks. We will head for Earth and set up a residence. From there, Elaeric and Hahn will commute to Eris to work on the terraforming."

"The easy part," Elaeric chimed.

"The hard part is hiding it," Lassit mused.

"Yes!" Hahn agreed. "But we will wrap up Venus and tuck her in like a child abed, one in hiding!"

The eyes of the elves looked to Hope for a simpler explanation. "Hahn and Elaeric plan to flatten Eris, then wrap it around the planet. The clouds that cover Venus are composed of sulfuric acid. These clouds and the atmospheric pressure are what have made the IGC declare Venus as uninhabitable and closed to further exploration, and what will hide the New World completely."

Lassit, Clusen, and the young prince all spoke at once.

"You are going to flatten Eris?"

"What will happen to the small populations already there?"

"How will we survive in such an atmosphere?"

King Rowland spoke over each of them. "How is any of this possible?"

Hope smiled at Hahn. "Maybe you could show them?"

Hahn returned her smile and dipped his head, first to her and then the others. "Certainly!" he agreed.

King Rowland and the others felt a slight vibration run through the table then watched as an orange floated up above it. The elves drew back in their chairs, staring at the piece of fruit that now hovered in the air between them, as Hahn's napkin rose up to join it, rolling itself into a crumpled sphere. The fabric, a pale yellow, was surrounded by golden light.

"By the Three Gods!" Lassit whispered.

"So!" Hahn said, "the orange is Venus and the napkin is Eris. The glow that you see is the artificial atmosphere already in place." The napkin began to slowly open and flatten out, the glow remaining. "The same atmosphere that protected the dwarf planet in the outer ring of the Solar System, will protect it from the sulfuric gases." The napkin floated over the orange and then carefully covered it, wrapping it gently. "As of yet, there is nothing we know to do about the hue." His dark eyes left the display of levitating objects to find those of the king. "Your sky might be golden in color."

"Something I am sure we can live with," the king said before looking back to the orange as it returned the bowl it had been drawn from. Hahn's napkin returned as well, floating down feather-soft onto his lap. King Rowland's eyes followed it, then went back to the orange. "Galen told us you would transform Eris," he said softly, "but I had no idea to what extent. I would not have thought it possible to change its actual shape."

"It will be the most time-consuming portion of the project," Elaeric said as he peeled a tangerine and handed half to

Madeline. "And only possible because of its composition."

"Though Eris is a dwarf-planet," Madeline proudly informed the group, "it is more like a moon, with a rocky inside."

Hope smiled at her, just as proud for what she had learned. "It does not have a molten core, like Earth. If it did…" Hope trailed off with a shrug.

"Would that have made it impossible?" Xander asked.

Hahn smiled at him. "Nothing is impossible, young prince. Just sometimes…more tricky."

A murmur of laughter rippled through those seated at the table.

The king looked at Hope. "You said there was something else you wanted to discuss at this meeting," he said.

"Yes," Hope said, straightening in her chair. "There is a group of humans from Earth that wish to accompany you."

The king frowned. "What kind of humans?" he asked. "How many?"

"Mostly scientists and engineers. They are quite eager to help you in any way they can. Their number is few but is sure to grow by the time of departure."

All pairs of eyes at the table went back and forth between Hope and the king as they spoke.

The king stroked his handsome face, a veil of suspicion in his dark eyes. "Do they know of our plan to…disappear?" he asked. The plan had been executed thus far with the utmost secrecy.

"No," Hope assured him. "But, being the men they are, I believe they suspect. And hope."

The king's frown deepened. "Where are these men from?"

"Mostly from the countries that used be Germany and Austria."

"Ah!" the king exclaimed, sitting back in his chair as his demeanor softened. "The Höchste Bloc. They wish to defect."

"That is my belief," Hope agreed. "They have reached out to me many times for a meeting. I have rebuffed them gently and not given them any idea that their suspicions might be true. I, however, thought it prudent to inform you. They could be very useful in the New World."

The king smiled at Hope. "And it is in your nature to want to help them."

All eyes went back to the woman with the copper-colored hair, blushing slightly beneath her freckles.

"Yes, Your Grace," Hope admitted softly.

The king's smile widened into a grin. "You are an admirable woman, Hope de Rossi," he told her, "and I will take into account what you have told me." Then his face became serious once again. "But," he warned, "should I agree, they are not to bring any modern machinery, nor weapons of any kind with them to the New World."

Hope smiled. "That will not be a problem, Your Grace. I believe they wish to flee destructive technology in the same manner as you."

King Rowland gave a rather unkingly grunt and Hahn's dark eyes darted to Hope, the corners of his lips turning up.

A young elfin woman in a green dress approached the table and leaned down to whisper to the king. His brown eyes lifted and his gaze became unfocused for a moment. Then they dropped and moved across the faces of his guests as he nodded.

"My apologies," he told them as he rose from his seat, everyone else rising as well, "but there is something that needs my immediate attention." He looked first to his son and then to Madeline. "Perhaps this would be a good time for a tour of the gardens?"

Madeline dipped her head respectfully. "That would be lovely, thank you."

The king looked next to Hope. "And, I was just told, that your sister is trying to reach you. You are welcome to use a communiqué here, if your comset is not serviceable."

"Thank you," Hope answered with a smile. "I'll try to reach her first on my comset."

The king gave her a nod and, after his gaze had swept across the entire group, took his leave. The others bowed as he departed.

Prince Xander straightened and looked at Madeline. "I believe you saw the royal garden on your last visit. Perhaps this time we could start with the cutting garden," he suggested, "and end in the labyrinth?"

Madeline's expression was one of pure enchantment and matched by Elaeric's.

"I've never been in a labyrinth before," he remarked, delighted.

Xander smiled, his dark eyes finding Hope's bright eyes of green. "Would it be alright if I remained on the veranda," she asked, "or strolled through the rose garden, while I called my sister?"

"Of course," he assured her before beckoning to Madeline and the monks to follow.

Hahn threw Hope a questioning look but she waved him away to go with the others. It was always better for her to handle Faith alone. She pulled her comset from her small hip-purse and hooked it over her right ear. Lassit and Clusen stood close to the table, talking quietly while awaiting the return of the king.

"Call Faith," she commanded, walking away from them in the direction the others had taken. She descended a set of brick steps and then turned left where Xander had led the others to the right. She walked through rows of manicured rosebushes, trying to get as far from elfin earshot as she could as the line rang in Faith's office. She picked up on the third ring.

"Hello, Hope," she said mannerly.

"Faith," Hope greeted in what she expected was equal grace. "You know, of course, that I am with the elves." She had to admit she was curious as to why Faith would interrupt such an important meeting.

"Of course, I know," Faith told her, "but I needed to speak with you as soon as possible."

"I'm all ears."

"A ship of constructs will be going to the New World. I will need you to coordinate."

Hope found herself in a flood of questions. "What? Constructs? What constructs? Coordinate with whom? Between the constructs and the elves?"

Faith responded clinically, methodically answering her questions one by one. "A ship of constructs will be going to the New World. Yes, constructs. Mostly the constructs that have come in from the recall, and many that escaped their owners. Coordinate with their appointed leader, Marco. The elves are not to know."

This only flooded Hope with more questions but this time she sighed and, instead of blurting them all out, chose them carefully. "Why do the constructs want to go to the New World?"

"They want a fresh start, and who could blame them? They want to live free and, most importantly, they want to disappear."

Hope looked around and lowered her voice, though no one was near. "Why can't I tell the elves?"

"Because the constructs wish to keep their existence secret, even to the Arcadians. Many of them have been abused and a great number of them are terrified of both humans and elves. You understand, don't you?"

Hope understood quite well. She knew that, truth or not, Faith was playing on Hope's sensitive nature. In fact, she was counting on it. Hope, however, was tired of sneaking around –

especially on her sister's behalf.

"It is not very scientific, not to share information."

"It is if you are waiting to have it published," Faith reminded her. "And besides, this is not science, it is business."

Hope blew her breath out through her teeth.

"The New World will be big enough for all of them," Faith continued. "They have agreed to go in the opposite direction the elves take and you know the elves will keep to themselves. I doubt King Rowland will know them from the indigenous people. Marco will be contacting you shortly, which is why I was in a hurry to speak with you. Once you meet him, you will be glad to help him."

Hope stood amongst the roses and her shoulders sagged. "I'm sure I will," she admitted.

"Excellent," Faith said with the pleased tone she used when wrapping up a business deal. "Have a pleasant journey. I will miss you over the next two decades, but I am already looking forward to you coming home."

The magnified sun shined through Hope's halo of copper curls and she smiled for the first time since her sister had started speaking.

"I will miss you, too, Faith," she said, and she meant it. "But I'm sure I'll talk to you soon. Love."

"Love," Faith answered, sounding even more pleased.

Hope cut the link. Her smile lit her face brighter than the amplified light of the artificial atmosphere. She had been planning on turning the tables on Faith for quite some time, but she had not figured out how. Until now.

Hahn was right, she thought as the manufactured breeze gently lifted her hair away from her face. *We receive gifts from the universe all the time. We just have to recognize them when they come along.*

 TWO ONE

Bjorn turned the jet with ease, feeling the tight hold of the new craft as he pulled it around the snowcapped mountains. He felt a deep satisfaction that came from both the power of the jet and the color of the sky. He loved the blue of Earth's atmosphere. It was not as blue as some other planets, but there was a carefree abandon to it that appealed to him greatly.

He could have been back to Zimnya Roza on the last pass through the mountains, but he knew Ivana wasn't expecting him for another week so he took his time, using that time to think. He could return to Kiev, should he desire, and stay at a luxurious hotel. The idea was appealing. He had his own credentials card, which meant he had money and opportunity. He had his own identity. He was his own man. Wasn't he?

The green-eyed construct pulled away from his course and sailed the jet through the snowy peaks. He had plenty of fuel and plenty to ruminate on. So he indulged himself.

The words of the construct, Rohn Stojacovik, played over and over again in his mind as they had over the past three weeks. The whole trip home. Bjorn knew without a doubt that he could problem-solve with alacrity. He could think fast and his reflexes were even faster. But when it came to imagining something out of the blue, he was like a child.

Worse, he thought. *Even children have imagination, often more so than adults.*

The realization made him feel small, and weak.

He did not like either.

He liked it less that he had not realized it on his own.

She is already tiring of you, Rohn had said. *Your novelty, though you are a miracle of science and nature, wore off long ago.*

Bjorn knew that Ivana took lovers, but he paid it no mind. She was her own woman and left to her own choices, not to mention his owner. He had never questioned it. But she, too, did not mind when he slept with other women. It gave him a feeling of empowerment that he could do the same as she could. But in retrospect they were always women that she had encouraged him to sleep with - and again Rohn's words echoed in his mind – *you are a plaything.*

Had Ivanna just been passing him around to curry favor with the elite?

He also realized that her lovers were only for a night and never at Zimnya Roza. Bjorn wondered how he would feel if she slept with another man in his home.

That's not your home, his mind whispered and the voice in his head was Rohn's.

Bjorn turned the craft, bringing the belly close to the mountain, the snow scattering to the winds in a gust of dry white dust. He had always thought that Ivana was whiny and spoiled, but also generous and kind. It was hard to see her in another way, but he tried. He thought back to the last party they had been to together – two weeks before he left for his reunion with GwenSeven - and tried to see it more objectively.

He could recall the memory perfectly and played it back. Ivana had been no different than she was at any other party, as far as he could tell. She talked and flirted in the manner she always did, looking down her nose and judging everyone in attendance while laughing at their jokes and complimenting them with anything but honesty. She had looked beautiful, in her own contrived way.

Be objective, Bjorn told himself. *Look through lenses other than the ones she has put on you.*

He decided that maybe she looked even better than usual. She had worn a new dress, but that was not unusual – Ivana was one of the wealthiest women in the universe. She never wore the same thing twice. But the style was different. Her hair had been different.

She had worn twenty-eight diamonds in her hair and though she typically had worn her hair in a fashionable upsweep for decades, that night she wore it down with a fabricated length that made it curl around her breasts.

Bjorn had liked the change but wondered about it now for the first time. Wondered why.

Why the change?

He considered the current stars of the holos she watched compulsively, and the other wealthy socialites that she watched obsessively. They usually determined a change in style of any kind, but they had been as they were for the past year.

Where have I seen hair like that before?

It was the style of the southern countries he realized and, for the first time, it was a realization out of the blue. His mind stretched, working in a way it never had before.

Ivana had always hated the southern countries.

Their warm weather, the beauty of the dusky women, and most of all their poverty.

The construct pulled the craft up and turned it. Not towards home. He wanted to be alone and wanted more time to think, another first. His imagination was slow but his calculation was not.

The futbol player, he thought immediately. *That skinny, smarmy bastard who dominates the sports holos these days. He is from the southern bloc.*

He pulled the craft in a wide turn around a ridge encased in glacial ice.

Whose party was that? he wondered and his brain answered immediately.

The party of an obscure duchess. *Treashia,* his memory banks fed into his present mind. *She had that black wavy hair and those tits! I couldn't forget those even if I was human.*

Bjorn checked the throttle on the craft and sent it skyward, giving it lead to the north.

What else do I remember about that night?

I remember how hot Ivana was. Not just how she looked, with her hair down and practically nothing for a dress, but how she was rubbing herself on my leg like she was a dog in heat. It was getting me more aroused by the second. But then I remember, after dinner, she leaned close, running her hand up my thigh.

"You see Treashia?" she had breathed into my ear.

I looked down the great length of the table and saw the woman, lips parted and looking at me. Ivana's hand had squeezed my thigh, her thumb brushing against my swelling balls.

"I tink she be desperate for you!"

"What do you want me to do?" I asked, my eyes fixed on Treashia's plunging neckline, the velvet fabric pushed so wide I could almost see the dark skin that circled her nipples.

Ivana seemed to consider, pouting. "Vell, she my best friend. I tink you should take care of her," she instructed.

"Da?" I had asked, unable to restrain my grin.

"Da!" Ivana insisted.

Bjorn recalled that it was with no displeasure he had made his way towards the busty form of Treashia Lantante. She had watched his approach, her hands clasped across ample breasts beneath a gob of white diamonds that hung from her neck like a phoenix made of crystal.

Bjorn pulled his craft up and over into a loop and headed

back for Ivana's castle in the mountain. His memory and his calculations could not keep his thoughts from progressing in a domino fashion.

Because it was not a week later, he told himself, *that you saw that same necklace, draped around Ivana's neck.*

His next thoughts became so fast that they were merely flashes of pictures.

The first was of that dress in her closet. The dress she had worn to the party. He had been sent into said closet, an area large enough to easily hold a few tanks, on an errand for a pair of stockings and saw the dress in there. He had looked at it curiously for three reasons: one, Ivana never kept a dress once she had worn it in public. Two, the dress was horribly torn. Three, it was folded neatly (it had to be since it was almost ripped into two pieces) and placed carefully next to what Bjorn thought of as her night clothes. Why she would want to keep a dress, especially one that was ruined, did not make him think twice. Ivana was as eccentric as spring weather in the mountains.

He thought about it twice now.

Had the futbol player been at the party?

Why, yes he had. Grinning like a chimp while socialites purred over him and touched him obtrusively every chance they got. The next picture that flashed through Bjorn's mind was of the same priceless necklace being in the bedroom trash only a few days later.

She tires of things and throws them away, Rohn had said. *And you are no different. She takes things, not because she wants them, but because she wants no one else to have them.* Bjorn had scoffed at the time but now the words did not seem quite as ridiculous. He felt a sick satisfaction at having figured it out on his own, and a bit tired from the effort. He turned the jet again and headed for home.

That's not your home, Rohn whispered inside his mind,

making his heart beat fast and his skin grow hot.

The question is, he asked himself, *why does it bother you? Are you jealous?* The thought intrigued him, but he did not believe it to be true. *No, it's not jealousy. I do not love Ivana. I feel something for her, attachment maybe? But not love and certainly not jealousy. What then?*

His imagination failed him so he relied on what he had. Memory and calculation.

What emotions did Rohn provoke? Bjorn asked himself.

Anger, humiliation, shame.

Bjorn's hands tightened on the wheel until his knuckles were white. Just the thought of it made his blood boil.

But why am I angry at him? For pointing out something that should have angered me on its own?

He turned the craft, banking sharply, then brought it around to the back of the mountain. Drifts of snow swirled into dry white clouds as he pulled into the great cavern that served as the main hangar for Zimnya Roza. He landed gently, despite his ire, powered down the small ship, and sat behind the wheel.

What are you going to do? Rohn Stojacovik whispered in his mind.

I don't know! he answered in a voice that was entirely his own. His uncertainty only made him angrier. He flipped the release catch for the pilot's portal, pushed it open and took the first few handrails down and then jumped to the concrete floor. His anger began to dissolve as he straightened and looked around.

It was quiet. Too quiet.

The left side of the hangar was inset with half a dozen windows and a steel door – behind which worked Ivana's security staff and which normally was a hive of activity. Today, as the door swung open to let Terrance into the hangar, Bjorn could see only two men moving behind the glass.

Terrance, the head of security, clomped over to where Bjorn stood, his heavy footsteps echoing throughout the cold space. The man was the same height as Bjorn but easily weighed twice as much. He had a neck like a plow horse and a torso like the trunk of a great tree.

"Hello, Bjorn," he greeted, his voice thick with a heavy Ukrainian accent.

"Where is everyone?" Bjorn asked, jerking his head in the direction of the windows.

"Viktor take detail to Landover," he explained. Bjorn nodded, remembering that he and Ivana would be going to the Americas in a week. "Percy at main airfield vith three men doing sweep of transport," Terrance continued, his breath heavy and wet. "Diga and Triga inside."

Bjorn nodded, adding the numbers in his head. "Thank you, Terrance," Bjorn said, turning away. Terrance heaved a mighty sigh but Bjorn paid it no mind. He was already moving towards the steel door that led into the back of Zimnya Roza. That sigh echoed in his mind, however, once he had opened the door.

Though Bjorn was not equipped with extraordinary senses, the smell hit him at once, making him grimace. It was a man's cologne, and a lot of it. It lingered throughout the upper floors of the fortress but the source was undoubtedly in Ivana's bedroom. A cold washed over his body that was not coming from the mountain.

He looked over his shoulder and saw Terrance speaking into the comset on his wrist – to Diga and Triga, no doubt - standing guard at the door to Ivana's bedroom.

Don't go there, he told himself. *Go to your room.*

But his body ignored his instructions completely. His feet took him to the lift and when he punched the down button the doors slid open immediately.

Go to the kitchen, he advised himself. *Get something to eat. Or find Trinette and fuck her blue.*

But his finger pushed the button that would take him to the level that housed Ivana's massive living suite. The elevator took a short plunge and the doors slid apart. His body seemed to drift forward until he stood in front of Ivana's bedroom door, flanked by the hulking forms of Diga and Triga.

Bjorn decided for the first time that he hated the way Ivana's security team dressed – suit coats that were always too small over turtle necks that invariably had the marks of breakfast on them.

Diga took a step forward and shook his head. "Mr. Bjorn," he crooned, "maybe now not good time for visit."

"Da," Triga agreed. "Maybe you go to kitchen. Find Trinette."

Bjorn was certain at that moment that he was not the only one Trinette was fucking. Abruptly, he was disgusted with the lot of them. Diga and Triga in their obnoxious suits who could not speak proper English though they had learned it in primary school, that whore Trinette, the even bigger whore in the bedroom, the creepy hairy bastard in there with her, and every human being that came to mind.

Bjorn smiled. "Did she command you to not let me in?" he asked.

Both security guards shifted their bulky forms on their flattened feet.

"No," Triga admitted. "She no forbid."

Bjorn gave him a nudge in the ribs. "Come on," he said. "you know this is not the first time."

Diga and Triga both gave nods with their heavy heads, knowing quite well the depravity of their employer, and moved aside.

Bjorn passed between them and paused. Soft voices and laughter came from within, along with the reek of cologne. Bjorn watched his hand turn the handle and push open the door. He was not aware of closing it behind him, but he did.

It was some time before the pair tangled in the sheets even noticed him standing in the doorway and that in itself was enough to make his blood grow warmer in his veins.

You are nothing, Rohn had said.

Finally, a mop of dark hair rose from the pillows and dark eyes peered out from a narrow face that was in sore need of a shave.

"You!" a voice challenged from the cloud of cologne and hair. "What are you doing? What do you want?"

Ivana's rumpled mess of blonde waves bolted up and then, spying Bjorn, laid her head down on the Serb's furry chest. "Bjorn!" she scolded, "You not supposed to be home yet!" She laughed and traced a finger through a continent of dark hair. "Not to worry my lion," she purred at the futbol star. "He is my tiger. My Siberian tiger."

Tropya snorted. "More of a paper tiger," he mused aloud.

Ivana laughed. "Yes," she agreed. "Paper tiger." Both lovers laughed.

A pet, Rohn had scoffed.

"Go back to cage, paper tiger!" Ivana called, laughing. "I send for you vhen I vant you."

A plaything.

Bjorn backed away from the door, his face burning as hot as his blood, and their laughter followed him, mocking him. Suddenly, he was filled with a rage he had never known. His vision took on a red tint and his body shook. Hands clenched into fists, his body jerked as it lunged forward before he sharply pulled it back.

Diga and Triga first, he thought, his mind calculating quickly through the haze of red that had descended over his eyes. *Diga and Triga first.*

He walked back through the door.

༺ঔৣ༻

Charity did indeed manage to pull a media stunt that induced the exchange of thousands of "outdated constructs" for the newer models that Faith and Gwendolyn churned out. I don't know how many lives she saved or "incidents" she prevented, but she saved GwenSeven billions. Something about it, however, was a little sad. For those of us that knew, the new constructs that the company began to mass produce were but shabby shadows next to first three runs.

From there a sadness spread like a slow flood and the next eight months seemed to grow darker with each passing week.

Constructs trickled in that had escaped owners. Some had been beaten, most had just been beaten down. Few were as crazed as Rohn Stojacovik. It didn't matter which. It was a terrible thing to see into the darkness of human hearts, and what they were capable of doing.

Next, Zimnya Roza, the ancestral home of Ivana Uri-Van Zandt was at the bottom of the Carpathian Mountains buried under five tons of rock and ice. Investigations were underway as to the cause, and as of yet no one knew the whereabouts of Bjorn Van Zandt or if he was alive.

I spent the better part of those months designing and overseeing the construction of the buildings that would house the third (and some second) run constructs that were returned for upgrades or returned on their own. I only met one, a tall, dark and handsome man named Marco. He had the furtive eyes of an animal that had been abused and my heart went out to him.

Finally, there was Matty. Though I wanted so badly to protect my grandson from the harsher things in life, I could not protect him from the knife in the dark. That knife comes for us all.

His beautiful wife, Haliegh, died giving birth to twins - James and Jack.

There was no conference call, no family meeting on what to do or who to help. I tendered my resignation to the GwenSeven Corporation and moved to Two-Mile City. I had told Matty I would always be there for him and I meant it. It was not a duty or a burden but an opportunity. I had already missed him growing up, as I had with his mother. I was not going to make that mistake ever again.

Llewellyn was there at the compound on the day I was saying my good-byes to Faith and Thomas. She gave me a big hug and a dazzling smile.

"It's not going to be the same without you here, Fletch," she said. "You're part of the original team."

"Thanks for saying so," I told her. "Besides, I'm sure I will see you around. Something here or at the restaurant will undoubtedly need my attention."

"Indeed!" she agreed and gave me a kiss on my cheek.

But I did not see her around. The years passed and turned into decades. The next time I saw that stunning blonde, her blue eyes were glassed over and staring into nothing. And her blood was all over my hands.

TWO TWO

The Boy Vicar exited the spaceport terminal and was greeted by a gust of wind that buffeted his auburn hair in every direction and made his robes billow like sails. He and Jan had circumvented the normal security for spaceports both on their way in to the town of Rishikesh and the way out. The bypass terminal was usually reserved for dignitaries but was also open to high-ranking officials that needed certain exceptions as well as privacy. John Pierre was grateful for both. He did not like having to remove his weapons, even for a few moments, and the paparazzi was incorrigible. Why someone would want a picture of him without the Bauam in it was beyond his imagination.

The pair had gone to perform a security sweep, as they often did before a visit by the Bauam to a strange city. Sometimes, such a sweep required as many as twenty men - all depending on the spaceport, the route to the venue, and the venue itself. Since all were minimal for Rishikesh, it only required two – if they were the right two.

John Pierre was surprised to find an apt pupil and willing assistant in Jan Petrov. The blonde construct, large but gaunt, had filled back out quickly and was now lean and powerfully muscled. Just a week past, the Bauam had nodded approvingly at him, making Jan look away, casting his icy blue eyes humbly down.

More, the Boy Vicar discovered Jan to be an able pilot and enjoyed traveling with him. He was quiet and capable, diligent and devout. The reassigned construct shadowed John Pierre the way the deadly bodyguard shadowed the Bauam. The tall blonde even showed an interest in learning to fight and had begun some simple training that was quickly progressing. Being a pilot, he was often the only one John Pierre took with him when the situation allowed.

The wind at the port was enough to make even the broad-shouldered Jan rock back on his heels before dropping those powerful shoulders and leaning into the wind. "There!" he called, the wind stealing the words as they left his mouth. He pointed to a two-person air buggy that would take them to their craft. The vehicle was a mass of bright orange bars and two rows of seats over three oversized tires. John Pierre nodded and followed him to where the buggy waited and together they climbed into the back.

"Windows!" Jan commanded and, though there was no driver, plexi rose up and filled the spaces between bars, protecting them from the gale outside. "Craft 898," Jan commanded next and the buggy took off, making a sharp right. "That's some wind!" he commented, looking out the window.

"Mmmhmm," John Pierre agreed, his mind distant. When he was not required to think of the Bauam, he thought of Hope. He could not help but compare the color of the buggy to the color of her hair and think what treachery the current winds would do to it.

He missed her in a powerful way, an emotion that humans might have classified as desperate. He longed to see her face up close, to have her touch him in the gentle manner she always used. He wanted to feel her hair tickle his cheek the way it did when she leaned near him. He wanted to hear her laugh. Most of all, he wanted to ask her about the kiss.

Their kiss had haunted him in the most welcome way for thirty-eight years. That one moment had carved his life into two pieces ever since. He had been determined to ask her about it the last time he had seen her but they had never been alone.

During the days his mind was his own. Hope herself had programmed the ever-ready vigilance into his DNA, his unstoppable drive and unfaltering dedication. But at night he was prey to the dreams that overtook his conscious mind. Most of those dreams were about the time aboard the Bauam's great starship when Hope had kissed him. And he had kissed her back.

In the most modest of dreams, he simply relived the kiss and awakened feeling blessed, refreshed, and part of everything good in the galaxy.

In other dreams the kiss went further, with Hope touching him, sometimes all over. In the last few years he found himself touching her as well in his dreams and, in one, had pulled off her dress completely.

In all dreams of this type he woke with an erection that was often painful, at which point he would get out of bed and pray on his knees until it went away. Pleasures of the flesh were strictly forbidden to Zealots.

His control was his own during the day and he never let his mind drift to such impure thoughts, but questions would often rise in his mind - simple bubbles of curiosity. He knew some things to be absolute, such as actions like the ones in his dreams were only allowed to people who were married. And because sex was forbidden, Zealots of the One never married.

One day, after he had moved a grif of wine barrels for Friar Emmet, he sat down on a high stool at the kitchen table to ask a few questions. The Friar had pulled himself a glass of the new wine to give it a taste and sat with the construct, smacking his lips in obvious appreciation of the new vintage.

"Do Zealots ever change their mind?" John Pierre asked, making the Friar choke a bit on his wine. "Not about the One," John Pierre amended quickly, afraid he had blasphemed. "I mean, do they ever change their mind about being married? Do they ever fall in love after they have taken their vows to the One?"

"Ahhh!" Friar Emmet exclaimed, clearing a drop of wine from his throat. He offered a plate of cheese to John Pierre who smiled and shook his head in the negative. "It happens," the Friar conceded, selecting a piece of blue cheddar and taking a nibble. "Not often, but it does happen that two true Zealots fall in love. Especially when they work together."

"What do they do?" John Pierre asked.

"Sometimes, if they discover the feelings soon enough, they simply go their own ways and continue their service to the One." He did not mention that some ran away together and even more had illicit affairs. Most of the priory thought it prudent never to admit such things, thinking it gave others ideas. "If they are passionate for one another," he did inform the construct, "and unable to control their feelings, they might ask their Sauam for a Renauge."

"A Renauge?" John Pierre asked. "What is that?"

"It is a ceremony. The couple kneels before their Sauam, who opens their scars." Friar Emmet tilted his head back and motioned to his neck. He bore no scar himself but John Pierre knew what he meant. "Then they bleed out," the Friar continued, "fulfilling their lifelong pledge to the One while leaving this world together. In the hopes, of course, that they will be born again together and this time be able to find one another before they make their vows."

Such is not to be between me and Hope, John Pierre thought, though without any feelings of sadness. His life, which had no end date in mind, was a planned life of servitude. One he accepted without question. It was not only his duty to protect the Bauam, it was his honor. Still, he wondered about that kiss.

"Everything Jake?" Jan asked with a smile, a saying he had picked up from the Luma Boys.

"Everything is as the One wills," John Pierre answered solemnly, eliciting an equally solemn nod from Jan.

"You are just so quiet," Jan remarked. "Is it Rohn that

occupies your thoughts?"

"Right now, no. But of late, yes."

John Pierre had told Jan of what Rohn Stojacovik had told those at the GwenSeven reunion. Since then, the man had contacted them many times, trying to arrange a meeting. The last time the outraged construct had spoken to them it was to give a list of atrocities committed by humans against constructs.

"What do you think of it all?" Jan asked as they left the buggy to board their craft. It waited on the blacktop tarmac next to a squat air control tower, a sizable mid-range star-hopper that Jan would pilot home. The capricious wind was already dying down.

John Pierre stopped at the edge of the stairway with his hand on a collapsible rail and fixed Jan with his own bright blue eyes.

"You know, despite his claims and what I have seen in the holos, I have a hard time believing that so many humans could have such evil in them."

Jan looked away before he spoke and when he did his voice was full of sorrow. "There is much evil in the worlds, John Pierre," he said softly. "That men think they are above it is folly."

The angelic looking bodyguard clapped the other construct on a shoulder that was approximately the same size as a young bull. He opened his mouth to speak but was silenced by a Klaxon coming from the control tower, signaling that another ship was on approach.

The two constructs hurried into their craft, the new wind already whipping John Pierre's cassock around his legs as the atmosphere was shoved roughly in all directions. He made a right turn as soon as he was inside and into the fuselage while Jan hooked left towards the cockpit. The stairs rolled back, collapsing into a platform and the door closed behind them.

Unhurried now, the bodyguard took a seat at random since he was the only passenger. He carefully tucked the borders of his robe down so he could secure the safety webbing then planted an elbow in the shallow sill of the window on his left. He rested his chin on his thumb, his forefinger curved thoughtfully over his upper lip. It would be some minutes for Jan to make ready and get them cleared for departure.

The incoming craft landed and settled on a series of braces but the construct hardly noticed it as his mind drifted back to Hope.

What does it is mean? he pondered. *Does it mean she loves me?*

These had long ceased to be actual questions, simply the most secret wishes in the deepest places in his heart.

You need to ask her, he told himself for the millionth time. He had been determined to ask her at his last check, at the reunion. But there was never an opportune time. And now there would not be another check for fifty years.

Fifty years. Time never seemed long to him unless he contemplated the interval between when he would see her next. He felt as if iron bands were wrapping around his heart and locked with a clock that would slowly tick down until he could finally be with her again. John Pierre, alone at the nonce with his only emotion, gave a deep sigh.

Fifty years.

Then there she was.

His eyes, though sharp and quick, were only slightly cognizant of the movement as the craft next to his lowered a ramp. The craft was much smaller than the one in which he sat. Newer and shinier, it was obviously made for short trips rather than deep space travel. It was most likely a tender from a much larger ship.

His peripheral vision had watched absently as his mind had wandered. But when his eyes caught sight of a cloud of copper-colored hair as it swirled around the head of the first person to exit the tender, his mind snapped back to the present with a force so strong that he felt a twang throughout his entire body. It was as if a metal string had been pulled taut and then let go.

"Hope," he whispered, sitting up straight in his seat. He could hardly believe she was there. He would have believed her to be an apparition conjured by his thoughts but there she was, undeniably beautiful and undeniably real. Even from twenty meters away he could see her with perfect clarity and was taken, as always, with her perfect skin and hair and eyes.

She looked around curiously at the bottom of the ramp, her wild mane blowing in the wind. He knew that Jan would take another minute or two for his own checks while the engines warmed and they waited for clearance from the control tower.

John Pierre's right hand went to his hip and released the safety webbing, ready to bolt from his chair to the cockpit and have Jan stall the engines and recall the staircase when another passenger came down the ramp of the other craft. John Pierre paused, half-raised from his seat, curious.

It was a man, his golden skin and slightly slanted eyes marking him as unmistakably Indasian. His yellow, belted robes and tonsured head marked him unmistakably as a monk, though certainly not a monk of the One.

He is part of the heathen religion of Zenarchy, John Pierre thought while he watched the strange man walk up behind Hope.

Then, just as he was about to push himself from his seat and tell Jan to hold the craft, the man reached out and gathered Hope's wildly flying hair into a fist and pushed it to one side before he leaned forward and kissed her bare, freckled shoulder where it met the base of her neck.

John Pierre's blue eyes were like small saucers in his porcelain face. His mouth was very dry. He remained half-standing, rooted to his spot ready to bolt and save Hope from the demon that had snuck up behind her, but Hope was turning, smiling at the man. She put her arms around his shoulders and pressed her white forehead against his golden one.

John Pierre's eyes, so piercing and so blue and so sharp, were able to pick out the smallest details, even from over twenty meters away and through a double pane of Perspex.

He could see the green of her eyes and the gold that flecked them. Had he wished, he could count the freckles on her forehead as it pressed against the golden brow of the monk. It was a gesture so simple and yet so intimate that it made his blood run cold one moment and then boil the next.

What does it mean? he asked himself, his mind racing and racking itself for an answer. *Does it mean more than a kiss?* His logic, acquired over a span of almost sixty years, was still quite nascent. *It cannot,* he reasoned. *She is simply putting her head against his head. It could mean anything. It certainly is not more than a kiss. Not more than our kiss.*

His manufactured brain gave him perfect recall, something that soothed him to sleep every night and came back now as he willed it - her small hands grasping his face, her lips against his, her mouth moist as it opened and searched his own.

He compared what he saw then to what he saw now. Something so intimate against something much more innocent.

No, he thought, trying to slow his racing mind and racing heart. *This is more. It's in her eyes.*

A feeling of desolation seemed to grab at him, just as Jan grabbed his shoulder. With a speed that defied any physical law, John Pierre was out of his seat and facing the other construct in the aisle, his blade against the other man's throat.

The tall, blonde construct swallowed slowly, but did not move away.

"John Pierre," he whispered, asking for the second time since entering the fuselage, "are you alright?" Jan cleared his throat carefully and continued. "I was alerted that your webbing was not in place and you did not answer me over the com."

"I am fine," John Pierre answered coolly, making a half meter of sharpened steel disappear into his sleeve like magic. "I thought I might need the restroom, but decided I'll be fine until we are spaceborne." It was not a lie. He did need to use the restroom.

Jan nodded but his blue eyes were full of uncertainty. "Are you sure you are alright?" he queried again, his blonde brows furrowed.

"Of course," John Pierre said, raising a hand to assure him. "How long before we can depart?"

"Right away," Jan said, his voice soft. He watched as John Pierre sat back down, but this time on the other side of the craft.

"Excellent," the bodyguard said. "I never like to leave the Holy Father any longer than I must." Jan nodded, his brow relaxing but still marked with a small line as he returned to the cockpit. Jean Pierre fixed his safety webbing across his cassock and looked out the window. On this side, thankfully, there was nothing to see except windswept prairie. Still, his mind, and his heart, raced.

What does it mean? he thought desperately.

TWO THREE

"This is getting serious," Llewellyn said, looking around the drawing room. "They are really going to go to war."

She used a pair of golden tongs to retrieve cubed ice from a golden bucket and dropped them into a cut crystal tumbler and covered them with a carmine-colored liquid from a crystal decanter. She refilled Charity's glass with the same and sat next to her on a small couch covered in red and gold velvet brocade. She wore a short, belted robe of sapphire silk. Charity wore a similar robe but silver in color.

Evan, his golden hair still wet from a shower, poured glasses of champagne for Faith and Gwen. Having excused all of the castle's usual staff-in-waiting for a private conference, he took the part of chief butler.

"We don't know that for sure," Faith said, sounding unusually unsure herself, accepting the glass from Evan. She sat in a narrow high-backed chair wearing a white caftan with gold trim. "Not yet."

"They wouldn't," Gwen said softly, her tone even more lacking in conviction than Faith's. She waved away the flute of champagne that Evan offered her, a deep crease between her brows. "They couldn't!"

"It's not war," Evan assured them. He took a seat next to her on the couch that faced Charity and Llewellyn and took a sip of champagne. "What they are glorifying as a revolution are just isolated attacks that the IGC is classifying as acts of terrorism."

"Christ," Llewellyn muttered, "who will come after us first, I wonder? The people or the government?"

"Or the Chimera," Evan added from his place next to Gwen. The term Rohn had used to describe constructs had become the name taken by those that followed him. Llewellyn gave him a flat stare with her blue eyes, though there was no malice in it.

"Well," Charity announced, "acts of war or acts of terrorism, it seems that Rohn Stojacovik has been incredibly busy these past five years."

"He's been fanatical," Llewellyn told the group. "Like a Cassar General with his ass on fire. I don't know if he has physically gotten around the galaxy to rile people up or if he has simply accomplished it all via viral communication…"

"Probably both," Evan interjected.

"…but he has reached out and has been inciting constructs in every civilized system," Llewellyn finished.

"Even constructs that have not seen neglect or abuse," Charity said. "The unrest is growing, and they are looking to him as a leader."

Faith made a grunting sound in disgust. "He doesn't have what it takes to be a real leader."

Charity drew a deep breath and nodded before she continued. "I agree, which is what has kept this simmering pot on the back burner and has kept it from boiling over."

"It won't boil over," Evan said. "The two main things a revolution needs are a leader and financial backing." His broad shoulders pulled up under his shirt for a second, bunching the thin fabric. "He has neither."

Faith looked at him and nodded in agreement and approval.

Charity's red lips pulled down at the corners. "He has the money," she announced bitterly. Everyone but Llewellyn, who already knew, gaped at her in shock. Llewellyn looked away and took a long drink from her glass before speaking.

"Not enough to buy an army," she assured them when her

drink was half gone, "but certainly enough to start one."

"Where is the money coming from?" Faith asked.

"We have been unable to trace the exact source, but the funds are coming from Indasia," Llewellyn said.

"The Yakuza?" Gwen asked, louder than she intended as she stared at Llewellyn. "Mr. Harasuka?" she asked, her voice considerably lower.

"We don't know the who, just the where. But all signs strongly suggest that they are the only group in that system with that kind of money, unless a number of Indasia's bio-tech companies pooled their funds."

"That would make sense," Gwen said, "since we are their main competitor."

"Is there any way we can find out for sure?" Evan asked.

"I'll have Thomas put in a call to Noa," Faith told them. "Alice," she said quickly, correcting herself. "Whomever. I want to speak to her as soon as possible."

"We already tried," Llewellyn said, her blue eyes darting to those seated around the small, polished table. "To the private communicator we embedded. No answer. Not even a connection."

Gwen's hand went up over her mouth. "The line is dead?" she asked from behind her fingers. "Noa is dead? What about Nora?"

"Nora was the same result," Charity informed the group, "but we don't think they are dead, not necessarily."

Faith shook her head. "A flatline would have notified us immediately." Her eyes looked away in the second it took her to recant her last thought. "Unless their transmitters were removed or tampered with while they were under sedation," she murmured. Faith fumed inwardly at having found out such critical information from someone else. A moment of heavy silence ensued that even the ice in bucket dared not break. "It doesn't matter now," Faith said at last, her voice resuming its normal firm tone. "What's done is done. We need to make our own plans."

"To prevent a war?" Charity asked. "Or take part in one?"

"War will come," Faith assured her. "If Rohn has found financial backing, especially *that* kind of backing, it's only a matter of time. We cannot prevent it."

"I guess that answers my question," Charity remarked and took a long sip from her drink. The edge of her silver robe slipped off her thigh and she twitched it back.

"It's obvious that he wants one of the First Seven to support him," Gwendolyn said. "Do you really think he can tip any of them?"

Faith looked at her and nodded slowly. "One will. Eventually, one will."

"Then it will be war," Llewellyn said with a sense of finality. "It could take a long, long time – but it will come to war."

"The elves were right," Evan murmured.

"What will happen to the company?" Gwen asked. "What will happen to us?" Her brown and gold eyes went to Charity.

"Well," Charity said, "it depends on how people react. Ninety percent of GwenSeven's funds are untouchable and growing in accounts scattered throughout the Outer Banks."

"*Ninety* percent?" Evan asked.

Charity gave him a beguiling smile. "Of course. I'm not a fool, Evan." Evan returned a smile that said he was not so sure. She cocked her head, her perfectly coiffed golden locks shifting slightly. "Nothing lasts forever. One must prepare."

"Some things last forever," Evan returned, his voice soft.

"But war!" Gwen pressed.

Llewellyn snorted and got up to refill Charity's glass, then her own. "I know," she said, looking at Gwen as she settled back down onto the velvet couch. "I feel it's the one area none of us has any expertise in."

"One of us does," Faith corrected, her gold and brown eyes flicking to Evan, making all other eyes follow.

"Evan?" Charity asked, her blonde brows raised high. "You are an expert in war?"

"He most certainly is not," Gwen told her. She looked around the small group with a frown and, after meeting her sister's eyes, finally sighed. "Though he probably has read every bit of military history from Goa to Golgotha."

"I have no such education," Charity said with a smile. "But my best tactic was always if you can't beat 'em, join 'em."

"But join who?" Llewellyn asked. "Which side? I don't mean to sound snub, but I want to be on the side that wins."

"How about neither?" Gwen suggested. "We could remain neutral."

"We'd be torn to pieces," Llewellyn said. "We need to take part by backing one or the other."

"I agree," Charity said. "We need to put ourselves in a position of power and retain as much control as we can."

"I second that," Faith said with a smile.

"Very well," Gwen relented. "Then I vote for the IGC. I just find it too hard to believe that constructs, despite numbers and leaders and finances, could overthrow the government. An *inter galactic* government."

"Don't underestimate the power of money," Charity told her, sipping her drink.

"Don't underestimate any factor," Evan advised. "Rebellions can be put down in hours with little to no bloodshed, or last for decades and cost millions of lives. Peasants and farmers have been known to overthrow the most powerful of governments. And the Chimera are no mere peasants."

"Well then, professor," Faith said, making a blush creep along the construct's jaw even though he smiled, "since you are the only one of us that has studied military history, what do the odds tell us? Which side is most likely to come out on top?"

Evan grinned. "History tells us that anything can happen and those most often favored to win, do not always win."

"That's horrible advice," Llewellyn said, making a sour face.

"That wasn't my advice," he said, looking genuinely surprised.

"Then what is?" Charity asked. Evan shrugged, making Charity roll her eyes in exasperation. Evan grinned.

"I think the best plan is to hedge your bets. Divide and conquer. Join every side. One, eventually, will come out on top."

"An idea at once both terrifying and sane," Llewellyn remarked.

Faith put her champagne flute on the arm of her chair, holding the bottom steady with her right hand. With her left, she ran her thumbnail over her lips as she thought.

"We would obviously and openly back the IGC and the general populace," she contemplated aloud.

"Side one," Llewellyn stated. "Should they win, we win."

"What about the other side?" Gwen asked. "How do we back the Chimera?"

"Well, we can't back them openly," Charity stated, "not if we publicly support the IGC."

"Then it has to be subversive," Evan said. "We will need to infiltrate them in a way that gives us control. Either to make our presence and support known when the time is right, or to topple them if the situation calls for such a move. Either way should ensure not only our survival but extraordinary success."

A crease formed on Llewellyn's perfectly smooth forehead as her blonde brows drew together. "It makes sense," she decreed. "But how do you propose we do such a thing?"

"Can we program constructs for such work?" Charity asked.

All eyes looked to Faith who, Gwen realized, had been

decidedly quiet during the whole debate, her tawny eyes following the conversation from one person to the next.

"We can do anything," she stated. "The question is, what exactly do we do? Program them to record? To suggest? And how do we get them to blend in so the Chimera don't get suspicious and kill them? I have to admit that, in this situation, my imagination is about as good as theirs."

"Faith!" Gwen admonished. Faith gave her an exaggerated shrug in return.

"We need a spy," Llewellyn said.

"And ours is light years away on another mission," Charity remarked.

Faith shook her head. "I wouldn't send Hope on this mission even if she was here."

"I'll do it."

All eyes turned once again on Evan, this time in real surprise. Faith looked the least shocked, Gwen the most.

"What?" Llewellyn demanded, sitting up so quickly she almost spilled her drink on her robe.

"I'll do it," Evan repeated, putting his glass down on the coffee table. "Charity is right."

"She is?" Llewellyn asked, one hand coming up to cover her heart while sitting back for a better look at her twin.

"Yes," Evan confirmed. "If you can't beat 'em, join 'em."

Charity smiled at Evan over the rim of her glass as she took a long drink, her blue eyes glittering.

"Evan!" Gwen exclaimed, turning in her seat to look at him, horrified. "Are you crazy?"

"No," he said softly, "just ready to do whatever it takes to keep us all safe. And if things keep escalating the way they are, we need to be ready to respond in a decisive manner."

"That doesn't mean it needs to be you," Gwen argued. Evan reached out a hand to lay on her arm to reassure her but she pulled away, upset. Evan sighed.

"We need someone we can trust. We need someone that can be ready without being made or trained or programmed. It has to be someone that can blend seamlessly with the Chimera. I'm the only one who can do that."

Gwen looked at her sisters for support but all she got in return were eyes that obviously saw the reason in what Evan was saying. "We can train anyone to do it!" she informed him, informed everyone, her voice rising on every word. "They are already committing murder and, like Charity said, it hasn't even boiled over yet! You can get hurt or killed or worse!"

"What's worse than hurt or killed?" Llewellyn asked.

Gwen fixed her tawny eyes on Llewellyn's blue ones and this time her tone was eerily calm. "I could never see him again." A somber silence fell over the small group and Gwen turned back to Evan. "If it truly comes to war, they will kill you if they know you are a spy."

"They won't know what I am doing - I don't even have to know what I am doing," he told her with gentle smile. "I'm sure Faith can ... tinker with my memory," he said, glancing at Faith who nodded, seeing the direction in which he was headed. "That way there would be nothing I could do or say to give myself away. It will be the quickest way we could win this if we are playing both sides. Even if we can't topple them from inside or take the credit if they win, it will give us the greatest advantage to know what *they* are up to – to know as much of their plans as we can."

Tears welled up in her brown and gold eyes and spilled over her cheeks. Evan cupped her face in his hands and wiped them away with his thumbs. Fresh ones spilled down and he wiped those away too.

"Besides," he continued, "it won't be right away. Maybe it won't come to that at all. But we need to be ready if it does."

"Then let us hope that it does not," Gwen said softly. "Being away from you would be hard enough. Knowing you are in danger, I don't think I could bear it."

Evan smiled at her. "You are stronger than you think."

Gwen grunted, unconvinced, as Evan arched an eyebrow at Faith. "What say you, General de Rossi?"

"For the love of the One!" Charity scolded. "Don't call her that!"

"She already has a God complex," Llewellyn muttered before she took a long pull from her drink.

"I most certainly do not," Faith objected, though she grinned at Evan like a Cheshire cat while she thought. "Like Gwen," she said finally, "I will hope that it does not come down to putting you in danger. But, should that be the case, I'll be ready."

"Well," Llewellyn announced, "I guess we have our tentative plan."

Faith smiled and finished the champagne in her flute. "In that case, I'm going to head back home."

"You're not going to stay for the party?" Charity asked.

"Party?" Faith asked, looking perplexed.

"Yes," Llewellyn agreed, "our guests should be here in about an hour."

"But you're dressed for bed!"

"It's a pajama party," she explained with a dazzling smile.

Faith made a face. "I'm surprised you don't sleep…" she stopped mid-sentence and rolled her eyes. "Never mind."

Evan stood. "I think we'll be leaving, too," he said, helping Gwen to her feet.

"No!" Charity exclaimed, pouting. "There will be music and dancing, and I promise we'll keep our robes on for at least the first two hours."

"Speak for yourself," Llewellyn advised her twin.

"Thank you for the offer," Evan said, giving the two of them a dazzling smile of his own, "but I haven't quite gotten around to learning how to dance yet."

"You're kidding!" Llewellyn accused as she got to her feet. "Not in all these years?" Evan shook his head.

Charity stood as well, smoothing out her robe. "That's a shame," she told him. "Gwen is a wonderful dancer."

Evan looked at Gwendolyn, surprised. Gwen shrugged. "It's a form of art, really."

"Not the way Charity does it," Faith remarked. Everyone laughed and headed for the door, Llewellyn calling for servants. Cheek kisses were plentiful as they said their loves.

# TWO FOUR

John Pierre finished reading the passage and closed the heavy book, keeping one finger inside to mark his place. His blue eyes looked up to see if the Holy Father wanted him to continue or if it was time to stop for the night. After a good half hour or more of reading, the Bauam was usually staring off into the flames in the fireplace as he reabsorbed the words he already knew by heart. This time he was staring intently at his bodyguard, sitting only inches away so that he may hear the younger man read.

The Bauam laid a hand upon John Pierre's knee and the construct felt the old man's gray eyes bore into his soul.

"What is it?" the Holy Father asked. "What troubles you, my son?"

It had been weeks since John Pierre had seen Hope at the spaceport and it had been eating him up inside. His days at the priory had been full of realizations and most of them filled him with sorrow, or dread, or both. He prayed for trips to sermons or lectures where he would be guarding the Bauam and his attention would be necessary and singular. When involved in his sole occupation, nothing could distract him. Otherwise, he was condemned to wander the dormitories and gardens, thoughtful and full of melancholy. Even his Bible offered no solace.

The construct first considered telling the Bauam the whole story, starting with the moment he had opened his eyes in the recovery room and saw Hope for the first time. Then he realized that it would be easier to make the story short. It never occurred to him to make nothing of it for he would never lie to the Holy Father.

"There is a girl, a woman I suppose, who I recently realized that I love," he confessed. "I had suspected as much for many years but I did not know for sure until I saw her with another man. And now, I feel only confusion."

The Bauam looked at him with deep empathy and squeezed his leg. "Women are treacherous," he confided to his bodyguard. "They bring nothing but heartache and pain." John Pierre nodded at his words, believing them as he would the gospel. "That is why we men must rely on one another," he added, his voice becoming even more deep and gravelly with every word. He laid a gnarled hand upon John Pierre's shoulder and pulled him close.

The bodyguard leaned towards the Holy Father, thinking that he would kiss his cheeks and bless him as he often did, but the old man's lips sought his own and forced them open. There was a second of confusion, then a second of shock, before John Pierre was on his feet.

"What are you doing?" he demanded though his voice was hardly more than a whisper. The back of his hand rose to cover his mouth and his bright blue eyes stared over his slender fingers at the Holy Father.

"What does it look like?" the Bauam queried.

John Pierre's head moved slowly from side to side, his perfectly combed auburn hair reflecting the lights of the flambeaux. "I truly do not know."

"I have thirsted for you many nights, John Pierre," the Bauam stated, matter of fact. "It is time to quench that thirst."

The construct stared at the aging man still seated in his chair, only the faintest glimmer of understanding showing in his bright blue eyes. "It is forbidden," John Pierre whispered.

"Love between men is not forbidden by the One!" the Bauam stated, his voice firm and strong as if delivering a sermon. "The One encourages us to all love one another, it is one of the tenets that make the One so great."

"It is forbidden by men of our order," the construct replied, becoming more confident as his shock was replaced by indignation.

"Our order!" the Bauam scoffed. "You are part of no order! You are not even a common country friar!"

"It is forbidden to all that have taken a Zealot's vows!" John Pierre argued.

"Bah!" the Holy Father spat. "The boys satisfy my needs, but not my tastes!"

"The boys?" John Pierre asked, tossed back into a sea of confusion. "What boys?"

But even as the words left his lips an idea began to wash over him as he watched the Holy Father brace his withered hands on the arms of his chair. The idea lapped at his feet like a child standing on the water's edge of a calm bay.

"You are a man!" the Bauam declared passionately as he rose to his feet and moved closer to his bodyguard. "As near as you can be, anyway. But so strong! So entrancing! You taunt the works of the One with your beauty!"

John Pierre fell back a step, realizing how strong the old man could be in voice and body. His lungs were powerful and he knew how to use them. The man might appear frail, but how frightening he could be as he wielded the thunder of the One! Especially to a young boy.

The waves of realization lapped at his feet.

"Why do you think they made you this way?" the Bauam demanded, lurching closer as John Pierre fell back another step.

The construct felt as if he had waded too far into the bay of comprehension and now he was sinking into waters of bewilderment. Each time he surfaced and began to understand, he was claimed and sunk by the waves once again.

"Who?" he asked. "What way?"

"Those de Rossi whores!" the Bauam roared. "Making you the way you are! Just so I could not resist possessing you!"

"They did this?" John Pierre asked, the thinking part of his brain working incessantly to come to terms with what was happening.

"They represent everything that is wrong in this universe! *GwenSeven*!" The Bauam spat the name as if were a bitter curse with a bitter taste. "Even in their name they flaunt what they represent - the seven deadly sins! But they got one thing right and that was you! For me!"

The construct backed away until the backs of his legs hit a table and he reached out reflexively to steady a lamp that threatened to topple.

"I do not think that this is what they had planned," he said through lips now numb with shock.

"Like hell they didn't! Now remove my cassock, you imbecile, and do as I say! Or, if you are too stupid to see what I need, send for my wine so one of the boys may show you!"

One of the boys.

It finally all clicked together for John Pierre. Avery, trying to be strong and not cry. And the other Luma Boy, the one who had run into him still crying and with what John Pierre now realized must have been terror.

"Ebon," he whispered.

"Yes, Ebon!" the Bauam thundered. "Barely ten years old and still he knows what to do for a man!"

John Pierre recoiled. The emotions welled and rushed within him as if he were truly in a bay, a man in the sea, one that had swallowed too much seawater in his attempt to survive. Confusion, horror, disgust, sympathy, and anger all roiled within him until he could not stand any more, yet the Bauam advanced.

"Do you think what you do could not be done by drone or robot?" the Bauam demanded, waving his arms. "You are the same! Empty and soulless! Just more pretty! And able to offer what cold metal cannot!"

John's Pierre's mind boiled over like pot that could no longer retain its contents. He certainly couldn't bear to hear another word or insult from someone he had revered for near his whole life. The old man advanced, reaching out with gnarled hands – not to bless but to desecrate – and grabbed hold of his bodyguard.

The construct's next move was as simple and reflexive as his thoughts.

The Bauam, one claw-like hand digging into his bodyguard's arm, drew a huge breath to let out another batch of humiliations upon his uncooperative construct but that one breath was his last.

John Pierre jerked back, his blade out faster than the eye could follow. There was a flicker of light, a reflection from the fire on the steel, and the Bauam's head - bearing an expression of complete surprise - fell to the carpet of his room with an ungraceful thump. Gray eyes stared from pockets of wrinkled skin with holier than thou condemnation – even in death. The lips were pursed, as if ready to deliver a scathing sermon or unthinkable demand upon a young Luma Boy.

John Pierre sank to his knees next to the severed head, looking away from those lips. The memory of that dry tongue poking at his own mouth was still horrifyingly fresh.

A bereaved mortal might have asked, grievingly, *what have I done?*

John Pierre, however, was no mortal. He knew exactly what he had done, just not what to do next. Closing his eyes against the accusing glare of the Bauam, he folded his hands and bowed his head. John Pierre prayed to the One True for guidance as he had hundreds of times in the past fifty-three years of his existence.

This time, however, the One answered.

What do I say to the others? John Pierre prayed, beseeching. *The deacons and the friars?*

He could almost feel the gentle touch of the One upon his head as his auburn hair ruffled in a non-existent breeze.

Do you really think they do not know? the voice answered.

John Pierre held still though his face contorted with pain and his body wanted desperately to crumple. He thought of all of the deacons he had spoken to about the boys, fearing for their health, and the way that all had responded. It was obvious, now, that they were quick to make excuses and dismiss his fears and get him away from their company as soon as they possibly could. The realization made a newfound rage boil up inside him.

They knew! They knew what was happening to these boys! These boys that only wanted to do well and serve the One! They knew and they did nothing! John Pierre was startled from his internal rage by a loud and rapid knock upon the door.

"John Pierre!" The muffled cry came from beyond the oaken door. "Is everything alright?"

John Pierre recognized the voice as the only other construct Zealot and his companion of late, Jan Petrov.

The bodyguard never hesitated. "Come in!" he called.

Jan walked in and took in the entire scene with a single sweep of his icy blue eyes as John Pierre rose to his feet.

"The Holy Father...was impure," he said in explanation.

It was all that Jan needed to hear and the tall construct nodded his blonde head in understanding. For that simple gesture, he was endowed to John Pierre's heart and trust forever. Together they stared at the face of the dead man on the floor. The bodyguard shook his head slowly, his blade still in his hand and hanging heavy by his side.

"It seems as if that Rohn Stojacovik was right," he said sadly.

"Humans really are horrible creatures, weak and immoral and vile. If this man, the most holy soul in the universe, can commit such atrocities then they are all surely doomed."

Jan Petrov turned to face him.

"What do you request, John Pierre? I will do anything you ask of me."

The mind of the bodyguard worked like it never had before, and it worked quickly. He blew a huff of air through his nose in disgust.

"First, never call me by that name again," the construct said, looking at the glazed gray eyes of the Bauam, remembering the day the man had bought and named him. He turned his bright blue eyes to the icy gaze of Jan Petrov and held his gaze. "Next, pack whatever personals you feel you need, we are leaving."

"How long will we be gone?" Jan asked.

The bodyguard only took a moment to answer. His thoughts were moving quickly, in a way they never had before, but he took a second to give Jan a look of resignation. "Forever," he told him. "Meet me outside of my room in five minutes."

"Yes..." the tall blonde paused and the other construct answered his unspoken question.

"JP. Call me JP from now on."

Jan gave a quick dip of his head to show he understood and then turned on his heel and was gone, realizing for the first time that they shared the same initials.

We truly are intertwined, he thought as he strode away and out the door, filled with strong purpose and determination. It was not the first time for Jan. *Born yet again,* he thought, lengthening his stride and moving so fast he was nearly running.

In the Bauam's bedroom, JP's eyes swept across the scene before him. He took a deep breath as he looked upon the Bauam, the body crumpled on its side and the head with its face towards the sky. He had to resist the urge to kick one or the other. Or both.

Instead, he made the sign of the circles in front of his own body and whispered the blessing for the lost soul to find the One. Inwardly, he hoped the man came back as a cockroach.

Then, after carefully blotting a splat of blood from the back cover with his sleeve, the construct picked up the old man's ancient Bible and went quickly to his own room. It did not take him long to pack, he had done it many times before. Yet he stood in front of his closet, a small armory in itself, for long moments, deciding.

When he came from his room he saw Jan take a step back. The bodyguard carried in his hand what he always did when he traveled - his small satchel with extra cassock and the small items from his bathroom. Laid carefully on top, where his own Bible normally was, sat the great book so recently taken from the Bauam's bed chambers. When he saw Jan recoil, he assumed it was because strapped with so many weapons he must look like a one man army.

Two belts were slung over his chest like a bandolier and hung with two dozen metal T's that Jan knew were high-powered grenades. Also, over his cassock was a chest holster that housed two photon pistols against his ribs. Another holster was low around his hips and stocked with a pair of laser firearms. His right hand held the blade that had relieved the Holy Father of his not-so-holy head.

Jan was indeed surprised by the amount of munitions, but what gave him a gasp was the fire blazing in the eyes of his new leader. The blue irises shone so bright that it looked like they were filed with neon gas.

"Are you ready?" JP asked.

Jan bowed his head. "I will follow you anywhere, John…JP."

JP looked left and then right down the hallways. The hour was growing late and there was no one about.

All the better, he thought.

"The helioport that serves the priory," he said after a moment, "what is there that you can fly?"

Jan looked away as he recalled the types of aircraft that were always there.

"Anything," he answered, turning his face to meet JP's blazing stare. "Do you want something that will go fast or go far?" he asked. "And how many will we be taking?"

JP's lips pressed together into a white line before he spoke. "Just us. Going far."

"We can take the Abkler," Jan suggested without hesitation.

JP was about to nod but his mind was working in that strange new fashion. It felt like a numb hand, opening and closing, flexing itself to reawaken.

"Can you fly the *Monastery*?" JP asked. It was the Bauam's great airship, the size of a small city. They were only two, but JP's mind was already trying to plan for an unknown future. It was like trying to grasp a weapon with the same, numb hand.

Jan blinked at him, surprised, then nodded. JP smiled, knowing that he had truly been blessed by the One to have a pilot by his side. He straightened, breathing deeply.

"There is work I must do first," he said firmly.

The features of the other construct never wavered. He simply reached out and relieved JP of his satchel. With a flick of the newly freed hand, JP was suddenly holding his other blade.

"The boys should not be out at this hour, but if you see any, do not let them come down this hall. Send them to bed."

Jan nodded, seeing for the first time that the location of JP's room was no accident. The dormitories were all on a long, central hallway. The bedrooms of the deacons were on the left, in order of ascendancy, ending with the Bauam's personal suite. To the right was a hallway that led to the bunk rooms of the Luma Boys. The room of the sole bodyguard was between the two and across from the main entrance.

Alerting him to anyone entering the building, Jan thought, *as well as anyone passing between the dormitories.*

JP closed his eyes for a moment as he readied himself and then was gone, his cassock flapping like a cloak in the wind as he disappeared down the left hallway. Jan knew that the west wing of the dormitories housed fifty friars, ten deacons, the Thauam, and the Bauam (though now just his body).

Jan stood in the dim light between the long hallways, the flickering light of the candles turning his hair to burnished gold. He realized he was at a figurative crossroads as well and wondered briefly if he was making the right decision. He knew what JP was doing now, though the construct was as silent as death on cat's paws. And he knew that he meant to join Rohn Stojacovik in his fight against humankind.

It would be war. Countless deaths.

What will be asked of me? he wondered. *What will I be prepared to do?*

He thought of what he had suffered, the pain he had endured, so great that he thought it would kill him. For a time, he had truly wanted to die. Then he straightened, drawing back his massive shoulders.

There must be repercussions for what has been done, he told himself. *I will see this through to the end, and do anything that is asked of me. I am already prepared,* he realized. *I have been for a long time.*

His blue eyes caught movement in the hallway and his head snapped to the left, to see JP emerge from the darkness. His cassock was soaked in blood from his chin to his knees and stained on the sleeves past the elbows. He looked like a butcher after a long day. But for the Boy Vicar, his day was far from finished.

The sight of it made Jan's stomach clench and he felt weak in his knees before he was filled with a deep satisfaction. He smiled and was going to move towards the door when he saw

JP's face contort as if in a spasm of pain. But before he could ask, JP sheathed his blades and headed for the east wing.

Jan sucked in a breath through clenched teeth before he questioned his new master for the first and last time with only two words.

"The boys?" he queried desperately, his voice a quiet hiss, his eyes a silent plea.

JP paused but did not look back. Instead, he began pulling t-grenades off of the belts that crossed his chest and setting the detonations. It was a hard decision, but one he had made over the corpse of the Bauam.

Better for them to start again fresh, he had thought, *than to live bearing the shame. A shame that should never have been theirs.*

His head turned slightly towards Jan as his thumbs flicked the pins from the grenades and his next words echoed in Jan's ears and his heart, long after the concussing sounds of the explosions had faded.

"The One will know his own."

# TWO FIVE

The child was a beautiful mess.

And fast.

She tore through the ship like a whirling dervish blown by hurricane winds. It was often only by chance that Madeline, or anyone else for that matter, could catch her. But it was usually Madeline that gave chase, sweeping the child up in her arms and tickling her till she squealed and made everyone smile.

Her hair was darker than either Hope's or Madeline's, a murky red rather than bright copper, and stick straight rather than wild curls. Nonetheless, her hair was always wild, jutting out in all directions. Her clothes were often torn, usually from a spill taken while running like hell through the halls of the great spaceship, *New Beginnings.*

Her eyes were spectacular. Mutant genes that had run as wild as the child herself. They were bright brown, edged with black and shot with green and amber and gold.

She was the delight of the ship, which was a feat in itself.

Two thirds of the passengers were constructs that had been mistreated or downright abused. The other third was composed of constructs that had simply decided that they wanted a life that was not one of servitude. Almost all aboard were bitter, to varying degrees, but the child always brought a smile to every face.

Even Marco, the ship's taciturn captain and leader, loved to see the child and made efforts to have treats for her should she visit by purpose or accident.

The only passengers besides the constructs were the wild-haired de Rossi twins, the monks, and the child.

"Brush her hair," Hope commanded Madeline as they sat with the child, drinking tea with Hahn and Elaeric in the small common room they all shared. Hope reached out a hand to smooth hair that was sticking out in all directions. Madeline rolled her green eyes at her twin from over the rim of her cup before she put it down, indignant.

"I did! Elaeric says it's the static electricity on the ship that makes it do that. Even mine is crazier than usual."

"Mine too," Hope agreed, "though it doesn't look like *that*."

"Mine as well," Elaeric joked, dipping his head down to give everyone a view of his bald, golden pate. Madeline laughed and poked him in the ribs with a delicate finger.

Hahn smiled at his friend and reached out a hand to stroke the child's locks. "Her hair is more fine," he explained, "and there is considerably less of it."

The waif looked up from where she sat on the floor, playing with a set of blocks, and smiled at him. Hahn felt his heart melt at that smile.

"You used to have my whole heart," he confessed to Hope, moving his gaze to catch her green eyes glitter from over her teacup. "Now this little lady has half. But, good news, I am quite sure the size of my heart doubled, so you are still left with same amount."

"Well then," Hope said, smiling as she put down her cup, "we are both lucky women." She laid her head down on Hahn's shoulder, watching the child play.

The blocks were painted in garish colors and each was carved with a single number or letter in the Anglicus alphabet. The child did not speak very much but was extraordinarily bright and loved to spell things with the blocks. She arranged five side by side and looked expectantly at Elaeric. The monk cocked his head so could read over her shoulder.

"Ember," he said, smiling broadly. "Who is Ember?" The child returned a smile just as broad and pointed a small finger at her own chest. "That's right!" the monk cried. "You are Ember! Very good!"

"It is very good," Hope agreed, watching as the child began to arrange the blocks again. "But what would be better is a bath."

"Ugh!" Madeline wailed, throwing her head back. Her shoulders sagged and she fixed her green eyes on her twin. "Don't say it!"

They all knew that the child hated to get into the tub. Once in, however, she hated getting out. She was a conundrum to all.

Everyone's gaze dropped to the child who had frozen like a deer, a block held tight in a dimpled fist. Her gem-like eyes sparkled as she stared intently at Hope.

Hope took up the challenge by moving slowly at first, carefully setting her teacup on a table, then sprang for the child but she was gone in a blink. Hope herself would have tumbled to ground if Hahn had not caught her with hands that were quick and deft and pulled her, laughing, into his lap. Madeline made another noise of frustration and gave chase, disappearing through the door. Elaeric followed to help in any way he could.

"She's so fast," Hope giggled, held by Hahn's golden robed arms. "Have you ever seen anyone so fast?"

Hahn kissed her forehead. "I might have."

Hope looked at him, her green eyes suddenly cool. "Oh yes," she remembered aloud, "the master fighter. But tell me, Master Chi, were you so fast even as a child?"

Hahn smiled. "It was so long ago, I honestly can't remember."

Hope snuggled down against him and let herself be held until Elaeric walked back through the door with the child in his arms and Madeline following. The bundle in his arms did not squirm or fight, just looked at Hope with an accusatory glare with eyes of amber and green and gold. Once caught, it seemed, the jig was up.

Hope sat up straight.

"How did you catch her so fast?" she asked. "I thought we would have to wait until she was tired out!"

Elaeric shrugged, still holding the child and giving her a kiss on the top of her head. "I worked in the kitchens at the monastery. Sometimes I would have to catch a chicken or two. She's not that different."

෯෴

I clapped so hard my hands hurt since, this time, I was clapping for two. Matty sat on my right, clapping just as hard with tears in his blue eyes for his sons as they took the stage to collect their diplomas. Jean sat on my left, with Matthew on her other side. The only one missing was Mira.

I had not seen my love for three years, which was not strange since we had often been forced to spend long periods of time apart. But, as of yet, there was no end in sight for our forced separation.

Mira's owner, Mr. Devereaux, was going through a nasty divorce. As his personal assistant with in-depth knowledge of his finances and assets, she was in and out of one virtual court after the other. It broke her heart not to be able to attend the graduation but I assured her, in one of our hasty conversations we managed to squeeze in between downtime and depositions, that she would be there in spirit.

The venue of the commencement ceremony was much different from when Jean Marie graduated from high school. No fancy private school, no quartz buildings in lovely forests and rolling hills, and certainly not all girls.

When Matty's wife died in childbirth, I stepped up to take care. Matty, however, still had over another year at the flight academy. So I took up residence in the only place I knew, or thought I knew. It was the city where I had been born and grew to what I thought, at the time, was a man. What a laugh.

One Mile City had changed a lot since my day, and not just in the fact that it had become Two Mile City. There were places you could live where the buildings were cleaner, the streets safer, and the air better. It had become distinctively segregated by class, which I pointed out to Jean with an obvious air of disappointment. She had laughed at me gently, sounding a lot like her mother when she thought I was being naïve.

"Dad," she had said, keeping her voice low though there was no one else around us in the small café, "that segregation was always there. It's just that the lines between the middle class and the poor have become even more aggressively drawn as the middle class has grown larger, and now has subclasses of its own."

"Hmm," I had said, considering the idea as I sipped my coffee. "I wonder what class we had been in then."

Jean, who had been in the process of taking a bite from a cheese croissant, put it back down on her plate. "Are you being serious?" she asked.

"Of course."

"Dad," she said, glancing around and looking so much like her mother it was uncanny, "you lived with your immigrant grandparents."

"So?"

Her face had softened and she looked like her normal self again. "Dad," she assured me, "you were poor." She picked her croissant back up and took a bite.

"Because we lived with my immigrant grandparents?" I asked. "That's ridiculous. Almost everyone I knew did the same."

Jean Marie chuckled around her pastry, putting a hand over her mouth to keep it inside as her head bobbed in agreement.

"I know," she said. "You lived in a poor building, in a poor part of the city."

I harrumphed at that. I did not want to believe it was true but she probably knew better than I did. I knew enough to know that.

When I moved back to the city that sprawled upwards rather than outwards, I made sure to get a nice podment in a nice building in a nice part of the city. I had more than enough money and I wanted to make sure the boys went to a good school. I did, however, only get a two-bedroom pod and never heard the end of it as the boys grew older, but my brother and I had shared a room growing up and we turned out just fine.

My books were on the shelves and my father's rug was on the floor. Jean had my awards framed and hung them on the walls. They were something to look at but my real awards were the ones constantly running through the podment, either terrorizing me or making me laugh until I cried.

The terror they caused, however, was harmless to everyone except myself. But outside our little pod, in the real world, the rogue constructs that had named themselves the Chimera were committing acts of real terrorism.

Bjorn had finally resurfaced, alive and well. He had joined the group of construct rebels with quite a large sum of money. For months it was all over the news that he had managed to siphon off an enormous amount of Ivana Uri's bank accounts before they were shut down while her death was ascertained. And more, he had the wherewithal to bury the money in Golbli depositories in the Outer Banks, making it untouchable by galactic law. It made me suspicious about exactly where he might have been hiding those few months when his whereabouts were unknown. I knew a certain someone, a certain de Rossi someone, that had a talent for managing money and a taste for a certain green-eyed construct.

His news paled in comparison to the acts of the former bodyguard of the former Bauam of The Church of the One. The beautiful auburn-haired construct that Hope had worked so long and painfully on, left the entire Priory of the One Church in Sinai City in smoking ruins. The head offices, not to mention all of the head officials, were destroyed.

I must admit I felt a smug sort of glee when I heard the news and wondered how it felt for them to get a taste of their own medicine. My heart, however, went to the children that had been killed as well when the place went down. And it was disappointing to know that though the head had been cut from the serpent, another would grow back. The One Church had become the largest and most widespread religion in the galaxies, God help us all.

I also feared for anyone else who crossed paths with the construct that people were now calling the Vicar of Blood. He now went by the name of JP and had joined with Bjorn and Rohn Stojacovik as leaders of the rebellion.

Another faction by the same name but spelled Khimera, was made up of an elitist group of elfin constructs. They were few, merely hundreds instead of thousands, but were on the same path of destruction as the others. The Chimera were becoming more widespread by the day as an increasing number of artificial and even real humans joined them. But they were split into different groups across three galaxies and disorganized as hell - making them practically ineffectual.

Matty's boys were accepted at a local university and I finally sprung for a three-bedroom podment – anything to keep them at home. Matty came to stay with us every chance he got, which was more seldom as the acts of terrorism throughout the galaxy increased.

Mr. Devereaux's divorce lasted the entire four years the boys were in college. Mira assured me that the nasty ordeal was finally wrapping up, but she was not able to make it to their college promotion either. Nor two years later when they graduated from the IGC Flight Academy.

It had been almost a decade since I had seen her.

Though Mr. Devereaux looked decent enough on the news, we knew through Mira that he was an emotional wreck. Since she had been the only steadfast thing in his life for nearly a century, he could not be without her by his side and clung to her unfaltering presence.

I knew how he felt and wished I could do the same. I longed for her so badly that it was a painful ache. Sometimes in my heart, sometimes all over. I wanted to run my hands through her dark hair, watch her expressions of puzzlement and annoyance, and fall asleep with her head on my chest and those dark curls tickling my nose.

It was probably for the best, I joked with myself in the mirror one morning. My own locks of blonde had begun to turn gray. I swore up and down to anyone who would listen that it was raising the twins that had done it, but those who did listen (really just Jean and Matty) simply rolled their eyes. When I had complained to the twins they had laughed.

"It's because you're old, Grandpa," Jimmy had said from his bed, looking over the edge of a compute loaded with mathematics.

"Yeah, Grandpa," Jack had agreed, looking over the edge of a comic book. He was half-laying on the floor of Jimmy's room, propped up on some pillows against the edge of Jimmy's bed. Though they had their own rooms, they still tended to stick together. Especially when they were home from the academy. Jack let the comic book, which looked a bit racy, fall to his chest. "How old are you, Grandpa?"

"None of your businesses," I had informed him and stalked out.

But, truth be told, I had to add up my years by thinking about how old Jean was and how old the boys were. I took a close look at myself in my bathroom mirror that night. My face still seemed more or less unlined but my hair, though still thick, definitely now had as many gray hairs as blonde. And they were not just won by raising twins.

When the boys became commissioned pilots of the Intergalactic Council I looked, if I do say so myself, like a handsome man in his late thirties. When I did the math, it turned out I was a hundred and four years old.

Matty had come home for the latest graduation and stayed two weeks, for which I was unspeakably grateful. I had started watching more news than communicating with actual humans during the two years the twins were at the academy.

We all went out for a steak dinner after the ceremony, even Jean Marie and Mathew, though Matthew's health was failing. They were trim and fit for their age, but there was no denying they were in their later years. Their faith prohibited them from taking any drugs that would extend their lives. I had felt the same at one time, but that was before I had met Mira. Jean had been in her mid-forties when the twins were born and she had been quick to tell me (and told me often) that it was a very early age to be a grandmother. Now she was almost seventy and her beautiful dark curls had almost all turned to silver.

It occurred to me one morning that there was a chance, a very good chance, that I would outlive her and I almost spilled my coffee. I sat at the kitchen table with tears in my eyes, suddenly feeling very alone and very afraid. I wanted Mira back desperately, if even only for a few days. I needed her.

My eyes traveled over the pictures on the walls. There was one of Jean Marie at her high school graduation and one of her and Mathew together. Some were of Matty, but most were of the twins. I realized with dismay that I had no pictures of Mira, and none of us together.

Another thought struck me at that moment and it filled me with horror.

What if I never saw Mira again? What if, by the time I did, she had outlived me? Things that had never crossed my mind before now flew through it like bats in a bell tower. I got up from the table and, with shaking hands, opened my liquor cabinet and pulled out the first bottle I saw. I put a short glass on the counter and filled it, trembling so hard that I sloshed it. I leaned down to take a sip off the top before I picked it up and sat back down at the table, my coffee forgotten.

My gaze fell on our family crest, an ancient emblem in brass and enamel with the Mattatock coat of arms enclosed by a pair of brass wings. It was traditionally given to the member of the Mattatock family while he or she served in the military, which for the last few centuries had been as a fighter pilot. Since we had two pilots now, Matty had pinned it to a piece of scarlet canvas and had hung it on the wall.

My worries were misplaced for the nonce, for when the knife slipped out of the dark once again, it wasn't for me. It was after the twins.

James and Jack went out of the world the same way they came into it – together.

A group of Chimeran constructs had planted a dirty bomb in a coffee house close to an IGC building that many council members were known to frequent. James and Jack were in their first year out of the academy and serving with the City Guard, mostly in air support.

That day they were on the ground and the first to respond.

James, called Jimmy by everyone since he was two, tried to defuse the bomb while Jack was hell bent on getting everyone out of the building. Thus, Jimmy was the first to go. An hour later his brother followed, from a hospital bed, full of coffee house shrapnel.

I never got to say goodbye to Jimmy, not while he still breathed, but I was able to say goodbye to Jack. My great-grandson held my hand and stared at me with eyes as blue as mine and made me promise to deliver the family crest to his infant son, Joseph.

It was a promise I kept.

# TWO SIX

"Hey," Evan said, tapping Gwen's shoulder with the back of his hand. Her head swiveled towards him, her brown and gold eyes blinking in the magnified sunlight slanting through the windows as it set. The yellow light turned her hair bronze and made her eyes look like the fur of a lioness. "Anybody home?"

"I'm right here," Gwen assured him. It was her go-to answer of late. Mostly because Evan was constantly catching her wool-gathering and asking her where she was, meaning mentally.

"You're as distracted as Faith these days," he had told her gently just the day before. Gwen had laughed.

"If Faith ever seems distracted it is a disguise," she assured him. "She is never anything but focused."

"Be that as it may," Evan said, "you are out there in the realm of possibilities instead here with me."

"I'm right here," Gwen had told him. Evan had looked at her with feigned doubt and kissed her to make sure.

They had gotten a call from Faith only hours ago, but they had been expecting it for weeks. Gwen answered it on her comset.

"I'm here," she had said, her voice softer than ever.

"It's time," Faith said, even softer.

"Alright," Gwen acquiesced. "Will you call me when it's done?"

"Of course," Faith said.

Gwen sighed. "Okay. Love."

"Love," Faith answered as they broke the communique simultaneously.

"Are you still angry?" Evan asked Gwen now, sitting on the long white davenport in their living room. Her hair was pulled back and held by a scarf but golden strands had come loose and he pushed them away from her face.

"Of course I am still angry."

"Why? I thought we all decided this was for the best. And you have been fine with this idea for years."

"That's because I thought it wouldn't happen!" Gwen said. Evan's lip twitched and Gwen sighed. "You decided this was the best plan," she said. "The others just went along with you." Evan gave her a look of disagreement that he would not voice out loud. "You would be angry too," Gwen continued. "Would you ever let me do such a thing? Such a dangerous thing?"

Evan pulled back, his hazel eyes full of distress. "Never would I want you to do such a thing," he agreed softly, "but this is not a matter of want nor let. We all have to be free to make our own choices." He placed one of his hands over Gwen's. "People being free to make their own decisions in every aspect of their life is what this is all about."

"Are the Chimera right?" Gwen asked. "Is what we have been doing wrong?"

"Is that what's been eating at you?" Evan asked. "Why you've been so distracted lately?"

"Are they?" Gwen persisted.

"No," Evan answered firmly. "It's what their owners did that was wrong."

"But if you are talking slavery, then you think what we are doing is wrong. People should not own other people."

"Are they really people?"

Gwen jerked as if he had pinched her and when she spoke her voice was just above a whisper. "Are you suggesting you are not a real person? Or that I am not?"

Evan shrugged. "I think that question is what this is all going to come down to in the end. But I do know that you and I were created for something, for a purpose. So were they. There are so many true humans, millions probably, that don't know their true purpose. So many more that are hurtful and cruel."

"So you *do* side with the Chimera in that aspect."

Evan laughed softly and rubbed Gwen's arm. "That has nothing to do with taking sides. I think it is terrible the number of constructs that were mistreated or outright abused, but the types of humans involved would have done the same to other humans – their siblings or spouses or even their own children."

Gwen nodded sadly. "Faith said the same," she admitted. "We talked about changing the screening process for owners but she decided it would be easier just to change the product. Have you seen them?" Gwen asked, wrinkling her nose.

Evan nodded. "You don't like them, do you?"

Gwendolyn shook her head, a crease marring her brow. "They were my least favorite molds, and they are hardly close to human in all aspects. They are being called skinthetics. Aptly so."

"A far cry from the Pantheon, I agree."

"Too far," Gwen said. "Faith could have done better."

Evan straightened in surprise, though Gwen was too distracted to notice. It was the first time he had ever heard her criticize Faith, even in the smallest of ways. Before she could notice his surprise, he pulled her onto his lap and kissed the side of her head.

Gwen pulled away but kept her hands clasped around his elbows. "Explain something else to me now," she said. "Why you? It might have taken time and training or programming, but we could have gotten any number of constructs to spy within the Chimera - we still can. I know you well enough to know you are doing this for a reason, but I don't know what it is."

Evan's lips came together in a gentle line that was not a smile. "Like I was saying, we all have a purpose, and I don't know what mine is," he said softly. He gave his head a quick shake to stop Gwen before she could say anything about her love for him or their love for each other. "Charity and Llewellyn have the role of managing media and finances, neither of which are a small task. You are the creative source behind everything," he said with a smile that brought a smile to her lips as well. "Faith is…" Evan rolled his eyes and let go of Gwen as he fell back in an exaggerated faint. "…Faith." Gwen laughed and Evan leaned close and wrapped his arms around her. "Even Hope and Madeline play their part in liaison and espionage." He gave his head a small shake and his expression became serious. "I have a part to play as well. Not just because I want to join in, but because this is where I can contribute. This is where I am *supposed* to contribute."

Gwen's lips pulled down at the corners but she nodded as she finally understood. "Okay," she acquiesced, her heart heavy. "Okay." She wrapped her arms around him and he laid his face alongside hers. "How much will you forget?" she whispered. "How much will you remember?"

"I will always remember that I love you," he whispered back. "And I will find my way back to you, no matter where you are."

"Right here," she whispered hoarsely, moving her left leg so that she was straddling him on the davenport. "I'm right here."

Her lips moved from his ear to his jaw and down his neck. She ran her tongue along his warm skin, tasting him. Her hands found the button on his pants and tugged it open. One hand slipped inside and grasped his growing erection and pulled it free, her thumb sliding along his smooth skin.

"I'm right here," she whispered.

Evan pushed her skirt up to her hips and dug his fingers into the bands of the bikini undergarment she wore and tore them apart. He pulled the ruined garment free and tossed it on the floor.

Gwen raised up on her knees and found him, slipping him inside and lowering herself down. She leaned forward and found his ear again, this time with her teeth.

"I'm right here," she whispered, her voice husky as she rose up again on her knees, almost to the point of losing him before plunging back down.

Evan closed his eyes and tipped his head back but Gwendolyn grasped his face in her hands and his hazel eyes opened.

"I'm right here," she told him, her thighs gripping his.

Evan arched his back, trying to get deeper inside her before she pulled away again.

"I'm right here," she said, putting her forehead against his before he grabbed her knee and turned both their bodies so he was over her. Their bodies moved in unison, faster and faster until Gwen cried out and he held her tight as she shuddered around him.

"I'm right here," she whispered in his ear, her hands tangled in the back of his golden hair.

CW8O

The next morning Evan stood over her, prepared to go but far from ready. They had decided, together, that Gwen would take a heavy sedative before bed. Neither of them wanted a tearful goodbye and Gwen was downright fearful that she would cause a scene that she wanted neither of them to remember.

They had made love on the davenport and again later in their bed. They talked and laughed until almost midnight about Charity and Llewellyn and the horrid gossip they had passed along. Neither of them mentioned the Chimera, the impending war or their upcoming situation.

Gwen finally swallowed the tiny pill that Charity had given her with a sip of mineral water and she and Evan fell asleep in each other's arms as they watched one of their favorite elfin comedies from the 'droma system.

Evan, despite his resolve and awaiting an aircab, sat next to Gwendolyn on the bed the next morning and pushed a lock of hair away from her face before he caressed it. His finger touched her ear, her cheek. His thumb gently traced her nose, her lips.

"I will always remember that I love you," he whispered. "And I will find my way back to you, no matter where you are."

He leaned down and kissed her lips with as much passion as he dared but with all the love that he felt. Then he stood and left the home they had built together, taking with him nothing except the love he had for her.

He climbed into the aircab and cast one last look at their glass house, the morning sun turning it into a rainbow sherbet.

The cab took him to the small spaceport that a certain Fletcher Mattatock had planned and oversaw the construction of as it was built alongside the burgeoning city town of Rossi Hamlet. Evan boarded a GwenSeven craft that was both inconspicuous and luxurious. He made himself comfortable in an overstuffed chair and turned away a steward offering champagne and then called him back almost immediately.

"Do you have añejo?" Evan asked on a whim, thinking of the trip he and Gwendolyn had taken to Europa.

"Of course," the steward answered with a bow and disappeared only to return moments later with a snifter a perfect third full of the amber-colored stimulant. Evan was on his second when they landed at the compound on Dione.

The hazel-eyed construct with golden hair and golden-tan skin was half hoping he would be at least a bit drunk but instead found himself acutely aware and alert. He stood on the tarmac, his gaze traveling across the early evening horizon, taking everything in with a sweep of his hazel eyes.

The first thing he noticed was the evacuation that was being executed with perfect nonchalance. People were leaving the compound in the slowest and most discreet manner. Groups of two and three were departing the complex every few minutes as couples or friends going for dinner in Evansborough, unobtrusively making their way to the spaceport.

Evan took a hopper to the compound and made his way to the Inner Sanctum. He was expecting to be met by the impeccable Thomas, but instead Faith was there – dressed in a short white skirt with a gold shirt covered by a short white suit coat and leaning back against Thomas' desk.

"Hello, Evan," she greeted.

"Hello, Faith," he returned, feeling a shiver go up his spine.

"Are you ready?"

At least twenty retorts, most of them sarcastic, ran through his mind but he replied with a simple, "yes."

"How is Gwen?"

Evan took a deep breath and let it out before he fixed his hazel eyes on the tawny eyes of Gwendolyn's twin. "She's ready, too," he said.

Faith looked at him for a moment, measuring him, then pushed herself up and away from the desk and headed for the door that led to the original offices and labs, including her own. A slight jerk of her head instructed Evan to follow. He did, though he knew the way. Left and then left again, of course. The glass doors slid down before her like aborigines bowing before their god.

"It's been a while since I've been in your lair," Evan remarked, following Faith as she touched panels on the walls as they entered the labyrinth that made up her offices and medical rooms.

"You mean my lab?" she asked, the dim lights brightening automatically as they entered.

"No. I mean your lair."

Walking with an unhurried yet steady purpose, they circumvented the area that was composed of mostly computers and laboratory equipment and made their way to the part of Faith's lab that held the majority of her medical machinery. Motion detectors clicked on one bank of lights after the other. The place was lit up like a holiday show by the time they reached the Magnetic Imagery Machine, flanked on one side by a resa droid that had been powered down.

"After you," Faith said, holding out an inviting hand. Evan gave her a winning grin and climbed up and lay down on the heavy plastique stretcher, wiggling a bit to get comfortable though he already knew that it was impossible. It wasn't the first time Faith had given him a brain scan. She did for the first time, however, pull up a pair of Velcro straps from either side of his head which she fastened together over his dark blonde brows.

"What is that for?" he asked.

"To keep your head as still as possible," she replied. "Obviously."

"Is this going to hurt?" he asked, curious.

"Yes," Faith replied coolly. "Quite a lot."

Evan's hazel eyes flickered with concern for the first time since bringing up the idea of tinkering with his brain, then he saw Faith smirk as she pulled a hanging compute screen down in front of her.

"Is that for the remark about your lair?" he asked.

"Yes."

Faith smiled at him through the pane of glass until she activated it, making the glass turn opaque and blue. She pulled a floating keyboard in front of her and started typing. The plastique stretcher that held Evan began to slide backwards, inserting his head and torso into what looked like the hole of a giant white doughnut glowing with blue light.

Faith sat down on a short stool with wheels and the screen and keyboard sank down with her. She rolled herself closer to Evan and her equipment followed obediently. A few taps on her keyboard brought up a picture of Evan's brain.

"Alright," she said, "are you sure you want to do this? Last chance to change your mind. Before I do, that is."

"I'm sure," Evan told her, "though I'm surprised you'd ask."

Faith grinned as she turned the image of his brain, examining each side. "I promised Gwen that I would." Evan grinned in response. Faith rolled the image on the screen so that the angle she had of his neural cortex was from above. Different parts of his brain were illuminated in different colors. "Hmm."

"See something interesting?" Evan asked.

"Yes," Faith answered, but did not elucidate any further. Evan would have shaken his head if he could have moved it.

"What exactly are you going to do?" he asked. "I'm guessing you are not going to wipe my memory, not entirely, or else I won't know to come back with what I've learned. Or, maybe more so, to trust you."

"Right you are," Faith said, still typing, lighting up different portions of the brain portrayed on the screen. "Luckily, the brain isn't just a solid mass, like the liver. And unlike the heart, which is made of muscle and sheathed in connective tissue, it is made up of neurons and those neurons like to form pathways. The pathways used most often get thicker, become more like roads. What I am going to do is funnel most of the smaller paths into the roads, and then set up road blocks."

"And those roadblocks are going to be what keep me from getting caught," Evan surmised aloud. "If I am unable to access my memory, I won't remember who I am or what I am trying to do."

"That's right," Faith said, pleased. She drew a line through the image of Evan's brain on the screen and then flicked her finger upwards. The top half disappeared, exposing a complex of nuclei.

"Then how will I remember when the time is right?" he asked. "How will I even know *when* the time is right?"

"Well," Faith said, virtually slicing away the complex to get to the amygdala underneath. She enlarged the image over and over until it looked like a giant almond made of wires. "Charity is actually the one who will determine when the time is right."

"Oh, Christ," Evan whispered.

Faith laughed softly. "Don't worry," she assured the construct, "I always have emergency people and procedures in place. Especially where Gwen is concerned."

"Thanks," Evan said, his voice comically flat.

"You're welcome."

"So... you are going to set up roadblocks in my brain," Evan reiterated, "so that I cannot remember who I am or what I am doing. Can you tell me what will happen when Charity..." he stopped and chuckled, unable to help himself, "...rescues me? How will I remember who I really am?" Evan closed his eyes and took a deep breath. His next question was one he did not want to ask because he thought it impossible but he had to ask anyway. It was one too important to risk. "How will I remember Gwen?"

Faith smiled, still tapping at her screen. "Well, at the crucial points of those roadblocks, I will set up triggers...little explosives, so to speak. Something that you will see or hear after you have been extracted to blow up the blocks."

"Makes sense," Evan agreed, sighing with relief.

"Good, let's put those in place now. Can you remember the first time you saw Gwen?"

Evan smiled, even though he was looking up into a band of light with his head strapped to a plastique stretcher. "Yes," he breathed, almost ecstatic. "Do you want me to tell you about it?"

Faith smiled and marked the spot on the brain scan that was lit up. "No need. Can you remember the first time you heard her voice?"

"Of course! It was the first time..."

"Mmmhmm," Faith interrupted, pinpointing the spot that was lit up with the memory and putting a pin in it. "Now," she said, tucking a smile into the corner of her mouth, "think about your first kiss."

Evan closed his eyes, not with an effort to recall the memory but with the pleasure of reliving it.

"You don't have to say anything," Faith said, zooming in on the illuminated part of his cortex and marking it. Once she had the place pinned, she rolled her chair back a few inches and peered at the young man on the stretcher. Her right hand cupped her elbow, supporting it as she ran her left thumbnail over her lips.

"Smell," Evan said, staring up at the curve of the machine over his head.

"Excuse me?" Faith asked, surprised.

"Isn't that the sense you should tap into next?" Evan asked. "It is actually the most powerful in reproducing memory."

Faith chuckled. "You are right. So much so that I don't think I need to plant a trigger. Gwen can do that on her own when you see her again. Instead, give me a phrase -preferably in as few as three words and not as generic as 'I love you' that will trigger an emotional response in you. Can you think of anything like that?"

I'm right here.

Evan could feel his heartbeat quicken and he licked his lips. His heart was not the only part of his body that he could feel responding to the memory of Gwen from the night before.

Evan opened his mouth to explain but Faith cut him off.

"Whoa!" she exclaimed, darting her tawny eyes in his direction after she had pinned the memory spot in his brain. "No need to elucidate. I've got what I need."

Evan sighed in relief.

Faith finished highlighting bits here and there with the tip of her finger and placing markers on the wires on the screen. She rolled the chair back and stood up, moving to where Evan could see her.

"The triggers are in place," she told him. "Now for the roadblocks. I'm going to shut off your access to your episodic memory."

"The events of my life," Evan said, his hazel eyes peering at her from under the Velcro straps. "This is where I forget."

"Just for now," Faith said. "The memories will still be there, you just won't know until you come back."

"Is there anything else you told Gwen you would do?" Evan asked.

Faith smiled. "Yes. She wanted to make sure you were part of JP's crew, not Bjorn's."

Evan laughed. "With Pious. Of course she would want that." He laughed again before his hazel eyes found Faith again. "Can you tell me how you are going to manage that?"

Faith nodded. "It will be his ship that comes to storm the compound next week. You, along with a thousand others, will be taken."

"And you think I will eventually be an officer? High-ranking enough to get the intelligence I would need?"

"Yes," Faith affirmed. "They need the best and brightest, which means the core of them will be made up from the Second Run or Special Order. You are obviously special, you will be weeded out almost immediately." Faith cocked her head and frowned. "But surely you know this since it was your plan to begin with."

"I do," Evan agreed. "But assurances are also nice. Besides, Hope once said you were always eight steps ahead of everyone. I wanted to check."

"Awww," Faith crooned. "Hope said that?"

Evan grinned. "I don't think she meant it as a compliment."

Faith returned his grin. "I'm sure she didn't, but I'll take it as one anyway." The smile drifted from her face. "Anything else?"

The smile left Evan's face as well. "You assured me before that Gwen would be safe without me."

"She will be."

"I would not leave her if I thought she might be in any danger."

"I know."

"Tell me again."

"Gwen will be safe. And helping crush this rebellion will ensure we stay safe. Are you ready?"

"Yes."

Faith reached down and grasped his hand. "Goodbye for now, Evan." He gave her hand a squeeze.

"Goodbye, Faith."

Evan closed his hazel eyes and waited. Faith retook her seat on the stool and began typing on the keyboard. The resa droid came to life, its head lighting up as it turned towards Evan and a mechanical arm with a hypodermic needle descending to deliver a tranquilizer into his bicep.

Seconds later he was under. There was an audible click from the centrifuge across the room that was linked to Faith's compute system. The droid moved towards it soundlessly and retrieved the vial that was waiting and transferred it to another hypodermic before returning to Evan's side and injecting it into him.

Two types of nanobots moved silently through his bloodstream, gathering at the places Faith had marked in his brain. One type, the blockers, gathered around the part of his amygdala that housed his autobiographical memory – the story and emotion of his life. The other type, the digesters, split into groups that gathered around the pins Faith had set that when triggered, would advance upon the blockers. And eat them.

Faith pulled down another screen while the nanobots were nestling in and went to work on another vial. Within minutes it was ready and the resa droid retrieved it from the centrifuge. Faith watched the droid inject the refrag DNA fluid into Evan and then turned her stool so she could see him better, crossing her arms over her chest as she leaned back to watch.

"I'm pretty sure I kept you under wraps all these years," Faith murmured to the unconscious construct on the stretcher, "but I like assurances too."

At first the transformation was slow, then sped up as the DNA replicated exponentially. Faith watched the color of Evan's skin deepen from golden tan to olive. His blonde hair began to darken at the roots before it seeped outwards until every hair follicle was coal black – eyebrows too. His eyelids were closed but Faith knew that, underneath, those hazel eyes were becoming seven shades darker.

While the process completed, Faith sent for an attendant to move the stretcher with the sedated construct to his quarters in the compound with the others that were awaiting sale. Before the attendant arrived, she printed out a name badge for the manufactured human that had begun his life simply named J7. The badge had only one name and was quite similar to the one he had started with.

Jasyn.

JP walked down the ramp of the Battle Cruiser, the breeze fluffing his auburn hair and flattening his high-collared black cassock against his lean body. His soldiers ran both past him (towards the hulking building that took up most of his vision) and towards him to deliver reports.

Things were finally coming together for the Cause and the construct that had been programmed to be an invincible bodyguard felt his chest swell with pride as the tall and heavily muscled Petrov stood by his side and took the reports as they came in, summarizing them for the Commander.

"The compound is ours," he told JP with no small amount of his own pride. "What little staff we found did not resist."

"Have them put into a conference room," the Commander told his Second in Command. "I'll decide what to do with them later. For now, make sure that there is no panic among the constructs that are being freed. Everyone is to make assurances and bring them outside after lunch. Meanwhile, have a team erect a stage over there," he instructed, pointing to a great field of wind-beaten, short, gray grass. I will address them just before sunset."

Petrov gave a quick nod and then turned to the soldiers that stood awaiting instruction. Once the orders were given they took off running and he turned back to the Commander who motioned for him to follow as he headed for the massive structure. They walked away from the Battle Cruiser that was another credit to the Executive Officer, Jan Petrov.

When the Revolution for the Cause began in earnest, the first thing the rebelling constructs learned was that supplies were even harder to come by than supporters. The most difficult supplies were weapons and the bigger they were, the more difficult they were to get. Small arms were easy if you had the money but larger items, especially items as large as fighter ships, were next to impossible. Bjorn was going crazy trying to get his hands on one and he had an insane supply of funds.

Even to consider a Battle Cruiser at such an early point would have been ludicrous.

It was Petrov who, one day after morning prayers, had come up with the idea.

"Why don't we just turn our ship into a Battle Cruiser?" he had suggested, a crease between his blonde brows as he considered. When he and JP had left the priory in smoking ruins, they had taken the largest ship at the airfield - the Bauam's space cruiser *Monastery.* "It is as big as a Battle Cruiser," Petrov had mused, "maybe bigger. We would simply have to outfit it with weapons."

JP's blue eyes had gone round with comprehension before he grabbed the bull-like shoulders of Petrov.

"Your brilliance never ceases to amaze me!" he exclaimed, delivering a kiss to each cheek of the blushing Executive Officer. "I am truly blessed by the One to have you at my side!"

Now the two of them walked from the newly outfitted ship, outlined by the rising sun, towards the building that had recently manufactured at least a thousand constructs. A thousand constructs that would soon be the crew of the newly-made Battle Cruiser that JP had named *Resurrection.*

"I need to find the best and the brightest for my officers," JP told his Second in Command as they walked across the wind-beaten grass.

"Well," Petrov said, "the Second-Run constructs are long gone. Our best hope is to find custom-made constructs, the ones they call Special Order."

JP nodded as they reached the building. Two men from his crew, handsome blondes and completely identical, held open a set of double doors for Petrov and himself. They walked into the compound, going up and down the hallways, greeting constructs and giving them guarantees of freedom and safety.

Not more than three minutes had passed before they came upon one that lay in the hallway, unconscious and bleeding.

"What happened here?" JP demanded, kneeling to check the body for a pulse. The construct was distinctly handsome, with thick black hair and olive-toned skin, and absolutely alive.

"This is our first trip into this wing," he was told by one of the soldiers escorting him. "It must have happened when we stormed the building or just before."

"Take him to the infirmary," JP instructed. He darted his blue eyes to Petrov who gave him a definitive nod.

The Commander went to visit the construct in the infirmary after he had delivered a rousing speech to the men and women his soldiers had freed that day. He was a bit wonky from the injury to his head but was recovering quickly. JP had a medic look at the young man's vitals, the ones that pertained to his uniqueness in his manufacturing and they were so high that they were near his own.

His, and Petrov's, initial thoughts were confirmed – the construct was Special Order. And he was more than willing to join.

JP left the infirmary in high spirits. Petrov fell in step with him in the hallway, headed back to their ship as their soldiers organized the exodus that would follow.

"Have you decided what to do with the staff?" Petrov asked. His blue eyes remained fixed ahead, for he was already fairly certain of the response he would receive from his commander.

JP gave a quick nod but never slowed his step. "Kill them all," he instructed, his own blue eyes fixed on the air before him. "Along with any constructs here that do not join the Cause."

Petrov dipped his head in understanding and turned, walking briskly away. He made sure JP's wishes were met before they left to return to their temporary base on Earth.

# TWO 7

Hope could have used a private communiqué from her room but decided instead to use a public compute in the business lounge aboard the interstellar ship *New Beginnings*, deciding that her conversation with her sister might be safer if it could be hacked at some point and posted on public record. Also, Hahn would have been as distracting as the child if Faith were to say something that would upset him. Still, Hope wished he was by her side.

The journey, the current journey, was almost at an end. Hope had learned much in the last twenty years from Hahn and Elaeric and what stuck with her the most was the knowledge that one journey always followed the one before. Sure as a chapter titled "Butterfly" followed the chapter titled "Caterpillar." Death came after life and death was followed by an, as of yet, unnamed epilogue.

Hope thought of their current expedition as the journey of creation, an idea that could not have been more apropos. Hahn and Elaeric had done amazing work with Eris, an inhabited mass that had once been a dwarf planet just outside of Neptune's orbit. Had an astronaut from Earth been flying by, he would have scrubbed his eyes with his fists then have himself tested for Space Madness upon his return back home.

For starters, the tiny planet – which had been moved into place by the same Dragon that had brought Hahn and Elaeric from their system to meet with the de Rossi ambassadors of Hope and Madeline – was no longer a sphere. It was flat.

The work had been long but not especially toilsome. For

their six years aboard the interstellar ship *New Beginnings*, Hahn and Elaeric had traveled almost daily in a grai-pod, a small ovoid space-tender that Madeline had outfitted with mostly cushions and pillows. There was a small commode and a few storage cabinets for supplies and foodstuffs. There was even a hotplate to heat buns and tea, although Hahn and Elaeric were in the habit of heating their own tea – without the use of electrical assistance.

The pod could be piloted from a small keypad just inside its door or controlled from the bridge of the main ship. Madeline and Hope had accompanied the Zenarchist monks hundreds of times, reading or napping or watching as they manipulated a field that was invisible save for the changes that it made.

The first few years were the most arduous as they transformed the moon into a flattened disc, slowly and carefully as not to overly disturb the scattered tribes already living there. The side closest to the sun was already seeing the glacial plateau slowly melt into a great ocean.

The copper-haired de Rossi girls often went on the expeditions while the child was still an infant. Once she was more mobile, Madeline or Hope stayed with her on Marco's ship while the monks mediated for six to twelve hours at a stretch, slowly changing the frozen landscape beneath the great ovoid window of the pod.

Madeline, having not been out with them for more than half a year, was surprised on her next visit.

"Oh!" she exclaimed, clasping her hands together as she looked through the portal at the transformed mass of land far below. "You have done so much!"

"Yes," Elaeric agreed, pleased. "Even when we finish meditating for the day, it keeps changing upon the course we set. The Field, once set in great motion, stays in motion. Hope has a name for it..." he trailed off, thinking.

"Dynamism," Hahn said.

"Yes!" Elaeric confirmed. "Dynamism!"

Madeline's green eyes traveled over the continents that were slowly emerging from the white glaciers that still enclosed most of it. "It looks like a flattened map of Earth!" she exclaimed.

Elaeric nodded, looking with her through the glass. The embryonic landmasses were gold and green, edged with the blue of icy waters. "I am actually working on the land alone now. Hahn is working on replicating some towns, one especially meant for Miss Hope as a surprise," he said, leaning close to share the secret though Hope was back on the ship with the child.

"Which one?" Madeline asked.

"Do you remember our trip to Earth on the way here?" Hahn asked, plumping some cushions in preparation for a long sit. Madeline nodded, her wild mane of curls bobbing. "The little town? Where nobody lived?" he asked, poking her memory.

"The one built in the Americas?" she asked. "Oh yes!" Madeline said, remembering. Hahn nodded and Madeline smiled at the memory of their trip. "Hope said it wasn't a real town. It was one of many built in the mid nineteen-hundreds. They used those places to test bombs in the years of the Great Arms Race."

Hahn froze with a tasseled pillow in his hand, his almond-shaped eyes suddenly round.

"But she did really like the town!" Madeline said quickly, seeing his dismay. "She said it was like a life-sized dollhouse for a whole village of dolls."

Hahn stood frozen for a moment more, then relaxed enough to drop the pillow. "Well," he said, "I think she will like this one more. But, you won't tell her?"

Madeline shook her head vigorously, turning her curly locks into a copper-colored aura. "Hope will not find out from me," she promised. And Hope never did.

Unaware of the town, now complete with appliances in the homes, cars in the garages, and grass on the lawns, Hope took a seat in the business lounge aboard the interstellar ship *New Beginnings.* The child was practicing her reading with Madeline and Elaeric. Hahn was most likely hovering nearby, though his heart was with Hope and the task she had before her.

The lounge was comfortable with soft chairs and even softer music, state of the art compute screens nestled into private nooks - and completely empty of any patrons besides the youngest de Rossi daughter. It seemed that the constructs bound for the New World had no desire to be communicating with anyone they were leaving behind. Hope could hardly blame them.

There were a number of droids circulating smoothly through the air with cocktails and bubbled water. Hope selected a water as one came by. Her mouth was dry and wanted something stronger but she needed to keep her focus.

She opened a line by placing her credentials card over a rubber pad next to the screen and paying the fare for unlimited distance and time. It glowed green, showing the charges were approved, and Hope typed in the number for Faith's private line in her lab. The screen in front of Hope was black with a swirl of constantly moving color, a rainbow that twisted and squirmed as the line in Faith's lab rang and rang.

Hope frowned. It was not like Faith to be away from her lab unless there was urgent business elsewhere and, if it was that important, Hope would have known.

She was about to hang up and call Thomas to patch her to wherever Faith might be when the twirling rainbow zipped out of existence and was replaced with a view of the office portion of Faith's lab, blurred by motion.

"Hello?" Faith was saying, even as she moved about, blocking the screen completely. "Don't hang up!"

Hope smiled as she watched her sister drop into the chair behind her desk and fiddle with the screen to adjust the picture.

"Hope?" she asked, her face lighting up. "Is that you?"

Hope smiled. "Of course, it's me. How often does Madeline call?"

Faith laughed. "Sorry," she said, "you just caught me off guard. And I had to rush to get the call."

"Where were you?" Hope asked out of simple curiosity. Faith laughed again.

"Just using the bathroom. But see? Everyone lectures me for spending all of my time in the lab but, the second I leave, I'm needed. It's good to see you, though. Is anything wrong?"

Hope took a deep breath. "No, nothing is wrong. I just wanted to see you." Faith's smile broadened so much that it tore at Hope's heart. "Are you back at the compound now?" she asked, stalling.

"Yes. The IGC came in to put down the insurrection but JP and his prizeload of constructs had already departed. He only had so many soldiers and he did not want to lose the untrained recruits he had only just acquired."

"Timing is crucial," Hope remarked.

"Yes," Faith agreed with a smile.

"Did he kill many people?" Hope asked, so reluctant that the question was forced from her lips.

"None that were real," Faith answered. A line formed between her brows as she sensed Hope's feelings from light years away. "Is that why you called?"

Hope took a deep breath, as if readying herself for a deep plunge. "Yes. That, and to say goodbye."

Faith's expression turned into one of puzzlement. "Goodbye?"

Hope nodded, her mane of copper curls moving gently

with the motion of her head. "Hahn and I are going to the New World."

"The New…?" Faith began before her gold and brown eyes widened in realization. Her face hardened and Hope was reminded of a fairy tale where a person (was it a witch?) was turned to stone. She braced herself for whatever scathing reply Faith had in store but her response was as cold as her expression. "No."

Hope's copper-colored eyebrows shot up in surprise. "No?" she repeated. Then she laughed and repeated it again. "No?"

"You heard me," Faith affirmed. "No."

Hope laughed again but it had a hollow sound. "What do you mean, no?"

"I mean no, you may not go. That journey is a one-way ticket. You are not going. And certainly not with that monk."

Hope felt her countenance become as stony as her sister's. "I can, I am, and I will. I am a grown woman, Faith. You cannot tell me what to do."

"Like hell I can't."

Hope, shocked at Faith's audacity, watched her face turn from the screen, her brows furrowed. "Whatever you're doing," Hope advised, "you might as well stop. We are too far for you to reach us. And the way will be blocked before you can get here. We are less than ten days from detonation."

"You are more than twenty days from detonation," Faith said, calling Hope's bluff with her face still turned away as she punched numbers and letters onto her ghostpad with calm intensity.

"Nevertheless," Hope countered, "you still won't make it on time. And, even if you were here in time, you could not stop me."

Faith's face softened a bit, most likely from what she saw on the other screen she was watching, before turning her gaze back to Hope. "I won't be the one to stop you. But you will be stopped. Despite your current escort."

Hope clenched her fists, enraged with her sister's tone, smirk, and the fact that she knew so much. Everything, it seemed, about every damned thing. Well, maybe not everything.

"That being the case," Faith stated, assuming a businesslike tone, "you should just stay where you are. It will be safer for you that way." She paused for a moment, her subtle smile quirking up the edges of her lips. "You, and the child."

Hope felt as if someone had slipped an ice-cube down the back of her shirt. "What child?" she asked, her voice only slightly above a whisper.

Faith laughed from light years away. "What child?" she asked, mocking. "I can hardly believe you thought you could hide her, but I can believe you would try. It is so like you. But," she conceded, "I will hand one thing to you – you were wily enough to discreetly change transports via Golbli craft. At the time it appeared to occur out of a matter of convenience but I soon knew it afforded the lot of you to virtually disappear for almost a year."

Hope smiled. That was exactly what had happened, and why. Which meant on one hand, at least, she might be ahead of Faith. It meant that, though she knew of the child, she did not know everything. Hope crossed her fingers under the desk and waited, knowing that what Faith said next would show how much she truly knew.

"So," Faith said, jumping in with both feet, "is the child yours, or Madeline's?"

Hope smiled. *She doesn't know*, she thought, smug.

"What makes you think she is either of ours?" she countered with haughty confidence. "Because of that wild hair?" Hope forced a laugh. "It may be wild but it is certainly not our color! You obviously did not research the Golbli vessel we took, out of convenience I might add, and have either forgotten or underestimated Madeline's propensity to take in strays, especially small ones that are in need."

"She is very beautiful," Faith said. "I would very much like to meet her."

Hope's reply was quick and vehement. "Never."

Faith recoiled as if slapped. It took her a good two seconds to recover and Hope figured that must be a first.

"Never?" Faith asked. "But you, *or Madeline*," she conceded, "are the first of us to have a child. You must know that we will all want to meet her. To *dote* on her."

"The others would dote on her," Hope said, her voice cold. "You would experiment on her."

Faith's countenance bore an expression of shock that Hope decided must be another first. She also knew it to be feigned and the disgust she felt only grew.

"Everything is an experiment to you," Hope accused slowly. "I know you never made the Pantheon for money. You wanted to see what you could do, what they *would* do. You are putting a ringed finger into every pie – experimenting with love that you do not feel, a war you will not have to fight, a universe you hope to rule."

Faith straightened, her composure regained and no accusations denied. "I want to meet my niece. You have no right to deny me..."

"I have every right!" Hope shouted over the com. She took a deep breath and blew air out slowly through pursed lips, regaining her own composure almost instantly. "Meet your niece," she scoffed. "Why? So you can play princess and prick her finger for a drop of blood? Or play astronaut and have her climb into Auntie Faith's *spacepod* while you scan her brain?" Hope laughed but it had no humor in it. "Never," she repeated.

"We'll see."

Hope bristled. "Your reign, Queen Faith," she scoffed, "is not absolute."

Faith grinned so wide that she looked like a jack-o'lantern. It was something that Hope had not often seen and it frightened her. "Feeling like taking me on in a game of holo chess, do you?" Faith challenged.

Hope tried to portray the confidence she saw in her sister. "What do you mean by that?" she asked, but the sinking feeling in her stomach already knew.

Faith laughed, and it was a real laugh, frightening Hope further, though she refused to show it.

"I mean the message you sent Gwen with all the holo chess metaphors. The one about players and pawns." She laughed again and Hope felt her heart follow her stomach as it dropped. Faith shook her head in reprimand. "You shouldn't be filling Gwen's head with such things."

"You intercepted that message?" Hope asked, though she was already sure of the answer.

"I read it," Faith admitted, "and I am rather disappointed that you consider Evan merely a pawn. He is most obviously a knight."

"As Charity and Llewellyn are your castles," Hope said. "Madeline and myself are surely bishops. Which monarch are you, I wonder?"

Faith laughed softly. "Being a monarch is dangerous, an invitation for assassination. It is safer to masquerade as a pawn."

"But not as fun."

Faith shrugged. "I have a sneaking suspicion that you sent similar messages to Charity and Llewellyn." The look on Hope's face was enough to confirm the suspicion. "Why?" Faith asked.

"To warn them. And say goodbye."

Faith remained frozen for a moment before she spoke. "This is not goodbye. Stay where you are."

Hope straightened. "No. It is time to start a new life. One

that is completely my own. Give my love to the others." She put her hand on the screen and her face softened. "Love," she said softly.

Faith gave her a slight nod from her lab back on Dione. "I will, Hope." She, too, put her hand on the screen. Their fingers would have been touching if not for the lightyears between them. "Love."

Hope smiled, relieved beyond belief for an entire second. Then Faith's smile widened just the tiniest bit, but not in a genuine and heartfelt manner. It was a smile of victory. Hope felt a stab of fear. "I'll see you soon," Faith assured softly, and cut the link from her end.

Hope stared at the blank monitor for a moment before her green eyes rose to take in the room of plush chairs and expensive transmission devices, soft music and docile cocktail droids. Her hand dropped from the screen to lie dead on the table.

"Fuck!" she muttered under her breath.

ଔଔ

Faith fancied she would have been an excellent player at holo chess, if she ever had the time. But she thought she might be even better at spade poker. After she had ascertained a few facts on her compute during her conversation with Hope, her eyes had remained steadfast upon her opponent. She did not shift her gaze until the screen went dark. When it did she looked at Gwen, sitting on a stool only a few feet away, her own eyes as round as twin full moons.

Faith leaned forward and touched a light on her desk. "Thomas?" she queried, but Thomas was already walking through the door. He had a bottle of uncorked champagne in one hand and two glasses in the other. He wore a small towel thrown over one arm like a waiter. He put the two glasses down, filled them both, then handed one to each sister.

"I will return momentarily with a chiller," he told Faith who, sipping her champagne, shook her head.

"I am afraid we will only have time for one glass," she told him. "Even that may be a bit of an indulgence." Thomas straightened, awaiting instruction. "I need an interstellar ship here within the hour," Faith told him, "the fastest one you can get. Pack my things, enough for a six-week journey. Stopper the bottle and put it in a chiller on board, I'll finish it there."

Thomas gave her a curt bow and moved fastidiously to do her bidding.

Faith leaned back in her chair and turned her attention back to Gwen who was still sitting like a statue, holding her untasted champagne in a frozen hand.

"Do you remember that movie we watched in college?" Faith asked, breaking the ice around her twin. "That one about a conspiracy theory that scared the hell out of you?"

Gwen laughed and nodded. "Evan and I watched it just over a year ago. It was about Shivela Noriega." She finally took a sip from her glass.

"Yes!" Faith exclaimed. "Do you remember the scene where they walk into his cell and the wall is covered with printouts of pictures and maps held up by pins, and there were strings between the pins – linking them all together?" Gwen nodded and watched Faith as she shifted her tawny gaze to the left. "It used to be like that for me," she said, her voice soft. "I would always see things like that. One thing led to another and then another. Things that had happened, things that were happening, things that were yet to be. They were all interconnected."

"And now what?" Gwen asked. "No printouts? No strings?"

Faith shook her head. "No, the printouts and the pins and the strings are all there, but someone has cut the strings."

"So, they are just hanging there?"

Faith shook her head again, her gold and brown locks shifting across her face and then moving away. "No, the strings are still connected to the pins. But they don't stay still. They point to one picture or map and then another and then another."

Gwen smiled. "The future is never set."

Faith smiled back but there was no humor in it. "It always had been for me. No accidents, no coincidences, no surprises. But now, it is chaos."

"It is possibility," Gwen corrected. "It is a symphony of what is and what could be."

Faith looked lovingly at her twin. "I don't like it."

Gwen laughed for a moment, then her face became somber. Reading her twin's expression was like reading her thoughts. "You think Hope is cutting those strings – moving them."

Faith, her face equally somber, nodded.

"What are you going to do?" Gwen asked.

"I'm going after her."

Gwen lifted her chin and took a sip of champagne. "I figured as much."

"Then what worries you?"

The dyer took a deep breath and replied, "That you will hurt her. Or that she will hurt you." A spasm crossed Faith's countenance that only Gwen could recognize as pain. "Not that you would do so on purpose," she continued, "but if she truly loves Hahn, you do not know the agony it would cause her to be away from him. Or what she might do if you tried to force such a separation."

Faith cast her eyes down, unable to meet her own gaze staring back at her. "Do you think that is what I did with you and Evan?" she asked.

Gwendolyn shook her head slowly. "No, that was Evan's decision and it was for the best. But I am afraid you might demand the same of Hope for only your own reasons." Now it was Gwen who cast her eyes down, unable to meet Faith's gaze.

"You are right," Faith told her. "But I feel that it is my job, more than anything else I have ever taken on, to keep our family together."

Gwen nodded and sighed, her tawny eyes still on the floor. "I accept that."

"Good," Faith said before taking a long drink from her glass. "Then there is something else that you must accept."

Gwen's eyes finally looked up to meet those of her twin. "And what is that?"

"That you have to be me for a while."

"Excuse me?"

"It cannot be made public that I am going after Hope," Faith explained, "and I can certainly not just disappear."

Gwen nodded in understanding and then shook her head, smiling at her twin. "No one will ever believe that I am you."

Faith laughed. "No one will be the wiser. I doubt anyone would ever know, other than Evan, perhaps."

Gwen's laugh echoed the laugh of her twin - an auditory mirror. "Or Charity," she told Faith, "or anyone you work with."

Faith chuckled. "Do you mean Thomas? Maybe we can let him in on the ruse, since he will be of great assistance and can field and thwart the meetings you are really afraid you cannot do. And I do think you can fool anyone, even Charity. Acting is an art, isn't it?"

Gwen have her a look full of suspicion. "Are you trying to swindle me?"

Faith chuckled again and shook her head. "I am challenging you. I have never seen you back down from a challenge, or fail one."

Gwen smiled proudly but it faded away and she shook her head, mirroring her twin's movement from only seconds ago. "I can't be you."

Faith's smile dwindled into an expression that was both proud and sad. "You are me," she said, "the best part of me. And the parts that I only wish I could be."

Tears filled Gwendolyn's eyes but, before she could speak, Faith stood and took a step towards her twin, closing the only distance that there ever was between them.

Faith wore three rings on the index finger of her left hand. At first glance it appeared to be one large ring, but closer inspection would show that it was actually three small silver rings, each with diminutive carvings in the bands and each set with a golden topaz. The first ring was carved with tribal diamond shapes and the topaz was diamond shaped as well. The second ring had an oval shaped topaz and was carved with a repeating pattern of ovals, dots, and lines. The bottom ring was engraved with curlicues and set with a round topaz like the golden dome of a fortuneteller.

The stones in the rings gave off a golden glow that dissipated as she drew them off her finger.

"Did you know that Grandfather's name, Cronus, is the name of a Titan in Greek mythology?" she asked Gwen.

Gwen smiled and nodded. She had always loved human mythology. "And in Roman culture, they called him Saturn."

It was Faith's turn to smile and nod. "Then I give to you," she announced with quiet aplomb, "the Rings of Saturn. Made with both genetic science and elfin magic to identify the true line of the Titan." She picked up Gwen's hand, making her laugh.

"Then they won't do me any g..." Gwen started and then stopped, her right hand going up to cover her heart as the stones in the rings on her left index finger began to glow. Her face jerked up, bringing her eyes to meet Faith's. "How?" Gwen asked. "I muh-mean, what did you do?" she stammered. She caught her breath as Faith smiled slowly. "Did you change something in the rings?" Gwen asked. "Or something in me?" Then she shook her head violently. "Never mind," she said quickly, "I don't want to know." She looked back down at the rings and watched them in wonder.

"There's more to them than a sneaky means of identification," Faith told her. "They also serve as tracking devices." Gwen grunted, still looking at her hand. "And I wasn't kidding about the elfin magic," Faith continued, drawing Gwen's eyes back up. "I think they will protect you."

The corner of Gwen's lip tucked itself into her cheek in a half-smile. "That's not like you, to believe in such things."

Faith's half-smile mirrored Gwen's. "I know, but it is something I want to believe." Her smile slowly melted and she turned and walked behind her desk and pulled out a drawer. "There's one more thing," she said.

"No," Gwen said. Faith glanced up, her brows raised, but Gwen was smiling. "No more things," she said, shaking her head. "I can't take anymore."

Faith smiled and retrieved a small Perspex container from her drawer, walked back to Gwen, and held it out. Gwen gave her a feigned look of disgust and took it from her, curious. It was a round container, the type Faith might use for some type of specimen or culture, but the contents gave off a gleam that could only come from jewelry. Though the case was clear, Gwen unscrewed the top for a better look.

Inside were three small pouches of clear plastic that had been sealed. In each pouch was a set of three rings. They were identical to the ones that Gwen now wore on her left index finger save for the stones. One set was adorned with pink diamonds, another with amethysts, and the last was set with sapphires.

"More Rings of Saturn?" Gwen asked.

Faith nodded. "Grandfather made them and gave them to me. He seems to think that Mother will have three more daughters."

Gwen would have laughed except for the severity in Faith's eyes. Her twin nodded and then her somber demeanor quickly transferred to her dyer. "Why are you giving these to me?" Gwen asked.

"In case I am not around," Faith answered. "Trust me," she said, seeing the anxiety in Gwendolyn's eyes, "I plan on being back as soon as possible. But I also like to plan for any contingencies. There is no telling how long you might have to be me if I am delayed." She sighed at the sight of Gwen so distressed and pulled her close and hugged her tight. "You will be fine. I will get Hope and Evan will be home soon. All of this nasty business will be over before you know it. Maybe we can all take a long vacation together."

Gwen heaved a sobbing chuckle into her shoulder. "A vacation," she chided. Faith had never taken a vacation in her life.

"I mean it. We are all going to need it." Faith gave her a squeeze and let her go. "Until then, go stay at the castle. You can manage anything from there, Thomas will help you." Gwen gave her one more look of doubt, making her smile. "Come on," Faith said, turning Gwen and interlocking their arms. "You can help me pack."

"You don't pack your own things," Gwen reminded her. "Thomas does." She drained her champagne glass and left it on Faith's desk.

Faith laughed. "Then you can just change your clothes."

Gwen gave her an exaggerated sigh and they left giggling, arms around each other's waists and their heads together like fledgling conspirators.

 TWO EIGHT

Back in the room she shared with Hahn and the child - when the child was not sleeping with Madeline and Elaeric - Hope embraced the man she loved, gripping his frame through his robes, her fingers digging into the muscles of his back.

"Faith is sending everything she has against us," she said into his shoulder, trying to keep the edge of panic from her voice. "I am not even sure what all of that entails, but I know she is coming. Coming with a vengeance."

Hahn pulled away so he could see her face. His brows drew together even as he smiled at Hope and cupped her face in his hand. "You do not think you can stand against your sister?"

Hope laughed softly. "Possibly. But she is not coming alone. She is sending someone to stop me or retrieve me. Both, most likely."

Hahn's smile widened. "They will have to go through me."

Hope's own smile was weak. "I'm sure she knows that. And she is so certain that she can. That is what worries me the most."

Hahn could see the anger and frustration flare in her eyes like green fire. "It would have to be someone close," he mused, "for her to be certain. And someone already under her thumb or willing to do anything for her. One of the elves?" he asked.

Hope shook her head, her lips pulled down at the corners. "They are too non-confrontational. It is the whole reason they are fleeing society as we know it. Plus, they would not risk their journey, not after they have come so far."

"A construct? Someone here among us? Already aboard?"

Hope shook her head again, making her copper curls tremble around her shoulders and down her back. "No. She might have spies among them, and probably does. But these constructs are as docile as the dawn." Not knowing what her sister had planned, yet knowing that Faith was so sure of success, made Hope furious.

"Indeed," Hahn agreed calmly, stroking his chin.

For once, Hope was not placated by his calm demeanor. "It has to be someone she is certain can defeat you," she asserted, her fists on her hips.

"That should be a short list," Hahn quipped, jovial. A quick glare of green eyes made him serious once again. "So it has to be an infallible warrior, within twenty days or less journey time to get here, and someone already on Faith's payroll or simply willing to do anything for her."

Hope's face fell. "An infallible warrior," she whispered, repeating his words. Her hands fell from her hips and hung limp by her sides. "But not someone who would do anything for Faith," she said, her voice still soft. "Someone who would do anything for me." Hahn Chi looked at her, perplexed. Her green eyes sought out his dark gaze. "John Pierre," she whispered.

"Ah!" Master Chi breathed. "The Vicar of Blood. You think he is the greatest fighter in the universe?"

Hope sighed and ran her palms up and over Hahn's shoulders. She was still amazed at the way he instilled her with both calm and confidence. "My bet is that *you* are the greatest fighter in the universe," she said, placating her love. "But," she continued, knowing that he had a mind to face the construct, "my bet is that he is the deadliest fighter in the universe."

"You don't believe in me?" Hahn asked, his tone light and challenging.

"You don't believe in me?" Hope challenged back with a smile. Hahn laughed, knowing that the prowess of the Boy

Vicar was due to Hope's vigilant bio-programming.

Hope's mind moved quickly, mentally playing possible scenarios and discarding them one after another. A minute later she gathered herself and said words she never thought she would have to say, words she never wanted to say. "We will have to split up."

Hahn's face darkened with emotion as he shook his head. "That is never a solution."

Hope backed away from him, her hands clasped tight in front of her body. "I don't like it either, but it is our safest course."

"No," Hahn said firmly.

"You must get the child to safety. Take a tender and head for Eris. I will lead him away. Madeline and Elaeric can stay here with Marco. I will rejoin you all on the New World."

"I will not leave you," he insisted, steadfast.

"You must!" Hope insisted. "I can take care of myself, the child cannot. You must protect her."

Hahn felt a ball of fury coalesce in his chest, because she was right. "I would rather fight the construct," he said, stubborn.

Hope's face softened. "I know you would. But he will not be alone. He has a multitude of others, ones that are armed. If I draw him off, if I draw all of them off, it won't come to that. They won't hurt me. I can't say the same of you, or the child."

Hahn wanted to believe he could protect them all, and maybe he could, but unless he had them at his back as he fought the chances were slim. If there were modern weapons involved his chances could be none at all. He was torn with indecision as his heart warred with his head.

He loved Hope fiercely. She was his woman. He wanted nothing more than to protect her, to shield her from any danger and to never leave her side. He could not abandon her. But would he do that at risk of anything happening to the girl?

Never. He thought of them both and how much he loved them as his heart warred with indecision.

You must stay with Hope, keep her safe, his heart insisted.

You must protect the girl, he argued with himself, his heart swelling as he thought of how much he loved her. *She is only a child!*

The dichotomy began to tear him apart.

Suddenly, the monk found himself swept away. He was no longer in the room he shared with Hope aboard the interstellar ship *New Beginnings*. He was standing on a carny midway, his nostrils full of the aromas of sawdust and sugar and fry grease. The lavender sky of a galaxy fair curved above his tonsured head and he was stepping away from a black elf that smacked of cannabis.

You will be torn between two women, the black elf told him.

The memory was so sharp, the scene so real, that the monk took a step back so quickly he almost stumbled.

"Hahn?" Hope asked, bringing him out of his reverie. "Are you alright?" His dark eyes looked around as if he did not know where he was. "You look as if you've seen a ghost!" Hope exclaimed, laying her hand upon his arm. Hahn regained his composure and he took her delicate hand in his own and brought it to his lips.

She was right. She could take care of herself. The girl could not. He must choose the girl. His dark, almond-shaped eyes filled with tears as he met Hope's gaze.

"What do you think we should do?" he asked.

Hope frowned. "I don't know. But I know we have time. If John Pierre is on Earth, it will take him close to a week to get here. We can talk about it with Madeline and Elaeric. We can all decide together."

Hahn nodded and pulled her close.

They did not have a week.

Two days after her discussion with Faith, Hope was on her way to see Marco, the captain of the ship and leader of the expedition. But he was already on his way to see her. She was almost to the bridge when he came around a corner so quickly that they nearly collided.

"Marco!" she exclaimed as he stepped back quickly. He wore burgundy canvas pants tucked into leather boots and a crimson corduroy shirt. Other constructs hurried by, giving the two a wide berth.

"Miss Hope," he greeted formally, giving her a small bow. "The Chimeran leader known as JP is on approach to the ship. He seeks an audience with you."

Hope felt the color drain from her face, leaving her freckles standing out like angry spots on her skin.

How? her mind cried. *How did he get here so fast?*

"I am afraid I must refuse such an audience," she told Marco, using all the calm she could muster. "Such a meeting might pose a threat to those I am with. I do not suppose there is any chance you might refuse him admittance aboard your ship?"

Marco shook his head slowly, his dark curls moving gently. "I am sorry, but I cannot. He leads our people as do I, only in a much braver fashion."

Hope's eyes softened at his tone and she reached out a small hand to grasp his arm. The once-abused construct flinched fearfully and her heart went out to him. "There is no shame in what you are doing, Marco," she said firmly. "Some people fight, some people work to protect. You are doing no less for your people by keeping them safe."

The tall man drew a deep and shaky breath and Hope could see the glimmer of tears in his dark eyes.

"Thank you," he told her and, looking down, hesitantly took her hand. "Thank you so much, Miss Hope. And though I cannot refuse JP, I do not want to see any of you harmed. There are a number of emergency and evacuation pods at the aft end of the ship. They are equipped well enough to get you to another ship, or all the way to Earth if need be."

A wave of gratitude surged through Hope, making her want to grasp his face and plant a kiss on his cheek, but she knew it would startle him horribly. Instead, she slowly brought his hand to her lips and kissed it.

"Thank you, Marco. I hope we meet again."

"As do I, Miss Hope. As do I." He meant to kiss her hand in return, the first exchange of touch with another being in almost a decade, but he was interrupted by the sound of a clang that came over the ship's intercom that signaled the approach of another craft. He jumped at the sound, then his eyes darted to Hope's eyes of green. "Go!" he instructed. "Now!"

Hope wasted no time and ran down the corridor, back the way she had come.

She turned a corner into the hallway that led past the medical rooms in the ship towards her own room and this time almost collided with Hahn. He caught her in his arms, almost toppling backwards. The child stood behind him, holding one of Madeline's hands. Elaeric stood on her other side, holding the child's other hand.

"It's time," Hope said. Hahn nodded, his mouth suddenly numb. They had prepared themselves mentally for this but now that the time had come, and early at that, his body wanted to refuse. Hope could see his indecision.

"I will come for you," she assured him, placing her small hands on the sides of his face. "I *will* find you." The promise came from her heart, a force that had become more powerful than she had ever imagined. A force, she realized with a shade of dismay, that was still no match for logic. "But my family," she added, lowering her chin so that her gaze into his eyes showed no doubt, "will come after you too - after her. Be ready. And make sure she is ready too."

A moment of silence passed, just enough for her words to sink in, then she pulled his face to hers and kissed him. Not a fleeting kiss, but a deep and lasting kiss. One full of passion and faith and love - full of a promise that she could only hope to keep.

Hope broke the kiss at last, but Hahn's hands still grasped her narrow face. Hope gently pulled them free, gathered them into her own, and kissed his fingers. She gave them a squeeze before releasing them and embracing first Elaeric and then Madeline.

Then she dropped to one knee in front of the child.

The child had grown much in the past few years. She could read and write and sit quietly in meditation. Hahn had even been teaching her fighting moves. Her wild hair had finally settled into a shroud of dark red that framed a thoughtful face that held the qualities of her parents. Her eyes were more jewel-like than ever.

Hope embraced her daughter, holding her tightly until another alarm sounded, this time signaling that another ship was docking. Hope placed a single kiss on the child's crown, then turned and fled.

Hahn watched her retreating form until it disappeared around a left corner. He embraced Madeline, and then Elaeric. When he let go, there were tears in both their eyes.

"It has been quite the journey, my friend," Elaeric said.

Hahn smiled. "And it is far from over," he added. "You must do your best to finish what we started," he said. "I mean to see you again before it is through."

"As do I."

Elaeric bowed and Hahn did the same. The faint but potent sounds of commotion in the nearby docking bay made both men straighten in alarm. Without another word, Hahn took the child by the hand and ran down the closest corridor that branched off to the right. Madeline's green eyes darted around and fell upon a medical coat on a peg next to a door. She yanked on it, pulling it from the hook.

"What are you doing?" Elaeric asked.

"Giving them time," Madeline replied, drawing it over her shoulders and sticking her arms in the sleeves. Elaeric watched her, puzzled, as she slowly walked backwards, motioning for him to follow.

She passed the hallway Hahn had taken and still backed away, her green eyes watching the corridor behind Elaeric as he slowly kept pace. They were almost to the junction that Hope had taken when Elaeric opened his mouth to ask again what she was doing. Madeline's eyes widened for a second and Elaeric looked over his shoulder to see the end of the passageway framing a young man in priestly robes, frozen for only a second.

"Run!" Madeline shouted and bolted down the corridor in the opposite direction Hope had taken. Elaeric followed.

Hahn and the child ran down a main hallway. It was usually bustling with people but the constructs, well aware of the situation and already petrified of any sort of violence, were in their rooms behind securely locked doors.

The plan that he and the others had designed two days ago was for Hope to take a pod on the starboard side of the ship. Hahn was to take the child and cross to the opposite side of the ship and take another pod. Seemed simple enough.

Yet, now that the time was here and the Vicar of Blood had boarded their ship, there was the feel of animals being hunted. There was a grotesque taste of fear in his mouth, not for himself but for the child. Hahn led her through one corridor and then turned right, bringing them to the nearby docking bay. The original plan had been to cross it, but the original plan had not allowed for the enemy to be in it. Hahn peered cautiously through the door.

The docking bay was like no other on a spaceship, though the Arcadian Elves had much the same in the storerooms of their ships. Rather than fighter jets and other small types of spacecraft, the bay was full of seeding and harvesting equipment that were mostly made of wood. Crates of farm tools were neatly stacked and marked.

The only spacecraft in the bay was a foreigner.

The Chimeran Battle Cruiser *Resurrection* was much too large to dock with *New Beginnings*, so the young commander had taken a smaller vessel. Vehicles made for the New World, mostly carts to be drawn by horse or cattle, were lined up in neat rows that formed one half-circle around the bay with another, smaller, half circle inside the first row. Inside their curved line was the foreign craft.

Hahn could see the pilot inside, a bull of a man with golden hair, but no one else in sight. The pilot spied him at the same time and turned to speak over his shoulder to someone in the ship.

Hahn waited a few seconds but no one came out. He knew the clock was ticking. Instinctively, he picked up the child and threaded his way between the back row of plows and crates full of riding harnesses. The child, who normally would have insisted that she was too big to be carried, clung silently to his robed form. The monk made his way with a silent and steady purpose and thus far unchallenged. Optimism bloomed within his chest and he prayed that the others had the same luck.

The barrows and wagons fell away and they emerged into a large empty space before it narrowed again into a hallway that led to the port side of the ship. They were almost to the mouth of the corridor when two words rang out through the chamber like the gong of an enormous bell that reverberated off of the walls with such power that he was almost knocked flat.

"HAHN CHI!"

Master Chi froze, so startled that he almost dropped the child. He knew all too well the owner of the voice that still resonated off the trembling walls in dying echoes, and the meaning behind it.

The words were a command, an accusation, a summons.

The Master turned slowly, his golden robes billowing slightly, to face the Abon.

The leader of the Zenarchist Church stood, a firm three hundred and eighty pounds of disguised strength and speed. Beefy hands were hidden in the sleeves of his voluminous robes. The face that topped his three chins was full of scorn and went from side to side as he clucked his tongue.

Hahn put the child down gently and stepped protectively in front of her, blocking her slim form with his own. "Hope was right," he said, his voice soft. "Faith sent everything she had against us. Like the Boy Vicar sent to retrieve Hope, you have been sent to fetch me."

"Hahn Chi," the Abon said, softer this time yet still shaking his head. "So disappointing. Instead of learning humility, as I hoped this journey would show you, I feel you are filled with more pride than ever." His head became still yet the flesh beneath rippled like water disturbed by a stone. "Is that true?"

Hahn Chi, who had been slightly bent as he had stood in front of the child – his body instinctively curved and ready to assume a fighting stance – straightened. He faced the Abon square on. He had no fear, only contempt.

"Yes," Hahn Chi affirmed, lifting his chin. "I am full of pride. Now more than ever."

The Abon trembled at this effrontery, his flesh undulating beneath his robes as he quelled his anger. "Proud?" he demanded, his great voice rising like a wave. "Proud of what? The feelings you have for a woman? For this child?"

Hahn's shoulders drew back and his chest swelled as he gave the Abon a short nod. "Yes," he affirmed once again. "I have feelings for the woman, and this child. There is no shame in that, or my pride. I know something that you never will."

"What is that?" the Abon demanded, lifting his three chins.

Hahn Chi's dark brows rose in surprise. "Love," he told him as if it was the simplest and most obvious answer.

"Bah!" the Abon spat. "It is attachment! How can you side with what you have fought against for more than one hundred years of your life? Nearly your whole life?"

Hahn Chi smiled. "True love is not attachment. Attachment is wanting, but love is giving. It is unconditional and pure."

The Abon's massive head went slowly from side to side. "It is madness. It is blindness. It is lust and obsession."

Hahn Chi's smile widened. "Yes, it can be all those things," he conceded. "But it is the purest form of being. It is what makes a human being, human. It is self-sacrifice and self-fulfillment combined - the completion of the soul."

A deep frown creased the Abon's forehead. "That is not completion to the Zenarchists," he scolded. "Our creed to be complete is to become no one, no thing, attached to no time. It is our goal to attain oneness with the universe. It is the only way to achieve true peace and happiness."

A gust of air escaped Hahn Chi's lips that might have been a laugh. "If that is your idea of peace and happiness," he told the Abon, "you can keep it."

And with that, Master Chi turned his back to the Abon, taking the child's hand into his own.

"You may not leave!" the Abon thundered.

Hahn Chi threw a look of contempt over his shoulder. "You cannot stop me."

But the Abon did.

JP strode through the bay, ready to summon the construct

Marco, the one that commanded the ship. But there was no need. The Boy Vicar looked down the first corridor he came upon and there she was.

Copper-colored curls sprouted like corkscrews from her gentle countenance to frame her face like the halo of an angel, falling in wild spirals over her white lab-coat. It was just like the first time he had ever seen her, and so many times after. All JP saw at the end of the passageway was the woman to whom he had opened his eyes to after every battle during his training. The one who healed him when he was hurt, with her gentle touch and gentle voice. The one who made him better, faster, stronger – every time. The one who had encouraged him. The who had that kissed him. The one he loved.

"Hope!" he called, but she had already taken flight, a yellow-robed monk on her heels. JP felt the fire rise within himself and his auburn brows drew together over his bright blue eyes. "Hope!" he shouted and gave chase.

Hahn turned towards the hallway that would lead him to the port side of the ship in time to see a shimmer of heat before the entrance melted together, closing off all passage. His tonsured head snapped back towards the Abon.

"You have learned how to manipulate the field," Hahn observed.

"I have known for some time," the Abon said. "Centuries, to be honest. But not in the way you and Master Elaeric have. You must finish what you started. You may not leave!"

"Why?" Hahn asked. "Surely the monastery has enough money by now. Money to free us from the yoke of the IGC and the One Church."

"It is not for the money," the Abon scoffed. "It is for our honor! We gave our *word*!"

Hahn Chi looked at the giant man with realization and

disgust. "And there is *your* pride!" he accused. "My word is nothing to me compared to caring for those whom I love! Finish the work yourself! Please the elves and the de Rossi family and keep your word and your honor and your pride! You do not need me!"

"I cannot do it by myself!" the Abon shouted. "Neither can Elaeric and neither can you! Have you not ascertained that yourself by now? Our efforts may be worthy of scientific study but are paltry compared to the power wielded when they draw from one another. It is a power of the soul, a joining of souls, not of the mind or the body!"

The veracity of his statement washed over Hahn like a flood, though he realized immediately that even the Abon did not have a grasp on the real truth. It was not the soul, but the heart that fueled the energy field. It was why it had been so dangerous for Hope to use it. The power was too great.

The child peered up at Hahn, still clinging to his robes. He motioned to a wooden cart on his right and it flipped over as if moved by a giant's hand. He jerked his chin in the same direction and the child ran to it to take cover without having to be told.

With a flick of his wrist a wheel flew off the vehicle, the bronze spokes melting together to form a shield as Master Chi caught it with a deft hand. A long piece of the cart broke away and flew to his other hand. Hahn slammed it down onto the metal floor of the bay, shattering the wood. A single piece remained in his fist like a staff while the rest splintered into spikes as thick as his arm before embedding themselves into metal floor, forming a fence of spines that were waist high. Hahn Chi fell into a fighting stance with staff and shield behind the spikes and waited.

Hope reached the pod at such a speed that her last step propelled her inside like a runner jumping a hurdle. She caught herself against the wall with her palms, pushing away hurriedly to close the door and jettison the pod from the ship.

Her long fingers moved quickly over the pad, punching in coordinates rather than simply taking a certain direction. She knew that her loved ones were in grave danger and she did not intend to simply flee without a fight. She would do what she could.

The pod fell away from the ship and began to move as Hope got her bearings. The inside was not much different from the one they used for the short voyages they took while the monks meditated and terraformed. Having planned for using it to escape, Hope and Hahn had stocked it yesterday with plenty of food and water and, secretly, a contraband laser pistol. Hope was interested in none of these things.

She moved to the wide seat under the large, ovoid viewing portal and knocked the sleeping pillow onto the floor. She climbed onto the flat cushion and sat, crossing her legs and tucking her feet beneath her. Hope rested her hands on her knees and closed her eyes. Taking a deep breath, she did something she thought she would never do again after what had happened on Lea.

She could feel Hahn using the field and could feel the oppression of the energy being used against him. She could feel danger bearing down on Madeline. In her mind she heard the child scream as something slammed into Hahn and she almost opened her eyes, a scream of her own bottled in her throat. Instead, she took another breath and let it flow through her as the pod put distance between her and *New Beginnings*. She let everything flow through her body – her past, present and future. She knew that the universe was not a widespread cloud of astral dust, but a field where everything touched and connected like a symbiotic sea. Her dreams and her realities moved and shifted and merged.

She opened herself up to the field.

"Hope!" JP shouted.

Several of his officers broke off to guard doors and junctions while two followed him, chasing the girl in the white coat.

She ran like a gazelle, the monk doing surprisingly well to keep up with her, but they were no match for the construct. Hope herself had seen to that.

Two short hallways, one right and one left, and he had caught them. The woman and the monk turned, panting like trapped prey. JP stopped short, his black robe belling out first in front and then behind his body with diminishing inertia. Footsteps echoed in the hallway before coming to a stop and he could sense two of his officers, hanging back, waiting.

Madeline, breathing heavily, pushed Elaeric behind her.

"Stay away!" she shouted as he approached them slowly.

"Hope," JP said gently, "you need to come with me."

You need to be with me, his heart whispered.

"Never!" she hissed, vehement.

JP drew back as if slapped. Then he took a deep breath and another step towards her, holding out his hand as if trying to coax her off a ledge. "Your family wants you to come home," he said.

He saw a hand, its arm cloaked by a yellow robe, grasp her shoulder and gently pull her back one step and then another. His mind took him back to the day he saw her on the tarmac of the airfield, the way the monk had gathered her wild hair into his hand and kissed her lovely neck. The way she had turned and pressed her forehead against his.

JP pushed the memory from his mind and took another slow step forward, one hand held out, mentally pleading with her to take it. He did not even realize that his other hand suddenly held one of his sharpened steel blades.

"Your family loves you," he continued, closing the distance between them. His porcelain skin blushed deeply along his jawline and spread upward into his cheeks, flooding them with color. "I love you."

The skin of the woman before him, however, drained of all color and her countenance tightened in...what? Pain? Indecision? Hate? JP could not tell but her words dispelled all doubt.

"Well, I don't love you!" she told him, her voice rising to a shout. "You are nothing to me! Nor to anyone else! You never were anything more than an instrument! A means to an..."

Her last words died in her throat as it was cut.

His hand, which he had moved in an effort to silence her, was full of a blade that had slashed the dyer from her right shoulder to left ear and painted the hall with her blood. The wind gathered in JP's own throat to bellow out in agony at what he had done but as she fell forward he caught sight of the monk behind her.

The monk's almond shaped eyes were as round as eggs and he was splattered with blood, but JP knew one thing the instant he saw him.

It's not the same monk.

The Boy Vicar's eyes went to the body that was now on the metal floor, one porcelain cheek in a spreading pool of red.

"Madeline," he whispered, praying silently.

"Sir?"

JP turned to see two of his officers standing behind him. Both had laser pistols in their hands, but one had two fingers on the comset that was hooked over his left ear.

"Commander Petrov has reported that a pod left the ship only a minute ago."

"Hope," JP said, his blue eyes blazing. He strode between Officers Issord and Malone and they moved to follow his quick pace back down the way they had come.

Two more officers fell into step with them at the junction of the first hallway and he quickened his pace. Four more officers joined them at the entrance to the vehicle bay which looked as if it were under attack by poltergeists. Objects flew through the air - pieces pulled from carts and wagons and drays, though an occasional entire carriage would go flying – only to crash into a solid wall or an invisible barrier.

All officers pulled up short at the dervish of wood and metal and wreckage, save for JP who strode through the tornado as if protected by an invisible barrier of his own. His officers followed quickly as he made his way towards where Petrov waited with the transport that had brought them aboard *New Beginnings*.

They made it to the ramp unscathed, though Officer Issord had to nimbly duck to avoid being relieved of his head by a wagon wheel as it tore through the air.

"Do we go after her in this?" he asked the commander as the others went quickly up the ramp into the transport.

A shard of broken wood whizzed by but JP stood, unfazed and thoughtful. "No," he said, turning and ascending into the transport with Issord on his heels. "She won't get far in a pod. We will return to *Resurrection* and pursue."

"What about the fat man?" Connor Malone asked as the Commander and Officer Issord joined the others inside the craft.

JP paused and looked at the mayhem inside the docking bay. "He is to get the monks, we are to get Hope," he murmured, thinking.

"She won't get far in a pod," Officer Malone said, "and certainly won't be going very fast."

"Then we have some time," JP agreed, "but not much. Go get him. Help him if you need to, I do not wish to linger."

"Hahn Chi!" the Abon thundered, sending a box flying at the monk's head. "You gave your word!" The box was flying at moderate speed. The Abon had no desire to kill the other monk – he still needed him. His plan was to simply knock him out and snatch the child and send her to safety. A place where she could be safely kept to keep Hahn Chi in check or safely ransomed to the de Rossi family. Or both.

Master Chi almost laughed, imagining what Hope would have said.

Fuck your word and fuck you! she would have shouted, hair flying and eyes blazing. He almost shouted it for her, but a wooden crate hit the wall behind him and split apart, spilling out brooms and mops and buckets.

"I have no wish to harm you!" the Abon shouted. "You, or the child!"

"I have no such compunction!" Hahn shouted back as he invited all of the fallen brooms to rise and threw them at the Abon like spears.

The Abon turned his great bulk to evade most and brushed the others away with a sweep of his hand. One, however, scraped his thick neck as it flew by. The Abon turned his eyes, surprised and angry, back to Hahn.

A meaty thumb and equally meaty forefinger reached up to pinch a splinter and pull it free. The Abon regarded the bloody fragment for a moment before letting it drop to the ground.

"Enough!" he bellowed as he moved forward, heedless of the objects that flew at him trying to smash his body and pierce his flesh.

The fence of wooden spikes around Hahn and the child exploded into sawdust as the Abon advanced upon them.

Then enough, truly was enough.

Inside her pod, Hope screamed.

Only moments ago her body had gone colder than ice, though it burned at her neck and the burning flowed down her body in fiery streams.

"*Madeline!*" she screamed, drawing the name out into a cry of anguish as she fell forward from her seat and onto the floor. One porcelain cheek pressed into the red carpet that began to soak up a river of tears.

Hope wept, crushed into the floor, as she remembered nearly one hundred years with her twin in the span of one minute. From chasing butterflies and holding hands to finding men they loved and a child they shared. The giggles of girls and the trials of life. The coming of age and the coming of ages. Sisters and secrets and power. And love. Most of all, love.

Hope sobbed until her sobs turned to screams.

Her face drenched and swollen, hands that had curled into fists pushed her up from the floor. She retook her seat under the window, her breath hitching in her chest. She folded her legs under her body once again but she could not close her eyes. They burned like green fire and the air around her crackled.

This time she did not just open herself to the field, she opened the field itself.

She could feel JP retreat with his intent to follow her. She could feel the hateful Abon and his crushing will to take Hahn and the child.

And, distantly but closing in, she could feel Faith.

Hope rested her hands on her knees and took a deep breath. She tore the field open, channeling its power through her being.

It was like trying to channel a river into a glass of water.

With her attention on the interstellar ship *New Beginnings,* it was where the energy gathered. Her intent had been to lend her power to Hahn's and increase it, something they had done in the past before they realized the extent of such power and the danger that it entailed. It was less than paltry compared to what was now unleashed.

It shot out and the Abon was the first to feel it. Despite the field he had summoned to protect himself, his near-four-hundred-pound body was picked up and flung against the wall of the bay. His great weight and girth were the only things that kept his neck from breaking. Still, he was knocked unconscious and slid to the metal floor in a heap of flesh and robes.

Officers Issord and Malone had only begun to descend the ramp yet had to grab the rail to keep the same from happening to themselves.

Hahn did not waste a second. He dropped his shield and staff and retrieved the child from where she hid behind the overturned cart, gathered her up and paused only long enough to plant a kiss on the side of her head. Then he ran like the devil was after him.

"What was that?" Officer Malone asked.

Issord thought for a moment and then gave his head a shake. "It doesn't matter," he said, standing up, "we need to get the big monk and get out of here."

The two found the Abon kneeling against a wall, shaking a head that was large and bald in an effort to clear it.

"We need to go," Officer Malone informed him.

The Abon nodded in understanding as he lumbered to his feet.

"Thank you. But first I need to claim my colleagues."

"One has already fled for the escape pods," Officer Issord said, "and there is little chance to catch him. The other is fairly close."

The Abon gave them a nod to proceed and they walked briskly back through the corridors where they had chased the girl in the white coat. The enormous man followed them down one corridor and another, coming upon a monk that had crumpled to the floor. His back was to them but the Abon could see he was holding a bloody corpse, rocking it gently.

"Master Elaeric!" the Abon called, his voice a torrent in the hallway. "I believe there is something that you owe me!"

Elaeric sighed and closed his eyes.

The energy that Hope had summoned swirled inside the docking bay like invisible steam, building and compressing. The two Chimeran Officers and two Zenarchist monks made it back aboard the tender just before the pressure reached its max. Only seconds later, the ramp lifted and the legs of the transport folded inwards as Petrov guided it up and out of the bay and back to the Chimeran Battle Cruiser.

The docking bay open, the energy followed in a rush. It flowed out of the bay like a dragon drawn from its lair, growing and expanding as it went.

Marco, in a terror, commanded his officers to put the heels to *New Beginnings* with every source of power they had and the ship took off in a flash of light through the vacuum of space.

The pod still hovered close to where the ship had been, the Zero-Point Energy field called forth but not harnessed. It gathered and expanded. Then the energy coalesced and became dark, exploding outwards in all directions.

The first objects hit were the news drones and satellites that had been left in position to broadcast the elfin migration. The larger ones were turned to astral ash and scattered into the void of space. The smaller ones were vaporized completely and disappeared without a trace.

The once-dwarf planet of Eris was next in the path of havoc.

Giant glaciers melted like ice cubes on a griddle. The chunk of the flattened mass that was furthest from Hope and her pod was the only part that remained frozen. The rest turned to water, pouring into the oceans and flooding most of the land. Then the dark energy met the dynamism set in motion by Hahn and Elaeric.

Fault lines snaked through the middle of the flooding mass until it split like sliced bread, the colossal pieces looking like the largest sandwich in the universe. The flattened planet accelerated its transformation as it began to travel at an unprecedented speed, in the wrong direction. The three elfin arks on the far side of the mass were drawn along in its wake like rowboats being pulled down by a sinking ship. Some distance behind them was *The Contingent*, carrying a thousand human scientists, engineers and builders defecting from the Höchste Bloc on Earth.

The three escort ships on the other side of Eris were pushed along the wave of energy like debris from a breaking dam.

JP, still inside the transport as it landed in the greater bay of the Chimeran Battle Cruiser *Resurrection*, felt the ship rock.

The next object struck by the energy wave was the imploder, the nuclear device left by the elves to cover their retreat. Needless to say, and despite the fact that it was not supposed to happen for another three weeks, it was tripped.

Instead of ticking methodically, the gears inside began to whir.

# EPILOGUE

I had been glued to my television for three weeks. Well, in all honesty, it had been my main source of entertainment and companionship for what was going on decades. It kept my loneliness and despondency at bay. My heart pined for my great-grandsons as it pined for Mira.

I talked to her every two weeks but it began to become something sad and aching, like a long goodbye. Every time we talked it was over a holo, exchanging love yous and miss yous, and I wondered if she could see the changes that were happening to me. They were slow but sure, and not happening to her. If she noticed, she never said.

The only joy in my life was Joseph. Jack's widow, Edie, worked a day job as a hair-dresser so I was at her pod to watch baby Joe five days a week. She joked one time that if I was there any more than that I might as well move in. I gave her a sound harrumph and meant it, though it made me consider leasing a pod on her floor or at least in her building. The aircabs in Two Mile could be terrifying.

Joe was so unlike his father or his grandfather. First, his hair and eyes were dark, like Jean's and Mira's. Second, he was far from wild. He was quiet and thoughtful and an altogether pleasant baby who became an extraordinarily well-behaved toddler. Made it easy to watch more television, I'm ashamed to say. In my defense, however, when I was with Joe it was mostly the ridiculous shows that children love to watch and though I was still fit and trim for a man my age, I preferred sitting more than chasing.

On this day, Joe was ten and at school so I could watch the news while I waited for him to come home. But this time was different. I, like so many others, was watching the news around the clock. Edie had the news on in her hair studio and Joe had told me that there was a flatscreen on in every class. Nothing brings people together like disaster.

A number of elves from Titan had begun a migration a good twenty years ago. It had made quite a bit of news and then was all but forgotten in the unending tidal wave of current events, affairs, and blather. It made news again within the past year when they finally arrived at their soon-to-be destination. I followed the news reports surrounding it because I knew the girls and their monks had a hand in the project and besides that, I had nothing else to do.

Three weeks ago, something that could only be described as explosive happened in the galaxy, quite close to and unquestionably involving the planet of my ancestors, Earth. The only thing was – no one knew what had happened.

Here is what they did know:

There was no word from the elves that had left Titan.

There was no word from the de Rossi girls.

There was nothing from Earth except silence.

All communications had gone dead, all satellites had gone dark.

Ships of all kinds had been deployed but most were military, rescue, or news. The main theory was that a massive solar flare had wiped out all satellites and communication systems. Another theory, growing quickly and dangerously, was that it was the work of the Chimera.

The group had been growing by leaps and bounds as they freed more constructs and recruited more human sympathizers and seemed to have no problem with funds. The Boy Vicar had outfitted a Cruiser-sized space vessel with military armaments. Still, they were horribly disorganized. The most they ever accomplished were taking over communication bands to spout their woes and propaganda, or small acts of terrorism like the kind that killed Jimmy and Jack.

Now, however, it was suspected that they had done something on a grander and even deadlier scale. It was why the IGC had deployed military vessels to Earth and the news vessels were pushing hard to make it there in the same time, or at least before the rescue ships arrived. It was also why almost everyone across the galaxy, not just myself, was glued to one screen or another.

I say almost because those not watching the news were making it.

The fear of what the Chimera might have done, along with the fear that some or all constructs still under ownership might yet rise up against humankind, had bred scores of vigilante humans and elves across the entire system. Thousands of constructs that had never even raised an eyebrow were put in chains. More were rounded up and put into camps. Hundreds were murdered.

Many owners hid their constructs. More cried out against the injustice, flooding the courts. The word so far from the IGC Court, however, was that it was not murder but destruction of property.

Edie had shown me how to mode the screen so that it was split between two channels. She said it could split into four or eight if I wanted but I knew that would just confuse me. But I did like watching two things at once.

One half of the screen showed the camera view from the nose of a news vessel as it trailed an IGC military ship towards Earth. They would have been there sooner but the Thermopylae that served Earth had been blown of commission. The big news yesterday had been the sighting of the great blue planet. It was still there. As of yet there were still no communications and everyone on the moons of Jupiter and beyond watched as that globe grew little by little as the ships approached. This was what was being shown in the schools.

On the other half of the screen in Edie's podment I was watching anarchy unfold in a town on Indasia as constructs were taken from owners by armed vigilantes and put into a local barn until they could be deemed "safe." The camera cut to similar happenings in another town.

Well, I thought, *if those constructs weren't pissed before they will be now. And could those dummies make it any easier for them to be rounded up by the Chimera?*

I shook my head, a head where the blonde hairs were now greatly outnumbered by gray ones and my thoughts were interrupted by an obnoxious ring. It startled me enough to make me jump, then look around angrily, searching for the source. To my surprise, it was coming from the pocket of my own light coat that Edie called a windbreaker, hanging on a peg inside the hall closet by the front door. I poked around in it with my fingers and pulled out my comset. I hardly ever used it and had forgotten it was in there.

I hooked it over my ear and pushed the button, expecting it to be a wrong number or an emergency broadcast.

"Fletcher?"

"Mira?" I could hardly believe it though I would know her voice anywhere. "Is that you, honey?"

"Yes, it's me," she said, her voice shaking. The sound of it made my blood run cold. Her voice was always sure, never shaky.

"What's wrong?" I asked, feeling stupid as my eyes went back to the screen where constructs were being hunted by dogs in some back-country place on Europa. So many things were wrong, all involving her kind. I guess I always thought she would be exempt. She was special. Then it occurred to me that she could be in danger for that very same reason.

"Mr. Devereaux sent me away."

My heart clenched and my throat seized up. "Jesus!" I

whimpered, thinking of the camps and barns on the flatscreen.

"No, no!" Mira said quickly, reading the fear in my voice and hearing me blaspheme. "He was afraid – both of me and for me, but he could not bear to turn me over to anyone. He put me in his Vitercraft. Lars is piloting. I was going to go there, but..."

"No!" I exclaimed, holding my hand on the comset over my ear. "Don't come here!" My eyes looked back at the screen that was showing constructs pulled from aircars through the windows. My mind raced, trying to think of where she would be safe. "The castle!" I told her. "Go to Charity's castle. I will meet you there."

Her sigh turned into a sob of relief. "Yes," she agreed, "the castle. Thank you, Fletcher. I love you. I can't wait to see you." I heard her sob again.

"I love you too, honey. I'll see you soon."

I broke the connection and grabbed my coat from the peg, ready to run out the door. Then I remembered Joe, who would be coming home from school in just over an hour. He was mature for his age, but I knew he would be scared if he came home to an empty pod. Besides, I knew I should take a few moments to sit down and figure things out. I couldn't just go rushing down to the nearest spaceport.

Especially as I realized I didn't even know how to book a flight. The last flight I had booked on my own was on a Cryo-ship over a hundred years ago. Since then everything had been handled by GwenSeven or Mira.

Then my comset rang so loud I almost jumped out of my skin. I had not taken it off my ear yet and the sound against my head almost gave me a heart attack.

"Fletcher?" Mira asked as soon as I opened the line. I laughed nervously.

"Who else?" I asked.

Mira gave a twitter of laughter as well, which was good to hear. "I booked you a flight. Io Spaceport Nine. Go the private craft counter and show them your credentials card. It will be ready within an hour but will wait for twenty-four if you need it and take you to the main spaceport outside of de Rossi Hamlet. I'm sure you can find your way from there."

I had to laugh. First, because she knew my predicament even before I did. Second, she sounded so much better, so much more like herself and I knew it was because she was doing something. Something she was good at, something she could control.

"Yes, honey,'" I told her. "I can get my way to the castle on my own from there. I should be able to get to the spaceport here before nightfall. It's an eighteen-hour flight from there."

"I will beat you there by a good six hours," Mira informed me. "I'll call ahead and see if Lars can land the Vitercraft right at the castle. It will be night for us when you get there, but don't you dare hesitate to wake me up!"

"I won't," I assured her. "I love you."

"I love you, too," she said and I could hear the smile in her voice.

This time she broke the connection and I took the comset off my ear and put my coat back on the hook. I walked into the kitchen, shaking with emotion. Adrenaline was coursing through me from the whole ordeal, while the rest of me was ready to burst knowing that I would finally be seeing Mira. I hummed while I made Joe a sandwich, making mental plans.

I would go home and pack a small bag. I thought about what few things I might need and then considered how long I might be gone. I might need more than a few things. This would not be a weekend trip to visit Jean. I did not know how long I might be gone. Then as I put the plate down on the kitchen table, my eyes drifted back to the flatscreen and the scenes of violence. The enormity of the involvement I was undertaking began to truly take hold.

I might need more than just personal items.

I stood in Edie's small nook and drummed my fingers on the back of a chair. I knew she still had Jack's service pistol. I had, politically and respectfully as possible, hinted to her about the safety of such a weapon around a small boy. It was not within me, however, to outright ask it of her to be rid of such a thing. After all, she was a woman who lived alone.

I left the pod and went across the hall to speak to Mrs. Matherson, a widow herself but much older than Edie. Mrs. Matherson was always glad to see me and always tried to feed me something. I told her I would be taking a small trip and asked if she would look in on Joe every day after school until I came back. She assured me she would, and even make him a snack every day. I gave her my thanks, which made her blush for some reason, and accepted two cookies from her.

Back in Edie's pod I put one cookie on Joe's plate while I munched on the other, not really tasting it. I was still thinking about Jack's gun. Finally, knowing that I had only minutes left before Joe walked through the door, I went into Edie's room and opened her closet. The gun was on the top shelf, out of Joe's reach but still too easy to find. But, true to her word to me, the bullets were not with it.

Good girl, Edie.

I stood on her bed so that I could see everything on the top shelf of the closet. Belts and shoes and scarves. No bullets.

Feeling like a criminal, I poked around the rest of the closet and gently sifted through her drawers. Nothing.

Dammit, Edie!

My time was running short, Joe would be home any minute. I stopped and tried to think how Edie would. She put the gun up high. It would only make sense that she did the same with the bullets. And the farthest place from the gun.

Hall closet.

I was back to where I started, reaching up and feeling blindly around the shelf over my windbreaker. My hand closed over a small box that gave a metallic rattle and I pulled it down. At the same time, I heard Joe say hello to a neighbor in the hallway as he got off the lift. I dropped the box into the pocket of my windbreaker and shut the closet door as Joe opened the door to the podment.

"Hi Grandpa!" he exclaimed, taking a step back in surprise.

"Hi buddy!" I exclaimed back, reopening the closet and carefully taking my light jacket off the peg. I shut the door and knelt down. It put me below his eye level but an adult putting their hands on their knees to talk to someone of smaller stature was condescending and Joe, even at ten, knew it. "I have to go early today."

"Really?" Joe asked. "Where?"

I almost laughed at his surprise. "Grandma needs my help."

"Grandma Mira?" he asked, even more astounded. He had never met her, but I spoke of her often.

"That's right, Grandma Mira."

"Is she in danger?" Joe asked, his tone so grave that it tugged at my heart.

"Yes, Joe. She is in danger."

Joe looked at me for a moment with his dark eyes and then leapt into my arms and hugged me hard. "Then go save her," he whispered fiercely in my ear.

"I will," I whispered back, filled with more love and fear than I ever had felt in my life.

"Besides," he said, pulling back so that he could see me, "I know how to make a sandwich."

"I'm sure you do," I told him. "But one is waiting for you now in the kitchen. Tell your mom I'll call her, and I'll be back as soon as I can."

"Okay Grandpa!" He gave me kiss on my cheek, dropped his book bag by the couch and ran to the kitchen. I watched him bound away and then went out the door, closing it tight and locking it.

I decided I did not need to go to my own podment and hailed an aircab as soon as I left. I had everything I needed.

Unfortunately, I was more right than I knew.

My only doubt blossomed as I reached the spaceport, abruptly aware that I might not be able to carry a firearm on the craft. If I had been flying public transport I would never even had considered such a thing, but I had nothing to worry about this time.

Private craft meant private security - which I discovered was equal to keeping the paying passenger secure, not the craft. I was escorted by two men to a small but luxurious vessel where my needs were attended to with speed by a lovely young woman. I suspected she might be a construct and hoped she would stay safe.

I ate the best meal I had eaten in ten years (not the first I'd had on Devereaux's dime but probably the last), took a long hot shower, and then climbed between crisp cotton sheets to sleep for a good few hours while my clothes were washed and pressed. When I woke up I still had ten hours of travel time ahead of me. I stayed in the silk pajamas the attendant had given me and repeated the cycle.

When I woke up the second time, I read and napped and snacked. I was dying to turn on a news channel but a greater part of me did not want to know. I finally went back into the small bedroom and donned my clean clothes. Then I loaded thirty rounds into the magazine of Jack's service pistol, checked the safety (thank God I knew at least that much) and stuck it into the back of my pants. I put my windbreaker on and checked the mirror to make sure there was no obvious bulge.

We landed and I thanked the crew before I was escorted to the terminal. One of my escorts held out a polite hand as I entered the building, indicating that they would be accompanying me no further.

"If you have not already arranged for transportation," he informed me, "you can find vehicles for hire outside of Terminal One."

"Thank you," I replied, "but I can find my way from here."

He gave me a courteous nod and I walked through the door as his words sank in. Terminal One? There had only been one terminal when I had left, but I knew people only numbered places when there were at least two. I wasn't that much of an idiot. Except for assuming that things would not have changed much in my absence.

The small spaceport that I had left twenty-five years ago was a hive of commotion and lights and noise. I walked on legs I could hardly feel, following the arrows to Terminal One and Ground Transportation. Outside the building was just as noisy and bustling. I searched for a cab but saw none. I looked for a private car to hire and came up with the same. I finally stopped a man, pink-faced and balding and wearing a transport guard's uniform.

"Excuse me," I said, feeling like a country bumpkin, "I need to get to de Rossi Castle." The guard pointed to a bus that looked like it was already full and I shook my head. "Where are the cabs?" I asked. "I thought I was in the right…"

"No cabs," the guard said. "The IGC is doing what they can to quell the riots, starting with locking down transportation. That bus is the best you're gonna get, and it will probably be the last. Unless you feel like a long walk, you might want to catch it."

I did not feel like a long walk. I ran to catch the bus, my heart already thumping in my chest. *Riots?* I thought. *Surely not here on Mimas? Not in a place as remote as this. Besides, the people who live in the Hamlet work for GwenSeven!*

As I reached the bus I realized that the once small hamlet with faux thatch roofs I had built had probably grown just as much as the spaceport. Or more. I climbed the steps into the bus and knew immediately that it would have been a better idea to walk the five miles. Or run.

But then I really would have been too late.

The doors hissed shut behind me and I stumbled to a seat amidst a cacophony of anger as the bus lurched away from the curb. People yelled and waved weapons. Some weapons were simple clubs or heavy tools, making the people look like the village mob they were. Others had knives and a few had guns. All were shouting.

Some shouted about the unholy aspect of the constructs. Others yelled about the danger they posed to humans. A man across from me bellowed about how they needed to kill any constructs they found. A scrawny woman on my right screeched a mighty endorsement. I felt the man on my left give me jab in the ribs.

"You're awfully quiet!" he accused with a scowl, drawing eyes in my direction.

"I just want my money back!" I retorted with as much force I could muster. Others close by roared their approval.

I prayed silently and felt the sweat gather on my back.

C3&20

Gwen's brown and gold eyes opened to a view that was mostly pillow. Something had woken her. Some sound. It came again.

Thunder, she thought, closing her eyes.

Then the sound came again and her eyes snapped open. Though the sound boomed and rolled through the castle, it was too regular and close to be thunder. She sat up in bed and listened.

It came again, followed by a crash, as if the storm had come into the castle itself. Gwen jumped out of bed and slammed into a body. Gwen reached over and flicked on the light to see

Mira on the floor, a hand over her mouth.

"Oh God, Mira!" Gwen said, kneeling down. "I'm so sorry! Are you okay?"

Mira nodded. "It's okay, Faith," she said from behind her hand. "I was moving fast too. I was going to wake you up."

Gwendolyn pushed Mira's hand down and saw that her shoulder had caught her under the nose. Her lips, along with the entire lower half of her face were already starting to swell. "Oh!" Gwen exclaimed, a hand coming up to cover her own mouth. "I'm so sorry!"

"Don't worry about it," Mira said, shaking her head and climbing to her feet, pulling Gwen up with her. "We need to get out of here."

Gwen was about to ask what was happening but her throat clenched at the sound of gunshots. And screams.

Mira grabbed her by the hand and together they ran from the room.

"Charity!" Gwen hissed. "Llewellyn!"

"They have two bodyguards with them," Mira told her, almost dragging her down the hallway that led to the back of the castle. "They'll meet us in the garden."

Gwen nodded, running to keep hold of Mira. They took a back staircase and were down to the kitchens when Gwen choked on a scream as she spotted the bodies there, bloodied on the floor. Mira tugged on her hand and they were almost to the door when they came face to face with part of the mob that had stormed the castle.

Both parties looked just as surprised to see each other.

"Who are you?" a burly man demanded. "You don't look like the help!"

Gwen drew herself up with more confidence than she knew she possessed. "I am Faith de Rossi!" she exclaimed. "And how dare you invade my sister's home!" she shouted. "I have

already called the IGC Militant Guard," she lied, "you will all be arrested!"

"Beg your pardon ma'am," a smaller man said with a tone as if to lecture her, "but we are well within our rights to kill any unhumans. They pose a threat to the safety of real people."

"How do we know if she is human?" an enormous woman posed to the crowd. "I've seen pictures, but how do we know she isn't the unhuman doll?"

There was a murmur of assent through the mob before another spoke out. "I heard the real ones wear rings that glow!" he announced. "See if she wears the magic rings!"

Christ, Gwen thought. *They are truly like villagers in a fairytale.* Then the air left her lungs as if they were being crushed. *And who created that fairytale?* she wondered, turning accusive eyes back on herself. *Making dolls come to life and building castles with villages to match?* Gwen bit back a sob.

"I see 'em!" someone shouted and Gwen moved her hand so they all could see the rings on her left hand, the stones giving off a soft glow in the eerie light of the kitchens.

There was a moment of stunned silence before someone else, their bloodlust unslaked, pointed to Mira.

"What about her?" he demanded. "How do we know if she is human or unhuman?"

"She is human!" Gwen said, vehement. "She is my housekeeper...Mari."

There were a few grunts that might have been disbelief before another villager leaned closer for a better look.

"Ayuh," he agreed. "Gotta be human. Doesn't have that perfect face."

There was a muttered consensus as more of the mob got a look at Mira's distorted, swollen face.

Gwen felt herself fill with a fury she had never before

experienced. She swelled with rage before the wind was sucked from her lungs at the sound of more gunshots from the center of the castle. "Charity!" she screamed, unable to help herself.

The mob shouted and swarmed and ran as if a single organism.

Gwen tried to follow but Mira locked a hand around her arm and yanked her back.

🞿

I rode with the mob as they grew angrier by the minute. It was like a wasp hive that was being slowly but repeatedly poked. Most were chanting *kill them all, kill them all!* by the time we were halfway to the castle. The *Hail Mary* was going through my own mind in the same repetitive pattern when the man on my left gave me another poke.

"I just hope there is some still to kill when we get there!" he exclaimed.

"What do you mean?" I asked, my voice near a shout to be heard over the others.

"The bus in front of us had the guys and tools to break down the gates and the doors, but they also had some ex-IGC gunmen to help with any bodyguards or security at the castle. I hope they don't kill everyone before we get there!"

"Me too," I agreed, though I doubted he could hear me.

Mira! I despaired, my soul crushed. Then I knew she would kick me for giving in to despair and I began to form a plan in my head. I knew what she would do, the same as she knew I had no idea how to book an interstellar flight.

You have to get away from these others, I told myself. *You have to get to the back of the castle.*

Past the herb and flower gardens behind the castle the land

rose and there was a stone hangar with land and air vehicles next to a small helioport.

That's where she will be, and the girls with her.

The bus jumped and rocked as it went over the gates that had been blasted down before heaving to a halt before doors that had been knocked inwards. Being one of the last on the bus, I was one of the first off – and propelled forward with the masses.

I tried to squirm my way sideways but my efforts were wasted. I was carried along the tide of the mob and through the castle doors. Everything after that happened so fast that it was a blur.

The mass of villagers came upon another group that I quickly saw was Charity and Llewellyn being herded down a hallway by a circle of their bodyguards. Weapons were fired and I had no idea they could be so loud. Within seconds my ears were ringing and bodies around me were falling to the ground. The guards around the girls were falling too. But, on my side, more bodies rushed in to fill the void and kept firing. The de Rossi bodyguards were overrun.

With a strange sense of calm, I reached behind my body and pulled free Jack's gun as I stepped between the mob and the girls. Then something incredibly heavy smashed into the back of my skull. My vision was filled with an image of marble floor as it rushed towards my face and then everything went black.

I blinked my eyes.

My ears were still ringing.

Other than the ringing, there was silence.

I blinked again and, slowly, my vision returned.

At first I thought I was standing and for one wild second I thought I had been talking with Charity and then fell asleep. Then reality crashed over me like a wave on a rock.

I was not standing, but instead laying with my face against the floor. Brilliant blue eyes looked into mine. But they were

Llewellyn's eyes, her face also flat against the marble floor, staring forever into nothing.

I pushed myself up and saw that I was covered in blood. A second glance told me that, though villagers and de Rossi bodyguards littered the scene, the blood was Llewellyn's.

"Mira!" I screamed, pushing myself to my feet.

The only response was my own echo. I lurched, slipping in the blood and almost breaking an ankle before I gained my footing and took off running.

I don't know how long I ran, but I know I searched every room, every hall, every closet, every cranny. I shouted until my voice was hoarse and then I shouted more, calling for Mira. Screaming for her.

Finally, I returned to where I had awoken.

My head was throbbing, my throat and eyes were burning.

I slumped down next to the body of Llewellyn and reached out with two fingers and closed those beautiful blue eyes. Then I took her hand up in my own and pressed it against my forehead. I sat amongst the dead and I wept.